DRAGON'S TREASURE

Also by Elizabeth A. Lynn

A DIFFERENT LIGHT

THE SARDONYX NET

THE CHRONICLES OF TORNOR

WATCHTOWER

THE DANCERS OF ARUN

THE NORTHERN GIRL

DRAGON'S WINTER

DRAGON'S TREASURE

Elizabeth A. Lynn

ACE BOOKS, NEW YORK

THE BERKLEY PUBLISHING GROUP
Published by the Penguin Group
Penguin Group (USA) Inc.
375 Hudson Street, New York, New York 10014, USA
Penguin Group (Canada), 10 Alcorn Avenue, Toronto, Ontario M4V 3B2, Canada
(a division of Pearson Penguin Canada Inc.)
Penguin Books Ltd., 80 Strand, London WC2R 0RL, England
Penguin Group Ireland, 25 St. Stephen's Green, Dublin 2, Ireland (a division of Penguin Books Ltd.)
Penguin Group (Australia), 250 Camberwell Road, Camberwell, Victoria 3124, Australia
(a division of Pearson Australia Group Pty. Ltd.)
Penguin Books India Pvt. Ltd., 11 Community Centre, Panchsheel Park, New Delhi—110 017, India
Penguin Group (NZ), Cnr. Airborne and Rosedale Roads, Albany, Auckland 1310, New Zealand
(a division of Pearson New Zealand Ltd.)
Penguin Books (South Africa) (Pty.) Ltd., 24 Sturdee Avenue, Rosebank, Johannesburg 2196, South Africa

Penguin Books Ltd., Registered Offices: 80 Strand, London WC2R 0RL, England

First American edition: September 2004
Previously published in Great Britain by Tor in 2003.

Library of Congress Cataloging-in-Publication Data

Lynn, Elizabeth A.
Dragon's treasure / Elizabeth A. Lynn.— 1st American ed.
p. cm.
ISBN: 0-441-01196-9
1. Kings and rulers—Succession—Fiction. 2. Brothers—Fiction. 3. Twins—Fiction.
I. Title.

PS3562.Y443D725 2004
813'.54—dc22

2004048254

PRINTED IN THE UNITED STATES OF AMERICA

10 9 8 7 6 5 4 3 2 1

Dragon is a fearsome creature. It is born of the sun, and so incendiary is its nature that neither stone nor water nor air nor any other element can withstand the fire that lives in its blood. A young Dragon comes whole from the womb of its mother. Even as it is born, the mother dies, and the young one feeds on its flesh.

Dragon is so strong that not the most extensive space, nor the highest obstacle, can contain its flight. It may kill by claws, fangs, or fire. The significance of its color is as follows: azure for wisdom, white for patience, black for ferocity, silver for fidelity, gold for incorruptibility, red for sacrifice.

The span of Dragon's life is short, far shorter than the span of human lives.

—A. Panati: *An Uncommon Bestiary*

DRAGON'S TREASURE

PROLOGUE

AN ICE STORM blew across the hills that night. It left the tree branches bowed and crystalline. All night the lovers heard them tinkling and snapping.

"It sounds like an army moving through the wood," the woman murmured sleepily.

"Not my army," the man said. "My men are quiet when they travel."

The woman laughed, and rubbed her face against his shoulder. Despite the freezing cold outside, the cottage was dry and warm. Quilts lay unheeded at the foot of the bed. Across its single room a pine-scented fire burned in the hearth, but the warmth came mostly from the man. He was clean-shaven, fair-skinned and golden-haired, and extraordinarily beautiful. Although he was young, scarcely twenty years of age, his face was an adult's, not a boy's: he was a man who could command armies, and did.

Beside his long, densely muscled frame, the woman appeared even slighter than she was. She was compact, with a narrow, heart-shaped face. Her rich dark curls were the color of new-turned earth. She trailed her fingers along his chest.

"Wake up," she whispered.

He snaked his arm up from the bed and pulled her on top of him.

After lovemaking they lay side by side. The pale March light slid through the cracks in the window shutter. The man stirred. "I should go." The fire woke beneath his blue gaze. A candle leaped to life in its sconce. He reached for his clothes. The woman twitched the soft silk shirt from his fingers and twined it teasingly around her shoulders.

"I like this shirt."

"Give it back."

Grinning, she shrugged into it. It fell below her knees.

"Iva, give it back."

In response, she went quickly to the door of the tiny cottage, unbarred it, and walked barefoot into the winter dawn. He followed her.

"Iva!"

She fled, laughing and shivering, around the rear of the hut. He caught her. He scooped her into his arms. His body was warm. She butted him fiercely in the chest.

"I want this shirt. Give it to me."

"It's yours." He carted her inside the cottage and dumped her on the bed. She pulled a quilt around her like a shawl and sat cross-legged.

"How are the boys?" she asked.

"They are well. Kaji wants a sword, so he can come with me to fight the Isojai." For four years now bands of Isojai had come across the border into Issho, looting and burning. Pohja Leminin had sent his couriers riding through Ryoka, to call the lords together with their armies. The Black Dragon had led his men to war, and brought them back triumphant.

"A sword! He is not yet three!"

"Changelings grow more swiftly than other children," he said. "And dragon-children develop especially swiftly. I was a man at twelve."

"And Tenjiro? Does he also want a sword?"

A shadow crossed Kojiro Atani's face. "No. He is not so vigorous as his brother."

She had never seen his sons. She pictured them—flame-haired imps, the image of their father—in Dragon Keep, chasing through corridors and down stairways into the fragrant, seething kitchen where Jon Duurni, the castle cook, was king. She knew those corridors well. She had been born within the Keep. Her mother, Wina, had been maid to Atalaya Atani, the Crimson Dragon, ruler of Dragon Keep, this man's mother, and her father had served in the garrison.

Kojiro Atani had been her lover for over two years. After his wife died he had stayed away for a few months, but then he had returned, hungry for her. She had not been a virgin. He did not care. She was older than he was. It did not trouble him. He wanted her because she matched his lust, and because she was not afraid of him. Hana Diamori, who had died birthing his sons, had feared him to the point of terror. His soldiers feared him, too. They had good reason. She knew what punishments he meted out. She had seen the broken bodies hanging on the castle walls. Outside Talvela, her father had told her, he had ordered a deserter flayed. Earlier that winter his men had brought him a man accused of raping his own daughter, a child of twelve. The lord had ordered that he be stripped, tied to stakes, and left to die in the snow.

He could also be extraordinarily generous. Four years before, on a battlefield outside Ruitsa, in Issho, Reo Unamira had flung himself between a charging Isojai and his unhorsed liege. For that loyalty Kojiro had given him land and gold, enough to build a house, and to hire other people to serve him. He talked now as if he were a lord himself.

"What news from the border?" she asked. "Will the raiders return?"

"Not now. It's winter. No one makes war in winter."

"Do you think they'll come again?"

He shrugged. "If they do, we'll kill them again." He reached for his boots. "Where's your father?" he asked.

"Gone to Sorvino. He left yesterday. He has a woman there."

"Does he indeed? The old bull! Who is she?"

"Her name's Lena. She's a widow. She's cousin to the lord of the city."

"You've met her?"

"Yes. I like her."

Resting his big hands on his knees, he said, "You know your father has been after me to marry you."

"I know."

"I told him I wouldn't."

"Good. I don't want to marry you, my lord."

"Why not?" he demanded.

She arched her back, and moved her body in the silken shirt. "I like it when you come to me."

"Are you so certain of me?"

"Are you bored with me? Ah, well. I suppose I shall have to find another lover."

Kojiro Atani's big hands flexed like claws. "You do and I'll kill you both," he growled.

She laughed, and bit his ear.

SHE WALKED INTO the snow to say farewell to him. He climbed the hill to the ridgetop, and Changed. Night draped the hill an instant, and he rose gleaming from it, immense and terrible, his ebony wings soft as cloud, his great arched neck crested with scarlet.

She watched him fly toward the Keep. Her eyes stung briefly with tears. She scrubbed them away. Tears were useless. She returned to the cottage. Sitting on the bed, she smoothed the shirt over her delicate, rounded belly with her palms.

It was too soon for the babe inside to move, but she knew it was there. She had felt her body changing. She had not meant to have a child. She had taken fennel, but the herb did not always work, especially when used against the dragon folk.

Her father did not know, yet, that she was pregnant. He would know soon enough, of course. There was no way to hide it. He would want to know the father's name. She had no intention of telling him. He might guess, of course, but there would be nothing he could do if she refused to tell him, except beat her, and she did not care about that. She had made the arrangements months ago. She was going to Sorvino. Lena had invited her to stay with her. *I will introduce you to Marion,* the woman had said. *His wife's left him; run off with some doctor, I heard. He needs consoling. You would captivate him, I know.*

Marion diSorvino was older than she was, closer to forty than thirty, Lena had said. He had given his wife two children, both girls, but she had taken them with her when she left him, and he had, not surprisingly, disowned them both. She had never met a man she could not dazzle. Pregnant or not, she was certain she could make him want her.

Kojiro would be angry when he learned that she had left his domain, but he would not come after her: his dignity would not allow it. He would forget her, and find another lover. Karadur Atani, the little flame-haired imp who would one day rule this land, would never know his half brother. It was necessary. Cruel as the dragon-kindred could be to their subjects, they were lethal to one another. She was of Ippa; she knew the stories. Lyr the dragon-king had killed his wife. The sons of Lyr had killed each other. Atalaya Atani, the Crimson Dragon, had disappeared in the middle of a thunderstorm, and it was said (very softly) by some in the domain that she and Kojiro had quarreled, and in the heat of that dispute the dragon-lord had killed his mother. Iva did not believe that, but knowing Kojiro Atani's temper, she understood how it was that the whispered tale persisted.

Even the small sons of Kojiro Atani had been touched by the dragon curse. Tenjiro, the youngest, had come from the womb bleeding from the claws of Karadur, his brother. Those same claws had torn Hana Diamori Atani inside. She had bled to death.

It would not happen to her. The baby growing in her womb was not a dragon-child. She was sure of it. When first she realized she was pregnant she had considered pennyroyal, but the thought only lasted a moment. She wanted this baby.

She folded the quilts, and laid them away in the chest. She fastened her knife about her waist. It was a good knife, sharp and well balanced. It had come to her from her grandmother, her mother's mother. She put sand on the fire. She took her staff from its place beside the door. The sun had risen: the peaks of the snowy mountain were alight with flame. The day was warming. She turned her back to the cottage, knowing that she would not come there again, and walked up the treacherous slope of the hill toward the ridgetop, and home.

PART ONE

1

IN THE HOUSE on Coll's Ridge, the outlaws were arguing again.

Wakeful in her upstairs chamber, Maia Unamira diSorvino sat silent in the moonlight. The Hunter's Moon, full and diamond-bright, blazed over the dark tree-covered hills. The men in the hall below were drunken and joyful. They had ridden out at sunset, her brother at their head. They had returned hours later, clamoring as if they had conquered a kingdom.

The noise rose to a crescendo. Fenris, motionless in her place beside the door, swiveled her fine pale ears back as if the shouting hurt. Morga lifted her dark narrow head and gazed at her mistress.

"It's all right," Maia said. "They'll stop."

Someone whooped. "I win!" a man roared. She thought it was Nils. "Pay me, you luckless devils!" Suddenly the shouting ceased. Treion had tired of the noise at last. The yelling did not resume. Maia stretched her arms above her head. Her muscles ached.

In the chamber next door, her grandfather, oblivious to what was happening in his house, snored. He, too, was drunk. He was constantly drunk, now. He had started drinking before her mother's death, and since that event, a year ago New Year's Moon, he kept a bottle always nearby. But his sickness—the falling, the tremors—had begun before then. Nothing she knew of Master Eccio's lore would help him. He refused the tonics she mixed for him. On good days he was lucid. On bad ones he marched through the house shouting incoherent orders, half-naked, breathing wine fumes into the faces of those who had once obeyed him. They had no time for the sick old warrior. They were Treion's, now.

A door opened, and someone shouted below. At first she thought it was her brother.

Then she heard the rush of footsteps through the house. Booted feet came down the hall. The dogs came silently to their feet. Fenris faced the door, her silver pelt erect. Morga growled deep in her throat.

"Hush," Maia said softly. She moved to the window and peered through the gap in the shutter. The clearing in front of the manor was ringed with armed men. Moonlight glinted off sword blades. She backed from the window.

The knife her mother had left her lay beneath her pillow. She strapped it on. A fist hammered on the door of the chamber next to hers. Her grandfather yelled a stream of drunken curses. A quietly competent voice told him to be still. She waited for them to pound on her door. But they did not. She heard her grandfather's plaintive voice, and the sound of booted feet retreating down the stairway.

She opened her chamber door, and gestured to the dogs. They went downstairs together. The hall was devoid of life, except for a bloodstained cat grooming in a corner. It raised its head to growl at the dogs.

The front door was ajar. Through the opening she saw Edan and Nils and the rest of her grandfather's men standing in the clearing. Their weapons lay in a heap in the dirt.

She looked for Treion among them. He was not there. The Hunter's Moon made the night bright as day. Her grandfather, barefoot, wearing only his night robe, stood in the center of the clearing, hands on his hips. His white hair was wild.

"Iva," he called shakily to his dead daughter, her mother. "Iva, we have guests! Bring wine!"

Before him stood a tall, fair man. He said, "Do you know where your band of cutthroats went tonight, old man? To Thorin Amdur's farm. They stole the horses. They killed Thorin and his son Garth. They fired the house and left everyone in it to burn."

His voice was very deep. His face was bleak as winter. Although Maia had seen him only once before, and that at a distance, she knew who he was.

Her grandfather said, whining a little, "I did not tell them to do that."

"Did you not?" the dragon-lord said. "It does not matter; it's done, and you must answer for it."

She knew the stories of the dragon-kind: their strength, their startling generosity, and their terrible ferocity when defied. She put her hand flat on the door and pushed. It was stuck; it would not move. Her fingers trembled.

Her grandfather leaned forward. "You should not speak so to me," he said, with a drunkard's mad dignity. "I saved your father's life in battle. He granted me this land."

The dragon-lord said, "I know it. You have traded on that service for nearly thirty years. Out of respect for my father I grant you one day's grace. But by sunset tomorrow, you and your kin must be gone from my domain."

"What of my men?" Reo Unamira demanded.

"They killed my people," Karadur Atani said coldly. "Their lives are forfeit." He looked at the encircled outlaws. "Which of you is Edan?" No one spoke, but heads twitched. The dragon-lord leveled a finger. "You. Step forward." Edan obeyed. The other men moved away from him. "Finle. Kill him."

From where he stood beneath a copper beech, a slender dark-haired archer lifted his bow and shot in one smooth motion. An arrow seemed to grow out of Edan's broad chest. He curled his hands helplessly around the shaft, and fell.

Reo Unamira cackled. "*That* for the gratitude of the dragon-kind." He genuflected mockingly toward the dragon-lord. "Iva! Iva, hurry up. We are leaving. Maia! Treion! Come quickly. Our gracious liege is dispossessing us from our home!" He spat in the dirt.

Maia pushed the door open with her shoulder. With Fenris and Morga flanking her on either side, she descended the steps. They all turned to look at her: her grandfather's men, the soldiers, and the dragon-lord.

He was taller than she was. The amber moonlight seemed to settle on his shoulders. But she was Iva Unamira's daughter. She would *not* be cowed, even by a dragon.

"Treion is gone, Grandfather," she said. She saw him in her mind, circling soundlessly around the soldiers' perimeter, finding a horse, mounting, riding, over the ridge, and gone. . . . He would not have been drunk. He drank—he had an especial fondness for her grandfather's merignac—but in all the months he had lived among them, she had never seen him drunk.

She faced Karadur Atani. "My lord," she said, and was pleased to hear her voice emerge steady, "as you can see, my grandfather drinks more than he should. It makes him foolish."

His gaze was like a weight. "Who are you?"

"I am Maia diSorvino. My mother was Iva Unamira."

Her grandfather said jauntily, "You were supposed to marry her, boy!" He giggled. "Your father and I planned it all. But then he went mad. Mad Dragon." He ran his hands through his white brush of hair.

The dragon-lord said, "I remember. Your grandfather wrote me a letter four, no five years ago. He wanted me to marry you." He looked at her oddly. "I thought you were younger."

She remembered that letter. Her grandfather had sent it without telling her mother. When finally the old man let it slip, Iva Unamira had been furious.

Greedy thieving sot! she had said. *What did you ask for in payment? Gold? A case of wine? My daughter is not a horse or a sheep, to be bartered to the dragon-kindred in exchange for a bottle of merignac.*

She said, "I was younger. Five years ago I was thirteen."

"You're from Nakase?"

"I was born in Sorvino. My father is Marion diSorvino. My mother and I returned six years ago."

Reo Unamira cackled. "You want her, my lord? Twenty nobles, and I'll throw in the dogs." He snapped his fingers at the moonlight. "You, there. Bring me some wine."

Karadur Atani said, "Your mother—is she still alive?"

"She's dead. She died in January last year."

Some emotion, perhaps surprise, perhaps compassion, she could not tell, moved in the dragon-lord's brilliant blue eyes. He said, "I am sorry. I know what it is like to be motherless."

Reo Unamira whined, "I want a drink. Treion took my merignac, the little bastard. Little bastard." He turned in a circle. "She would never say his name, no matter how I beat her. But I knew. I saw them. I saw them." He giggled senselessly, and crouched to pat the dirt with his hands.

Karadur Atani's face went stony again. Maia said, "My lord, I beg you, ignore him. He does not know what he is saying. He has been like this for months."

"Has he indeed." His face changed suddenly. "Of course. He did not lead the raid tonight. Who did?"

She could tell him it was Edan. But no, one could not lie to the dragon-kind. They always knew a lie, and it made them angry. Her mother had told her that. She did not want to make him angry.

"My half brother Treion led the raid. Ask any of his cohorts, those that are sober enough to talk. They will tell you."

"And where is he?"

She said, "Gone, I am sure. He must have heard you coming, and escaped."

"Herugin!"

A lean, grim-faced man with a badge on his sleeve said, "One man did get out the back ahead of us, my lord. But he won't get far. Huw and Elief are out there."

To her horror, a familiar voice said, "My sister tells the truth. I do not deny it." Sweet Sedi, it was Treion. He sauntered into the center of the clearing. He held his bare sword in his right hand. "However, I must correct her inference that I ran away when your men arrived. I did not run away. I merely moved faster than these cretins." He cut a contemptuous look at the encircled men. Arrogant, impossible, stupid Treion . . . The outlaws looked at him hopefully. Fools, Maia wanted to shout at them, he will only make it worse. Her fingers curled into fists. She wanted to hit him.

He bowed theatrically, almost derisively, to the dragon-lord. "Treion Unamira, my lord, at your service. They call me the Bastard."

"I have no interest in your parentage," the dragon-lord said. "Was it indeed you who led tonight's raid?"

"It was. Though I did not kill the old man. Edan did

that." Treion nudged Edan's corpse with his toe. "He's paid for it, I see. Dragon's justice."

The dragon-lord's eyes glittered like blue flame. "Herugin. Take him."

Drawing his sword, the grim-faced officer walked confidently toward Treion. Treion turned to face him. He looked relaxed, even lazy, and entirely unafraid.

Suddenly his drooping sword sliced upward. The Atani soldier's sword spun from his hand. Treion touched the point of his blade to the disarmed man's throat.

He said tautly, "I am not so easily taken, my lord. Tell your men to lay their arrows in the dirt. Otherwise, he dies."

No one moved. A ghostly bird called across the forest. A second answered.

Then Herugin turned his head to look at his lord.

Karadur said, "Do it." The archers unfastened their quivers and laid them on the ground.

"Move away from them," Treion said.

The dragon-lord nodded. His soldiers stepped back.

"You drunken, stupid pigs," Treion Unamira said scathingly to the outlaws. "Find your weapons and meet me where we left the horses. Go." The men scrambled to obey.

"My lord, as you have ordained, we will leave. You will not see us again, though you may hear of us. I intend that you shall hear of us. I will take your officer with me, however; he shall be my safe conduct till I leave your land. Once we're beyond your borders, I'll let him go. Edric, get a rope. Tie his wrists together in front. Now, get me a horse. One of theirs. The rest of you take their horses. Hurry." Edric brought him a horse. "Tie the end of the rope to the saddle." The tip of his sword had not deviated an inch.

He waited until the rope had been secured, then mounted. "I understand you brand brigands in this country." The sword point slashed across the bound man's face, and returned immediately to his throat. "My brand," Treion said.

He touched his rigid captive lightly in the center of the chest with the tip of the sword. Blood from the wound on his cheek ran down the man's face and into his clothing.

Karadur Atani's voice was soft and deadly. "If he dies, make no mistake: I will find you."

"I believe you," Treion said. "I wouldn't want you to do that. I'll keep him alive. Farewell, Grandfather. You are a vicious drunk. I hope your death finds you soon." For a moment his eyes met Maia's, and she saw the pride and the rage there. "Farewell, sister dear. Walk, you." He urged his mount into the trees. The Atani officer, blood streaming down his cheek, loped at the horse's side.

The dragon-lord's soldiers scrambled to retrieve their weapons. Maia's legs were shaking. The dogs pressed protectively against her.

The delicate, insubstantial birdsong went on. The moon, its light diminished, had fallen behind the trees. Dawn was approaching.

Reo Unamira whined, "Iva's little bastard. It was my thought to name him Treion. It means treasure. I meant it as a joke. The joke's on me. The boy took my treasure. Stole my soldiers. Drank my merignac. Bad dragon. Mad dragon." He glanced archly at the dragon-lord. "Mad as your father."

"Old man, for the gods' sweet sake, be quiet," the dark-haired archer said.

"Hah." The old man drew himself up. "Who are you to talk to me like that? My lord, your men are rudely mannered. Mad Dragon. They say you killed your brother for his treasure. Chests of gold and jewels." He waggled his bony fingers in the air. "Poof! *I* had chests of gold and jewels once. Gone, all gone. Treion took them. He took my merignac, too. It was the dragon's gold he stole. Your father gave it to me. Kojiro Atani, the Black Dragon. I wanted him to marry her, but no, he wouldn't do it, not Iva Unamira, not *my* daughter.

"He fucked her, though. She would never admit it, but I saw them, I saw them, I saw them lying beside the stream. I knew it.

"I knew the Diamori bitch would never satisfy him."

The dark-haired archer flinched. Karadur Atani's eyes burned like stars. A hot wind rose out of the earth, bowing the tall trees as if a giant's hand had swept across their tops. Dust and dirt and tiny pebbles whirled in circles. Half-blinded by the swirling dust, Maia grabbed for the dogs' collars. She could not find them. The hot wind thundered in her ears. She saw her grandfather's mouth fall open. Then fire sheathed his head, and he screamed.

A bright light seared the clearing. The Golden Dragon soared above them, great wings spread like sails. His deadly exhalation fell upon the house. White flame dripped along its walls, its heavy timbers. . . . Fire filled her vision. The trees were burning. Her grandfather howled in pain. Fire whipped about her, devouring the air. She panted, fighting for breath. A terrible, inhuman bellow shook her to her knees. She struggled to her feet.

Pain shot through her scalp. She yanked the bronze hair clip from her head, and flung it away. A searing silver rain spattered at her feet. Flame erupted from the dry forest floor. She ran, and fell, and ran again. A tree crashed in front of her, showering her with sparks. Eyes tight shut against the bitter smoke, she felt her way around it. A body cannoned into her.

"This way!" a man's voice cried. "This way. Get to the river!"

Suddenly her legs went out from under her. She fell, and

slid into a sour, enveloping coolness. Near her, someone sobbed. She clutched at the riverbank. Far away, a horse screamed in agony, a terrible rending sound.

The sobbing man cursed.

EVENTUALLY, THE FIRE passed.

Maia sat on a rock. She had no idea how she had gotten there: she did not recall leaving the haven of the river. Below her the land sloped down toward a scorched hollow. Debris littered the ground: shards of blackened wood, which had once been the thick beams of a house, her house.

Morga shivered at her feet. The black hound had somehow remained with her through her flight through the woods, and even to the river. Her coat was caked with mud; she trembled, but appeared to be unhurt. Fenris was gone: dead, no doubt. Maia's limbs felt sluggish and sore, as if she had been beaten.

Her gown was charred. She still had her knife, though; somehow, through long hours clinging to reeds in the river, it had stayed in its sheath.

Clouds like feathers streaked the pale mauve sky. A shadow passed over the sun. She looked up. High above her, the Golden Dragon, terrible and beautiful, glittered in the autumn air. His immense pale wings were evanescent as gossamer. She wondered if he knew what he had done.

A place on her side pulsed with pain. She heard Master Eccio's cool, astringent voice in her head, reminding her that tea, or a paste made of old-man's-beard, would ease the pain of burns and scalds. She had no tea.

Atani soldiers, worn and grim, accompanied by one sorefooted horse, moved slowly along the ridgetop. They halted when they saw her. After a moment, one of them maneuvered down the slippery, ash-strewn slope. He was hairless, even to his eyebrows. His face was streaked with mud and ash, as was hers. Morga growled at him. Maia stroked the dog's sleek head.

"Hush."

He said, "You need shelter. Come with us."

"To Dragon Keep?" She shook her head. "I think not."

"Where will you go?"

"I know a place." She had a picture in her mind, of a place where the river widened into a pool beside a tangle of berry bushes. Near it lay a stone cottage, a trapper's hut. Her mother had brought her to it, soon after they arrived from Sorvino.

What is this place, Mama? twelve-year-old Maia had asked.

Her mother had said simply, *A place where I was happy. I wanted you to see it.*

"You're sure?" the soldier said.

"Yes," she said. "I'm sure. Thank you."

He left, limping. Her legs ached, and her chest hurt from breathing smoke. She was stiff. The longer she sat, the stiffer her body would be. She rose. With the wolfhound at her heels, she ascended the slope. At the crest of the ridge, she stopped. Below her spread a meadow, and beyond it the blue-green tinge of forest. A glint of silver caught her eye: the river, curving through the amber meadow grass. She trudged down the slope. The river was farther away than she had thought.

By the time she reached the cottage she was shivering. A ghost of a path led to a vine-covered entrance. She struggled through the thick tangle. A thorn hidden in the glossy leaves left a bloody scrape on her arm.

"Come on, girl," she whispered to the anxious dog. Morga whined and wriggled through after her. The cottage was small, but it seemed dry. Morga snuffled in the corners. A shutterless window, a simple square, graced the south wall. A rude chest sat below it. Maia lifted the lid. Inside it, someone, some trapper or hunter, had left a blanket, a bowl, a jug, and a coiled, dry bowstring.

Thank you, she said to that unknown stranger. She wrapped the blanket around her shaking shoulders.

"Hey, girl." The dog came to her. "What shall we do now, eh?" The dog licked her chin. The cottage was dim. Light, she thought. Fire.

Methodically she felt about the hearth until she felt a loose stone. She pried it up. As she had hoped, a small leather pouch lay in the exposed hole. Inside was a bit of dry puffball, and three jagged bits of flint.

Not too far from the hut grew a cluster of white-trunked birches. Chips of bark, some of them long as her arm, littered the ground. She gathered bark in her blanket. With her knife, she cut swaths of meadow grass. Fingers chilling, she struck flint against the knife blade. At last a spark leaped into the puffball. She blew on it; it flamed. She thrust a spear of grass into the flame, and, when it lit, held it to the hearth.

It caught. The fire sang in its bed. She dragged the chest across the hard dirt floor and positioned it athwart the doorway. An owl hooted across the meadow.

Some creature of the twilight, hunter or prey, rustled through the tall grass outside the hut. Morga's head lifted; she rose to her feet.

"Morga, no! Stay." To Maia's relief, the dog obeyed the croaked command. "Lie down." They curled together beside the fire. Dragons tussled in its glowing heart. Maia's stomach growled with hunger. In the morning she would look for food. She knew how to fish. Treion had taught her. Savage, dangerous Treion . . .

He was dead, of course, he and all the men who rode with him. He could not have escaped the fire.

A chill breeze blew through the exposed doorway. It smelled of ash. Her hair was filthy; she needed soap to get it clean. She needed warm clothes, candles, a pot to cook in, none of which she had, nor any way to get them. She was alone. Her mother was dead. Fenris was dead. Her grandfather was dead. Treion was dead.

Her eyes stung with tears. She forced them back.

She would not weep. She was Iva Unamira's daughter; she would *not* weep.

2

THE BURNING OF Coll's Ridge made news across Ippa.

In Castria Market, where the first sketchy tales were told, the farmers and shepherds spoke of it with grim satisfaction. They were not a vengeful folk, but Thorin Amdur and his family were well-known and well respected throughout Dragon's domain, and all of them had suffered, over the years, from Reo Unamira's attentions.

The merchants from Mako and Ujo and Averra were pleased. Dragon Keep's soldiers were well trained, but they could not be everywhere, and more than one trader, over the years, had found his wagons waylaid in the twilight by Reo Unamira's men, and forced to hand over a few barrels of wine or oil or grain.

"Consider it a toll," the old outlaw had been wont to say, grinning.

In the days that followed, the news grew bleaker. Ten of Dragon Keep's soldiers had lost their lives in the fire. More had suffered burns. Macallan, the Keep's physician, was dead. So was Elief Ivarson from Castria, and Huw Udall, whose parents farmed land outside Chingura.

No one was quite sure what had caused Karadur Atani to burn Unamira's house. Those who had survived the conflagration did not speak of it. This was not surprising. Murgain Ohair, fifteen years archery-master at Dragon Keep, who knew something of Karadur Atani's temper, shared a beer one night at the Red Oak tavern in Sleeth with Egain the tavern keeper, and Niall Cooley, the leather-worker of Chingura, new come from Dragon Keep.

"How is it at the castle?" he inquired.

"Very quiet," said the leather-worker. "The men are mending. Finle Haraldsen has burns on both arms; he had the worst of it, I think."

"What of Dragon?"

"He's barred himself in the tower. No one sees him, save Azil Aumson."

Murgain said, "What angered him?"

Egain said, "I heard it was Reo Unamira's speech. The old outlaw gave the lord some insult."

Niall lowered his voice. "It was the insolence of the man who led the raid. Yellow-haired, smooth-tongued; called himself the Bastard. Took Herugin with him as safe conduct. Said he would not kill him, but what worth does the word of an outlaw have? Dragon went wild. His father come back again, men said it was."

THE DAY AFTER the burning, Angus Halland went out to mend the stone fence that ran along the eastern border of his farm.

He was very weary. Neither he nor his wife Maura had slept for two nights. Their daughter was sick. In the five years since her birth, Rianna had often suffered random fevers and coughing spells. But this episode seemed more severe than the others. Angus had sat up with her most of the night.

"Papa, it hurts," she whispered hoarsely, holding her throat. "Why does it hurt so much?" He could not answer.

"It's the ash from the fire," Maura said quietly, bathing her face. "My sweet, it will pass."

A light pall of smoke marred the sky to the east. Northward the peaks of the Ippan range stood sentinel. Dragon's Eye, steepest of the peaks, held a dusting of white along its crevices. The air was soft, no hint of frost. He found a gap in the fence. The ground around it was imprinted with the marks of many horses' hooves. The riders coming from the ridge had jumped the fence and tumbled the stones. The biggest of them was sunk in mud. He rocked it and kicked at it, but the ground held it firm. He would need a stick to pry it loose.

He went back to the barn and found an old ax handle. As he levered the stone out of the sucking soil, Anni, the aging black-and-white shepherd dog, growled. A tall woman stood on the other side of the fence. A lean black wolfhound pressed close to her side.

She was clean, though her blue gown was soiled and stained. Her brown hair was shoulder-length, and so uneven that it looked to him as if someone had chopped at it with a knife. He had never seen her before. The dogs gazed fixedly at each other.

"I could help you with that," the woman said. She had a pleasant voice. She stepped through the gap. While the dogs walked stiff-legged around each other, sniffing, the two of them rolled the big stone into place. Angus put the remainder of the stones on top of it, fitting each one as he knew it had to go. He walked along the fence, looking for more dropped stones. She kept pace with him. He found a fallen stone, and put it into place again. When they reached the gate, he held it open and walked his fingers in the air.

"You want me to come with you?" He pointed toward the farmhouse. "You can't speak?" He nodded again. She followed him to the farmhouse door. He pushed it open.

Maura looked up from her work. He pointed at the stranger, and touched his fist to his heart.

Maura rose. She filled a cup with cider.

"Welcome," she said, holding out the cup. "I am Maura Halland. This is my husband, Angus. Come in."

THE HOUSE WAS warm, and it smelled of new bread. A ginger cat looked up from its place on the windowsill to gaze suspiciously at the black dog.

"Grace to the house," Maia said. She took the cup the woman handed her. She sipped. The cider's fruity wine taste made her momentarily dizzy. "My name is Maia."

Angus Halland smiled at her. He was a good-looking man. A pity he could not speak. She put the cup down.

"Sit, please," Maura said, indicating a bench beside the table. "Have some breakfast." A platter on the table held a loaf of bread and some thick slices of cheese. Maia laid a slice of cheese across a slab of bread, and bit into it. The bread had bits of pumpkin in it. Her fingers shook. She made herself eat slowly. Maura set a bowl on the floor for the black-and-white dog, and another, on the other side of the room, for Morga.

Maura Halland was an ugly woman. She was not deformed; her limbs were in the right places. But her proportions were wrong. Her torso was long, and her legs stumpy and short. She had massive hips, and almost no chest. Her face was ill-fashioned as well: her nose was too big, her eyes too small, and her mouth too wide. Her hair was lovely.

Midnight black, thick and glossy, it fell smooth as a waterfall to the middle of her back.

"Did you mend the fence?" she asked Angus. He nodded. His fingers drummed a gallop on the tabletop. "How many riders were there?" His fingers flashed, then spread apart. "They were Reo Unamira's men, weren't they? I wonder what mischief the old devil's up to now. By the smoke, it looks as if he's burned the ridge down."

Maia said, "He's dead. Karadur Atani killed him."

"Tell us, please, what happened." She did. At the end of her recital, Maura said slowly, "This is quite a tale you have told us. Thorin Amdur dead, and the Unamira house burned to ash, and Unamira with it."

Maia said, "It is true."

"Oh, I believe you. But who are you?"

"My full name is Maia Unamira diSorvino. Reo Unamira was my grandfather."

Maura said, "Then you are Iva's daughter. I heard she had returned from Sorvino, and that she brought a girl-child with her."

"That was me."

"I heard she was ill."

"She was. She died in January—not January this year, but the year before that."

"May the Mother receive her." Maura bowed her head a moment. "Why did she leave Sorvino?"

Maia said, "She left because my father did not want her—or me, either."

Maura said, gently, "That must have been very hard for you." She poured more cider into Maia's cup. "So, your grandfather is dead. Your brother is gone, perhaps dead, perhaps not. Your home is gone, too. What will you do now?"

"I don't know. I slept last night in a cottage by the river. I would like to stay there."

A child's voice said, "Mama? Who are you talking to?"

Rising, Maura lumbered to the near sleeping stall. "We have a new neighbor, Rianna, sweet," she said. "She has come to visit us. Her name is Maia."

"What does she look like? I want to see her."

Maia stepped to the sleeping stall. A small child half-lay, half-sat in the narrow box-bed. She had Angus's light reddish-brown hair, badly tangled now, and his fine, regular features. Her cheeks were flushed. Her eyes were bright with intelligence and fever. A toy lay athwart her legs: a wooden doll, dressed in scraps of silk.

"Hello," she said. "Why is your dress torn?"

Maia said, "I was walking in the woods."

Rianna shook her head. "You shouldn't, you know. There are bandits in the forest. You have to be careful." She coughed, a painful barking sound.

"You are right," Maia said. "I shall be, I promise." The ginger cat jumped on the bed, turned about twice, and began to wash.

Maura coaxed Rianna to drink. She straightened the bedclothes, crooning.

When she emerged, Maia said, "How long has she been like this?"

"Three days. She is better today than she was yesterday. She strengthens with the sunlight. But then at night the cough returns."

"If you will lend me a pot, and a flask of wine, I will brew a tisane to help control the cough."

Maura said, "You have skill in such matters?" Maia nodded. "I will give you a pot." She brought one from a cupboard and set it on the table.

Maia said, "She is a beautiful child."

Maura nodded. "Yes. By the Mother's grace, she has Angus's form and features, not mine."

"He is a fine-looking man," Maia said carefully. "And he seems very kind."

"He is the sweetest soul alive."

"You have just the one child?"

"Yes. I wanted more, but I lost two before they were born, and two died after. Rain the midwife says there will be no more."

WHEN MAIA LEFT the Halland farm, Angus went with her. She carried a clean blanket in which reposed a pot, a skein of thread, three bone fishhooks, a needle, a jar of soap, half a dozen candles, a shirt, and a pair of Angus's pants. Angus carried a coil of rope, a hammer, and an ax.

That afternoon, Maia swept and cleaned the hut. Angus mended the walls, plugging grass and moss into the chinks between the stones. While Maia pulled sweet-grass and reeds from the riverbank to make her bed, he found the door hidden beneath a mat of brush, and fastened it back onto its pegs. Maia went fishing, and caught two trout. She cut off their heads, grilled them, and seasoned them with rosemary plucked from the woods. As the sun moved slowly into the western sky, Maia looked for herbs. She found bellflower. She found basil and thyme. She found yellow agrimony, lemon balm, and hemlock. She found parsley in the field below the house, and licorice beside the river. She even found some elecampus root.

That evening Maia ate stewed squirrel by candlelight. She slept on dried sweet-grass, under a clean blanket. In the morning she took soap and her new clothes to the river. Using the pot, she scooped the cold river water over every inch of her body. She scrubbed her feet, and her hair. Shivering, but clean, she washed the blue gown. Then, moved by an impulse she did not understand, she gripped it between both hands and tore it down the middle.

The next day she brought Maura the tisane she had promised. It held elecampus root, licorice, and bellflower. She had guessed at the proportions. Master Eccio had always warned that herbals meant for children should be more dilute than those made for adults.

"Let her drink this when she coughs. You can put honey in it if she finds it too bitter. How is she?"

"Not so well as yesterday. Angus is with her."

Angus lay stretched on the small box-bed. Rianna was curled in his lap. Her face looked drawn. Her father rocked her. The ginger cat watched from the foot of the bed.

"She won't eat," Maura said. "She says it makes her cough."

"She must eat," Maia said. "She needs the strength. Don't give her milk. Give her water, or soups if you can." She tried to remember what she had heard Master Eccio say when the cook's children were sickly, as they were, every winter. "Rub her chest with grease, and bind it lightly with flannel. It will help to keep her warm."

The following day, she was in the meadow, her arms full of grass, when Angus appeared. He was ruddy-faced, and breathed as though he had been running. He *had* been running. The grass slid through her fingers.

"Rianna," she said. "She's worse?"

His grin was wide as the ocean. He mimed sleeping, and eating. Then he extended the flask in which she had poured the tisane. It was nearly empty.

"I will make more," Maia said.

IN THE MONTHS that followed, Maia realized that happenstance—*the gods' will*, Maura said, but then she was a devout woman in her way—had given her a friendship, one without which she might barely have survived the winter, and certainly not in any comfort. She had anticipated solitude, and that she had.

In November it grew cold. In December the storms blew over the mountains, veiling the fields with snow. Throughout December and well into January, days went by when she saw no human face. But then a gloved fist would pound on the door, and she would open the door to find Angus at her doorstep, fur-clad, breathing steam, pulling a laden sledge. Sometimes it held salted meat, once a half round of cheese. Often he brought bread. Maia knew how to bake, but her bread never seemed as tasty as Maura's.

In times of thaw, she sometimes went back with him to the house. She sat beside the hearth, petting the ginger cat, listening to Rianna spin elaborate tales with wooden dolls. *Once upon a time there was a beautiful princess. . . .* There were many dolls. They were, Rianna declared, all kings, queens, wizards, warriors. They were gorgeously dressed, in lace and fur, silk and wool, taffeta and satin. Their heads and trunks and limbs were wood. Angus whittled them, and Maura dressed and painted them.

"What do you do with them?" Maia asked.

"Sell them at Castria Market." She picked up one with red wool for hair and a haughty look on her smooth painted face. "This one is for Chloe, Nini Daluino's daughter.

"Mama, you must call her Elisabetta. That's her name," Rianna said severely. She took the red-haired doll from her mother and walked it over the table.

Rianna had given all the dolls noble names: Gaharis, Atalaya, Genevra. She was a loving child, playful and quick-witted. She adored her father, and seemed to find it unremarkable, even natural, that he had no speech. Angus, in turn, would have walked through flame to bring his child a cup of water. He was a strong man, a knowledgeable farmer, and clever with his hands. . . . His bound tongue seemed his only deficit.

Once, when the two women were alone in the house, Maura spoke of how she and Angus had come to wed.

"We made a bargain. He did not wish to remain on his family's land: they treated him like a lackwit, which he is not. He needed a wife who would help him. I wanted children. And no man who was not simple or blind would marry me if he had other choices."

"The farm is yours?"

"Aye. My mother left it to me. She inherited it from her mother, and she from hers. It is not so big, but it serves us. We have a cow, a horse, a goat, chickens, and bees. And Angus can do anything other men can. He simply cannot speak."

TWICE THAT WINTER Maia glimpsed others in the forest. Once it was a bearded stumpy man dressed in rags. He wore a shapeless cap on his head. She asked Maura about him.

"I don't know his name. He lives with his brother in the woods," Maura said. "In autumn they come out to help with the harvest."

The second time, she was gathering bark from a slippery elm when Morga growled: the low steady rumble that warned a stranger to come no closer. Maia turned. A woman stood watching her. Her white hair blazed about her seamed, strong face. Her clothes were stained, shapeless, and ragged.

Maia said, "Good day, Grandmother. Is there something I might do for you?" But the woman did not answer. Maia returned to her task. When she next glanced behind her, the woman had vanished. She asked Maura about that, too.

"You saw the old woman? Not many do. She lives deep in the forest."

"Who is she?"

Maura shrugged. "I don't know. She's lived there forever. My mother used to leave bread for her on the step. Folk in Castria think she's a hedge-witch."

"What do you think?"

"I think she's harmless." Maura stirred her stewpot. "I leave bread for her, too, in winter, and meat sometimes, when I have it. What can it hurt?"

AFTER NEW YEAR'S Moon, soldiers from Dragon Keep visited the Halland farm. They brought a load of wood, a bag of winter apples, and a huge slab of salted meat from the castle storerooms. They also brought news.

"Herugin Dol has returned," Maura said to Maia the next time she came.

"Who is Herugin Dol?"

"The cavalry officer your brother took with him for safe conduct. He came back last week."

"Came back—from where?"

"From wherever your brother is, I suppose."

So Treion had survived. Maia closed her eyes, giving thanks to whichever god had saved him. No doubt it was Vaikkenen, patron of thieves. She wondered if any of the others had lived: Edric, Nils, Nittri, Ulf. . . . Some, she knew, had not. Their bones had been found on the hillside, and buried with those of the Dragon Keep's soldiers and the luckless horses.

In Dragon Keep, the men of the war band, and particularly the riders, rejoiced to have the captain home. He arrived wearing ragged furs, on a swaybacked, weary horse. The cut across his face had scarred. Karadur came striding down the tower stairs to greet him in the courtyard. Relief and delight were plain on his face. He clasped the rider's hands in both of his. "Welcome back."

"Thank you, my lord," Herugin said. "I'm glad to be here."

Later, in the close, octagonal chamber of the tower, Karadur questioned him. "Where were you? Where did they take you?"

"Into Nakase, my lord, to the hill country north of Yarrow. He has gathered men to him. They call themselves the Bastard's Company."

The singer Azil Aumson spoke from his high-backed chair. "How were you treated?"

"It was not too bad," the rider said. "They fed me."

"Did they make sport of you?"

The scar on Herugin's face darkened. "No. Some wanted to, but Unamira did not permit it, and they obey him."

"Why?"

"He feeds them. He has gold. It was Reo Unamira's gold, I think. He's got quicker wits than most of them, and they know it. A quicker temper, too. They fear his sword."

Karadur asked, "What are his allegiances?"

"He has none, as far as I can tell. He's rootless."

"Does he mean to come north again?"

"No," Herugin said. "He has an enemy, some Nakasean lord. I think he means to ride south, and make mischief."

IN MID-FEBRUARY, ANGUS swam through snow to Maia's hut. His face was drawn. He mimed coughing. Maia wrapped herself in the cloak Maura had woven for her, and thrust beneath it two flasks containing Rianna's tisane. She had brewed it in October, and stored it through winter for just this moment.

The snowdrifts were high and crusty. A relentless wind blew without surcease out of the north. By the time they reached the farmhouse it was dark. Maia's fingers were numb beneath her cloak. Maura opened the door. Her face was the color of candle wax. Behind her, Rianna's coughing made a doglike sound.

Maia thrust the cold flasks into Maura's outstretched hands. "Heat it gently. Don't let it boil." She bent over Rianna's bed. "Hello, princess."

Rianna's eyes were hollow, and her lips had a blue tinge.

"I hurt," she croaked.

"I know," Maia said calmly. Master Eccio had always been calm with his patients. "But you shall be better soon." She gathered the little girl into her arms, feeling the unnatural heat of her.

"There's snow on your cloak," Rianna whispered. "Is it snowing? Where's Morga?"

"She's here. She is getting warm by the fire." Despite the vicious weather, the black dog had followed Maia across the field. She lay panting, while steam rose from her soaked, matted coat.

"I want to see the snow," Rianna said.

"All right. But just for a moment."

Maia opened a window shutter. Cool air swirled into the room. "It smells good," Rianna whispered. The wind dashed snow crystals through the narrow aperture. Lips parted, Rianna leaned into the cold. Her labored breathing eased.

Maura brought a cup. "My sweet, drink your drink."

Rianna took the cup between both hands and sipped. She made a face. "Bitter." She coughed again. "I don't want it."

Maura said, "Love, you must drink. It will make you better."

"Put honey in it," Maia said. "A little will do no harm."

Wind blew through the farmhouse; the candles would not stay lit. Maura kept a kettle at the boil: the moist steam eddying through the room seemed to relieve the hard coughing. With Rianna in his arms, Angus walked from one side of the house to the other. The house rattled in the incessant wind. Rianna coughed and sipped and coughed again. When Angus tired, Maia took his place.

"Tell me a story," Rianna whispered, and Maia told her the story of the wind-giant who lived in the north, and how he and his brother, the south wind, agreed to hold a contest to see which of them could blow the harder. . . . In the middle, Rianna fell asleep. A little while later she woke again, sweating heavily, and coughing as if her lungs would burst.

"Give her to me," Maura said. She took Rianna in her arms and walked with her, crooning to her as if she were a baby.

Maia curled onto the hearth rug beside her dog. Her face felt numb. A little before dawn, the wind died. Maia woke into the silence. She sat up, rubbing her eyes. Maura sat motionless at her loom. In the dark room she was a shape, a stone, a shadow.

Angus, with Rianna in his arms, lay across his and Maura's bed. Maia rose stiffly. Crossing to the window, she thrust the shutter back. A pale quarter-moon hung halfway up the sky. The storm had passed. The snow was wan, the sky a deep grey, as if some wizard's spell had banished color.

Maura lifted her head. "Listen," she said softly. From the bed came the sounds of the ginger cat's purr, and Angus's slow breathing.

Maia walked to the bedside. The ginger cat's purr grew louder. Rianna lay curled in the very center of the bed. Her chest rose and fell evenly.

Stooping, Maia laid the back of her hand against the child's cheek.

It was cool and dry.

3

IT WAS SPRING in Ippa, and Karadur Atani was looking for his kindred.

He had never flown this high before. The great wind of the sky, whose name, it had told him, was Inatowy, had iced his wings with its deadly breath. It was an effort for him to lift them.

Below him, through the deep blanket of darkness, lay the endless ocean. His home was behind him, days away. He had not meant to come this far. He had been hunting over Kameni, the easternmost province of Ryoka, flying in great slow circles, calling with his mind, as he had learned to do, and listening. . . . It was painful, listening to silence.

Then silence had been broken by a voice, a soft crystalline singing in the fissures of his mind. *Greetings, bright one. . . .*

A strange being hovered above him in the brilliant sky: a naked, white, winged man, whose hands and feet were talons. The winds rushed about it in a great whirling cloud, so that it moved within a vortex of air.

He answered, *Greetings, sky-dweller. Who are you?*

I am Inatowy, lord of the upper sky. Hast heard of me?

I have not. What manner of being are you?

I know not what men call it. I am Inatowy. I dance between earth and the Void.

O Inatowy, have you seen my kindred?

I have heard them, the winged being sang. *I have heard them, and I have seen them. I saw them flying over the sunlit sea, scarlet and ebony, white and gold, sapphire and rose.*

Every atom of Karadur's being blazed with sudden hope. *When did you see them, lord of the sky?*

Long, long ago. They were singing. I called to them to come and dance, but they did not hear me.

Where did they go?

I do not know. The extraordinary being bent toward him. *Thou art beautiful, bright one, as indeed thy kindred were beautiful. It has been long and long indeed since I danced with the dragon-children. Will you dance with me, bright one?*

I know not what you mean, he said.

And the white-winged being grinned, and opened its mouth, and a great, battering wind lifted him like a dry leaf and flung him through the azure emptiness, and dropped him. Furious, he spread his wings and found the thermal, and rose upon it. Inatowy swooped lazily under his nose. He flung fire at the wind, and it tore his flame to shreds and scattered it like dust.

For a brief, unaccustomed moment he had been afraid.

A voice sang in his mind: *Be not wrathful, bright one. We are kin. I would not harm thee. This is play.* The wind caught him again. This time he slipped its grip, diving beneath it toward the featureless land below.

Caught in a kind of madness, he played with the wind, now hunted, now hunter. At last the white being said to him, *Come, bright one. Let us see who is the faster, thou or I. I shall race thee to the sun!* And they raced, shooting eastward across the dun-colored countryside. But even he could not catch the sun; it drew farther and farther away from him across the endless sky.

And now it was night.

Far above him, the stars, his ancient brothers, shone. They saw him, fighting the will of the wind. They knew him. But there was nothing they could do for him. They dwelt elsewhere, in that great hollow place around the world that humans had named the Void. It felt very close, that place.

If he gave himself to the wind it would take him there. It howled against his skin, and the membrane of his spread wings grew cold. His spent muscles burned. The air barely touched his laboring lungs. His wings seemed not to move. Reason told him that he did not have to stay in this place, battling the wind, but he could not think what to do. His dazed mind seemed frozen.

Inatowy, he said, *release me. . . . I must go home.*

Come, sang a coaxing voice in his mind. *Are we not both great lords, thou and I? I have flown over thy land many times. Now let me show thee* my *kingdom.*

It was tempting. All he had to do was cease to struggle: to let the white wind take him.

It is no great thing, bright one. Only surrender.

Deep in his chilled heart, rage woke. Like fire in the night, it leaped through his sluggish muscles. His blood quickened, and with it, his mind began to work. Lifting his golden scaled head, he roared defiantly into the wind. Then he spread his wings, and began to drop through the murderous rushing cold toward the restless ocean.

* * *

MAIA DISORVINO WAS fishing in the river when she saw the dragon fall.

He was moving very slowly, his great wings barely holding him. He swooped so close that she saw quite clearly his great rending talons, spread to grip, and the delicate diamond pattern of his soft belly scales. He skimmed the top of the ridge.

Then he vanished, and did not reappear.

She stood trembling. She wanted to run, to thrust herself, like a wounded animal, into a dark, safe hole. She waited, knowing that this was the body's fear. After a while, the shivering went away.

"Morga," she called. The black dog crept from where she had been cowering. She looked ashamed. "It's not your fault," Maia told her. "I was frightened, too. Come."

Leaving her pole and basket where it was, she climbed to the crest of the ridge. A man lay in a clump of purple fireweed. His massive chest rose and fell. His eyes were shut. A wide gold band gleamed on his forearm. She went closer, noting the lines of exhaustion on his fair face. His limbs appeared unbroken. His clothes were shredded, and there was ice matted in his hair. He wore no sword. The hilt of a knife poked from a sheath in his right boot.

She listened to his even breathing. He was deeply asleep. She wondered if she should wake him. *Only a fool wakes a sleeping dragon.* She wondered if she could wake him. Sleep was physic, and from the look of him, he needed it. She had no fear for his safety. Even asleep, there was no mistaking who he was.

A bee hummed merrily among the flowers. Maia rose, and went back down the hill. In her cottage she found a pillow, and a jug with a stopper. She filled the jug with water, and returned to the slope. The ice in his hair had melted, but the dragon-lord had not moved. She laid the flask near his crooked right elbow. He would be thirsty when he woke. Then, carefully, she slid a hand beneath his head, lifted it, and eased the pillow beneath his cheek.

THRICE DURING THE day, between her tasks, Maia climbed the hill, Morga at her heels, to look at her visitor. He seemed peaceful.

The second time she found him turned on his side, an arm across his eyes. She lifted the water jug. It was empty. She went to the river, and refilled it. When she returned, he was sitting up. She halted. For a moment he seemed not to see her, and then the blue eyes focused. Her fingers tightened on the jug until she feared it would split.

He said, "It was kind of you to leave me a pillow. How long have I been asleep?"

His voice was very deep.

"Since dawn. I saw you descend. I thought it best not to wake you."

"You were wise," he said. "I was very tired. I don't remember that descent. I remember only wind and sea, and the shape of the hills."

She wondered if he recognized her. She held the jug out. He reached for it, and tipped it to his mouth. His hands were huge. He drained the jug, and started to rise. Morga, motionless and alert at Maia's right knee, stared at him suspiciously and growled a warning.

"Morga, hush," Maia said hastily. The wolfhound's feathery tail drooped, and her ears went down.

The dragon-lord snapped his fingers. "Come, Morga."

The wolfhound glided forward as if drawn on a string. He held a hand out to her. She sniffed it delicately, and then, to Maia's wonder, allowed the big man to stroke her narrow head and soft ears. "Thou shalt know me next time, eh?" Morga's ears pricked. Her tail began to wave. He glanced over the dog's head at Maia. "You are Maia diSorvino. I did not know that you were still in my land."

There was nothing she could say. If he wanted her gone, she would have to leave.

He said, "You needn't fear. I have no quarrel with you."

She had a loaf of poppy-seed bread in her house, Maura's gift, fresh-baked, and the rose-bellied trout she had caught that morning, still in its reed cooler beneath the riverbank. She had intended to cook it for supper.

She said, "My lord, are you hungry? I have food. Bread."

"Hungry. Yes."

She led him to the house. He halted on the threshold, taking in the wreaths and strings of dried herbs that hung from every ceiling beam. The cottage smelled powerfully of their mingled aromas. He stepped into the tiny room.

"Are you an herbalist?" he asked.

She was not sure how to answer. "I have some skill. I was never formally trained."

Morga curled up on her rug beside the hearth. Maia set bread and a pot of clover honey on a tray, and laid it on the narrow wooden plank that served her for a table. She filled a cup with water and set it in front of him. "Please sit, my lord."

He sat, and gestured to the second stool. "This is your house. You must sit."

The courtesy surprised her. She drew up the second stool, and seated herself opposite him. He slathered honey on a slice of bread and ate it in three bites.

His propinquity made the hut seem smaller than it was. It was not an effect simply of his size: she was tall, and she had known other big men. It was the sense of his power, the weight of his presence. She remembered the dragon's fiery inhuman gaze, and the sound of his rage.

That was the Golden Dragon. This is Karadur Atani, lord of Atani Castle.

But she knew they were one and the same.

"You bake good bread," he said. He took another slice.

She said, "It's not mine. It was made by my neighbor, Maura Halland."

"You said you were not an herbalist. But someone taught you."

"I used to play in the garden in my father's house when I was a child. Uta, my nurse, taught me to recognize and find common herbs. She was my first teacher."

"Who was your second?"

"Master Eccio. He was the physician who came to treat my mother."

"What did he teach you?"

"He taught me to measure. He taught me how to make pastes and tinctures. He taught me how to mix one element with another, and sometimes with wine, to make both more active. He taught me to label my work. He taught me to recognize and treat simple ailments."

"Could you treat a sword cut? A simple one."

"Yes."

"How?"

"I would wash it in water that had been boiled and allowed to cool, and powder it with comfrey. Were it deep, I might recommend that it be stitched."

"And could you do that?"

"Yes." In the six years she had lived with her grandfather's outlaws she had done it many times.

He lifted the cup, and studied her over its rim. "What happened to the man who taught you these things?"

The skin on her face and arms tightened. "He died."

"How?"

It had been a shameful death—a criminal's death. "My father had him strangled."

Her guest had demolished the bread. She brought the waterskin to the table and refilled his cup. As she reseated herself, her foot encountered something soft. One of Rianna's dolls lay prostrate and forlorn beneath the stool. She could not remember its name; something grand: Rinetta, Beatricia, Alisandre. . . . She dusted it off and set it in her lap.

Karadur Atani's wide mouth quirked. "Charming. Is this another of your skills?"

"It belongs to Rianna, Maura's daughter. She must have forgotten it the last time she visited." She held the little doll upright and made it bow. "Good day, my lord."

An expression she could not read crossed his face. He said meditatively, "When we were small, my brother and I had an Isojai warrior and a spearman with the dragon badge painted on his chest. We used to make them battle one another." He drained his cup, and rose. "I must leave you now. Thank you for your care, and for the meal."

"You are welcome."

"Forgive my shabby manners. A guest should bring a gift, but I have nothing to give you."

Was he mocking her? She could not be sure, but she did not think so. She matched his gravity. "I take no offense, my lord."

He held out a hand. She took it. His fingers closed lightly over hers. His hand was warm. The skipping rhyme that Uta had taught her scurried through her head. *Dragon sleeping, Dragon wakes, Dragon holds what Dragon takes, How many apples shall I see, growing wild on yonder tree, One, two, three, four.* . . . For an instant, she saw in her mind that other thing he was, a being of glitter and flame.

Her hand trembled in his. He opened his fingers.

They left the cottage. The sky was a bright pale blue. The dragon-lord turned to climb the ridge. Morga, tail flying like a flag, frisked playfully ahead of him.

"Morga, no," he told her. "Stay with thy mistress." The black dog's tail drooped. She retreated, to stand at Maia's knee. He turned once, halfway up the slope, to look back. Then he reached the crest of the hill. Lightning flashed along the ridgetop.

The Golden Dragon rose from the hillside. His vast bright wings beat. A hot dry wind seared the pliant grasses. His shadow swept over her.

Then the shadow lifted, and he was gone.

IN THE PROVINCE of Nakase, two weeks' ride from Dragon Keep, Treion Unamira watched a village burning.

Its name was Alletti. It was scarcely big enough to be called a village: it had a scant thirteen houses, along with a mill, a cobbler's shop, and a forge. The smith mended wheels, doctored sick horses, forged plowshares, and repaired the holes in kettles. It also had an inn, where travelers stayed while the smith repaired the wagons and the cobbler mended frayed tack. They drank the local liquor, which the miller brewed in a shed behind his house, and sometimes slept a night or two in the inn's lice-ridden rooms.

Treion had brought his men into town, as was his custom, at sunset. The town's constable looked at twenty armed, horsed men and at the confident face and ready sword of their leader, and offered no resistance.

But the grey-bearded innkeeper had loudly proclaimed what anyone could see was not true, that he had no money.

Treion hung him for the lie from the oak outside his own front door. When the innkeeper's wife foolishly refused to give up the strongbox, he had said, "Burn it down." The insect-ridden wood burned easily, fueled by the gouts of liquor his men had splattered. The fire had spread to the mill. The villagers had tried to save it; his men had killed three of them, including the miller, and now the rest stood glumly silent.

Treion stared into the fire. Fires were better at night. The sight and sound of flames burning into darkness brought a rush of pleasure to his blood.

He had always loved fire. As a child he had spent long hours gazing into the kitchen fires, speaking to them, certain that if he could only find the right words he could make the dancing flames obey his thought.

It had happened, once. Riding through the dry forest, as flames roared around him and a dragon soared overhead, he had spoken to the encircling fire, and it had let him and his followers pass through unharmed. He remembered the exhilaration and terror of that moment. Staring into the flames, he spoke to them again now, willing them to hear. . . . *Awake! Arise!* But nothing happened.

He watched the red blaze fall in upon itself. Edric arrived at his elbow.

"We found the money." He brandished a leather pouch. "It was under the stairs. It's mostly silver. Stupid, to die for a sack of coins with Alf Ridenar's ugly mug on them. You want us to keep looking?"

They had been here too long already. "No."

THEY CAMPED THAT night in one of their best hiding places: a huge cavern, easily large enough to hold them all.

A narrow, nearly invisible trail led to its entrance. Others had used it before them: they had found bits of metal and cloth and old glass fragments scattered about the place. An elaborate system of smoke holes—impossible to say whether they had been created by happenstance or design—sent smoke entirely in the opposite direction from the cave's mouth.

Treion sat in his usual place, cleaning his sword. Firelight glittered on the steel. It was a good sword, of Ippan steel, which was nearly as good as Chuyo steel. He had taken it from Evard diScala's armory the day he left Arriccio. Someday, maybe, he would have a Chuyo blade. In the depths of the cave, the men were buoyant with drink, and because they had something to entertain them: the miller's wife, who had turned out to be young and moderately pretty. Wiping the sword with oil, he sheathed it, and beckoned to Leo. "Tell Savarini I want to talk to him."

Leo slouched away. In a little while Niello strolled from the rear of the cave. "Chief. You called?"

"Sit," Treion said. Niello Savarini sat, gracefully. He did all things gracefully. He had come to them in February. Reo Unamira's intelligencer had been Nittri Parducci, known as Fat Nittri, or Nittri the Ear. Nittri had died in the burning. Nittri had been a gross man, foul-mouthed and filthy. Niello was entirely other. He was a handsome man, and a superb intelligencer. He could walk into a strange inn of an evening, and within an hour know whom the innkeeper's wife was bedding and what the weekly take was. He could be scholar or merchant or fishmonger. He had, he admitted, been expelled from Kalni Leminin's service for crimes that, the outlaws speculated, ranged from bestiality to cannibalism. His true name was not Savarini, but Ciccio. Only Treion knew that. He also knew the true nature of Niello Ciccio's crimes. He thought the man who had described them to him had been exaggerating, but could not be sure.

"Our take was poor tonight. We did much better at Embria." Embria was north of Alletti. Sensibly, the folk of that town had handed a sizable portion of the town's treasury to Treion three months ago.

"Embria's larger," Niello said. He reached for the wineskin.

Treion let him drink his fill before asking, "So—will diSorvino send troops to Alletti?"

"Of course," Niello said. "Just as he did to Embria. They're on their way; sent to find the miscreants who burned the inn and bring them to justice; thirty of his finest, under Captain Nortero's command."

Gilberto Nortero was a simpering sycophant whom Marion diSorvino had elevated to senior commander's rank. Treion snorted.

"Nortero's an idiot. He couldn't find stink in a midden." He took the wineskin back. It was empty. "Leo!" Treion threw him the empty skin. "Fill that. How's the rain?"

"Coming down harder."

"Send Oliver to check on the horses."

"Aye," said Leo. He walked to the rear of the cave and bellowed, "Oliver! Chief says go check on the horses!"

Oliver trudged glumly past the fire.

Niello said, "How did we do at Alletti?"

"Forty ridari."

"Not enough," Niello said.

It wasn't enough. The gold he'd stolen from his grandfather was almost gone, spent on food and beer and weapons and horses and winter quarters and bribes and information. It was possible that there was still gold hidden on Coll's Ridge. But he would not go back. Word had come from Ippa across the Nakase border: nothing on Coll's Ridge had survived the burning.

He did not mourn his grandfather; he had planned to kill

the old man himself, sooner or later. But the news of his sister's death had come like a knife thrust into his heart. She should not have been there, in Ippa, living among drunks and bandits: she should have been in Sorvino, loved, honored, sheltered by her family's name and money. That, too, was part of the score he had to settle with diSorvino.

He allowed himself to imagine Marion diSorvino pinned beneath a beam in the burning wreckage of his manor, as the inexorable flames crawled closer. . . . That vision, or a version of it, had sustained him through his childhood. But his company, though murderous, was too small to assault Sorvino, and so he had to be content with harrying farmers and innkeepers.

Frustration roared through him like a hot wind. Terrorizing farmers, skulking in a cave waiting for Gilberto Nortero's trackers to find him—this, *this* was not what he wanted. How had he come to this place? When he escaped Sorvino, his principal ambition had been to make a name for himself, to be known as a warrior, to ride in some great lord's war band. . . . But the glory he'd sought had not come. He had traveled about Nakase for three years, taking employment here and there, first as a caravan guard, then as a bodyguard in Secca. He'd spent two years in Arriccio, in Evard diScala's guard troop. It was not a happy time. DiScala's men were lazy, and his officers corrupt, little better than the thugs they were paid to apprehend. When he left, with little to show for his training except a taste for merignac and a strong mistrust of the nobility, the stolen sword had seemed a scarcely adequate payment.

In the rear of the cave, voices began to sing. *"Southern girls have yellow hair; Take her, Donny, take her. . . ."* If they made too much noise, even Gilberto Nortero's trackers would be forced to hear them. He signaled Leo.

"Tell them to be quiet."

Leo cupped his hands to shout.

"Hoy," he yelled, "chief says to keep it down."

Suddenly a man roared in fury. A woman, half-naked, plunged from the rear of the cave. Head down, long hair flying, she raced blindly through the fire, and flung herself toward the entrance. She ran headfirst into Oliver. He wrapped his arms around her. She kicked furiously. Gund loped after her. He was a big man, notoriously brutal even among the outlaws. He wore a bloodied shirt, and no pants.

"Damn that woman. I'm going to kill her."

Niello said, "Why?"

"She cut me!" he said. "She took my knife, my own knife, and cut me! Look at it." He lifted his shirt. Blood welled from the shallow cut and trickled down his belly. He bent snarling over the woman. She snarled back at him. He hit her. The blow snapped her head back.

"Cunt. Bitch. I'm going to snap your neck." He wrapped both hands in the woman's long brown hair.

Maia's hair was—had been—long and brown. She was a girl, really, younger than his sister. Her small breasts were purple with marks from the men's fingers. There was blood and dirt on her thighs.

Treion said, "Stop." Gund did not seem to hear. Rising, Treion drew his sword. "Stop," he repeated.

The big man opened his hands. He took a step back. "Chief," he protested, "she cut me."

"Too bad," Treion said. He looked at the crouching woman. Her eyes glittered. He remembered a cat that his men had shut into a barrel with a fighting cock. Its eyes had glittered so. She wanted to live.

"Oliver. Give her your cloak." Oliver hesitated. "Do it!"

Sullenly, Oliver took off his rain-soaked cloak. The girl snatched it from his hands and wrapped it around her shoulders.

"Go," Treion told her. Oliver stood in the entrance. "Get out of her way."

"She'll bring the soldiers."

"No, she won't. They'll use her just as you have, or worse. She won't go near them. You won't, will you?" he said to the girl. She shook her head. Then she slipped past Oliver, and was gone.

Gund was red with fury.

"You should have let me kill her," he said to Treion.

"Another time," Treion said. Gund stared at him, eyes burning. Treion held his eyes a moment. Go ahead, his stare said to the infuriated outlaw. Charge me.

Gund turned, and lumbered in the direction of the liquor. The rest of the men followed him. Sheathing his sword, Treion returned to the fire.

Niello said, "You take chances. You shouldn't."

"You mean the girl? She won't look for the soldiers. She'll go home, to her village." What was left of it.

"I mean the men. Gund won't forgive you. You shamed him."

"The girl shamed him."

"He'll make trouble."

"If he does, I'll kill him." He knew he could do it. He was strong, and faster than any of them with a blade. *They* knew he could do it.

He did not think Gund would make trouble for him with the others. It was not that they were loyal—except, perhaps, for Edric—but they had grown used to following his orders. Without him, most of them would by now be dead, or in some lord's prison.

Besides, they thought he was lucky. He had heard Edric boast of it. He was Treion the Bastard, who had faced the Dragon of Chingura, and walked away with his skin.

Still, he had to have gold. Lucky or not, they would leave if he did not pay them. A ghost of an idea flitted through his mind.

He said, "I know where we can find some gold."

Niello raised an eyebrow.

"Castella."

The intelligencer said, "You're mad. It's under Kalni Leminin's protection. You know that."

"So what? We'll be there and gone before he hears about it."

"It's walled."

"Walls can be climbed." Walls could be climbed, doors forced, strongboxes opened. . . .

"The Lemininkai has a garrison there."

"How big? Under whose command?"

"I don't know," Niello said.

"Can you find out?"

"Surely." He frowned. "You're serious about this, aren't you?"

"Maybe." If fate desired him to be an outlaw, Treion thought, perhaps it was time for him to embrace it. He would be Treion the Bastard, the man who sacked Castella. . . . "Maybe not. Don't say anything. It's just an idea. Have you your pieces on you?"

Smiling, Niello withdrew a keph box from within his cloak. The delicate carved pieces, half the size of those in a conventional set, glittered in the firelight.

Treion fished a ridari from his pocket. "Heads or tails."

"Heads."

The coin spun, and dropped into the dust, face side up. Treion turned the board, giving Niello the Summer pieces. Aloof in her carved elegance, the Summer Princess faced the Winter Warrior; the Wizard faced the Vampyre; the Eagle faced the Raven. The two Kings confronted each other gravely: mirror images, except that the Winter King was blind.

Niello nudged a pikeman forward. Treion lifted the Winter Warrior's pikeman in his fingertips and advanced it one square.

"Your move."

4

FOUR DAYS AFTER the unexpected visit from her overlord, a heavy knock sounded on Maia diSorvino's front door.

Morga, sleeping on her rug beneath the window, lifted her head. Her tail thumped. Maia was kneading bread dough. "A moment." She scooped the dough into its bowl and covered it. Wiping her fingers on a cloth, she opened the door, expecting to see Angus.

Karadur Atani stood before the small doorway. Tail thrashing, Morga frisked to him and stuck her head under his hand.

He scratched her chin. "Well, beast. Hast kept thy mistress safe, I see." Behind him, a big black gelding bent its head to snatch at the new grass.

He held out a wooden case. "This is for you. It's from my library."

She opened it. Nestled within the smooth wood lay a book. *The Properties of Herbs*, the printing on the cover read, *Prepared by Nennius Guerin, Being an Account of my Observation of the Properties of some Medicinal Plants, with Illustrations*. She opened it to the first page. *Aloe,* the text read. *A plaster of aloe leaf cures burns and soothes eruptions of the skin from the bites of insects and evil beasts*. She turned the page. *Anise. The seeds of this delicate plant will relieve cough, sweeten breath, and quicken a mother's milk*.

Master Eccio had had a copy of *The Properties of Herbs*. When she was small, he had kept her amused by allowing her to look at the pictures. As her interest in his work quickened, he had used it as a syllabus. After his death, her father had burned all his books.

She closed the wooden cover, and held it out. "My lord, this is a treasure. You should not give it away."

"It is mine, therefore I may give it if I wish. Do you want it?"

He was Dragon; she could not lie to him. She nodded. He smiled. She caught her breath, because of the way it changed his face. "Good. It's yours.

He closed the door before she could speak to thank him.

LATER THAT WEEK she had a second visitor. Miri Halleck's farm was adjacent to Angus and Maura's. She had heard about Maia from Maura, and had walked across the fields to meet her. She had brought a guest-gift: a lace-trimmed pillow, stuffed with lambswool.

"Here. Invite me in, girl."

She looked at the cottage with approval. "So, you're Iva Unamira's daughter. I knew your grandfather, thieving sheep-stealing scoundrel that he was. He was a handsome man, though. I always liked him."

Miri was past seventy, and thrice, she proclaimed proudly, a widow. She had five daughters and two sons. "Seventeen grandchildren. Twenty great-grandchildren, and two more due next month." She had lost her first husband to fever, and her second to an Isojai raid. "He rode with the Black Dragon into Ippa, the old fool. *Stay home,* I told him. *War is for young men*. But farming never suited him. He was happiest on horseback."

They spent the afternoon talking, or rather, Miri talked, while Maia listened. Miri knew everyone in the domain. She had known Wina Omara, Maia's grandmother, who had borne Reo Unamira a daughter, and died in the Fever Year. "She was a sweet woman." She spoke of Hana Diamori, the dragon-lord's mother—"She was a child, that Hana. She should have married some young man of her own country. But the children of the highborn do not make their own choices"—and of Atalaya Atani, Kojiro Atani's mother, who had ruled the domain for forty years, and vanished in the midst of a thunderstorm.

"Ah, she was a beauty. White, white skin, and hair the color of flame. She was wild. She never wed. She refused to even name her son's father. She said he was the North Wind.

"But it did not matter who Kojiro Atani's sire was. From the moment he was born, everyone could see that he was Dragon."

Mama, what's a bastard?

A child who does not know its father. Why?

Father called Treion a bastard. But Treion is my brother. How can he be a bastard?

Treion is your half brother. He is mine, but not your father's.

But, Mama—don't you know who Treion's father is?

Oh yes, Iva Unamira diSorvino said, *I know*.

Maia said, "What was he like?"

"The Black Dragon? He was a wild boy, and a fearsome man. His temper could kindle in an instant, and when it did, there was no escaping it. But those who served him faithfully he rewarded. Loyalty and courage mean everything to the dragon-kindred."

Maia said, "Did you know my mother?"

"I knew her. We were not close. You look like her, a little."

"Surely not," Maia said. "I am tall. She was small and delicate, and beautiful."

"It's so. She was beautiful, and shameless with it. Men fell about her like trees in a windstorm. Alf, my eldest, wanted desperately to wed her. She laughed at him, of course. I was glad. They would never have suited. I remember when she left, to go to Sorvino. I was surprised to hear of her return. Why did she leave Sorvino?"

Maia was growing accustomed to the question.

"She left because my father did not want her, and because she was sick."

When Miri left, she took with her a wreath of chamomile leaves and a bag of poplar-bark powder for her hands, which were swollen and painful, especially in the morning. As she crossed the threshold, she turned back.

"Do you make a remedy for headache? My daughter Arafel has fierce headaches."

"I know several remedies for headache," Maia said.

"I will send her to you," Miri said.

SHE KEPT HER word. In the weeks to follow, a steady stream of folk made their way to Maia's door, Arafel among them. Most had minor ailments. Maia did what she could for them. She made teas for headache, stomachache, and flatulence. She made tisanes for fevers and anxious nerves. She made syrups for a cough, and poultices for bruises and sprains.

Sinnea Ohair, who had been in service at Dragon Keep before she married Murgain the Archer, took away a salve to cure a sty. Rain, the midwife of Sleeth, came to the house, not for a potion, but to ask Maia to keep an eye out for the herbs she needed in her work.

"I keep basil and dill in my garden. Thistle and pennyroyal are easy to find. But raspberry, bearberry, slippery elm; often I cannot get to them. I am less spry than I used to be. My greatest need is for purple fennel." She looked at Maia somewhat dubiously. "Do you know—?"

"I know." *This is fennel,* Uta had said. *There are two kinds. We can eat the stalks of both, but the kind with the purple flowers has another use. I will explain when you are older*. She hadn't, but Master Eccio had. He had taught Maia how to crush the seeds to make tea, and told her, in his driest professional tone, that drinking fennel tea every day would keep a man's seed from quickening in a woman's womb. He showed her the relevant page in Guerin's *Properties. Purple fennel, although it prefers sun and warmth, is hardier than its yellow-blossomed cousin. In cold climates yellow fennel will wither, but purple fennel can survive all but the coldest climes. . . .*

"Do you have much need for pennyroyal?"

Rain said, "It has its uses. Some women do not want children. And some women should not have them; their bodies are too weak to bear a child. Men do not think of such things. It's not their concern."

Maia nodded. Women gave birth. The making, and sometimes the unmaking, of children was their business.

She prowled the woods looking for herbs. The trees were thick with new leaves; miniature flames, trembling at the ends of the red-limned branches. She cleared space for a garden behind the cottage. She filled the cottage with cuttings. When she tired of her own company, she visited Maura and Angus. The spring corn was up; she joined Angus in the fields, and learned to use a weed hook. When rain drove her inside, she sewed. Nini Daluino, the draper from Castria, had traded her a bolt of cloth for simples. Maura helped her cut it. She was an indifferent seamstress, but a dogged one, and she needed clothes. She made trousers, and a shirt.

She was not lonely. She missed her mother, though, and she missed Fenris. And she missed comfort: soft clothes, a hot bath, food she did not have to find or cook herself. But such desires were childish. Her mother had lived with a man she had not loved to protect her child, and left him for the same reason. She had endured his spite, and her father's drunken fits. She had lived in pain, and died without complaint. *She* was Iva Unamira's daughter. She could bathe in cold water, and eat root vegetables for days at a time, if that was what was necessary. Comfort could be forgone.

Often, during that spring, she would look up from her harvesting to see in the cloudless sky the great glittering form of the Golden Dragon. In Castria, where she went occasionally to trade her potions for the goods she could not fashion, she listened to the tales people told of the dragon-kindred. Some, like the story of Lyr, were ones she knew. Others, like the story of Iyadur Atani, the Silver Dragon, were new to her. Maura told her of the war Karadur Atani had fought against his brother Tenjiro.

"They were womb-brothers. But Tenjiro was always angry, jealous of his brother. He left the Keep to study sorcery. When he came back, he stole Dragon's magic, and vanished. No one knew where he was. Then Azil Aumson returned to the Keep."

"Who is he?"

"He is a singer, son to Aum Nialsdatter, steward of Atani Castle. He is Dragon's dearest friend. Tenjiro took Azil north with him and kept him there, a prisoner. Everyone thought he was dead. But he escaped, and came back, across the ice. That winter, last year it was, Tenjiro sent wargs into the domain. They killed twenty people. It was a bad time."

Maia said, "I remember it." The outlaws had kept close to home all winter.

"In spring, Dragon took the army north. He fought Tenjiro and took his magic back. They say a wizard helped him, a woman."

BEHIND THE SHIELD of its brick walls and hanging gardens, the village of Castella dreamed in the sun.

Rodolfo Mino, Governor of Castella, nibbled delicately at his sugar-topped muffin. It was an idyllic day. The air was warm, scented with chocolate. A mug of it, topped with cream and cinnamon, sat on the table before him, beside his second muffin.

In the meadow below his patio, a trio of village girls were exchanging secrets beneath the fig trees. Goats grazed on the verdant hillsides. A red-tailed hawk hovered hopefully above them, black against a luminous sapphire sky.

Across the green and placid meadows lay other villas, summer homes for the wealthy of Ujo and Firense. Their presence gave Castella its name: the Summer City. Like his own, they were old, elegant in design, filled with beauty. Most were empty; it was June, a little early for the summer visitors, though some had arrived already, like Remy Andujar, and Celia Bertinelli. He had dined with Celia two evenings ago. Even though she was nearly forty, she was still one of the most beautiful women he had ever seen. He had brought her a bottle of eighteen-year-old merignac. She had given him a crimson robe embroidered with a vine-leaf pattern.

"To keep you warm at night," she jested.

He had not misunderstood; she had no romantic interest in him, nor, to tell the truth, did he have in her. They were, as Celia said, winter friends.

Once he, too, had wintered in Ujo. But he found traveling less convenient now than he had when he was younger, and carried less flesh on his bones. He was a substantial man. He was also not ambitious, and therefore did not need to visit Ujo to remind Kalni Leminin of his loyalty. He was fortunate to have so powerful a patron.

He was fortunate, too, in his brothers, who were perfectly content for him to live in Castella, while they toiled in Ujo, managing the bank. They were good at managing the bank. He would have made a terrible banker.

He smelled smoke. Something was burning. He hoped that it was not his lunch. He heard a sound behind him; the scrape of a footfall on brick.

"Leander," he said, without turning, "draw my bath, if you would be so kind."

An unfamiliar voice said, "I am sorry, Governor. I'm afraid you will have to wait for your bath. Leander is busy."

He turned. Two strangers stood on his patio. The one in front was slender and fair-haired, rather good-looking. He held a drawn sword in his right hand.

"Who are you?" Rodolfo Mino said. He rose. "What are you doing in my house?"

The man with the sword smiled. "My name's Unamira. They call me the Bastard. Don't bother to call your garrison. I am afraid they also are busy."

He had heard of this man who called himself the Bastard. He and his outlaw band had been giving Marion diSorvino fits, threatening towns, stealing, burning. . . .

"What do you want?"

"We want your gold, Governor. Where is it?"

Mino said, "I will not tell you that."

"Niello," the man said. A third man, also fair-haired, with a vulpine face, stepped onto the terrace, dragging Leander with him by one slim wrist. He held a knife in his right hand. Leander was naked. His hands were bound, and a filthy cloth had been thrust into his mouth. "I think you will. Show him, Niello."

The other man smiled, and with a negligent flick of his hand, slid the knife along Leander's chest. A pebble of flesh—Leander's left nipple—fell to the brick. Blood streamed down his narrow chest.

"Stop," Rodolfo Mino said. "That is unnecessary. I will give you whatever you want."

"I thought you would," the speaker said. "You will lead the way to your strongbox. Quickly, please." His sword tip lifted threateningly. In the orchard, the girls were still singing. Leander's eyes were filled with terror. The scent of burning grew stronger.

Don't hurt them, Rodolfo Mino prayed. *Please don't hurt them.*

He stepped across the tiles, avoiding the blood.

THEY LEFT THE governor bound and gagged beside his empty strongbox.

"Now where shall we go?" Edric said.

Treion pointed at random to a nearby villa. "Let's go there."

"Whose is it?" Edric asked.

"I have no idea." He turned to ask Niello. He was nowhere to be seen. "What the hell . . . Where did he go?"

Edric said, "Don't know. Want me to look for him?"

"No." He stuffed the pouch with the governor's money into his saddlebag. They rode toward the villa, passed a deserted square, a fountain, an olive orchard. . . . Half the trees were alight. There were fires everywhere now. The flames were highest around the guardhouse. They had stacked hay around it, and blocked the door with the cart they had used to haul it in. They had purchased hay and cart from a farmer in Orvieto. Wisely, he had asked no questions.

Gund and Leo loped by. Gund had a swath of yellow silk wrapped about his shoulders. He was carrying an ornate silver candlestick in one hand.

What you find is yours to keep, Treion had told his men. *When you've got enough, get out. Separate, don't stay together. They'll be looking for us.*

Where shall we go? Oliver had asked.

Wherever you like. We'll meet again in Yarrow, a month from now.

THEY RODE TO the house. The front door was locked, but Edric broke a window. The house was exquisitely furnished, with fine wood chairs and stuffed beds, and silk over all the windows. The hearths were cold. Edric went upstairs. "No one's here," he reported.

"Damn." They went to another house. This one had already been ransacked.

As they left it, Oliver ran up to them. "Chief. You better come."

"What is it?"

"It's Ippo. He's dead. Someone shot at him with an arrow from inside a house. They won't let us in."

"Which house? Show me."

It was a neat stone villa with a bright blue door. They tied their horses to the garden gate. Two of his men stood in the garden.

"There's two, maybe three people in there," Oliver explained. "One's a woman. I saw her through a gap in a curtain. There are horses in the stable. We tried to break the door down, and someone shot arrows at us through a window." He pointed to a small round window set high in the brick wall. "The first one caught Ippo right in the chest. The others missed."

"How many shooters?"

"Just one, we think."

And not a good one, if all but one of the shots had missed. Not a trained soldier; probably a servant: a groom, or a cook.

"Right. You two stay here. Find something to make shields with. There's bound to be some pieces of wood lying around. Bang on the door, shout, make a lot of noise. Edric, Oliver, come with me."

They followed him around the side of the house. He pointed to the stairway leading to a balcony. Crouching, they wormed up it. The balcony was empty. In the front of the house, the men began to yell. "Now," Treion said.

Edric and Oliver slammed against the balcony door. It opened into a bedchamber. A black-haired girl in an apron was folded down to the floor beside the curtained bed. She stared at them in horror, and screamed. The chamber smelled of roses. The bed hangings were green silk.

A jeweled comb lay on a table beside the bed. Oliver snatched it up. He grabbed the girl firmly with the other hand.

"Shut up," he said to her.

Treion asked, "Who lives here?" She gazed at him, mute with terror. He turned his back on her and went out of the chamber and down a gleaming wood stairway to a wide, pleasant room. It had tall windows, curtains drawn across them now, and cushioned divans, and soft plush rugs.

A woman in green silk stood beside an ornate chest. Her hair was red. She was small and plump, and quite beautiful. Her delicate hands were covered with jeweled rings, at least one on almost every finger. She wore a green ribbon around her neck. There were pearls in her ears.

Outside, the men were still yelling. Treion said to Edric, "Let them in. Search the house, and bring me what you find." He turned to the woman.

"Give me your rings. The earrings, too. Where have you hidden your gold?"

Calmly, she began to remove her rings. "I have no gold." It was, of course, a lie. She had an enchanting voice, rich and deep and honeyed. "Who are you?"

He bowed. "My name is Unamira."

"I've heard men speak of you. They call you the Bastard, do they not?"

"I call myself the Bastard, my lady. I'm honored that you've heard of me."

Upstairs, there was a thumping noise. The girl screamed shrilly. The woman said sharply, "Teresa!" She started toward the stairs. Treion put an arm out.

She stepped back from him, snarling like a cat. "Don't touch me! Teresa!" The screams continued. "Tell them to leave her alone."

Treion said, "Sorry. Too late."

She batted at him. "Get out of my way." He did not move. "Damn you!" Her eyes sparkled with anger and contempt. She flung the rings at him. One of them caught him on the cheek. She scooped up a lamp from the chest and threw it. The oil spattered across his chest.

"Thief! Coward! Rapist! Your father was a rapist, too! Get out of my house. Get out! Get out!"

Fury roared through him. His eyes went red. For a moment, he could not see. Furious, he snatched his dagger from his belt and stabbed her in the throat. Blood sprayed from the wound. He leaped back.

She slumped to the floor. Edric entered, grinning, holding a burlap sack. "I found the gold, chief," he said. "It was hidden in the pantry." He stopped grinning. "Imarru. What happened?"

"Never mind," Treion said curtly. The dagger was still in his hand. He walked to one of the windows and wiped the blood from the steel with the velvet drape. He opened the sack. It held about twenty nobles and more jewelry. He picked the rings off the rug, all that he could find, and dropped them into it. A gold ring set with a large square-cut topaz looked large enough to fit him. He slipped it onto his little finger. His cuffs were wet with blood.

Oliver came downstairs, adjusting his clothes.

"Well," he said, "that was fun." He glanced without interest at the dead woman. "Ooh. That's a pretty thing." He scooped up an ivory letter opener.

Treion jerked his head at Edric. "Time to go." They went out the front door of the house. A man wearing an apron lay dead in the hallway.

Treion wedged the burlap sack into his saddlebags. Damn it, he hadn't meant to kill her. If she hadn't said what she had said, he wouldn't have killed her. *Thief! Coward! Rapist! Your father was a rapist, too!*

They rode past the burning olive orchard, toward the town gate.

Edric said, "Where are we going?"

"East."

"East? How far?"

"First to Secca. Then across the Kameni border."

"Why so far?" Edric said. "Secca's a good place. Why can't we stay in Secca?"

"Because," Treion said, "they'll be looking for us in Secca."

As they neared the guardhouse, the smell of burning flesh grew strong.

"Feh," said Edric, flapping a hand across his nose. "Hoy,

look." Niello, on horseback, emerged from the smoldering orchard. Edric shouted. Niello bent his head. His horse shot forward. It galloped down the avenue.

"Now where's he going in such a hurry?" Edric said.

"Good question," Treion said. He turned the grey into the trees. They followed the tracks to a clearing. It smelled of blood. Someone had slaughtered an animal—a pig, perhaps.

The horses tossed their heads uneasily.

Edric's horse stiffened. He wheeled in a circle.

"Easy," Edric said, "easy now, what's wrong with you?"

Treion rode forward. The beast, partially eviscerated, lay against the bole of a tree. A flock of crows flew up from it as he approached. Then he saw that what he had taken to be animal was, in fact, human, and breathing. Its face, such as it was, looked eyelessly up into the light.

His sword was in his hand. With no thought in his mind at all, he killed it.

WORD OF THE desolation of Castella came to Ujo from the lips of a carter. He was on his way north with a load of salvaged timber, and had led his mule team through the open gate just after sunrise, hoping to water his animals and quench his thirst.

What he saw, and smelled, made him empty his wagon, wrench his mules' heads around and urge them to the road as swiftly as they could be made to trot.

He reached the gates of Ujo after sundown. The gates were shut, but when the men at the gate heard what he had to say, they sent him, despite the lateness of the hour, to Kalni Leminin's palace.

Dennis Amdur, captain of the Lemininkai's first cavalry wing, was not an inexperienced soldier. He had served the

Lemininkai for eight years. He had fought outlaws, and Chuyokai, and even Isojai. He had seen dead men before.

Nevertheless, when his chief lieutenant brought him to the olive grove, and showed him the viciously mutilated thing that had once been a human being, he felt first a terrible revulsion, then a rage so great it dizzied him.

Martin Giambi, a gravely controlled man, was grim and white.

"Butcher's work. It's a child," he said. "Male, I think."

Dennis forced back his sickness. He made himself look again at the tortured corpse. It would have taken someone a long time to do this. In the trees, the waiting crows shifted from foot to foot.

"Cover it."

Martin threw a piece of sacking over the corpse.

They walked from the orchard. Smoke drifted from the terraced hillsides.

"Have you found the governor?" Dennis asked.

"Aye. He's dead. Oddly, he's not wounded. They tied him up and left him, and he choked on the gag. His strongbox is empty. There's another man in the kitchen, perhaps the cook. He's dead, too. A chest wound."

A man ran up. "Sir, we found a girl. Her name's Teresa. She works—worked—for Mistress Bertinelli."

"Worked?"

"She's dead, sir. Stabbed. The girl was raped. She's coherent, though."

They would need to make a list of the dead. The Lemininkai would want to know who had died, and who survived. He wondered what name he should put for the dead boy under the olive tree.

"Tell Carlo I want to see him."

The man saluted and loped away. In a little while, Carlo

arrived. He was a steady, quiet man, a little older than most of the troopers. He had been born in Firense, and served in that city's cavalry.

"I need you to take a message to Lukas Ridenar," Dennis said. "Bring him the Lemininkai's greeting, and his deep regrets. Tell him Mistress Celia Bertinelli was killed in an outlaw raid on Castella. Tell him what you have seen."

"Yes, sir," Carlo said. He turned on his heel.

Martin said, "Why—?"

Dennis said, "She was his mistress."

He sent Piero to Ujo with a report to Kalni Leminin, including his recommendation that men be sent from Ujo to rebuild and hold the guardhouse. He set men to the ugly business of digging graves. The rest of the troop fanned out through the town, dousing fires where they found them, and looking for survivors.

He took upon himself the gruesome, necessary task of burying the atrocity in the olive orchard.

5

THE RIDE FROM Castella to Secca took four days.

Under the bright summer sky, the wide brown road was nearly deserted. Behind them in the west ran one river; eastward lay a second: between the two the land was flat, and green. Barley and wheat grew tall in the fields. Black-faced sheep, newly shorn, grazed in their pastures, attended by black-faced dogs.

"This is rich country. Whose is it?" Edric asked.

The Genovese family had dominion over Secca. Treion had no idea if this was part of their domain, or not.

"I'm not sure," he said.

They passed a village: ten tiny houses clustered around a rectangle of common grazing land, surrounded by a palisade. A cow, accompanied by her calf, nosed steadily at the grass. Pigeons fluttered round a dovecote. A girl with a blue ceramic jar on her shoulder stood beside a well. She gazed at them with curious eyes.

"Hoy," Edric said to her. "What's the name of this place?"

She shook her head shyly.

Treion said, "Perhaps it has no name."

They rode sedately, but not slowly. Men in a hurry only called attention to themselves. They slept in the open, avoiding inns and travelers' shelters, where someone might notice them, or their horses. Edric fell asleep at once, snoring lightly. Treion lay still, staring at the darkness. He was, he realized, afraid to sleep. A monster stalked his dreams, a graceful, blond-haired monster with a knife in his hand.

Somewhere in Ryoka, Niello Savarini lay, his breathing light and steady, his dreams untroubled. Truly, the man was a monster. He had heard the rumor of it months ago in the gutters of Ujo. He had even, to his shame, made use of it. *Show him, Niello.*

THE MORNING OF the fourth day, they rode into Secca. The flag over the city gate showed the Genovese crest: a black viper on a red field, rampant. The guard at the gate did not even ask their names.

"State your business in the city," he droned.

Treion slipped him a ridari. "Entertainment."

They found Olin Marchioni at his place of business: a large, utilitarian warehouse, filled with pots. Marchioni was a legitimate pottery dealer. He was also a smuggler and a dealer in gems. He whistled when he saw the jewelry.

"This is fine stuff. Don't tell me where you got it. I don't want to know."

"I won't," Treion said. "What'll you give me for it?"

They haggled for a while, and finally agreed on a price.

They slept in the warehouse that night. Edric slept; Treion lay awake, listening for footsteps in the darkness.

The following morning they reached the Gorsin Bridge. The stones of the slender span were pitted with centuries of weathering. Two guard towers, equally ancient, flanked it on either side. They appeared to be empty. No smoke rose from the chimneys; no banners hung from poles. The noise of the river sang in their ears.

Edric gazed suspiciously at the long grey archway. "This place makes my head hurt. Where are we?"

"The Gorsin Bridge."

"Where does it go?"

"To Lienor."

"Lienor," Edric repeated. "The king's city." He tried not to look impressed, and failed. "Why Lienor?"

"It's a big city," Treion said. "Big enough for us to get lost in. We need to be lost, for a while."

"Is it as big as Ujo?"

"Bigger."

Edric frowned, clearly unable to imagine a city bigger than Ujo. "Why are those towers empty?"

"Because no one comes here anymore," Treion said. "There's a bridge to the south, a newer bridge, wide enough for carts. Everyone goes that way." He dismounted. "We'll have to lead the horses."

"Wait. I need to piss," Edric said. He walked toward the side of the bridge, loosening his clothes. "Oh, Mother." He stepped back, white-faced. "Vaikkenen's balls, we're high."

They coaxed the horses forward. The river streamed pewter. Sun glittered on its labile surface. A wet mist boiled to meet them out of the riverbed. On the far bank, a massive stele stood in the center of the path. They circled the stone. On the far side its makers had incised a crown, and below the crown, ancient markings.

"That's wizard's work. Runes," Edric said. He glanced anxiously at the tall pillar.

They mounted. Beyond the pillar, dark, spiky trees closed about them. Grey tendrils of mist seeped through the trees.

A narrow, stony road wound beneath their horses' hooves. The clip-clop sound echoed into the mist. There were none of the usual forest noises, no bird sounds, only the whisper of the wind sliding through the trees. The rushing sound was constant, inexorable as lust.

Edric said angrily, "This place isn't natural."

When night fell, they found a place to camp. Edric yanked his hood over his ears and lay down in the dirt. "Fucking wind," he complained. Treion leaned against a tree. His eyes were gritty. His mouth tasted of ash. He closed his eyes.

Monster, the wind wailed.

HE WOKE, AND found a blade at his throat.

He froze. Above him, cold eyes registered his return to wakefulness. Grey ghosts weaved silently amid the mist-wreathed trees. One held a torch.

The blade moved in a tight gesturing circle. "Get up. Slowly."

Very slowly, he pushed aside his blanket, and rose to his feet. It was not yet dawn. The sword tip touched his chest warningly.

"Who are you?" he asked. "What do you want?"

No one answered him. Hard, competent hands searched through his clothes. Neither the cloaks nor the gear of his captors bore any emblems, but he had no doubt that he was dealing with professionals. They took his sword, the pouches with the gold, his boot knife, and the knife in his sleeve.

"Boots."

He put his boots on.

"Hold out your hands." He obeyed. "That's a pretty thing. Take it off." Treion twisted the topaz ring from his little finger. "Captain, look at this."

The troop leader appeared silently out of the mist. He turned the ring in his fingers.

"How did you get this?" he asked.

Treion said, "A woman gave it to me."

Hands bound his arms neatly behind his back. They brought him to his horse and hoisted him on it. Edric, also bound, was already mounted.

"Where are you taking us?" Treion asked. Still no one answered. "Whom do you serve?"

The captain answered. "We serve the king. Now be quiet, or we will bind your mouth and your eyes." He raised a hand. "Ride out!"

They moved, swiftly. Treion clamped his legs around his horse's ribs and concentrated on staying in the saddle. That day they halted once, to rest the horses, and to eat. Then they pushed on. Forest gave way to cleared land. They passed a village, another, another. By nightfall, Treion was swaying in the saddle, his legs trembling with weariness. Their captors loosened their bonds so that they could eat and relieve themselves. Then they were bound again. They slept tied.

The following day they reached the outer gate of Lienor. It was massive, two stories tall. Guard towers flanked it on either side. Pennants fluttered atop the towers, each bearing a device: the red running horse, the blue arrow, the white wolf, emblems of the lords of Ryoka who had once sworn fealty to the kings of Lienor. The tallest of them was black. It bore three gold emblems: crown, sword, and star.

The captain advanced to the portal and spoke to someone on the other side of the gate. The iron teeth lifted. They rode through. Ahead of them stretched a long bare plain, and at the other side of it stood another wall. It ran north and south. Even across the distance it looked taller than the one behind them. It seemed to go forever.

The captain said, "Behold the King's Wall. They say it was built at the same time, and by the same hands, as the Wizard's Wall." Three abreast, they rode toward the immense granite barrier. As they neared it, the iron grate that barred the way to its other side lifted. They rode into a dark passageway. The smells of oil and burning wood and horse swirled about them. A wain filled with huge iron-shod barrels thundered past. Then they were through. Directly ahead stood a massive stone fortress. Squat and strong, it thrust out of the earth like a boulder. Men in dark cloaks hurried by, intent on unknown errands. Helmeted soldiers with sharp-edged pikes guarded its entrance. The horsemen dismounted.

"In," said the captain. Hard hands pulled the captives up the fortress's broad steps. They were hustled along a corridor, thrust through a door, and left.

The bare room held neither cushion nor chair, not even a chamber pot. The only illumination came from a slit high in a wall. Treion swore. His fingers, which were fat as sausages, ached horribly, and his wrists were near chafed raw by the cords. He was thirsty, hungry, and sick of his own stink.

The door opened: the rider captain entered, followed by an older man. He was clean-shaven, his greying hair shorter than Nakase fashion would have it, much as the captain's was, but he was broader than the wiry captain, and older by twenty years.

Hands on hips, he surveyed the captives.

"Which of you is Unamira?"

"I am." Treion bowed as smoothly as a man whose forearms are tied together against his belly can bow. "And you, sir, are—?"

The man shook his head. "I ask the questions. You answer." He paused. "You bear no travel pass, no letter or courier's emblem. You carry a fortune on your person. Given your name, I doubt you came by it honestly. What is your business in Kameni?"

Treion said, "My business is my own."

"Bran," said the grey-haired man.

The blow came straight at his head. He dodged, too late. The rider's gloved fist caught him on the left side of the jaw.

"Try again," the grey-haired man said. "What is your business in Kameni?"

Treion's jaw throbbed. He said, through shut teeth, "My business is my own."

Bran's fist hit him squarely. He reeled, and fell hard against Edric, who went over as well. His bound hands hit the floor. Blood popped painfully beneath his nails.

The grey-haired man said, without haste or heat, "Eventually you will tell me. It is a simple question. What is your business in Kameni?"

Slowly, Treion untangled himself from Edric's legs, and stood. He breathed a moment, tasting blood. He could take a beating. But they might move on to other methods. He did not want to be tortured.

He said, "I came to Lienor to hide."

"From whom?"

"Kalni Leminin's soldiers."

"Why do they want you?"

"I burned the guardhouse at Castella, and stole the governor's treasure."

"I see," the man said dryly. "In answer to your question, I am Honoris Imorin. You may have heard of me."

Honoris Imorin was Commander of the Royal Guard of Kameni, and Idaris Imorin's brother. He was, next to the king himself, the most powerful man in Kameni. Treion's skin went a little cold.

Imorin looked at Edric. "Who are you? What are *you* doing in Kameni?"

Edric said promptly, "My name's Edric Edricson. I came with him."

"Just the two of you? No one else?"

"Yes, sir," Edric said.

Imorin frowned. Then he said, "You stay here." That was to Edric. "*You*—come with me." Bran opened the door. Imorin walked out.

Treion followed him along the corridor to a door. Imorin pushed it open a little.

"Look there," he said. "Do you know that man?"

On a bench in the middle of a bare stone courtyard sat Niello Savarini. There were chains on his wrists and ankles. His face was puffed and marked with bruises.

Treion said, "I know him. He rode with me."

"What's his name?"

"While he was with us, he called himself Savarini."

"How long was he with you?"

"Five months."

Imorin said, "Do you know what he is?"

Treion flushed. A little stiffly, he said, "I don't know what you're talking about."

Turning his head, Niello stared at the two men in the doorway. A slow smile moved across his mouth. The emptiness in his eyes made Treion's skin crawl.

Imorin said, "I don't believe you." He gestured to the rider captain. "Put him in a cell. Find out everything you can from the other one."

"Aye, sir," Bran said.

He fastened a hand on Treion's upper arm. "Come on." He walked him down the hall to a cell. It was tiny, no bigger than a closet. Treion tensed. He hated small spaces. He considered resisting, for pride's sake. But his hands were useless; there was little that he could do to the rider captain, except try to bite him.

Wearily, he stepped inside.

WORD OF THE despoilment of Castella came late to Dragon's country. The gypsies, who went everywhere, were first to speak of it. According to their accounts, a troop of Chuyo pirates had crossed the border and rampaged up the Great South Road, ravaging and looting. This news caused a stir among the ignorant. But those whose knowledge of the world reached past the back side of their neighbors' fences pointed out that Chuyo was part of Ryoka, and that even if it were not, no Chuyo pirate would travel hundreds of miles inland to assault a village in the heart of Nakase.

A trader from Poros had more accurate information. A troop of outlaws had entered Castella, killed the governor and all the guards, and made off with the governor's treasure.

"The Lemininkai is fuming like a geyser. There are soldiers everywhere on the road, asking questions. They held me at Yarrow for four hours, and searched every wagon. Look at this!" He pointed to the slash marks in his fleeces.

IN THE WINDLE river valley, the noise of quarreling birds filled the forest: the forest jays were squabbling over their nests. The smaller females sat smugly in the pines as the bright-feathered males puffed up their pinions and flew at one another. Morga hunted squirrels and barked playfully at the aggressive jays. Wild with snowmelt, the river plunged and sang between its banks. The pool below the cottage, deeper now than in the autumn, filled with fish: yellow perch, black bass, blue-bellied trout.

Sitting beneath the willows, pole in hand, one warm, sun-dappled afternoon, Maia heard Morga's warning bark. She turned.

Karadur Atani stood at the top of the bank. The dragon armband shone high on his bare right arm.

She scrambled to her feet. "My lord," she said, "welcome."

He came down the bank. Morga pranced through the underbrush to the dragon-lord's feet. Panting happily, she thrust her head at him. He fondled the dog's soft ears. Folding beside her, he glanced into the basket, which held a water flask, one rather small perch, and several dozen snails, culled from her garden, for bait.

"Fishing for your supper?" he inquired.

"Yes," she said. She sat again. Her line quivered, as some inquisitive fish nosed at the bait. "Do you fish, my lord?"

He said, "I am acquainted with the concept." Morga sprawled under the willow and pretended to sleep. After a while he said, "May I hold it?" She passed him the pole. It seemed to shrink in his hand. He looked across the river.

Then he said, "Gods, this is difficult. I am sorry to disturb your peace. Have you heard the news from Nakase?"

She had heard no news for days. "No."

"A courier arrived from Ujo this morning. Six days ago, a troop of outlaws entered Castella. They burned the guardhouse with the guards inside. They killed the governor and his servants and ransacked the town for whatever treasure they could find. Their leader was a slender blond man, quick with a sword."

"Treion," she said.

"It would seem so." He paused, then said, "Most of those responsible have been taken. But not your brother, not yet. Kalni Leminin promises gold to anyone whose information leads to his capture. I expect they will find him soon."

Morga, sensing her distress, rose and padded to her. Maia stroked her head. Stupid Treion. Savage Treion. She said, "He won't come here."

"No," Karadur Atani said. His molten gaze was turned away from her. A courtesy . . . "I doubt he will. Though my men will watch the roads."

And if they found him, they would deliver him to Kalni Leminin, who would kill him.

"It was generous of you to come and tell me," she said. "Will you, of your kindness, tell me when he is found?"

"I will," he said. On the far bank, the marsh marigolds glittered like coins in the sun. "Will you tell *me* something?"

"If I can."

"Do you love him?"

"Yes," she said. "I do."

"Does he love you?"

The question startled her. Did Treion love her? She was not sure.

"I think so," she said slowly. "He taught me to fish."

"What else?"

"He gave me a kitten once. When it died, he helped me bury it beneath the persimmon tree. When we were young he did his best to protect me."

"From what?"

Loyalty and courage, Miri had said, *are everything to the dragon-kindred.* "From my father. His was not an even temper."

"Did he beat you?"

"No. He beat Treion, though." She remembered the morning Treion had interposed himself between an angry Marion diSorvino and a terrified servant, a serving-girl who had broken a glass. Her father, furious at the boy's defiance, had ordered a groom to thrash him.

Hours later, Maia, basket on her arm, crept into Treion's darkened bedchamber. Her brother lay rigid on his cot.

I brought you food. There's bread, and cold soup. . . . Treion, you must eat.

I will kill him someday, he had whispered to her. *I promise you, Maia, I will.*

Reckless, vengeful Treion. He had raged over Master Eccio's death, not because he had cared for the man, but because of what the death of the little physician had meant to her, and to her mother, whose friend he had been.

Karadur said, "Why did your mother leave your father?"

It was as if he had walked into her mind.

"She left because he killed her friend, and because he did not love her." She reached for the fishing pole. A cockawee called amid the marigolds.

"Why did she take you with her?"

"She loved me. My father didn't. He didn't want me, he wanted sons. I was a girl, and not a very satisfactory one: I was not pretty, or charming, or sweet. I preferred the company of an aging doctor to that of his friends."

The pole jerked in her slack fingers. She grabbed for it. The line pulled taut, dragging her into the water. She gasped as the cold slid up her thighs. The hooked fish thrashed, then leaped from the pool. It twisted in midair like an eel, and fell with a great splash. Her rod went horizontal. She hauled the tip of the rod upright. The fish leaped again. It was blue, with a sunset-red stripe along a swollen belly.

Her palms burned against the wood. If she let go of the pole, she would lose fish and pole both. She dug her bare feet into the greasy mud. Morga leaped and barked excitedly. Karadur, slithering down the bank, held out a hand for the pole.

"Give it to me!"

She passed it to him.

"Keep the tip up and walk backwards slowly." She splashed to the rocks and grabbed her net. The fish breached a third time. It was clearly tiring. Feeling with her toes for the bottom, she waded farther into the pool. The current nudged her legs and sucked at her balance. The trout bucked and spasmed, and then floated. She scooped it into the net with a shout. As she dragged it through the water it spasmed hard against the net. She yelped. The cold had numbed her hands. Forcing her frigid fingers shut, she half pushed, half pulled the net onto the rocks. A huge hand closed around her arm.

"The fish!"

"I have it." He steadied her with one arm, holding her against him. She felt his warmth through her shirt. She craned her head past him, looking for the net. Fish fast in its coils, it lay high against the bank. She grew conscious suddenly of her dishevelment. Her hair was matted and windblown, her tunic and borrowed breeches wet, stinking of the river, and streaked with slime and fish blood.

Her hands ached with chill. Grimacing, she stretched them into the sunlight. He drew her against him. "You are shivering," he said. "Stay still." An easeful, silken warmth enveloped her. Held as she was, she could feel his heartbeat; it had quickened.

So had hers.

"My lord," she said, "please let me go."

Immediately he opened his hands.

PART TWO

6

SHEM WOLFSON LAY on his back, gazing into an azure sky.

Heat from the kitchen chimney rose through the brick. Beside him, his cherished companion, the two-year-old hunting hound Turtle, snored lightly, one eye open. Dogs could sleep like that, with their eyes open. Humans could not. Shem had tried.

He rolled over until his head was pillowed on the dog's furry flank. Turtle grunted softly, and his tail thumped. The smells from the kitchen made his stomach fizz with hunger. He rose and hauled himself on tiptoe to look over the parapet. It was laundry day. Girls with bright kerchiefs on their sleek heads carried laden baskets to and fro. Sheets, towels, and blankets flapped on lines.

"Dog. You dog." Dropping, he nudged the sleeping dog with his foot. Opening both eyes, Turtle sneezed, and leaped up, ready to play.

Shem trotted down the outer stairway to the courtyard.

It smelled powerfully of soap. Turtle sniffed curiously at a dripping sheet.

A reaching hand waved from behind a basket. Shem crouched.

"Where've you been?" It was Devin. "I was looking for you everywhere."

"On the wall. I was hiding from Kiala. She wants to make me a shirt." Kiala had been his nurse when first he came to the Keep. Even though he was much older now, and slept at night beside Devin's mother's fire, with Devin, she still behaved as though she was responsible for him.

"Ah." Devin squinted. "Can you see Mira? She was behind the well, but now I can't find her."

They were playing Hunt. Shem was not permitted to play; his friends had banned him from the game ever since they realized that he did not need to see them to know where they were hiding. It was one of the ways he was different from them. There were others. They had mothers and fathers, and he did not. They were dead. It had something to do with the war. He could see in the dark, too.

It's because you're changeling, Mira had said loftily, as if she knew all about it. *Like Dragon*. The thought that he was like Dragon took the sting out of not being allowed to play.

He closed his eyes and found Mira behind the tallest of the baskets.

"You want me to tell? That's cheating."

Devin grinned. "I know. Tell me anyway." Shem pointed. Devin raced toward Mira's hiding place. There was a squeal from the other side of the courtyard. Mira leaped up, with Devin in pursuit. They weaved and dodged amid the baskets. Mira scampered through the blowing maze toward the whipping post. Devin lunged for her.

She slapped the post with both hands. "Lair!"

"Got you first!"

"Did not!"

"Did too!"

Bryony Maw, the laundry mistress, lumbered toward them.

"Out," she said, massive arms ominously extended. "Go on, all of you, get out of here."

"Race you to the kitchen," said Devin, dodging. They galloped across the courtyard toward the castle's kitchen. The doors stood wide. Turkeys, their featherless skins brown and cracked and running with juice, turned on the spits. Boris, face shiny with sweat, stood in the center of the steamy room, shouting at the undercooks. They ran frantically about with knives and pots and platters.

To Shem's horror, Kiala stood in the pantry. She pounced on him. "Where have you been?" she demanded. Her round face was flushed. "You knew I was looking for you."

He wriggled, but her grip was firm. "I was on the wall. Turtle was with me."

Simon the stew cook said, "Leave the brat alone, Kiala. What can happen to him?

"He's still a baby."

Simon said, "He's no baby. Look at him, he's big as Devin." Devin, swinging on the pantry door, grinned. "Beside, there's naught in Dragon Keep would harm him. He's Dragon's pet."

Simon had once threatened to cook Turtle for getting underfoot. Shem had bitten him. He stared at Simon, not smiling. Simon glared back.

"Come," Kiala said. She dragged him to the sewing room and made him stand on a stool while she measured his shoulders. "Mother of night, I swear you've grown a handsbreadth since the last time I did this."

"I have?" He wriggled. "Can I go now?"

"Go."

In the hall, Devin was waiting with the honeycake he had filched when Simon's back was turned. He broke the cake in two and passed Shem one of the halves. Turtle, who had vanished—he knew he was not allowed in the kitchen—reappeared. He laid his head soulfully on Shem's knee. Shem broke off a bit of cake and held it in his palm.

They returned to the courtyard. Devin pulled a piece of yellow string from his pocket. "Look what I found in the barn." It was a long piece, quite strong.

Shem tugged on it. "We could go fishing."

"We need a hook."

Shem felt in his pocket. But he had nothing sharp at all: only a dull arrowhead found at the archery range, an empty snail shell, and a flat rock glittering with mica.

Devin eyed the rock. "Where did you get that?"

"In the old buttery." Shem liked the ruined buttery. The scullions played dice there. It was cool and secluded: fat yellow roses clambered over the stones, and daisies trembled underfoot. An owl lived in the tumbled-down west wall; he had heard it, shuffling in the dim private place it had found, and grumbling to itself.

Devin said, "Eilon says there's a ghost in that place."

"What ghost?"

"A weeping lady, with long black hair and black teeth. He says it wails at night."

"Huh," Shem said. It sounded fearsome. But Hawk had told him that there was no need to be afraid of ghosts, that few people saw them, and that when they did appear, they were not dangerous, they were only messengers. *She* had seen a ghost once. She had refused to tell him whose it was. "*I've* never heard it."

Devin said thoughtfully, "We could go there now and look for it."

Their eyes met. They were not supposed to go beyond the

walls without permission. But if they asked Beryl's permission she might forbid the excursion, or find some tedious task for them to do. Devin grinned. Wordlessly, they scrambled up and trotted through the courtyard toward the storage barns. Luga the dogboy had showed them the hole in the wall behind the barns. A set of planks hung over a hole in the stone, but the planks could be lifted, and the hole turned into a tunnel. It was dark, but quite dry, and high, big enough for a grown man to crawl through, if he was not too fat.

Devin, who was stronger, raised the planks. Shem burrowed in. The tunnel was dark, and smelled of animal droppings. He wriggled through it quickly. Then he was out. Devin followed him, sneezing. Over them, the sky blazed white, like a fire. On the tower, the dragon banner waved, high atop its pole. They trotted across the fields and crept into the roofless ruin. Gorging bees dipped and dug amid the flowers. They climbed over the fallen beams, hunting for signs of a ghost.

Shem found a piece of pointy bone. It was smooth and yellow. "A dragon's claw!"

Devin found a square of bleached cloth, and a pole, and a bit of corroded metal. "An arrowhead!" he declared. He breathed on it and rubbed hard to make it shine. While Turtle chased squirrels through the scrub, they made the tumbled stones into the wall of a fort, and shot imaginary arrows at Isojai raiders. Proclaiming themselves victors, they threaded the cloth on the pole and propped it between two stones.

"It ought to have a device," Devin said. "Like the dragon. Or the blue arrow. That's the Lemininkai's sigil."

"How do you know?"

"My father taught me. He says a warrior has to know the sigils of all the houses."

Turtle leaped over a fallen beam and trotted to Shem's

side. He had something in his mouth. "Here, Turtle. Give."

The dog laid his prize down. It was a fluffy yellow-eyed bird, quite dead. It had a deep puncture wound in its throat.

"Good dog. Where did you get this?"

Turtle wagged his tail. The body was still warm. Blood seeped from the hole.

"One of the cats must have killed it," Devin said. It had huge round eyes and short stubby feathers, auburn on top, but underneath pure white. "It's a fledgling, look at its wings. I bet the barn cats raided the nest while the mother was hunting."

Shem wondered if it was the chick of the owl he had heard hooting in the west wall, and if the owl knew that its chick was gone. He imagined the cat gliding silently along the sun-warmed stones toward the hidden nest, tasting the bird's scent deep in its throat, every muscle taut, ready to cut off escape, while the fledgling, unwitting, breathed and slept. . . .

"Hey," said Devin. "What are you thinking? Your eyes are strange."

Shem blinked. "Nothing." He jumped up. "Come on. Race you to the fence." The fence marked the bounds of the riding runs, where men new come to the Keep and hoping to be soldiers learned that riding a warhorse was different from riding a plow horse. It was quite far, but Shem did not care, he just wanted to move. Legs churning, he pounded through the tall grass.

Suddenly he tripped. He hit the ground hard. His breath went out of him; he yelped like a puppy. Gasping, he lay still, arms and legs splayed into the dirt.

Devin bent over him. "Are you all right?"

"Uh." He sat up. His face and hands were covered with dirt. He pushed to his feet. "Yes." He walked in a circle. His knee stung where it had smacked into the ground, and his elbows were skinned. In the distance, Turtle was barking loudly.

Devin said, "Maybe we'd better get back." He looked a little alarmed. If it were discovered that they were out, they would get a scolding, and, if Beryl was very cross, perhaps a beating.

"Where's Turtle?" Shem whistled. The barking continued. "Turtle!" They moved toward the sounds. "Turtle, come!" It was hard to see through the thick grass. Shem pushed it aside with his arms.

Suddenly the grass was gone. They had reached the road. And there was Turtle, barking and barking at a lean man who sat calmly on a fine spotted horse. Shem dove forward and grabbed for his wayward dog's collar.

"Turtle! No! Bad dog! You know better than to bark at horses." He wound his fingers in the leather strap. "Sorry," he said, squinting upward at the rider. "He does know better. He forgets sometimes."

The man did not seem particularly distressed. "No matter. My horse is used to barking dogs." He sat gracefully in the saddle, with the ease of a man for whom horseback was as natural as walking. "I am going to Dragon Keep. Shall I find its lord at home, do you think?"

Devin looked at Shem.

Shem shook his head. "No."

Early that morning, half-asleep, curled in his place at Devin's side, he had felt the Golden Dragon spring from the mountainside and soar into the sky. He always knew when Dragon was near. That was another way he was different from the other children.

"He'll be back, though. He always comes back at sundown."

"Then I must wait for him," the rider said. He touched his heels to his horse's sides. The horse trotted forward.

Devin, quivering with excitement, said, "Did you see?"

"What?"

"His cloak bore the blue arrow. He's a messenger from the Lemininkai. That's the second in a month. Something's happening. Come on!"

THAT NIGHT SHEM and Devin ate in the hall. Crouched over a single bowl, they watched from the shadows near the hearth as the men dragged the long tables and benches into the center of the big stone space, and the servers brought platters of spring lamb and turkey and new potatoes and bitter greens and hot bread and pitchers of foamy red beer. They had not been beaten, nor even scolded for their transgression: in the fuss of the courier's arrival, no one had noticed two small boys slipping through the postern gate.

At the center table, big Olav and one of the recruits, a muscular farm boy from Sleeth, had clasped hands to test each other's strength. Huffing, the two big men strained against each other. Olav bent his opponent's arm to the table.

"Olav is strong," Devin said. "My father says he is stronger than anyone in the swordsmen's wing."

Shem said loyally, "He is not as strong as Dragon." The lord of the Keep sat among his officers at the table nearest the hearth. Azil the singer, as always, sat at Karadur Atani's right hand. Marek Gavrinson, Devin's father, was there: so was Herugin, the cavalry master, and Rogys, his lieutenant, and Captain Lorimir, senior captain of the garrison. The courier sat at Dragon's left hand. Hawk sat beside him. As usual, she looked very stern. Her sternness frightened people, Shem knew. So did her patch, and her crooked arm, and her fierce, one-eyed gaze, which seemed to look right through to bone. It did not frighten him. Hawk was his friend, as she had been his father's friend. Hawk was changeling. She, too, could see in the dark. She could hear a mouse whisper, the archers said, with admiration. And there were other things she could do, skills only changelings had, that he would someday have, when he was older.

Hawk did not Change, though. He did not know why. He had seen Dragon Change, many times. He thought—he was not sure—it had something to do with the war.

Devin tore a hunk of bread in two, and passed the larger piece to Shem. He dunked the bread in the turkey juice. Someone opened the doors to let the dogs in. Turtle galloped joyfully to Shem's side. Shem gave him the bread.

"You spoil that dog," Devin said. "You should keep him hungry. Hungry dogs make better hunters. Cuillan says so."

Deep in Shem's mind, so deep that he could not quite recall it, was the memory of a time when he had been hungry. He pushed it away. He would never starve a dog. He stroked Turtle's ears. Cuillan was the dog warden. But Cuillan did not keep the Keep's dogs hungry; Dragon would not have let him do that.

He looked across the room to the officers' table. Marek Gavrinson was speaking to the dragon-lord, and Dragon was laughing. Then he glanced across the room, right at Shem. He crooked a finger. Shem's heart beat hard, like a hammer. He scrambled up.

"So, Shem Wolfson," Dragon said. "I am told you and Devin Marekson were first to greet our guest today. What were you doing beyond the wall?"

Shem said firmly, "My lord, we were fighting Isojai."

"How many did you kill?"

"I don't know, my lord," Shem said. "Many. We didn't count them."

The men at the table laughed. Dragon smiled, and brushed his palm lightly over the top of Shem's head. Then he rose. The men quieted. Faces turned expectantly.

"Warriors of Dragon Keep," he said, "we have a guest. This is Laslo Umi, who comes to us from Ujo with a message from the Lemininkai." He nodded to the stranger. "Speak, courier."

The courier stood. "This is the message from the Lemininkai. To the lord of Atani Castle, Karadur Atani, from Kalni Leminin of Ujo, greetings. You are invited to share the city of Ujo's joy, and its celebration of the wedding of Selena Mariana Leminin and Cirion Imorin, Prince of Ryoka, lord of the city of Selidor, in Kameni, to be held during Midsummer Festival on the first day of August, this year."

The soldiers whistled and stamped. "A toast!" Dragon said. "A toast to a wedding!" Brian leaned swiftly to pour Dragon's wine. The soldiers held their mugs and flasks high. The dogs barked. Everyone drank.

The courier said, "My lord, the Lemininkai asked me to tell you he hopes you will come. A suite of rooms has already been reserved for you and your escort at the Hotel Goude."

Dragon said, "That was thoughtful of him. You may tell the Lemininkai I accept." He looked down the table. "Lorimir, do you want to go to Ujo with me?"

The elderly captain's beard glinted in the candlelight. "If you want me to go to Ujo, my lord, I will."

Dragon smiled. "I know you will. But I also know that you hate cities. Herugin."

"My lord," said the scar-faced officer.

"You shall come to Ujo with me. Rogys, while Herugin is absent, the cavalry is in your charge. Mind you keep it well. Finle, you shall ride to Ujo as well. Bring your bow. There will be contests. Tourneys, archery matches, wrestling, horse races: I expect you all to compete, and if you can, to win. Herugin, is Rosset ready to race?" The big red four-year-old stallion was the fastest horse in the Dragon Keep stable, and maybe in all of Ippa.

"My lord," Herugin said, "there's not a horse in the north can beat him."

"My lord," Marek said, "you have named an archer and a cavalryman: whom shall you bring from the swordsmen's wing?"

"Whom would you choose?"

Marek said, "Lurri is the Keep's strongest swordsman." Lurri looked pleased. "But Lurri has no manners. He's bound to quarrel with someone." Lurri reddened. "Take Edruyn. He is not as strong as Lurri, but he is skilled and quick, and he gets on well with everybody."

Karadur glanced at Lorimir Ness. "Lorimir?"

"I agree," the old swordsman said.

"Edruyn, then," the dragon-lord said. "Hawk, my hunter. You shall come, too." Hawk said nothing. Finle clapped her on the shoulder. She looked sideways at him. "Let's have some music."

At once, everything went still. Azil the singer rose from his place. "What would you hear, my lord?" he said. It was what he always said.

"Sing 'Ewain and Mariela,'" someone yelled.

"'Tree of Gold.'"

"'The Old Man's Beard.'"

The dragon-lord glanced at the visitor. "We have a guest," he said. "Let him choose."

Laslo Umi said, "My lord, I do not know your singer, and this is your hall. Of your courtesy, choose for me."

"Sing 'March to the Sea.'" "March to the Sea" was a victory song. It told how Pohja Leminin, the first Pohja Leminin, Kalni Leminin's great-great-great-however-many-greats-it-was-grandfather, had marched his troops from Ujo across the border between Nakase and Chuyo all the way to Balas Bay.

When at last they sheathed their swords, on the diamond-white sands before the Towers of Morning, hundreds had died. The soldiers loved it. Even Devin, who had no ear for music, shouted. Shem slipped back to Devin's side.

Azil bowed his head.

Then he lifted it again, and his voice filled the hall. Strong as Raudri's trumpet, soft as the whisper of snow in the early morning. *"Bright swords in the vanguard and sorrow in his wake,"* he sang, making poetry of slaughter.

When it ended, no one moved. Even the dogs were still.

Laslo Umi said, "My lord, I have never heard such singing, not in Kalni Leminin's hall, nor at any hall in Kameni or Issho."

The men yelled, and banged their knife hilts on the tables. "More!" they cried.

Azil raised his voice. "Be quiet!" They obeyed. "I will sing a song none of you have heard before.

I am a wanderer; this is not my home.
My home is far away, on the southern shore
Where the bright sea shines, and the white gulls soar;
My heart rests there, however far I roam.

My home is far away, by the southern sea.
Strangers smile when they speak my name,
And they pour sweet wine, and they bid me stay,
But the grey sea calls, and I must obey.

When the south wind sings, and the night is still,
And bright stars burn through the apple trees,
I will take the road; it will bring me home
To the southern shore, where she waits for me.

The plaintive melody was unfamiliar. It made a lonely sound in the quiet room. When it ended, no one spoke for a while. Azil sat on the bench, and Dragon put an arm around his shoulders. The singer leaned into it.

Brian came forward to pour wine.

Devin said dreamily, "When I am older, *I* shall be Dragon's page."

"I, too," Shem said. He could think of nothing more desirable than to be Dragon's page: to ride with his lord, carry his messages, serve his meals, and keep his long, bright sword free from stain.

"When I am grown I shall join the guard, like my father. I shall be a swordsman."

"I, too."

Devin sat back. "You won't, though," he said.

Shem frowned at him. A trickle of cold wormed along his spine. "Why not?"

"My father says a man must fight beside his own people."

"So?"

"My father says that your father's people live in Nakase, by the Crystal Lake, where the river ends. It is a long, long ride from Dragon's country, along the Great South Road, farther than Mako, farther even than Ujo. My father says that someday they will come for you, and you will go to them."

A log fell in the hearth, and a shower of sparks scattered out of the big stone mouth of the fireplace. A spark landed on Shem's bare knee. He barely felt it. The succulent turkey, so tasty in his mouth a moment before, turned to ash. He did not want to leave the Keep. The Keep was home, comfort, love. There was a place he had been before coming to the Keep, a place of malevolence and pain. His heart raced. He sprang to his feet.

"I won't," he said wildly. "I won't go!" Knotting a fist, he swung at Devin. The blow connected squarely on Devin's left cheekbone.

Devin fell over, mouth agape.

In the dark courtyard, the hounds had finished their own battles, and were lying in their places. Savage, the big bull-headed pack leader, lay regally beside the kennel, a lamb shank between his paws. He growled as Shem blundered past, but the growl held no animosity, only warning. Within the kennel, Luga the dogboy raised his head.

"Who is it?"

"No one," Shem said. Wisely, Luga blinked and put his head back down on Bessie's flank. Shem burrowed in the sweet-smelling kennel straw. In a moment, a cold nose snuffled at his neck, and a familiar body wriggled beside him.

"Dog," he whispered. "Dog, you dog." He hugged Turtle to him, sick at heart.

At last the queasy feeling diminished. Sitting up, he scrubbed his face. His stomach felt hollow. He felt angry, and ashamed. He had hit his friend. He had run away. A warrior never runs away. He wondered if he had marked Devin's face.

Wriggling from the dog-scented space, he brushed the straw from his hair and clothes. The big dark courtyard was quiet: empty, except for the softly breathing dogs, and the shadows. Turtle's nails clicked on the stone. It was strange, and a little frightening, to be alone in the empty space. The night breeze nibbled on his skin. He looked up. Torches flared on the ramparts: blurred saffron-yellow spearpoints of light.

But when he looked back there was a shadow in the center of the empty courtyard, a shadow that had not been there before. Turtle, tail whipping from side to side, whined a greeting. A deep, well-loved voice said, "Hey, cub."

A tiny light spurted out of nothing. Dragon sat on a bench beside the pillar. The dragon-lord snapped his fingers. Turtle pranced forward. Dragon scratched him under the chin and over the loose scruff of his neck.

The dragon-lord said, "You should be in bed, cub."

Shem said, "I wasn't sleepy."

"Is it so? Perhaps it was another boy I saw crawling from the dog pen, knuckling his eyes."

"I was in the dog pen. But I was not sleeping."

"Ah. I see. Come here." Shem obeyed. A warm hand brushed lightly over his head. "So Devin Marekson goes to bed with a bruise on his cheek, and Shem Wolfson stays wakeful through the night, grieving because he struck his dearest friend. What was the quarrel about, my wolf cub? Speak."

Shem took a long breath. It felt as if a heavy stone was lying on his chest.

"He said—Devin said—that *he* could join the war band, and be a swordsman, like his father, but that I—*I* will have to leave the Keep, and ride south to Nakase, and join my father's people. He said they will come for me, and I will have to go with them."

"Would that be so bad, cub?"

"I do not want to go," Shem said. "I do not *want* them to want me. I want to stay here, and join the war band, and be a soldier."

Again Dragon's palm brushed his hair. "It is no bad thing, to be wanted by one's father's people. But as for leaving: that shall not happen, not for some time. Dragon Keep is your home, cub. And even if you leave one day, to find your father's kin, or for whatever task you set your hand to, you will always be welcome back."

The stone lifted. The dragon-lord had said it, and it would be so, no matter what Devin or anyone else thought. Adults, Shem knew, did not always keep their promises, but Dragon did.

Suddenly he wanted to find Devin, to curl beside him, back to back, on the big soft pallet beside Devin's mother's fire that was their usual sleeping place. . . . Bootheels clattered on the paving stones. It was Cuillan, come to shut the dogs in, all but Savage, whose right and pleasure it was to roam the courtyard through the night. Cuillan was singing softly, an uncouth drone, and the smell of beer preceded him.

"Hey, Asa, hey, Blackie, heya, my Bess," he called. "Hoy, my beauties, come to bed now." Suddenly he stopped. "Who is there, fooling with my beasts? By the gods, I'll have the hide off you, so I will!"

Bright as a torch, light blazed into the night. Cuillan froze.

"My lord!" he said. "Excuse me. I didn't see you."

Rising, the dragon-lord held his hand out toward Shem. "Come, cub." Shem went to him and laid his small hand in the dragon-lord's huge one. They walked through the dark courtyard to the kitchen. "You know your way from here. Good night."

"Good night, my lord," Shem answered. Then he was within, among the smoke and lingering odors and the huge metal cauldrons, loosed from their chains now, brass bottoms bright where they had been scrubbed.

The scullions snored into their quilts. He picked his way carefully between them. Beryl and the children lived in a chamber beyond the kitchen. A red glow rose from the center of the hearth, where a thick log still burned. By its light, Shem saw Beryl's curtained sleeping place, and baby Elise's cradle. Devin's head was just visible beneath his blanket.

"Down, Turtle," he whispered. Grunting, Turtle turned in a circle thrice and lay down. Lifting up a corner of the blanket, Shem slid beneath it. Devin muttered, but did not wake. Shem pillowed his head on his arm. The fire gleamed. He gazed into it, until his eyes blurred and he saw, not a log afire, but a giant clutching a ruby in its fist. He wondered if he would dream. Hawk said dreaming was like memory. But Shem thought that really it was a kind of magic. There was a place he visited sometimes, dreaming. He could not see it clearly, but he could smell and taste it: a smell warm as new milk, and a taste sweet as honey on the tongue. In it there was a woman singing, and a cool softness, smooth as silk, against his skin. It made him happy to go there.

Hopefully he closed his eyes.

7

FROM EVERYWHERE IN Ryoka, caravans rolled toward Ujo.

They carried lace, silk, and velvet, for the gowns of noble ladies. They carried beer from Chingura, wine from Merigny; spices from Chuyo; silverwork from Taleva. In Mirrinhold, men packed blocks of ice in straw, loaded them on barges, and floated them down the river to Ujo. In Averra, the potters spun their wheels until their feet bled.

In Merigny, Allumar Marichal gave last-minute instructions to his wife, who received them with her usual placid competence. In Firense, Lukas Ridenar packed his second-best sword.

In Castria, Gerda Sorenson bemoaned the cruelty of the gods, who had given her a tavern in the northern mountains, instead of on the Great South Road.

"Imagine," she mourned to her husband Blaise, "all those travelers riding to the celebration, saddlesore, thirsty, desiring only a place to rest. If we lived farther south, we could be rich!"

IN DRAGON KEEP, the scullions were taking bets.

They all agreed on one thing: Rosset would win the horse race. No horse in Ippa could beat him.

Anssa, chief of the undercooks, said, "Finle will win the archery."

"I don't know," said Ruth the pastry-maker, sister to Raudri, the herald. "The Talvelai have good archers. So does the Lemininkai."

"Care to bet?" said Anssa. "Five pennies says he takes it."

"Where did you get five pennies?"

"Never you mind that. Will you bet?"

"Done."

After some discussion, it was further agreed that Edruyn would not win the sword contest, despite his youth and quickness.

"He's good," Simon the stew cook said, "but others are better."

The scullions scowled at their toes. It irked them to be forced to agree with Simon, whom none of them liked. Pico, the youngest, spoke loyally from beside the onion bin. "Dragon will win."

"Idiot." Simon aimed a cuff at him. Expertly, Pico dodged it. "Dragon won't fight."

"He would win if he did."

"He won't. He'll be too busy."

"Doing what?"

"What lords do," Simon said loftily. The scullions hooted at him.

"Will there be dancing?" asked Jess.

Ruth said, with heraldic authority, "Of course there will be dancing. There is always dancing at weddings. And this is not just any wedding, but the wedding of a prince. Pass me that bowl. No, not that one—the one with the cloth over it." She lifted the cloth and prodded the rising dough.

Fourteen-year-old Eilon, eldest of the scullions, turned from scrubbing the big copper pot with lemon to ask, "Is a prince a lord?"

Ruth said, "Surely. They're all lords."

Eilon frowned. "Then how's a prince different?"

Simon made a rude noise. "Hah. You don't know anything." Then he yelped, as a brisk, hard hand clouted his ear. The scullions ducked beneath the slicing table, all but Eilon, who was too big to hide.

"You don't know anything either," said Boris the head cook. He was a small, balding man who could hang his nose over any pot and tell from the steam how long the food had been cooking, and if it needed more spicing. Like many head cooks, he had a blistering tongue and an explosive temper.

"A prince is the son of a king. And a king, you ignorant slovenly jackass"—Simon flushed, and the scullions beamed happily at him—"is one who rules a country."

Deferential silence greeted this declaration. Then Jess said, "But this is Dragon's country. Is Dragon a king?"

"No," Boris said. "Listen, toads." The scullions ceased making faces at Simon and edged from beneath the slicing table. "This *is* Dragon's country. But Dragon's country is part of Ippa, and Ippa and Nakase and Kameni and Issho and Chuyo all together *are* Ryoka. And just as you and I and all the folk of Dragon's country are subject to Dragon's law, so the lords of Ryoka are subject to the king's law."

Pico tugged on the tail of Eilon's shirt and whispered a question.

"Does the king have a castle?" Eilon asked.

"Naturally he has a castle. It's in Kameni, in the east."

"What's the king's name?"

"Idaris Imorin. Cirion is his son." Picking up a spoon, the head cook absently stirred a pot. "Not that the title of king means much. The time of the kings is gone. All Cirion Imorin brings to this marriage is his land, and his lineage."

Simon said, "I don't know why they make so much of it. For all they are so great, under the sheets these lords and ladies look no different than you or I, or Jess in her shift."

The scullions cackled. Jess said, "How do you know what I look like in my shift?" She scooped a heavy rolling pin from the pastry table. Simon scuttled to the other side of the room. Boris's brows drew together.

"Simon, if that sauce burns, you shall be chopping onions for a week. Girl, put that down! Enough chatter. This is Dragon's business."

And since all in Ippa, especially those who served him, knew it was unwise to pay overmuch attention to Dragon's business, the folk of his household abandoned their speculations and went about their own business, which was dinner.

EIGHT DAYS AFTER Treion Unamira had been put into a cell in Lienor, they took him out and told him he was leaving.

"Where am I going?" he asked the man binding him. The man reminded him of Bran, same dark hair, same features. A cousin, perhaps. He had not seen the rider captain, or Honoris Imorin, since the day he had been confined.

"To Ujo," the man said. "Kalni Leminin wants you." He was not surprised. They had had no cause to execute him: he had done the folk of Nakase no harm; not a storehouse breached nor barn burned, not even an apple filched from a barrow. They walked him through the prison to a stable yard, and hoisted him onto a handsome, restive chestnut.

A few yards away, Niello Savarini, secured like himself, sat astride a black mare.

"Where's Edric?" Treion asked him.

Niello shook his head. "Don't know."

"Shut up," someone said. "No talking."

Guards closed round them. They rode through the prison gate. The pennants fluttered bravely on the towers of the wall. At the outer gate, their guards displayed passes. Treion hoped savagely for a diversion, something to distract the guards: a rearing horse, a falling roof tile, a mad dog loose in the streets. . . . But no mad dogs appeared.

The ride to Ujo took three weeks. It was not a pleasant journey. The midsummer heat sucked the life from all of them, even the horses. The captives were not allowed to talk to each other. They ate one-handed. They slept tethered. They were fed, and given water, but it never seemed to be enough.

As they neared the gates of Ujo, the road grew crowded. Bright banners fluttered from windows and cornices and rooftops. They rode through the East Gate. Guards took Niello roughly from his horse.

"Down," someone said to Treion. He slid down the horse's side. Two men took him into the guardhouse, down a torch-lit corridor lined with doors. They stopped in front of one. It opened, of course, to a cell.

It held nothing save a pallet, no water pitcher, not even a pot to piss in. A slit in the rear wall was set too high to see out of. It stank of urine and fear. The walls were covered with thin lines of writing. *I, Petros Antolini, swear by the gods that I am innocent of all offense. . . .*

I am Julian the scribe, who lives in the cottage behind the bakery on Peach Tree Street. . . .

I, Fulk of Secca, made these signs. . . .

"Where am I?" he asked. "What place is this?"

"Eastgate Prison."

"How long will I be here?"

"Probably not long," the man said. "That's up to the Lemininkai."

Treion had never met Kalni Leminin. He was Marion diSorvino's overlord. He was reputed to be ruthless, intelligent, and ambitious. *He's clever,* Niello had said once. *Cleverer than you. Possibly even cleverer than me. He plays keph, by the way. I hear he prefers the Winter pieces.*

"I'd like to speak to him," he said, with dignity. Perhaps Kalni Leminin was not as clever as Niello thought him to be.

The two guards grinned at one another.

"I'd like my uncle to die and leave me his fortune," the older one said. "Try again."

"I'd like a bath."

They laughed aloud at that.

"What happened to the man who came in with me?"

They stared at him contemptuously.

"You mean Ciccio?" The older guard wrung his hands slowly. "That gods-cursed piece of filth. He's going to be dead, very soon. Tonight, in fact. Is he a friend of yours?"

"No," Treion said.

They looked at him as though they did not quite believe him. Then the younger one said, "You have family? A mother, a brother? Anyone you want us to speak to?"

At that moment, Treion realized that he, too, was destined to die for what he had done at Castella: if not that night, then soon. He thought, briefly and with pain, of Maia.

But Maia was dead.

"No," he said, dry-mouthed. "There's no one."

* * *

UJO SMELLED LIKE a slaughterhouse.

The visitors from Dragon Keep entered the city through the North Gate. The smell of offal and roasting meat rose from the baked earth like steam.

Finle, riding at the tail of the small cavalcade, remarked, "Imarru's balls, they must have killed every pig in the city!"

Hawk, just ahead of him, did not answer. She was occupied in keeping Lily from bolting down an alley. A man, or possibly a woman, carrying the plaster figure of a griffin on his—her?—back, had scampered directly under the red mare's nose. Lily, normally as well behaved as any of Dragon Keep's steeds, had decided to take offense.

"Daughter of goats!" Hawk clamped her knees on the cavorting mare's sides and whacked her over the ears with the end of the shortened rein. The mare shuddered and stopped dead. More masquers danced past the troop. Lily rolled her eyes at them. Hawk crooned at her. "Come on, girl." Reluctantly, Lily moved.

The avenues and alleys were filled with people in costume, people wheeling barrows, people carrying hammers and harps and sides of beef and baskets filled with fruit. The noise from the roistering crowds was deafening. Hawk took a deep breath of the ripe, pungent air. She knew the odor well. She had lived fifteen years in Ujo. For twelve of them she had served in Kalni Leminin's Blue Arrow company; for six, as its captain. It felt strange to be back. She wondered how Tiko, once her apprentice, was faring with the bowyer's shop on Lantern Street that had once been hers.

Edruyn said, "It's hot. Is it always so hot in summer?"

"Yes," Hawk said. It was not that hot, for Ujo: it was late afternoon, and the lengthening shadows had begun to cool the streets. They pushed from the crowded avenue onto a side street. A man trotted past them, carrying a lute.

Herugin turned in his saddle to catch Hawk's eye. "Do you know a quick way to the Hotel Goude?" he shouted.

She hesitated. There was no telling which alleys were blocked. "I think I can find one."

"Lead us, then."

She urged Lily forward. Letting memory guide her, she coaxed her nervous horse down the narrow cobblestoned street, left, then straight three blocks, into Jugglers' Alley, past the Yellow Dog tavern, then right and left again onto a wide, silent street. The buildings' tall stone facades made an elegant fence. Trellises wound with yellow and red and white roses stood in front of every door. The street smelled strongly of flowers.

"What's this street?" Finle asked.

"The Avenue of Roses. This is the perfumiers' quarter. See that arch? The Hotel Goude is on the other side of it." They trotted down the boulevard to Three Lions' Square. It was not a square, but a circle of deep green lawn. In the center of the sward, three lions turned their wide marble countenances to the sun. Water sprayed from their mouths and fell into a pool at their feet.

The hotel was two floors tall, of gleaming pink stone. A broad marble stairway rose from the street to the hotel's entrance. As they reached the steps, a brigade of stableboys shot out of the shade of the hotel walls. Karadur swung from his saddle.

Amaral, the hotel's owner, hurried down the steps.

"Welcome to the Hotel Goude, my lord!" he called, bowing deeply to the dragon-lord. "Your rooms are ready." He snapped his fingers at the hovering grooms. Edruyn pulled the dragon standard from his pack. It would fly over the hotel while Karadur Atani was in the city. Hawk tossed Lily's reins to a waiting stableboy. As they strode through the hotel lobby she glimpsed Magnus at his post.

A page led them to the hotel's second floor. He opened a door. "The Gold Suite," he announced grandly, and withdrew. The rooms—a sitting room, a bedroom—were hung with cloth of gold.

Finle said, "My lord, they are bringing food and drink. Do you need aught else?"

"No," Karadur said. He went inside. The page showed Hawk and Finle to a room across the hall. It held four pallets, each with a chest. It had two narrow windows. Hawk took the pallet beneath the far window. Finle sank onto a bed. He rubbed his face with both hands.

"Tired?" Hawk said.

He looked up. His hair was standing straight up on his head.

"Gods, aren't you?"

She grinned at him, and went looking for a privy. When she returned, there were platters of food—grilled capons, a whole fish, a huge bowl of ripe figs—and a large pitcher of beer on the table. Finle handed her a capon leg. The sounds of the city echoed upward from the streets. In a little while, Herugin entered. He went straight to the beer and drank a mug without stopping.

"Ah, that's good," he said. He set the tankard down.

"How's Rosset?" Finle asked.

"Fine. His stall's bigger than this room." He reached for a plate. "How's Dragon's temper?"

Finle made a face. "The same." It had taken them five days to come from the Keep to Ujo. Karadur had been withdrawn and silent, with a smolder to his gaze that made them all walk softly near him. He had wanted Azil Aumson to come to Ujo with them, and Azil had refused. Why, none of them knew. Azil rarely refused the dragon-lord anything.

Hawk finished her meal. "I'll be back," she said. She found Magnus in the lobby. He had been head concierge at the Hotel Goude for twenty years: he knew every boulevard, every alley, every tavern and gamblers' den and moneylender's stall. He knew who sold the best wine, and where to get boots repaired, and which guard to bribe if you were caught outside the wall after the gates had closed.

He grinned. "Terrill Chernico. I heard you were in the north." They clasped palms. Hers had a gold piece in it. "So that's the Dragon of Chingura. He looks—severe. Is it true he stormed a wizard's castle, and captured a great treasure?"

"Of course it's true," she said. "Do you still know everything that happens inside the city?"

"Pretty much," he said. "What do you want to know?"

"Who else is in the city?"

He ticked the names off on his fingers. "Marichal is at the Hotel Bene. The Talvelai are at the Hotel Imago. The Oseppi and the diScala are with cousins. None of the lords from Derrenhold, Serrenhold, nor Mirrinhold are here."

"Any of the Chuyo lords?"

"Isheverin was supposed to come—the son, not the father. But at the last minute he cried off."

"That's not a good sign," Hawk said.

"No, it's not. What else do you want to know?"

"When's the wedding?"

"Tomorrow, at dawn, in the Temple of the Mother. It's to be very private: family, the abbess, a few witnesses. After, there is to be a feast at the Lemininkai's palace. The Lemininkai's proclaimed a three-day holiday. Footraces, horse races, wrestling matches and shoots, sword bouts, dancing, singing, two masques—and that's only the public sport."

"What happens tonight?"

"There's a reception tonight for the prince in the Hotel

Azure. Luke Ridenar is hosting it, but the Lemininkai's paying. All the folk of rank will be there, and anyone else who can beg or steal a way in. Your lord will go, of course."

THE HOTEL AZURE was six blocks from the Hotel Goude. There were no horses or wagons to be seen: between the sunset bell and midnight, only foot traffic was permitted in the center of the city. Karadur wore black: in an uncharacteristic show of wealth, he had covered his left arm from wrist to elbow with armrings, all different widths and weights, all gold. On his right arm, the golden dragon gleamed.

At the corner of Lilac Avenue and Silver Row, three buxom women, elaborately gowned and coifed, crooned throaty endearments.

"Ooh," one said, "look at the shoulders on that one, will you! And the hair!" Swiveling, Herugin scowled mightily at them. They broke into rapturous giggles.

They turned the corner into Willow Square. Instead of a fountain, a huge willow tree occupied the center of the square. Tiny lanterns, hundreds of them, red, gold, blue, green, swung from the branches. Three banners dangled from the Hotel Azure balcony. The one on the left showed the red fox, the Ridenar emblem, on a white field. The one on the right showed the Lemininkai blue arrow on a silver field. The one between them was black, embroidered with three silver emblems: a sword, a jewel, and between them, a crown.

The hotel doors were wide-open. Two sweating pikemen, blades crossed, stood ceremonially in front of the entrance. A man with a captain's emblem on his silver-and-blue shirt stood beside them. His eyes widened slightly as he took in the dragon badges, and the armband on Karadur's forearm. He bowed.

"My lord, welcome to the Hotel Azure." The pikemen

drew their weapons back. Karadur strode past them. The hall was thick with scent, and filled with people. Servants, trays propped on their shoulders, circulated through the crowd; their trays held wine, fruit pastries, and cups of raspberry sherbet. The sherbet was melting in the heat. A harpist, scarcely audible through the buzz of voices, played from a dais.

Hunter, Karadur said, *find me Kalni Leminin.*

She pivoted on her heel, listening and looking. Near the dais, a phalanx of richly dressed backs shifted to reveal the diminutive lord of Ujo leaning casually against the wall, talking to a taller, red-haired man.

There he is, my lord. The shorter man, in blue.

Karadur walked to the dais. The people near the Lemininkai drew back. Karadur halted. "My lord of Ujo," he said, "I am—"

"I know who you are. The Dragon of Chingura," the Lemininkai said cheerfully. "Of whom marvelous tales abound. They have been telling stories about you the length and breadth of Ryoka. Welcome to my city. You know Lukas Ridenar?" He jerked a thumb at the man beside him. "The lord of Firense is host of this overheated affair."

"The nominal host," Lukas Ridenar said amiably. He was older than Karadur, but younger than the Lemininkai. His elegant clothes hung gracelessly on his frame. "Everyone knows this is really your party. I have not even seen the guest list. Atani, you are welcome." He snagged a wineglass off a passing tray, and handed it to Karadur. "Your health."

"Yours." They drank.

"Where are you staying?"

"The Hotel Goude."

"How was your journey from Ippa?"

"Uneventful," Karadur said. "My lord of Ujo, I have a message for you. Erin diMako sends his greetings."

"I am happy to accept them, but I had hoped to see him in person. Is he indisposed?"

"He is quite well. He said to tell you that having seen four daughters wed in four years, he has had enough of weddings."

The Lemininkai laughed. "Gods, I don't blame him! I should not want to do this more than once. Not that I have had much to do. As my wife keeps telling me, weddings are women's business. You have not yet met my wife. Tomorrow you will, and when you do, you will understand. Sarita is a formidable woman."

"I look forward to our meeting," Karadur said politely.

It was going well. It was going very well. On the dais, the harpist cased his harp, and retreated in favor of a lute-player and a man with a drum. Silent figures stood like statues against the walls. Drifting into shadow, Hawk joined them. Most wore Lemininkai badges, but here and there she glimpsed other emblems: a red fox, a silver spear, a yellow diamond.

Herugin appeared, holding two sausages, each within a wrap of bread. Hawk shifted to make room for him. He handed her a sausage.

Suddenly Kalni Leminin left the corner. Striding toward the rear of the hall, he vanished amid a swirl of men in blue cloaks. He reappeared in a moment, followed by a slim, dark-haired man dressed in grey silks. A narrow circlet of silver glittered on his brow.

"Gods," whispered Herugin, "he's young."

Conversations stilled. With the Lemininkai at his elbow, the prince circled the hall, stopping now and then to speak to someone. They came to the corner where the dragon-lord stood.

Kalni Leminin said, "My lords, I would like you to meet Cirion Imorin, Prince of Lienor. Highness, this is Lukas

Ridenar of Firense, whom you know, and this is Karadur Atani, of Dragon Keep."

Lukas Ridenar bowed. "My prince. It's good to see you again."

"The lord of Firense I know well: he has visited my home, and he and his family have many times entertained my sister." The prince's tone was light, with a thread of gaiety running through it. "How fares your family, my lord?"

"They're well. How is your lovely sister Idana? Fierce as ever?"

"More than ever so. She sends greetings to you and your lady." He looked at Karadur. His eyes were grey, and clear, and acute. He seemed entirely at ease. "The Dragon of Chingura and I have never met, to my regret. A pleasure, my lord."

Karadur said, "The pleasure is mine." He bowed smoothly.

Herugin said softly, "He did it."

A dark-haired woman in a grey cloak glided to stand behind Cirion's left shoulder. She was lean and supple as a sapling. Her gaze touched Hawk's. *Sister hawk*, she said, in the accents of Voiana. *I greet thee.*

Hawk blinked. It was as if she looked into a mirror, and saw herself as she had been, twenty years before.

Sister, she said. *Who art thou?*

I am Jada Afar. I serve the prince.

Terrill Chernico. I am with Dragon.

At the other end of the hall, the rhythm of laughter in the gathering changed. Like figures in a military march, the revelers had formed themselves into two lines. A woman stood alone in the high-arched doorway. Her gown of sky-blue silk was trimmed at hem and neck with silver. A web of tiny diamonds glittered in her auburn hair. Smiling buoyantly, she walked between the lines. Cirion went to greet her. She put both hands out to him with tender grace.

A child toddled out of the crowd, carrying a bouquet of pink flowers nearly as large as she was. Selena took the bouquet. Cirion, laughing, swept the child up onto his shoulder, swung her into the air, and set her on her feet again.

A man in dapper satin spoke at Karadur's elbow. "They make a charming couple, don't you think?" He had a seamed, long-jawed face, and dark eyes, made prominent by deep eye ridges and the jet-black eyebrows that hung over them. "Permit me to introduce myself. I am Marichal."

"Atani."

"I know: the Dragon of Chingura. I knew your father. You look like him. We fought together under Pohja Leminin, twenty-five years ago."

Karadur said, "It's a pleasure to meet you, my lord. Were you friends with my father?"

"Friends? No. He had a damned imperious way about him, and a demonic temper. But his soldiers would have followed him to hell if he chose to lead them there."

Karadur said mildly, "So will mine."

Allumar Marichal smiled. "Is this your first visit to Ujo?"

"No," the dragon-lord said. "I have been here before, with Erin diMako." He did not elaborate.

"Kalni's proud of his city. As well he should be." He lifted a glass off a passing tray. "Proud of his girl, too. She's a beauty, is she not? Quite a triumph, this wedding."

"That's generous of you, Marichal," said a grating voice at Karadur's back. "Too bad that your own plans fell through. I heard you wanted the girl for one of your boys. Ario, I heard it was."

Marichal turned. For a moment, it appeared as if he was about to snub the interloper. Then he said, rather frostily, "My son Ario is happily married, my lord." He gestured. "Do you know each other? Karadur Atani; Marion diSorvino."

The dragon-lord said, "My lord of Sorvino."

"Atani. Yes. I heard that you were here." DiSorvino was a bulky man, with wide shoulders and a fleshy, ruddy face. "I have a bone to pick with you. You had Treion Unamira in your hands last winter, and you let him go. You know what he did in Castella. You should have killed the murdering bastard when you had the chance."

Karadur said, "My lord, what I do in my domain is my own business. But I regret I have offended you. I had hoped we could be cordial."

"Why?"

"I want to speak with you about your daughter Maia. She lives on my land."

"My daughter?" DiSorvino scowled. "You have been deceived, my lord. I have no daughter. My late wife Iva bore a pinched-faced whelp who lived in my house for a time. Who the bitch's father was is anyone's guess."

Repugnance, quickly concealed, crossed Allumar Marichal's ugly face. He said, "Atani, you must excuse di-Sorvino, he has no manners."

DiSorvino purpled. "Mind your own business, sir! My manners are my own. Should I wish for a tutor, I'll pay one." He nodded to the dragon-lord. "Take the girl if you want. Be warned, though. She's probably a whore, like her mother."

Karadur's face went still as stone. Then his eyes changed, from cobalt to searing, diamond-white.

The lute-player's fingers jangled to a halt. Herugin started forward. Hawk clamped her fingers round his arm. "Don't be a fool," she said. No one moved.

Suddenly Cirion stepped between Karadur and diSorvino. With a nod toward Marichal, and not even a glance at Marion diSorvino, Cirion said to Karadur, "My lord, forgive me for interrupting your conversation. There is a contest in the square you should witness. Your man is in it; the black-haired archer." He gestured toward the doors. "Join me."

It was, quite clearly, a command.

Cool grey eyes met that fiery gaze, and held. Hawk felt the shock of it through her nerve endings. Then Karadur Atani's preternatural gaze metamorphosed into something human, endurable. Calmly, Cirion turned. Karadur and Marichal both followed him through the chamber. Lukas Ridenar padded after them.

Herugin said softly to Hawk, "What the hell just happened?"

"I don't know," she said. Her head throbbed. "Come on."

The evening was balmy. A fragrance of honeysuckle hung in the air. The sky was tinged with lilac. A swelling moon, a hairsbreadth short of full, edged slowly over the city's rooftops. Selena Leminin stood on the lowest step, gazing across the shadowy lawn toward the huge willow tree. Facing the tree, at the far edge of the lawn, Finle Haraldsen stood, bow in hand. Next to him stood a second archer, a solid, stocky youth, not as tall as Finle. Finle lifted the bow and loosed an arrow. It hissed through the darkness. An amber lamp, the string that held it to its branch severed, fell to the ground. A page darted out to seize it. The other man shot. A blue lamp dropped from the tree. A page scooped it up. A trio of groundskeepers stood by with pails of water, lest one of the falling lamps ignite. The two men shot again in turn. Two lamps dropped.

There were four lamps left on the tree.

Marichal said, "You said this was a competition. I see two men."

Cirion said, "You missed the beginning. There were nine contestants to begin with. If a man missed a shot, he had to drop out. These two alone are left."

Lukas Ridenar said, "Allumar, one of those men is wearing your badge."

"That is so."

"And looks remarkably like your son Daniello."

Marichal said complacently, "Indeed, I believe it is my son Daniello." Again the men traded shots. Two more lamps fell.

Suddenly the great doors opened wide. Laughing and jostling each other, a crowd of merrymakers spilled down the steps. The archers ignored them. Finle aimed and loosed. A red lamp dropped from the tree. The second man shot. No lamp dropped. The shooter let out a crow of laughter.

"I'm done!" he announced gaily. "My friend, you have the prize."

Allumar Marichal said, "Daniello!" The young man turned. "Daniello, come here. Say hello to the prince, whom you know, and to Karadur Atani, whom you do not. My lords, this is my son, Daniello."

"My lady, my lords, I am honored." Daniello bowed, first to the prince, then to the dragon-lord. He looked very like his father. "My lord Atani, your man's skill makes the rest of us look like children. I counted myself a good archer, until tonight."

Lukas Ridenar chuckled. "By the gods, Atani, your man just beat Daniello Allumar at archery. Not very diplomatic of you to let him do that."

Carefully, Finle aimed at the lamp Daniello had missed. It dropped. Finle shot a final arrow. The last lamp dropped to the earth, guttered, and went out. Selena clapped her hands. "Ah, splendid!" She turned to Lukas Ridenar. "My lord, I wish to make a toast. Do you suppose we might arrange for wine?"

Ridenar said, "Certainly, my lady." He whistled shrilly. A page scuttled out of the darkness, and vanished again, to return carrying a tray loaded with glasses. A second page arrived with a jug. The rich scent of spiced wine rose into the night air. The pages filled the glasses.

Selena raised hers high. "To tomorrow's contestants! May they all win!"

"That's impossible," Daniello said gloomily. He drank, and brightened. "Ah. This is good. Father, there is merignac in this."

Marichal drank. "So there is," he said. "Lukas, I approve of your refreshments." Smiling, Lukas Ridenar tipped his glass up. Elsewhere on the lawn, a harpist struck a chord.

Selena, rosy-cheeked, said, "Then I wish to make a second toast!" Lukas Ridenar signaled. The pages filled the glasses a second time. "To the winners!" She drank. "My lord Atani, your archer deserves a prize."

The dragon-lord said, "Do you think so? Then he shall have one." He worked a ring off his arm. "Finle!" Bow in hand, Finle approached the steps. Karadur tossed him the armring. Finle caught it deftly. "My lady, allow me to present Finle Haraldsen, second-in-command of my archers' wing. Finle, make your thanks to the lady Selena."

Finle, bowing, said, "Thank you, my lady. You are as thoughtful as you are beautiful."

"A courtier!" Selena clapped her hands. "My lord Atani, I applaud your warrior's training. Are all of your men so quick-tongued?"

Karadur said, "My men have many talents, my lady."

A whippoorwill called into the warm darkness. A yawning page trotted to Selena's side. She bent her head to listen, and made a wry face at his whispered message.

"Alas, my friends, I must go. My mother reminds me that I am to be wed tomorrow, and need my sleep." She reached a hand to Cirion. Together they climbed the stairs and went into the hall.

Allumar Marichal said, "Indeed, it grows late. Daniello, time for us to return to our hotel. Lukas, my thanks; it was a pleasant evening." Shoulder to shoulder, father and son descended the stairs. Three men with Merigny badges fell into step behind them.

Lukas Ridenar nodded to the dragon-lord. "Till tomorrow, my lord." He mounted the stairs. The whippoorwill called again. A phalanx of groundskeepers with water buckets and brooms moved toward the tree. Karadur passed his glass to the waiting page. Finle took his habitual place at Karadur's left hand.

They were nearly to the boulevard when a harpist plucked a familiar tune. A voice lifted into the night.

The Red Boar came from the forest; the Red Boar came to the hills;
His tusks were iron and his breath was fire;
His bellow toppled the castle spire;
O, the Red Boar, the Red Boar of Aidu.

The harping was indifferent but the voice was true as a lodestone. Karadur halted in his tracks. Joy and astonishment chased across his face. The harping ceased; the singer fell silent. Finle whispered, "My lord—do you want—shall I—?" He gestured in the direction of the music.

Karadur hesitated. Then he shook his head.

"No," he said. "Leave them alone."

He started walking again, toward the hotel.

8

AT DAWN ON the day of the Midsummer Festival, in the city of Ujo, Cirion Imorin, son of Idaris Imorin, Prince of Lienor, and Selena Leminin, daughter of Kalni Leminin and Sarita Amarinta Leminin, of this city, knelt before the Goddess in the Temple of the Mother on Mirabella Square. Each drank thrice from the beaten copper bowl, and recited the words Isandre the High Priestess told them to say.

In Great River Market, merchants had been toiling since before sunup, laying out their wares. Stalls filled the square, selling every manner of luxury and trinket: fine cloth, shining brass bowls, mirrors and jewelry and leather sandals, willow cages filled with songbirds. The streets of Ujo were, for once, quite clean: they had been swept, and scoured, and swept again by a battalion of street cleaners. Stalls on every third corner, attended by competent men with flashing cleavers, and urchins whose sole task it was to chase away flies and stray dogs, sold ribs and sausages and pigs' feet. Vendors sold oranges and dates, ears of roasted spring corn, and taffy on a stick. On the river docks, costers sold live eels, which a cheerful man would slice into pieces and grill for you as you watched. White-winged gulls perched on the pilings, shrieking at one another, and fighting over the discarded eel heads. Even the shabbiest barges were festooned with ribbons. There was ample entertainment. Acrobats turned somersaults and stood on one another's shoulders. Musicians plucked lutes, blew on horns, jangled bells and tambourines. In the common room of the Crimson Lion, a man in a green robe with stars embroidered on its hem told fortunes. In the courtyard of the Steeplejack, a puppet master and her apprentices presented the drama of Pohja Leminin's victory over the Isojai to an admiring throng. In the Perfume Quarter, pretty girls in scanty silks invited visitors to sample the scents. On Lilac Avenue, girls leaned precariously over the balconies, tossing wrapped mementos down to the men. The favors held chocolates and little bells and occasionally a small gilt token, which entitled the lucky man who caught it to a free visit. Pickpockets wove quietly through the crowd, staring with feigned wonder at the acrobats, while deft fingers plucked pouches and wallets from hidden places. The city guards observed them indulgently; even cutpurses had to eat. But indulgence had limits. Word had gone out across the city to the pimps and thieves and thugs that for this day, and two days after, while petty infractions would be overlooked, visitors were not to be touched. Violence to their persons would draw immediate, severe penalties.

On the hill above the city, the archways and balconies and spires of the Lemininkai's palace gleamed like cut rubies. Below the palace, on the promenade, two snowy-white pavilions had been erected. Pennants floated on poles over the lawn. To the south, a long and level field sported man-shaped straw targets painted with bright concentric circles.

To the west, the lawn was chalked for the tourney. The lines were arrow-straight: the master of lists, a meticulous man, had personally supervised the placement. The grass was emerald-green. The sky was cobalt. It would be—the Leminkai had decreed it, and it would be so—a flawless, faultless, perfect day.

AS THE PARTY from Dragon Keep rode up the avenue, a herald stepped forward to greet them. Grooms appeared to take charge of their horses. "Careful with this one," Herugin warned as he relinquished Rosset's reins. "He's racing this afternoon." The red horse pranced a little at the unfamiliar touch.

Pages scuttled through the crowd, carrying trays of fruit and sweetmeats and jugs of wine. Men and women in bright silks moved across the grass. Karadur sauntered easily among them. His eyes were bright.

"These are the same people we saw last night," Finle said. "Don't they get tired of each other?" He unstrapped his bow case from the saddle and slid it over his shoulder.

Herugin said, "My lord, I'm going to the raceway."

A man with a pike over his shoulder plodded past them. Edruyn glanced hopefully at the dragon-lord. "My lord—may I . . ."

"Go," Karadur said. He touched Edruyn's shoulder lightly. "Good luck. Don't kill anyone whose rank is higher than your own."

Grinning, Edruyn sped away. *Hunter*, Karadur said, *stay beside me*. He strolled toward the palace. The Lemininkai's big red house shone in the sunlight. It looked like something on a tapestry.

A gently sloping lawn led to a terrace. At its center sat a stone fountain carved in the shape of a massive lily. Water poured into its bowl. Cirion, with Selena beside him, stood beside the fountain. Cirion wore silver-grey. Selena's gown was blue. A fire opal on a golden chain glowed at her throat. Set in red-gold, it was the size of a baby's fist.

Karadur said, "Hunter, is it true that there is a fountain in every room in the Lemininkai's house?"

Hawk said, "I don't know, my lord. I haven't been in every room."

He crossed the terrace to the newlyweds.

"Highness," he said to Cirion and to Selena, "Princess. Felicitations on your wedding."

Selena said, "Thank you, my lord." She touched the opal at her throat. "As you see, I wear your gift this morning. It is beautiful. Do you know its history?"

"Alas, I do not, my lady. I took it from Dragon Keep's hoard because it was beautiful. I am honored that you wear it this day."

Sister. Jada appeared at Cirion's left elbow. *Good morning.*

Good morning, Hawk said. *Did your lord get any sleep last night?*

Oddly enough, he did.

Did you?

Jada grinned. *Very little. A surprising number of people tried to interrupt the prince's rest, to congratulate him on his nuptials, of course. They kept us busy.*

Lukas Ridenar, brandishing a roasted chicken leg, strolled across the emerald lawn. "Good morning. My lady, my prince, felicitations on your marriage. I wish you joy."

Selena gave the swordsman a dazzling smile. "Thank you, my lord, and good morning to you also."

"Atani, good day. This is quite a festival the Lemininkai has given us, eh?"

Karadur said, "It is." He glanced at the sword on Ridenar's hip. "I see you plan to compete."

The swordsman patted his well-worn scabbard. "I do. My friends have come to expect it." A trumpet sang across the day. "That's the signal for the contests. The archery's first. Is your young man shooting this morning?"

"He is."

"I'd like to watch that."

The two men made their way to the front rank of the crowd that ringed the shooting range. Finle stood amid the ranks of archers. "What round is this?" Lukas Ridenar asked of no one in particular.

"Second," half a dozen voices said.

"What's the distance?"

"Sixty paces."

There were twenty-eight shooters all together. They shot in groups of ten. By the end of the second round, twenty-eight had shrunk to seven: Finle, Daniello Marichal, two of the Lemininkai's soldiers, two of Cirion's, and a boy. His long black hair was tied back from his face with a broad red band, Issho fashion. He was perhaps fourteen, with long hands and long feet like a puppy's.

"Who's the youngster?" Karadur asked.

"Juni Talvela, Ydo Talvela's second son. He's a good lad, a good archer. He's supposed to go to Serrenhold for training."

"You don't approve?"

Ridenar said, "You know what they say. Serrenhold's a bitter place. Koiiva trained there. But Koiiva's more like his father than any son I've ever met. Juni is different." Ridenar shrugged. "Of course, it's not my business. But I'd not send a son of mine to be trained by Bork Hal."

They moved the line to eighty paces. Daniello Marichal's sixth shot missed the target. The seventh shot eliminated the two from Ujo. An arrow went wide: one of the men from Lienor stepped back from the line. Now there were three men left. They moved the line one hundred paces from the targets. Finle lifted an arrow, nocked it, and sent it flying into crimson. A second and third arrow followed the first. Without hesitation, the other two matched him. The crowd breathed loudly. The Talvela boy's fourth shot went into yellow. The spectators groaned in sympathy. He stepped back, flexing his fingers. The soldier's next shot plowed into the grass. Finle's fourth, fifth, sixth, and seventh shots hit crimson. The Talvela boy lifted his bow. His next two shots hit red. His eighth shot hit the yellow.

Finle sent his last three shots smoothly into the target's red heart.

The spectators cheered. "Very nice," Lukas Ridenar said.

A pretty girl tossed a cluster of yellow roses at Finle's feet. He scooped them up. Karadur strolled to his side. "Well done." He nodded at Juni Talvela. "Both of you."

Color flooded the youth's face. He stammered thanks. A horn blew twice, and then again. The crowd began to slither toward the west lawn.

Lukas Ridenar said, "I must go. That's the signal for the sword bouts." He cocked an eye at the dragon-lord. "You don't compete."

"No."

"Your father didn't either. Care to join me?" Across the lawn, the red fox pennant fluttered on a pole above a tent. "My man is there, with my armor."

Inside the tent, a man with a seamed, calm face said, "My lord, you're late, as usual."

Ridenar said, "I'm always late to battles." He jerked his thumb at Karadur. "Nico, this is Karadur Atani, lord of Dragon Keep. Don't be rude to him." He unbuckled his sword belt and laid it aside.

Nicolas inclined his head. "My lord Atani." He pulled a light mail shirt from a worn chest and tossed it to his lord.

"Put that on." He knelt, greaves in hand. "There's wine, if either of you would like it."

"Not I," Ridenar said.

Karadur shook his head. He said, "You spoke of my father. Did you know him?"

Ridenar said, "I remember him from the war. I was thirteen; it was my first battle."

"Aye, and you were late to it," Nicolas said. "Your father was beside himself. He thought you'd been captured."

"Aye. He told me so, after." He stood. Nicolas settled his breastplate over his shoulders. "Your father . . . He was a big man, as you are, and he moved like flame. He was not so much older than I, but he was a man already, ruler of his domain and leader of his war band, and I was still a boy. I have to confess, I was frightened of him."

He ran his hand over the scratches in the breastplate. "Nico, is there anything you can do about these?"

"Not anymore," Nicolas said. "I've told you not to wear it."

"It's comfortable."

"Scratches draw the tip."

"I know." He held out his arms. Nicolas fastened leather vambraces over his forearms.

Karadur said, "You spoke of your first battle. When was your last?"

Ridenar frowned. "My last true battle? Gods, years ago. I don't count chasing outlaws."

Nicolas said, "You had that skirmish with the Chuyokai last year. September, it was."

"I don't count that either. They hardly gave us much of a fight." He rolled his shoulders. "I'm stiff."

"Getting old."

"Look who's talking. Old man. I'll never be as old as

you." They grinned at one another. Nicolas handed Ridenar his sword belt. "*You* fought a war in the north. Last year, April, was it not? They say you battled a demon, and took its treasure."

"Do they?" The dragon-lord's face was expressionless.

"Not true?"

"I fought my brother in the north," Karadur said. "I killed him."

THE WINNER OF the tourney, to no one's surprise, was Lukas Ridenar. The rangy warrior scythed and battered his way through all his opponents. Edruyn advanced as far as the third round. He was beaten by one of Cirion's soldiers, a tall man with an astonishing reach and reflexes to match.

After the tourney there were footraces, and the jugglers returned, followed by acrobats, and then by dancers, many of them young, female, and dressed in diaphanous, slithery costumes that draped and undraped strategically. The young men ceased their wrestling to form a rapt circle around the dance troupe. Toward midafternoon the horns blew. The crowd moved toward the racetrack. It wound around the palace in a great circle, through trees and rock gardens. Kalni Leminin's groundskeepers had built it especially for the occasion.

Karadur and Lukas Ridenar worked their way through the crowd to one of the better viewing points.

"I hear you have a horse in the race," Ridenar said.

"The red one," Karadur said. A groom was walking Rosset down the middle of the track. The red horse's coat gleamed like fine glass.

"He looks prime," Ridenar said. "Of course, so does that

one." He pointed to the big grey stallion that danced and fretted to Rosset's right. Its groom wore the prince's colors, black and silver. A slender man, also in black and silver, stepped onto the track and caught the stallion's rein. "Vaikkenen's balls. It's Cirion."

Kalni Leminin appeared on the terrace of the palace, Selena on his arm. A horn sounded. The horses moved toward the starting line.

"One's missing. There were supposed to be twelve," said Ridenar. "Ah, there she is." A sleek black filly trotted up the track. Her jockey seemed impossibly small.

"Whose horse is she?" Karadur asked. The jockey's robes were unmarked.

"I don't know." The trumpet blew a second time. The riders brought their horses to the starting line. The Leminkai lifted a hand. The trumpet blew again. The horses surged forward.

The black filly led the field from start to finish. She crossed the line a stride ahead of the big grey stallion. Rosset, battling hard with Dennis Amdur's bay over the last quarter of the track, finished fourth. The spectators cheered their lungs out, and pelted the horses with flowers. A groom grabbed the filly's head rein. The jockey leaped from the narrow leather patch that served as a saddle. Her white robes billowed about her. Her skin was brown, and her hair and eyes were ebony.

Ridenar said, "Gods, it's a girl." He swung his long legs over the rope and strolled down the track to Cirion's side. "My prince, you should have won. The black filly had an unfair advantage, bearing so light a rider."

Cirion shook his head. His hair, clothes, and skin were coated with dust. "Not so. I was outraced."

"Whose is she? I saw no colors."

"I don't know." Cirion beckoned to the girl. She danced

to his side. She was lithe and small as a child. "What's thy name, child?" he said.

She shook her head and spoke in a musical tongue. He answered in the same language. Her dark eyes widened.

Ridenar said, "I didn't know you spoke Chuyokai."

Cirion said, "I had a Chuyokai tutor for a time." He spoke again to the girl. She smiled broadly and gestured. A look of surprise crossed the prince's face. The girl laughed and danced away.

"Well?" said Ridenar.

Cirion said, with an apologetic smile, "It seems the filly's mine. A wedding gift from Sunudi Isheverin."

"Truly? Your own horse beat you? Ah, that's a fine jest."

Cirion said, "I shall have to write and thank him. Atani, that red horse of yours nearly knocked mine off the track. Your man's a fine rider."

Karadur said, "Herugin Dol is my cavalry master." He beckoned. "Herugin!" The rider came swiftly to his side.

"My lord?"

Cirion said, "My friend, you ride well! Someday we must have a rematch. Perhaps, if your lord permits, you will come to Selidor, you and your horse. It is a beautiful city."

Bowing, Herugin said, "Highness, I was born in Selidor."

"Were you indeed!" Cirion looked at Karadur. "My lord, once there was great friendship between the house of Imorin and the house of Atani. I would have it so again. It would give my wife and myself great pleasure if you were to come to Selidor, and visit us."

Karadur said, "Thank you. I would like to visit Selidor. And you, my prince—you must come north someday."

Cirion said, "If the king my father's health permits, I shall. I am told there is nothing in Ryoka to rival the northern mountains. Though I do not think I could live in the north. I would miss the sea."

"I do not think I could live in the south," Karadur said. "I would miss the mountains. And the music."

"There is music in the south."

"Not like our northern music," the dragon-lord said. "When you come to my house, you will hear it."

A horn called. "That is the signal for dinner," Cirion said. "You will forgive me, I hope. My wife will kill me if I keep to these clothes." He turned toward the palace.

Dennis Amdur appeared at Herugin's elbow. He said, "My lord!"

Karadur and the lord of Firense both glanced his way. Lukas Ridenar frowned.

"I know you," he said. "Amdur, isn't it? You're one of the Lemininkai's captains."

"Yes, my lord," said Dennis. "First cavalry officer."

"You rode well." Ridenar's mobile face went still a moment. "You and your men were first into Castella."

"Yes, my lord."

"You sent Carlo to me. I am in your debt." Then he said, "From the way the two of you battled down the track, I believe you know each other."

Herugin said, "We do, my lord. And I, for one, look forward eagerly to our rematch. Though I understand it may be delayed, since I go north, and Dennis east."

"Oh?"

Dennis Amdur said, "The Lemininkai has given my company to the prince, a wedding gift." Squaring his shoulders, he faced the dragon-lord. "My lord, Hern wrote to me. He said it was you who replaced the stock we lost, and that when he tried to recompense the builders for rebuilding our house, he was told it had been paid for already, by Dragon Keep. You must let me pay you back."

"No," Karadur said.

Dennis said stubbornly, "My lord, it's my responsibility."

Karadur just looked at him. Herugin stuck an elbow in his ribs. "Dennis, you fool. Shut *up*." He thrust an arm through his friend's. "Excuse him, my lord. His wits are addled."

HUMMING SOFTLY, THE gratified crowd streamed back toward the pavilions. Within the near pavilion, a meal lay ready on cloth-covered tables: an elegant pasturage of cold meats, smoked fish, cheese and soft bread and opulent baskets of fruit. Pages, bells chiming softly on their shoes, circulated among the revelers with glasses of wine.

As Karadur and Lukas Ridenar approached the tents, a belled page sprang, like a conjuror's pigeon, out of the ether. "My lords, of your kindness, the Lemininkai begs you to accompany me." He led them to the second pavilion. It, too, held a table piled high with meats, bread, and fruit.

The Lemininkai and Allumar Marichal sat facing each other at a small table. They had a keph board between them. The Lemininkai lifted a hand. He said, "Come in, my lords, and join us. It's crowded out there."

Resplendent in sky-blue silk, Sarita Amarinta Leminin sat majestically in a massive chair. She was a stately woman, twice her husband's size. A vase of orange lilies glowed at her feet. A stern-faced man sat on a chair beside her.

Karadur walked to her. "My lady," he said, "we have not met before. I am Atani."

She smiled graciously. "My lord, the city is honored by your visit. Are you enjoying your stay?"

"I am, very much."

"Good. Do you know each other?" She smiled at the man beside her. "My lord, allow me to introduce Karadur Atani of Ippa."

The man said, "Atani. Yes. I am Ydo Talvela." Juni Talvela slid forward, holding a plate of food. "This is my son, Juni." Ydo Talvela scowled. "Don't just stand there, boy. Get the lord some food."

"No need," Karadur said. "I am served." Edruyn had arrived with a plate of meat pastries in one hand and a chair in the other.

Ydo Talvela said, "I am pleased to meet you, my lord. I knew your father. You look like him."

Karadur said, "So I have been told. I saw your son shoot today. He did well."

"Not well enough," Ydo Talvela said. "He should have won."

Juni flushed.

A page brought Karadur a glass of wine. There was a slight stir at the entrance to the pavilion. Cirion, damp, and in fresh clothes, entered the pavilion with Selena on his elbow.

Behind them glided a dark-skinned woman. She was tall, regal as a goddess. She wore a gown of fluid gold. Night-dark hair sprang from her erect head like a corona.

Ydo Talvela said, "Who's that girl?"

Sarita Leminin said, "A singer, my lord."

Ydo Talvela grunted.

Azil Aumson, carrying a lap harp, followed her. He settled on a stool and laid the harp across his knees. Something glinted between his gloved fingers. He drew it across the strings. It made a hard, bright sound.

He did not look at Karadur. He spoke to a page. The boy brought him a glass of water. He sipped it. He tuned a string, another, then nodded.

The woman in gold put a hand on his shoulder.

The Lemininkai said, "My friends, pray silence for the singers!"

Let love be all and there shall be no weeping;
In every spring, sap rises in the tree;
Sweet summer calls; cold winter lies a-sleeping;
Let all be love when you return to me.

Let love be all; let song define our kingdom;
Let there be joy, and music unrestrained;
Let us delight; one to the other clinging;
Let grief and care be banished this domain.

For winter cold will silence summer's laughter;
And soon will come the turning of the year;
Yet love endures, through winter, and thereafter;
And spring returns, to vanquish every care.

Let love be all, and there shall be no sorrow;
In every song, let melody run free;
Winter will pass; the sun will rise tomorrow;
Let all be love when you return to me.

Supple voices blended in beauty. The pavilion was silent; no one breathed.

Then Selena said softly, "Sing another. Please."

Again Azil struck a chord.

The Red Boar came from the forest;
the Red Boar came to the hills;
His tusks were iron and his breath was fire;
His bellow toppled the castle spire;
O, the Red Boar, the Red Boar of Aidu.

The looks on most of the faces made it evident that most of the people there had not heard the song before. By the time it ended, they were clapping and swaying in their chairs. Karadur sat still, hands folded tautly in his lap.

"More!" said Daniello Marichal.

The woman in gold stepped back, leaving Azil alone on his stool.

Azil said, "This is the story of Kani and Tori." He stroked the harp again. His voice easily filled the pavilion.

Two brothers went a-hunting, upon an autumn day;
See the wild geese fly over, fly over.
Two brothers went hunting on an autumn day;
And the wild geese rise in the morning.

"Now, Kani and Tori were brothers, the sons of a king. Both men were fair and strong and beautiful. And Kani was a man of great heart, and he loved Tori. But Tori above all loved power, and so he hated Kani, for Kani, being the elder, was destined to rule.

"Consumed with hatred, Tori rose in the morning, and went to bed at night still hating. But Kani knew nothing of his brother's feeling. And it came to pass that Kani and Tori went hunting together one misty autumn morning.

"(See the wild geese fly over, fly over.)

"And on that soft autumn morning Tori took his brother prisoner, and bound him with chains, and brought him east, into the impassable desert, and imprisoned him in a tower without doors. He set his soldiers about it, and ordered them to kill any who tried to enter it. And he told his father and all the people that Kani was dead.

"And so it came to pass, as is the way of things, that the old king died. And the people came to Tori and said, 'Your father is dead, and your brother is dead. You must rule us now.'

"'I will,' Tori said. And they gave him the crown, and scepter, and the sword that had been his father's. It was an ancient blade, sharp and puissant, and none but the king could wear it. And he made a decree that throughout the kingdom no one, not even the smallest child, was to speak Kani's name, for—he told them—the grief that came upon him when he heard it was too great for him to bear.

"(And the wild geese rise in the morning.)

"But Kani had a friend, a good friend, who loved him above all things. That friend's name was Arum. And Arum did not believe that Kani was dead. One morning Arum went hunting.

"(See the wild geese fly over, fly over.)

"And a goose came flying from the east, and the feathers of that goose were gold. And the golden goose stooped over Kani's friend, whose name was Arum, and said, 'Follow me, and I will show you what you most long to see.'

"Arum followed the goose into the impassable desert, to the doorless tower.

"(See the wild geese fly over, fly over.)

"It was guarded by Tori's men. They carried spears, and bows. 'Go away,' they said, and leveled their spears.

" 'What shall I do?' Arum asked the goose.

" 'Mount my back,' the goose said.

"So Arum mounted to the golden goose's back. *(See the wild geese fly over, fly over.)* The goose rose up. The soldiers shot at it, but missed. It brought him to the window of the tower, and there, within a small, round room, Arum saw his friend. Kani was gaunt, but his back was straight and his eyes clear. 'Kani!' Arum cried.

"And Kani heard, and came to the window. Thus the dear friends were reunited.

"(And the wild geese rise in the morning.)

" 'My dear friend and king, let me take you from this place,' said Arum. But there seemed no way to do that. For the window was barred, and the space between the bars was narrow. Despite his leanness, Kani could not get through it. The friends despaired.

" 'Do not lose heart. I will help you,' said the goose.

" 'How?' Kani asked.

" 'You must kill me, and take my skin, and wear it.'

" 'I cannot do that,' Kani said.

" 'Then you will die here,' said the goose.

"*(See the wild geese fly over, fly over.)*

"And they saw that what the goose said was true. So the goose flew in the window, and Kani snapped its neck. He took Arum's knife, ready to skin the goose, but as he touched the golden feathers, they sprang from the goose's body in a brilliant cloud, and wove around him like a cloak. Then Kani was gone, and there was only a goose. It flew through the window. *(See the wild geese fly over, fly over.)* Arum mounted its back. The goose flew from the tower, past the arrows and spears of the soldiers, westward, into the mountains.

"And there, in the mountains, Kani regained his strength. And he rode out of the mountains, to the city ruled by his brother. *(See the wild geese fly over, fly over.)*

"And the people knew him, and followed him. He reached the citadel, where Tori lived. 'Call the challenge,' he said to his herald. The herald lifted his horn, and blew the challenge.

"Tori came from within the citadel.

" 'Who dares challenge me?' he cried.

" 'I do,' said Kani. He strode forward. The cloak of golden feathers shimmered in the sunlight. 'This kingdom is mine. You took it from me. Now I will have it back.'

"And Tori's heart shrank in his breast, for he knew his brother's claim was just. But the greed that had brought him to take the kingship from his brother still governed him.

" 'You will not,' he said, and drew the sword that had been his father's. 'Take up your weapon!'

"'I have none,' said Kani. He showed his hands. They were empty.

"'Then you will die,' Tori said.

"But as Tori advanced upon his brother, the cloak's golden feathers caught the sunlight, and dazzled him. He could not see. He staggered, and the sword dropped from his hand. Kani picked it up. *(And the wild geese rise in the morning.)* Then, in the sight of his people, Kani killed his brother, and regained the kingdom.

"He ordered that the body of his brother be entombed beside their father. *(See the wild geese fly over, fly over.)*

"And Kani decreed that there should be made a great banner, and ordered it to fly over his kingdom. The emblem on that banner was a wild goose. *(And the wild geese rise in the morning.)*

"And Arum and Kani remained friends all their lives."

9

THE HARP CALLED triumphantly, and went still. There was blood on Azil's gloved fingers. Rising, he bowed to Cirion, and to the Lemininkai.

Cirion raised his glass. "Honor to the singer!" They shouted it, and drank.

A page brought Azil a harp cover. He slid it over the instrument and handed the instrument to the page.

Ydo Talvela said brusquely, "Juni. Pour some wine for the singer and bring it to him." Juni Talvela's dark eyes were wide as a deer's; he looked dazed, as if he had a fever. "Juni!" Talvela cuffed the boy's head. Juni rocked where he sat.

Rising from his chair, Karadur walked to Azil. The singer rose and faced his friend.

The dragon-lord said softly, "You said you wouldn't come."

Azil said, "I changed my mind."

"You rode alone?"

"I wanted to," Azil said. "But Lorimir insisted I take companions. Arnor and Tallis are with me."

"When did you get here?"

"Yesterday."

"How did you know where to go?"

"I went to an inn in the Pleasure Quarter, and spoke to some musicians. They knew my name. They brought me to the palace. I asked to speak to Laslo Umi. He remembered me."

Cirion came up to them. "Thank you for your music," the prince said to Azil. "I have never heard a harp played like that." He smiled at Karadur. "My lord, it was the singer you missed, I think, not the song."

Servers entered, carrying trays laden with bowls of sherbet. Azil said, "You have not said that you liked the song."

"I liked the song."

"And that you are pleased I came."

Karadur lifted his hands and set them on his friend's shoulders. Then he slid his palms down the singer's sides to his rib cage. Azil caught his breath.

"Later," Karadur said softly, "when we are private, I shall show you whether I am pleased, or not."

The singer in the golden gown glided up to them. She said imperiously, "Azil, you promised."

Karadur lifted his hands. Azil said, "I have not forgotten. My lord, allow me to present Khorrem Hazari. She is part of a trio called the Golden Sparrows. She and her friends have been most kind to me."

Karadur said, "Khorrem Hazari, thank you for your music. You have an extraordinary voice. Do you and your companions travel?"

"We do, my lord."

"Come to Atani Castle, and play for me."

Spine supple as wire, the singer bowed.

"Sir," said a boy's voice. It was Juni Talvela. He held a wineglass. He extended it toward Azil. "You must be thirsty."

The singer smiled, and took it. The boy's gaze was worshipful.

Lukas Ridenar spoke at Azil's back. "That was an elegantly told tale. I've never heard it before. Did you make it?"

"Yes," said the singer.

"Very nice." He looked thoughtful. "Is that how it was, Atani? Your war?"

Karadur said, "Yes."

Outside the tent, a voice was raised in sudden anger. A fold of cloth was flung back. Breathing heavily, Marion diSorvino thrust his way into the tent.

"So this is where you are hiding!" he said thickly. "Kalni, I want to speak with you."

The Lemininkai glanced up from his keph game. "I am here," he said mildly.

Sarita Leminin said, "Will you sit, my lord?"

"I will not," said diSorvino. His face was red. "Kalni, you have Treion Unamira in your custody. I want him. You know I want him. Tell your men to release him to mine."

The Lemininkai said, "Marion, surely this can be kept for another time."

"No, it can *not*," diSorvino said tightly. He snapped his fingers at a page. "Wine, damn you. Merignac, if you have it."

Lukas Ridenar said quietly, "Kalni, is this so? Has Unamira been taken?"

"Yes," the Lemininkai said. "It is so. I have him. He was captured some weeks ago, in Kameni. Honoris Imorin sent to me, to ask what I wanted done with him. I asked that he be conveyed to Ujo for judgment. There was another man with him, who has long been under sentence here for crimes against children. He's dead now."

Ydo Talvela said, "I know naught of this. Who is Unamira?"

Lukas Ridenar said, "An outlaw."

DiSorvino said, "Kalni, I want Unamira. You know what he did in Bruna, Alletti, and Maranessa. You have to give him to me."

The Lemininkai said, "I know you want him, Marion. But the men who died at Castella were mine. Castella was under my protection. Rodolfo Mino was my deputy."

"Bah! A troop of incompetents and a glutton: small loss. Castella was one town. The bastard burned four of my villages! Where he did not burn, he looted and despoiled. I want him. Give him to me." DiSorvino's hands clenched into fists.

Conversation in the tent had ceased. The Lemininkai said, "Lukas, what do you think?"

Lukas Ridenar said quietly, "You know my feeling."

The Lemininkai glanced across the table at his keph partner. "You smile, Allumar."

Allumar Marichal's right hand was closed about the Summer Princess. He opened it, and set the ivory figure lightly on the board. Leaning back in his chair, he said, "The situation appears to me to be moderately amusing."

DiSorvino rasped, "I fail to see its humor."

The Lemininkai said, "What amuses you?"

"The knowledge that ultimately, whichever one of you executes him, for whatever crime, the man—Unamira, is it?—will still be quite, quite dead."

DiSorvino grinned with terrible malignancy. "You are right, Marichal. Give him to me, Kalni. My men are quite skilled, Lukas. I promise you, it will take him weeks to die."

There was no mistaking his meaning. The Lemininkai looked at Lukas Ridenar. Ridenar spread his hands. "I do not contest it," he said.

"Excellent! Then we are agreed." DiSorvino set his glass

on the table. "Tell your men to release him to my custody." He turned to leave the tent.

Karadur spoke. "A moment, my lord. I believe I have first claim upon this man."

DiSorvino whirled. "What? What claim?"

"Last fall, months before his attack on your towns, and long before the sack of Castella, Treion Unamira raided a farm in northern Ippa, and in that raid men were killed. You know this, my lord of Ujo: they were father and brother to Dennis Amdur, your cavalry commander." The Lemininkai nodded. "For those two deaths alone his life is forfeit."

"Two deaths!" DiSorvino reddened again. "Thirty died in Castella!"

"Thirty-six, actually," the Lemininkai said. "And one woman."

"No!" Marion diSorvino was shaking with rage. "Atani, I will not be denied in this. This man is mine."

Karadur said nothing. He stood, and let them look at him, at his height and breadth, and at the dragon armband that gleamed on his forearm.

Then he said, "I hold to my claim, my lord."

There was a silence.

Kalni Leminin said, "Allumar, what do you think?"

Allumar Marichal said, "Oh, I am not nearly so wise as to be able to resolve this dispute." He smiled benignly. "Judgment is the privilege of kings." He coughed, and tapped the board. "I believe this is my game, Kalni."

The Lemininkai surveyed his pieces. "You are right. It is." He tipped the Winter King on its side. "Would that all our conflicts might be resolved with such dispatch. I believe we need a mediator in this matter, someone who can be both impartial and wise." He raised his voice a little, though there was no need for it: the silken-walled space was utterly silent. "We need judgment. Highness, can you help us?"

If he was surprised by the question, Cirion did not show it. He said calmly, "My lord, I am at your service."

"Excellent." The Lemininkai spoke softly to a guard. He strode away, and returned carrying a high-backed wooden chair. He set it in the center of the pavilion.

DiSorvino said angrily, "What is this mummery?"

Crossing to the chair, Cirion seated himself, and folded his hands in his lap. He said, "What matter you bring before me, I will hear it." There was weight in the words, and ceremony. Somehow—it was not entirely clear how—the perfumed, silken tent had become a court.

Kalni Leminin said, "Allumar, you have no stake in this. If you would, present the arguments, all of them, so that his highness may understand what was determined, and why we cannot agree."

"Certainly," Allumar Marichal said. "My prince, this dispute regards a man, an outlaw, presently in custody in Ujo." Swiftly he set out first the Lemininkai's claim to Treion Unamira—the sack of Castella, a garrison burned alive, the death of a governor—then Marion diSorvino's claim—four towns plundered, men and women killed for resisting the looting. Then he made the dragon-lord's claim.

Cirion listened intently.

Then he said, "Of all these crimes, the destruction of Castella and the death of the garrison seems to me to be most brutal. Yet you, my lord diSorvino, claim that because the attacks in diSorvino's domain precede in time the attack on Castella, Ujo's right to take this man should yield to Sorvino's. Do I have it correctly?"

"You do," Marichal said.

Cirion's gaze was austere.

"My lord diSorvino, you cannot have it both ways. If your claim takes precedence to the Lemininkai's because the man's offense against you predates his offense against Ujo, then Atani's claim takes precedence to yours. The prisoner is Atani's."

Everyone in the pavilion looked at the dragon-lord. His expression, not surprisingly, gave nothing away.

Allumar Marichal pursed his lips. "This decision seems to me to be both equitable and logical. Well judged, highness."

"I agree," said Ydo Talvela.

"No!" said Marion diSorvino. "I do not accept this." His hands worked. "This is legalistic rubbish." He faced the Lemininkai. "Kalni, this is your city. You are the law here. Give me Unamira."

Kalni Leminin said, "I respect your passion, Marion. But does not our ancient compact state that we are subject to the king's justice?"

DiSorvino said furiously, "He is not king yet."

The Lemininkai said, "He will be." He nodded to Karadur. "My lord, my men shall bring Unamira to the Hotel Goude."

Karadur said, "Thank you, my lord. Edruyn, find Herugin." Edruyn bowed and padded away.

DiSorvino looked from the Lemininkai to Allumar Marichal to Cirion Imorin. His voice rose.

"This is no justice. Damn you, *I* see what it is. You are afraid of him. You fear he will burn your cities, as his father did Mako." He flung his glass across the tent. It hit a pole and broke. "You are fools, fools! Kojiro Atani would have taken what he wanted and burned you all to ash by now. Gods rot you all, you are cowards and sons of cowards!"

Jowls red as poppy, he stormed from the pavilion.

THERE WAS A long silence. Pages moved softly forward to sweep up the glass.

Then Ydo Talvela said gruffly, "DiSorvino is wrong. It's a

fair judgment." He held out his glass for his son to refill. He said to Karadur, "You'll kill the man, of course. Your father would have had him flayed. Or cracked his spine for him, and hung him living on the wall of his castle, till hunger or thirst or pain killed him."

"Yes," Karadur said, "I know. My lord," he said to the Lemininkai, "thank you for your hospitality. I must go."

"Of course you must," the Lemininkai said.

Karadur turned to Cirion. "Prince, I leave in your debt. You have my thanks."

Cirion smiled gravely from his seat. "My lord, I am pleased to have met you. Safe journey to you all."

Karadur strode from the tent. Eastward the sky was grey with twilight. In the west the sun lay low on the horizon. Shadows splayed across the grass. A light breeze blew through the trees.

Herugin arrived. He said, somewhat breathlessly, "My lord, you sent for me?"

Karadur said, "Treion Unamira is here in Ujo. The Lemininkai's men have him. They're bringing him to the hotel. Meet them there. Put him in the stable, under guard. We'll leave for home tomorrow."

LATER, MUCH LATER, in the privacy of his bedchamber—which smelled, very faintly, of lilies—Kalni Leminin lay staring at the ceiling. He was thinking.

He was quite happy. The week had proceeded almost exactly as he had intended it should. His beloved daughter was wed, to a comely and clever young man who was also heir to the kingdom. His city was peaceful, and very much richer than it had been: the multitude of visitors, lowborn, highborn, and in between, had spent a great deal of money in its streets.

He had had a number of very satisfactory conversations. He had spoken with Lukas Ridenar and Allumar Marichal, and confirmed their understanding of the political situation. With the internal situation in Chuyo as uncertain as it was, they knew how vital it was to fortify the south. Lukas, whose intelligence network was nearly as good as the Lemininkai's own, had promised to keep an eye open and an ear cocked for any hostile movement.

He had spoken with Dennis Amdur, and impressed upon the cavalry officer the importance of the work he was being sent to do. The captain had understood. The Lemininkai had no doubt that he would do his best. Dennis Amdur's best was very good indeed.

He had spoken with Cirion, and recommended that he strengthen Selidor's friendship with Merigny and Firense. He had suggested that Cirion keep a close watch on Evard diScala, who was a snake. Cirion had promised to do so. He had no doubts of Cirion. He would make a good king. He had captivated the city's elite, and charmed Allumar Marichal, that most clear-sighted observer. He was noble, clever, and unambitious, which was excellent, since the Lemininkai had more than enough ambition for both of them. Moreover, Selena loved him. He hoped there would be children soon.

That, of course, was up to his daughter.

It had been wise of Cirion to come to Ujo for the wedding, instead of insisting that Selena come to Lienor, as rank and custom dictated: it had allowed him to meet and assess men and women whom otherwise he would not have had a chance to meet. Ydo Talvela would never have gone to Lienor. He was sorry Sunudi Isheverin had not been able to come. The common folk of Ryoka had no idea how grim the situation was. They would not, the Lemininkai thought grimly, until the caravans that brought silk and wine and spices and sword blades ceased to come across the border. But that day might not come. At the moment, according to Danae Isheverin, the lords of Chuyo could scarcely sit in the same room together. *They hate you,* Danae had written, *but they hate each other more.* He hoped they would continue to feel so. He was not prepared to give up Chuyo. It was part of Ryoka. His progenitor had won it. *Bright swords in the vanguard and sorrow in his wake* . . . He smiled into the darkness, thinking of a battle he had not been alive to see.

Across the city, the temple bells rang the hour. The distant sound mingled with the nearby sound of water falling. It was not true that every room in the Lemininkai palace had a fountain in it. But most did. The one in this room was a water-spouting serpent.

He was sorry about Castella. The death of innocents was regrettable. He himself was not fond of country living, but the town had been a pleasant place. But the outlaws who had attacked it, nearly all of them, had been captured. Niello Ciccio was dead. Unamira would be dead soon. And the Dragon of Chingura, while formidable, had proved quite amenable to civilized negotiation. He liked him. Cirion, too, had liked Karadur Atani, though something curious had happened between them which the Lemininkai had not understood.

Kalni Leminin said aloud, to the only person in the world with whom he shared all his thoughts, "What did you think of Atani?"

Sarita Amarinta Leminin answered, "He's dangerous."

"As dangerous as his father?"

"Probably," Sarita said. "He is Dragon, after all."

"I liked him. So did Lukas. His bluntness has a certain charm."

"Kojiro could be charming, too. You remember."

"Yes." He remembered Kojiro Atani well. "But Kojiro was

savage, even at his sanest. This one seems quite restrained."

Sarita said, "Too much so. I would feel better if he had an heir."

"Allumar said he spoke of the diSorvino girl."

Sarita said, "I suspect *that* interest will wane, now that he's met her father. Gods, that man's an idiot! An idiot and a bully. He hates women, you know."

"How do you know?"

"He has three children, all daughters. He disowned all three. And both of his wives ran away rather than live with him."

"Why does he hate women?"

"Because he has no sons."

Kalni Leminin, whose posterity consisted solely of one beloved daughter, said, "That makes no sense."

"Of course it doesn't. But for some men, the begetting of a son is evidence of manhood, against which all other proofs are insignificant. Marion has no sons. It is the fault of any woman he has ever slept with, and possibly every woman in the world, that his seed throws only daughters."

The Lemininkai considered this. He himself had had no doubt about his manhood since the year he turned twelve. He moved his leg against hers in the fragrant darkness. They had been together twenty-two years. He had never wanted another woman.

"Is that why he repudiated his daughter? And why he hates the Unamira boy?"

"It's likely. One can't be sure; he hates easily. A flaw in his character: it makes him brutal, and stupid. Someday someone will kill him for it. You, perhaps."

THE GUARDS TOOK Treion from his cell sometime after sunset. They struck off the long chain that secured him to the wall of the cell and fitted him with manacles. He asked for a drink of water, and they gave it to him.

They led him into the city. It was a warm night. Overhead, the moon was brilliant. The torchlit streets were bustling with people. A juggler stood on a box, juggling plates and knives and torches. Vendors brushed by, their trays piled with food: skewers of meat, grilled corn, slices of sweet melon.

"A fine night," one of his guards remarked.

A trio of singers strolled by, two men and a girl, their voices raised in harmonious warble. A pleasant scent filled the air.

"Where are we?" Treion asked.

"The Perfume Quarter."

It was not a part of the city in which one would hold an execution.

"Why?" They did not answer. Ahead of them, across a smooth green lawn, stood an elegant edifice of rose-pink stone, flanked by a marble fountain. A long stair led up to its wide double doors. "What is that place?" Again they did not answer.

Two men walked around the corner of the building. One of them had a jagged raised scar across his face.

He said, "Treion Unamira. It's been a while. Do you know me?"

"I know you."

"Good," said Herugin Dol. He wrapped his fingers around Treion's upper arm. "Thanks, we'll take him now." The Ujo guards left. Herugin jerked him forward. They went round the back of the hotel, to a stable. They walked inside the horse barn. A man stood guard outside a horse-box. It was empty, save for a heap of straw.

"In," Herugin said. Treion walked in. In the left-hand stall, a horse stamped and snorted: a big horse, from the sound of him. An owl hooted in the hayloft. "Sit down. Not there. Against the wall."

Treion did as he was told. Herugin whipped a loop of rope around his neck and fastened it to a ring above his head.

He said, "There's water in the pot. The guard's name is Finle. He and two other men will be outside this stall all night. If you give them any trouble, they have orders to throw you in with Rosset." He jerked a thumb toward the left-hand stall. "He's a racing stallion. You'd probably survive."

HE WOKE TO fire. The stable was on fire. Columnar blue flames soared toward the ceiling. The very straw he lay on was burning. Desperately he bucked and rolled, stood, and lunged for the door.

He had forgotten the rope. The lunge almost broke his neck. The shock and the pain stunned him. For a moment he could not move, and in that moment he realized that the stable was not, in fact, burning. There was no smoke, no sound, no heat, only a dense blue shimmering. In the stall next door, the agitated stallion stamped and bugled.

The illusion faded. Darkness returned. Out of it a deep voice said, "That is what the guardsmen in Castella saw as they died."

Slowly he sat up. His neck burned. He eased the pain by sliding closer to the wall. The fire returned: not a conflagration this time, but a single point, a candle stub, set in a lantern. A breeze blew through the tiny circular window in the back wall of the stall.

Karadur Atani, holding the lantern, stood in the opening of the stall. He looked much as Treion remembered him, only bigger. Treion's lungs seemed suddenly inadequate to his need for breath.

The dragon-lord stepped into the stall. Shadows gyrated wildly. He set the lantern on the floor and crouched, so that their faces were on a level. The flame, quivering in the breeze, touched his hair and the planes of his face with light.

He said, "Marion diSorvino wants very much to kill you. So does Lukas Ridenar."

"Why?" The word came out a whisper. Treion tried again. "Why? I never burned *his* towns."

"Celia Bertinelli. The woman you killed in Castella. She was his mistress."

"I didn't know," he said.

"Why did you kill her?"

Why had he killed her? She had taunted him. He had lost his temper. "It was a mistake," he said.

"And Rodolfo Mino? The man was an administrator, not a warrior."

"I didn't kill him," he protested.

"But he died," Karadur Atani said. "You raided the Amdur farm, and Thorin and Garth Amdur died. I could kill you for that. I should kill you for that." His eyes burned suddenly, bright as the sun. The stall grew oven-hot. Treion's back and sides dripped sweat. He tried to look away. Karadur caught his chin in one huge hand.

He closed his eyes to shut out the inhuman glitter.

"Look at me!" Karadur said.

Treion opened his eyes.

"Last year, on Coll's Ridge, you could have escaped. Instead, you came back to the house. Why?"

His neck throbbed painfully. If he said the wrong thing, Karadur would kill him. A lie was unthinkable. His mind was empty. The words came from elsewhere.

"I came for my men. They followed me. They trusted me. I thought I could get them out. I had to try."

The heat in the stall eased. Somehow, somehow he had said the right thing. The dragon-lord dropped his hand. He rose to his feet. Scooping up the lantern, he walked to the door of the stall.

Gathering his courage, Treion said, through his parched, aching throat, "Are you going to kill me?"

"Possibly," Karadur Atani said. "Not tonight."

10

THEY ARRIVED AT Dragon Keep at sunset. A horn blew as they approached the gates. Boys came running to hold the horses. Girls in bright aprons leaned from the windows, calling welcome. Behind the Keep, the mountain peaks glittered red.

He had forgotten how clean the air smelled in the north. His scalp itched; vermin crawled in his hair. His clothes were stiff and mud-caked; they felt like armor against his skin.

The journey had not been too bad. They had fed him, at least. He had had to sleep bound. He had watched, hoping for a chance to escape, but of course there had been none. Like the riders of Lienor, unlike his own quarrelsome crew, Dragon Keep's warriors knew what needed to be done and did it without being told. They obeyed Karadur's orders without servility, and without question.

They feared him, of course. The only one who did not was the singer. Obviously they were bedmates: men did not touch each other as Karadur touched this man unless they were lovers. But there was more between them, a connection, a feeling that was present even when they sat apart.

He ached all over. The pain in his wrists and hands was so familiar that he had almost ceased to feel it.

"Get down," Herugin said. Wearily he slid from his horse's back. A dog barked at him from beneath a wagon. Karadur did not look at him. His attention was elsewhere; he was talking with a grey-bearded man, obviously one of his captains.

Two men took him to the post set in the courtyard and fastened him to it with ropes. The castle hounds, captained by a brown brute with a heavy, battle-scarred head, eyed him suspiciously, barking and growling. Children came to stare at him. A dark-haired boy with odd, light-filled eyes watched him for a long time. Loathing the indignity, he forced himself to piss and shit in a corner. He cleaned himself as best he could.

A bell rang in the ward; men streamed into the hall. Toward the end of the meal, as the hall began to empty, Finle appeared, with a platter of meat, and bread. He laid it on the stone. It was a kindness Treion had not expected.

"Thank you." Finle was still standing there.

"What's going to happen to me?"

The archer shrugged. "Don't know. Whatever it's to be, it'll be soon. Dragon doesn't linger over judgment."

IN THE KITCHEN: "Pay me," Anssa said to Ruth. "You owe me five pennies."

The scullions were curious about the prisoner. Pico, especially, was puzzled. "He's from Ujo, right? Who is he? What's he doing here?"

"His name is Unamira. He's an outlaw," Ruth said. "He's

the man who raided the Amdur farm, and took Herugin hostage, last year. He did something bad in Nakase. He ran east. They captured him in Kameni and they gave him to Dragon, to punish."

"Why?"

"Because he wanted him," Simon said. Pico wrinkled his nose. But Ruth and Eilon nodded in rare agreement. Even though it was Simon who said it, it made sense. If the lord of Dragon Keep wanted something, or someone, it was best not to stand in his way.

"What's going to happen to him?" Pico asked, turning toward Boris. The cook sat on a stool at the slicing table, keph board at his elbow. He had taken off his apron. He mostly played by himself, now. Macallan, the Keep's physician, had been his regular partner. But Macallan had died in the burning of Coll's Ridge.

"Don't know, toad," Boris said.

IN THE SMALL, octagonal chamber in the watchtower, two friends sat in a companionable silence. The room was warm. An empty wineglass sat on the floor at Azil's feet. Another perched on the bare desktop. On the wall, a single candle burned in its sconce.

Brian stuck his head round the door. "My lord, do you need aught?"

"No," Karadur said. Brian withdrew. The dragon-lord gazed into the shadows. His eyes were nearly closed. In the dimness, he looked like a stone.

Azil said, "When will you do it?"

"Tomorrow."

"Will he survive it?"

"He'll survive it. He's strong."

"And after?"

"I don't know. We'll see." His lips tightened. "I shall have to tell Maia."

Azil asked, "When will you tell her?"

"When it's done."

He'd known for years that one day Karadur would meet a woman, and that they would have a child. But for years Karadur had refused to even contemplate it.

My mother died giving birth to me, he said. *I will not do it. . . .*

Then he had met this girl. Azil had not met her. Karadur had said she was comely, and quick-witted, and that she loved her brother. Presumably she was healthy, sturdy enough to bear a child, and clear-sighted enough to know that the children of dragons were not like other children. . . . He would have to meet her someday.

It would be simplest if he could hate her. Only he could not, because Kaji wanted to love her.

Karadur's eyes opened. His gaze focused. "Azil. It changes nothing."

Azil did not reply.

He said, "What did you think of Cirion?"

"I liked him." Karadur's face grew pensive. "Something—strange—happened between us."

"What happened?"

"He—stopped me. I can't explain it. He touched my mind, and held me. . . ." He clasped his hands together, frowning. The dragon brilliance shimmered momentarily behind his eyes.

"Is he changeling?"

"No."

Sorcerer? The word trembled on the tip of Azil's tongue. But he did not say it. Karadur had no love for sorcerers. Tenjiro Atani had been a sorcerer.

A voice whispered in his head. *Traitor. I see you, traitor. . . .*

It was Tenjiro Atani's voice. His heart shuddered in his chest.

Illusion. It was illusion. Tenjiro was dead, and Ankoku, the terrible, malevolent being whose purpose Tenjiro had agreed to serve and who had ultimately devoured him, was defeated, gone, sleeping.

Karadur said sharply, "What's the matter?"

"Nothing. A memory: a bad one. It happens." It happened sometimes, at night, when he was very tired.

But never with the voice.

"The ice?"

"Yes." He shivered.

"I can do something about that." Rising, Karadur came around the desk. He pulled Azil from his chair.

The chamber filled with light.

AT SUNRISE, THE castle woke. The watch changed. Men came from the barracks. Some of them, carrying short bows and a supply of arrows, left the castle through a side door in the wall. Hawk went with them.

The dog keeper let the dogs out. They trotted through the ward, marking and scuffling. A few of them came to sniff at Treion, but the hostility of the day before had gone. He no longer smelled like a stranger.

The grey-bearded captain and Herugin sat on a bench in the sunlight. They talked; Herugin made marks on a slate.

Half a dozen men with wooden swords came into the yard and began to spar under the eyes of a black-bearded officer. They were novices: farm boys, probably. He wished he were with them, and not tied to the post.

The postern gate opened. Riders entered. He recognized the foremost of them, an elegant, erect woman wearing a wide-brimmed leather hat. She was the woman whose farm he had raided. The others were a ruddy-haired young man, and a towheaded boy on a pony. The boy, wide-eyed, looked about with wonder on his face. The woman folded her arms and stared rigidly at Treion. The young man put an arm around her shoulders.

Karadur came into the yard. He was wearing his sword. He looked at Treion without expression. Two men hauled a flat block of wood into the courtyard and set it near the post. The skin along Treion's backbone prickled. Men began to gather. His bowels knotted shamefully. He knew the stories of the dragon-kindred's vengeance.

Finle and three men he did not know walked toward him. A knife gleamed in the archer's hand.

"Get up," Finle said. Treion stood, heart racing.

They stripped his shirt off and unfastened the ropes. Clamping their hands about his arms, they pushed him to the wooden block. The crowd in the yard surged forward. The towheaded boy stood in the front. The young man stood behind him, hands on his shoulders.

Into a sudden quiet, Karadur said, "Treion Unamira. You are a despoiler and a thief. Last year, in my domain, you led your men to Thorin Amdur's farm, and stole his horses, and burned his house.

"Thorin and Garth Amdur died that night. The man who killed them is dead. But you were his captain. You must pay for what you did to them and to the family." He turned to the grey-bearded captain. "Lorimir, how would my father have punished this man?"

The captain said soberly, "My lord, your father the Black Dragon would have opened him from breastbone to gut, and hung him living on the walls for the condors to devour."

The listening men murmured. Treion's skin went clammy. A strong man could live for days in such torment.

Karadur's eyes met his.

I will not beg, he thought.

The dragon-lord said, "It might be fitting. But I am not my father. Stretch him out."

Hands pushed Treion to his knees. Someone brought a rope, and looped it over his right wrist, and drew it taut. He understood, then, and fought them, writhing and twisting, but they had him pinioned, and there were too many men. They pinned him to the stone, and stretched his right arm across the block. He closed his eyes. His face ground into the dirt.

Someone seized his head and forced it to turn. Karadur had drawn his sword. Red flame ran along the blade's edge.

I won't cry out, he thought. *I won't.*

"So do we punish thieves in the north." The sword flashed down. There was a bright pain in his arm. Blood ran into his mouth. He smelled burning flesh.

Then the pain swelled into an agony so brutal and fierce that he could not endure it.

GATHERING SPIKES OF sage and rosemary, attended by a dog, Maia diSorvino did not know that the lord of Dragon Keep had returned to Ippa.

Seated at her table, grinding sage into powder with pestle and mortar, she heard the rush and thunder of the dragon's passage. Morga, tail thrashing, flew up from her rug.

Rising, Maia set mortar and pestle to one side. She heard the footsteps on the path, and opened the door. Karadur Atani stood before her doorway.

She could not help the quickening in her heart.

"Welcome, my lord," she said. "When did you return?"

"Last night." He bent to run his fingers gently over the

wolfhound's ears. The dog leaned blissfully against his leg. His gaze was steady and a little sad.

"Treion," she said. "It is Treion, isn't it? He's dead." Her knees started to tremble.

Karadur caught her lightly by the upper arms. "He is not dead." The warm clasp steadied her. He led her into the garden. She sat on the bench Angus had built for her. He sat beside her. Single-minded, Morga slid her head between his knees.

"Tell me," she said.

"I have him," Karadur said. "He was captured in Lienor and returned to Ujo. The Lemininkai gave him to me."

A black-bodied bee bumbled up to her and nuzzled her as if she were a flower. She did not stir. It drifted away. She said, "I would like to see him, if I may. Before—" She could not finish it. She had heard tales of the dragon's justice. She hoped it would be quick, that Treion would not be tortured.

Karadur said, "Of course. You may see him as soon as he recovers."

Surely she had misunderstood him. "I thought he was condemned to death."

"By the Lemininkai. Not by me."

"You pardoned him?" Her heart thudded painfully against her breastbone.

"No," he said. "That I will not do."

She imagined Treion crippled, broken, eyeless. . . . "What, then?"

"I have taken his right arm." He paused, and then said gently, "You must not worry too much. He is being cared for. My senior captain, Lorimir Ness, is very skilled with wounds."

There had been a one-armed man in Sorvino, who sold ribbons and small trinkets in the market. She pictured Treion peddling trinkets in the market. He would die first.

He might die anyway. She wondered if the wound had bled a great deal. Poppy would ease the pain. Comfrey powder would keep the stump from festering.

Stubborn Treion. Savage Treion.

"What happens to him now?" she asked. "Will you release him?"

"No."

"Will you kill him?"

"Not unless I must. Have you forgotten what your grandfather said? It is possible that we may be kin."

Reo Unamira's vivid, obscene words leaped out of memory. *He fucked her, though, the lovely slut. I saw them lying beside the stream. . . .*

"You think what Grandfather said was true? He was old and sick with drink, and he babbled."

"He was old," the dragon-lord said. "But he saw what he saw. Your mother and my father were lovers. That is one reason I would spare him. There is another.

"Treion Unamira has a sister," he said slowly, "whose peace has become somewhat dear to me."

The lacings of his shirt lay open to the sun. The pulse of blood, slow and steady, beat in his throat. He laid his palms on either side of her face. She closed her eyes, trembling. He kissed her lightly on the lips. She set her hands on his bare forearms. Soft golden hairs shifted against her palms. She felt his body's heat. Her skin felt liquid. She slid her hands up to his shoulders.

Dragon sleeping, Dragon wakes, Dragon holds what Dragon takes.

"Maia," he whispered. "Maia, Maia, look at me." She opened her eyes. "When Treion is healed, I shall bring him to you. Will that please you?"

"Do you wish to please me?"

"Yes," he said, "I do. Very much."

* * *

AT FIRST IT did not matter to Treion Unamira if he lived or died.

The absence of his arm seemed as much a hallucination as the other hallucinatory dreams he was having. People hovered over him, talking. They prodded at him. His right arm hurt. But when he felt for it he could not find it.

The tiny, wood-walled chamber he lay in was no bigger than a cell, but it was not a cell. Beneath him were a straw pallet and a heap of sweat-soaked quilts. A ginger cat lay sleeping in a corner.

He dragged himself upright. He had expected to awaken in a field somewhere, surrounded by crows. He reached his hand to touch his aching shoulder. It was neatly bandaged. A pitcher had been set nearby. He lifted it. It felt odd in his left hand.

He drank. It was water, flavored with wine. Effortfully, he stood. Holding on to the walls, he shuffled out of the tiny chamber. A placid bay horse peered amiably at him from a stall. He tottered forward, taking shaky old-man steps. At the end of the long passageway he heard the click-clack of wooden practice blades. He followed the sound to a doorway. He leaned a moment to catch his breath. Then he stepped into the sunlight. Twenty feet from him, men in pairs circled and lunged. Beneath stair risers and in shady corners, panting dogs lay stretched on their sides. The heat was intense.

There was a shaded bench a few yards away. He took a step toward it. Black shapes danced across his eyes. The pain in his stump bit like an auger.

The clack of the swords slowed; the men were watching to see if he would fall. Sweat rolled down his sides. He walked to the bench and sat, breathing hard. A man shouted. The men resumed their practice. Children raced through the yard, calling to each other in high, challenging voices. He watched until exhaustion sent him stumbling back to the stables.

That evening, a stableboy silently brought him food: an oat bannock, some cheese, some bits of burnt meat. He did not want the meat, but he ate the bannock and cheese.

He was lying on his pallet, staring into darkness, when Herugin and Lorimir appeared at the entrance to the stall. Herugin was holding a lantern.

Lorimir said, "Let me see your arm."

Treion wanted to refuse. But that was stupid. He sat up. Slowly he worked the sleeve of his shirt back from the stump. Lorimir knelt. Treion set his teeth. But the old man was surprisingly gentle. He unwound the bandage. Herugin held the lantern close.

"It's healing," Lorimir said. "I see no signs of infection." He salved the stump with some strong-smelling ointment and retied the bandage.

As he rose to leave: "Wait," Treion said. "Please."

Lorimir turned.

"Am I a prisoner?"

The two men looked at one another. Lorimir said, "You're not a prisoner. I don't know what you are."

"May I have the light? I promise not to burn anything down."

Lorimir hesitated. Then he said, "Give it to him."

Herugin, expressionless, held out the lantern.

OVER THE NEXT few weeks, his strength returned. The stableboys brought him gruel. No one touched him, or gave him orders, or spoke to him. He was a ghost. He walked through the yard. He sat on the bench to watch the swordsmen. He ate in the stable, with the mice and the barn cats.

Lorimir—who was, he learned, the Keep's senior officer, captain of the war band—came regularly to examine and salve his stump.

When he could no longer bear his own stink, he found a clean bucket, filled it at the well, and hauled it into his stall. When he could walk from the stable to the well without stopping to rest, he decided it was time to get his own food. He made his way to the kitchen. A skinny youth in a dirty apron scowled at him, and muttered something, in which the words "thief" and "murderer" were prominent. But a sweet-faced girl placidly handed him a stew bowl and a hunk of bread.

That evening, when the men went to eat, Treion followed them. In this hall there was no high seat. Karadur sat with his men, at the long table nearest the hearth. Treion stayed well away from them. He found a shadowy corner, out of the torchlight. No one looked at him, or spoke to him. A serving-girl bustled by him, carrying a platter piled with vegetables and meat and bread. He waited until the men at tables were eating before reaching out to catch her attention. She gave him a bowl of soup and a slab of bread covered with butter. He set the bowl on his knee. The soup had bits of meat in it. He ate slowly. He was still clumsy with his left hand.

A shadow fell across the bowl. It was Herugin.

"Get up," the rider said. "He wants to talk to you."

A chill finger ran up Treion's backbone. He set the bowl aside. "Now?"

"Now," Herugin said. Treion rose from the stone.

As he approached Karadur's table, the hall fell silent. Karadur sat with his back against the cold stone and his arm around Azil Aumson's shoulders.

"You wanted to see me," Treion said.

At his back, Herugin said harshly, "You wanted to see

me, *my lord*." Treion ignored him. The men at the table—Rogys, Finle, Lorimir, the others whose names he didn't know—looked at him as if he were not quite human.

"I did," the dragon-lord said pensively. His eyes were half-closed; for a moment he looked asleep. Then he opened his eyes, wide enough for Treion to see the flame in them.

"Lorimir says your arm is nearly healed. It is in my mind that I need to do something about you. What shall I do with you, One-arm?"

"Give me my sword."

"What could you do with a sword?"

"Cut his own balls off, most likely," said Edruyn. The listening men laughed.

Karadur said, "Quiet." They breathed as one, and were silent. "What would you do with a sword, One-arm? You cannot fight us all."

He could not fight even one of them.

He said, "I know I can't fight you. Let me go."

"Go where? Where would you go, Treion Unamira? West? South? East? In Nakase and Kameni, there's a price on your head."

It was so, of course. The Lemininkai and Lukas Ridenar both had a grievance against him. If he left the Keep, they would find him, eventually. Someone would give him up. And when they found him, they would take him to Firense, or Ujo, and he would die a slow death.

Stubbornly, because he could not think what else to say, he repeated, "Let me go."

"If I let you go, what will you do?"

He said, knowing how foolish it sounded, "Kill Marion diSorvino."

Herugin laughed. But the others were still. The dragon-lord unwound his arm from Azil Aumson's shoulders.

"I think you will not do that. Indeed, I am not going to

allow you to do that. I am going to keep you, One-arm, and make you useful. Even a one-armed man can work. Can you clerk? Can you write with your left hand?" Treion shook his head. "Can you swing a scythe? I didn't think so. You will be no help in the fields, then."

Someone said, "Even a one-armed man can clean a privy."

Herugin said, "Give him to me. There's always work to do in the stable."

"No," Karadur said. "Boris!"

The bald cook walked out of the kitchen. "My lord?"

"I have a new kitchen worker for you. Can you find a place for him? He's clumsy, but he'll do what he's told."

The cook said tranquilly, "Certainly, my lord. Has he a name?"

"Treion. No. Taran." The word meant *wanderer* and, sometimes, *foreigner*. "His name is Taran."

Herugin said, "Keep him away from the spice jars, Boris. He might try to poison us."

Again, the soldiers laughed. Karadur did not. He said, "He won't do that. Will you, Taran?"

"No," Treion said.

Hawk the archer said, "He might try to escape."

Karadur said, "You think so, my hunter? What do you say, Taran? Will you run?"

He had thought of it, of course. He had strolled past the postern gates once or twice, just to see if the men on the walls were paying attention. They always were. And even if, by some miracle, he had been able to get through the gates unseen, he was too weak to get far.

"I won't run," he said. It was a pledge, of sorts. "I'll work, at whatever task you set me to, I'll make no trouble, I'll be docile as a puppy—for a year."

Orm, the archer chief, laughed his flat bark. "My lord, he's trying to bargain with you! Gods, he's mad!"

"And then?" Karadur said. "When the year ends?"

"Then you'll give me a sword, and let me go. I can learn to use it again. There are left-handed swordsmen."

Without warning, a huge shadowy head lifted from the flagstones. Up and up it rose, unfolding dark wings. Its lambent eyes burned silver. Heart pounding, Treion stepped back from it. It gazed down at him, and yawned, displaying serrated teeth.

"Don't be afraid," Karadur said. "It will not harm you." He gestured to the page to fill his glass. "So, Taran. Let us be clear. You offer to serve Dragon Keep freely and without stint for one year, in whatever task I set you."

"Yes."

"Anything."

"Yes."

"Cleaning privies."

"Yes."

"In exchange, you would have me promise that at the end of that year, I will give you a sword, and make you free of my domain forever. Is that what you want?"

His legs were trembling. If he stayed upright much longer he might fall. "Yes."

Karadur said, "So be it."

Herugin rasped, "You would trust his word? The word of a thief and a murderer?"

Karadur said, "Herugin, *be quiet*." The dragon-lord nodded at Boris. "He's yours."

"Come on, you," the cook said.

Treion turned to follow him. Karadur's deep voice called him back. "Taran. I almost forgot. I have news for you about your sister."

All the eyes in the hall were on him. They glittered in the dark, like the eyes of wolves. To his horror, Treion felt tears burning in his throat. He set his teeth against them.

Brusquely he said, "I know what you would tell me. I've known it for months. My sister is dead."

Karadur said, "Your sister Maia is alive, and under my protection. She lives on Coll's Ridge."

Treion stared at him, too shocked to speak.

"When you are healed, I will take you to her."

PART THREE

11

IN THE DARK old house in Issho, Ydo Talvela wondered if he was doing the right thing.

He loved his sons, both of them. He had never had any trouble with the eldest; or rather, he had always known what trouble to expect from the eldest: Koiiva Talvela had always done exactly what he had done when *he* was Koiiva's age. Now, at twenty-two, Koiiva was past his youthful rebellions and ready, almost, to take on the responsibilities which would one day be his as lord of the domain.

But Juni . . . The boy had no regard for swordsmanship, or horses. He had no interest in girls, though they were interested enough in him, nor boys, for that matter; he preferred solitude. His body was sound: he could run, and wrestle, and swim, and he did not lack courage: he faced his father's temper without flinching or excuses. He was—though it was not the sort of word Ydo Talvela normally used of his children—a superb bowman. But he hated hunting. And hunting, everyone knew, was training for war.

What he liked, as far as Ydo had been able to determine, was music, and tales about faraway places and far-off times. He was a romantic. That was the problem. Music and history were all very well, but a warrior had to know how to rule: himself and other men. Peace was short-lived; trouble could come at any time.

It had to be done. It would have been done earlier, had not there been all that nonsense about the naming. But that was over.

He heard footsteps and looked up. His younger son stood on the threshold.

"You sent for me, sir?" His voice was light; it had not yet broken.

"Come in," Ydo said.

Juni stepped into the room. His clothes were clean and dry. His hair was too long. He looked entirely too neat, Ydo thought with some irritation. A fourteen-year-old boy should have mud on his clothes.

"I received a letter today from Bork Hal," he said. "Now that the succession ceremonies are over, he has agreed to take you into his household."

"Yes, Father."

"Is that all you have to say?"

"Yes, Father."

"Good," Ydo said. "In that case, go pack, and don't forget to say good-bye to your mother. You leave tomorrow."

Juni's face whitened perceptibly. "Yes, Father." He bowed, and walked away.

Perversely, Ydo found himself wishing that the boy had argued, had shouted at him, something. . . . He knew Juni did not want to go to Serrenhold. But Koiiva had trained in Serrenhold. He himself had trained in Serrenhold, with the old man. Bork Hal was harsh, as all the Hal men were. But rigor would do Juni no harm. It had to be done.

In later years, the boy would thank him for it.

ON A BLISTERING hot day in early August, Maia diSorvino walked to Castria to get her boots repaired.

A light haze hung over the cornfields: harvest had begun. Reapers, sickles in hand, moved steadily through the tall corn, while crows and pigeons circled overhead, waiting for the gleaners to pass so that they might make their own harvest from the leavings. Thunder rumbled in the hills. Birds perched in trees, too stupefied to chirp. White and orange lilies drooped by the side of the road. Flame-winged butterflies, undeterred by the heat, undulated from blossom to blossom, looking for nectar.

She had stopped at the Halland farmhouse to show the boots to Angus, hoping that he would be able to cobble them back together. The soles were completely separated from the heels, and the leather was cracked and battered. But he signed regretfully that they were beyond his skill to mend. She asked Maura if Castria had a cobbler.

"Aye: Hoskil Iarsen. He's a sickly, sour man, but skillful. He may be able to fix them. If not, he can make you a new pair."

As Maia and the wolfhound passed through the village gate, a fawn-colored cur rose barking from its bed outside the wall. Morga bared her teeth and growled low. The other dog's ears flattened. Nacio the hunchback strutted down the street. *"Pretty ladies, lovely ladies, stop and see my ribbons, fine ribbons, who'll buy my ribbons. . . ."* He mimed a courtier's bow. "Pretty lady, want a ribbon? *I have red ones, blue ones, yellow ones, green ones. . . .*" He shook the pole on which the ribbons were tied.

The bright fluttering bands made Maia smile. Her hair was long again. "How much for a ribbon?" she asked.

"For you, sweet lady, a penny."

"Let me have a red one." She gave him a penny from her pouch. Threading the ribbon through her hair, she walked to the market. Beneath a drooping tree, Hennifen the scribe worked patiently at a letter.

Beside the well, three women with water jars sat talking. She knew two of them. They waved to her. Across the square, Graciela Parisi's red hair stood out like a flag. Some weeks ago she had approached the herbalist for a physic for her youngest daughter's eyes, which were red and swollen. Maia had made her an eyewash of elder tea. She crossed the square. In the stall beside Graciela's, hens squawked mournfully through their crate slats. Morga sniffed at them with interest. The stall was festooned with trinkets: mirrors, bracelets, fans, carved and painted animals, gauzy scarves, and strings of polished stones.

"Good morning."

"Oh, aye, the herbalist. How is it with you?" Maia assured her that she was well. "What brings you to town? Trade?"

"Necessity. My boots need repair."

A long-necked white goose ambled past the stall. It had what appeared to be a narrow red collar around its neck. Maia looked inquiringly at Graciela.

"That's Jansi's goose, loose again. You know Jansi, the butcher's wife? The bird's her pet. It has a bad wing and can't fly. It was the runt of the flock. She raised it by hand."

A barefoot boy scampered after the goose, rope in hand.

"See, here comes Small Toma to fetch it." The boy pounced. The goose honked and spread its wings. Fowl and child tussled in the gutter. The hens squawked. Graciela folded her arms. "Have you heard the news?"

"Likely not," Maia said. "Tell me."

"Sinnea Ohair is pregnant with her first."

"That I knew." Rain of Sleeth had told her.

"Her sister Muriella's come to stay with her. She'll know what to do; she has four of her own, and a fifth she took in when her cousin Lisa died of the birth-fever. Blaise Sorenson's mother is ill."

"I'm sorry," Maia said automatically.

"Oh, aye, she's old. She must be eighty. She was born when Saramanta Atani ruled the domain, her that was called the Dragon of the Mist." Graciela lifted a fan from the pile and fanned herself. "I got a letter from my cousin Amanda, who lives in Nakase. Hennifen read it for me. There's talk of war in the south."

"War with whom?"

Graciela shrugged. "Chuyokai pirates, Isojai raiders: who knows? I wrote a letter back to her, telling her she can bring the family to stay with me if she wishes. They won't come here. No one challenges Dragon Keep. Here, have a fig." She held out a bowl. Maia took a fig. The soft green flesh was achingly sweet.

"Mama, Mama, I want this bear."

A blond-haired girl child bobbed up under Maia's elbow. A second child, perhaps a year older but as like to the first as a big sister can be, pushed in beside her. Behind them came a towheaded boy and two women, one blond, one gray.

"Tina, don't be greedy," the younger woman said.

But the rapt child barely heard the admonition. She touched her finger to a painted red bear. "Mama, *please* may I have this bear."

A slender man with red-gold hair stepped up beside the woman. He drew a handful of coins from a pocket. "You shall have a bear, Tina. Placida, what would you have?" Unhesitatingly, the older girl took a wooden bracelet from the tray. "Is there something you would want, Timothy?"

Shyly, the boy pointed to a painted soldier.

"Excellent. Bear, bracelet, guardsman; we'll take them all." He handed Graciela the coins.

He noticed Maia watching, and grinned amiably at her. Their eyes were almost precisely on a level. He bowed slightly. He had the look of a horseman about him. He was a well-made man, though nowhere near the size and breadth of Karadur Atani. She found herself thinking of the dragon-lord, and flushed.

"Say, thank you, Uncle," the mother prompted.

"Thank you, Uncle," the children chorused.

The little girl cradled the red bear. "His name is Rudy," she declared. The two little ones began to chase each other. Placida slipped the bracelet onto her slender wrist and held it up for the older woman to admire.

"Granna, look! See what I have!" The woman laid her hand lightly on the child's shoulder. Their ease and trust with one another filled Maia's heart with a sudden, unanticipated ache. She wondered where their father was. Back at the farm, perhaps, mending a kettle, or at the mill, watching the miller weigh out his flour, or hunting across the meadow after a strayed sheep . . . The man limped slightly.

When she was certain they were out of earshot, she asked Graciela who they were. Graciela's sandy eyebrows rose. "That's Hern Amdur. And Leanna and her children, and Mellia, Thorin Amdur's widow."

"Ah." She felt a rush of shame, that she had not known them. She should have. A mirror caught her eye. The wooden frame had been carved into the shape of a climbing rose. The woodwork was marvelously delicate. She picked it up.

"Pretty, isn't it?" said Graciela. "It's from Orsia, in Nakase, the Lake country."

"It's lovely." Her mother had owned an oval mirror nearly as tall as she was, in a painted gold frame. Maia had been forbidden to touch it, less her grubby hands mar the gleaming surface. When she was very small she had pretended that her mother's mirror was enchanted, and that someday it would open like a door, and from it would emerge all manner of marvelous beings, like those in the stories Uta told: elephants, phoenixes, manticores, chimeras. . . . Like all luxuries of Iva diSorvino's life, the mirror had been left behind when she fled Sorvino. She laid the mirror back on the table.

"Take it," Graciela said. "The mirror. Take it. You can keep it."

"Are you sure?" Maia said. "Thank you." She cupped the mirror between her palms. A stranger looked back at her, a woman in a man's shirt, with shoulder-length, unbound hair and skin burned amber by the summer sun. She was not the skinny twelve-year-old who had fled her father's house, or the hollow-eyed sixteen-year-old who had watched her mother die, nor the woman who had stood in the moonlight beside her drunken grandfather, hoping to turn a dragonlord's rage. She was all of them.

She had become the chimera.

MAURA HAD SAID that the cobbler's shop was on the north side of the square, next to the glassblower's. She found it easily. The shop was windowless and dark. A wiry, narrow-faced man stood behind a counter.

His skin was almost grey. She had seen that look before. Her mother had had it, just before she died. She told him who she was, and held out the boots.

"Can you fix them?"

Iarsen turned the boots over in his hands. "No. They've been patched as much as they can be. I'll make you a new pair, deerskin, very strong, very supple. Half a ridari."

Half a ridari was a lot of money. But a good pair of boots

would last years. She nodded. "All right. How long will it take?"

"Come back in a week."

When she reached her house, she found Karadur Atani sitting on her steps.

Morga frisked to him, tail wagging furiously. He bent to stroke the wolfhound's ears.

"My lord," she said. "What brings you to my house?"

"Your brother. I told you I would bring him."

She went past him, into the house. Her brother was sitting at the table. The right sleeve of his shirt was cropped. His face was thinner than she remembered.

Morga growled from the doorstep.

"Hush," she said to the dog. "It's Treion. You remember Treion." Neck hair raised, Morga sniffed suspiciously at his boots. "Go lie down." She looked at Karadur. "Thank you, my lord."

"Finle will come for you at sundown," he said to Treion.

"I'll be here," Treion said.

The cottage was still hot. They went into the garden. Treion put his left arm around her shoulders. She laid her palm against his chest, feeling his heart beat hard against her palm. "Tell me how you are."

He made a wry face. "I'm alive."

She gestured at his right shoulder. "Does it hurt?"

"It did. Sometimes it still does," he said. "You look well. Are you?"

"I am," she said. "How do they treat you at the Keep?"

He shrugged. "I work in the kitchen."

"In the kitchen?" She stared at him. "Can you cook?"

He grinned like a ghost. "No. I wash, and clean tables, and carry pots. Sometimes Boris lets me stir the soup."

"Where do you sleep? Where do you eat?"

"I sleep in the kitchen, with the scullions. I eat there, too."

"Do they mistreat you?"

"No." His eyes searched her face. "The traders told me you had died in the fire. How did you escape it?"

"I went into the river."

"Fenris . . .? " She shook her head. "I'm sorry."

"How did *you* escape the fire?"

His mouth tightened. He looked away from her. "Firefly outran it."

"Where did you go?"

"East," he said. "I wasn't alone. Edric came with me. You remember Edric? We went into the hills, to the border country between Ippa and Nakase. And then we went south. We stayed there for a while."

She said, "I know where you were." She took a breath. "I know about Castella."

"No," he said bleakly, "you don't." There was shame in his expression, and something deeper, something he had witnessed, or done, some horror. They spoke of other things. She told him about her friends, about Maura and Angus, and the child Rianna, and about the Hallecks. She described a recent visit to Castria. The tale of Jansi's goose made him smile.

"I have a new name," he told her. "Taran." He described his bargain with the dragon-lord. "I promised him a year of service, in exchange for freedom at the end of that year. He agreed."

"Why?" she asked.

"I don't know," he said bleakly. "I still don't understand why he didn't kill me."

Just before sundown, Finle Haraldsen knocked on the cottage door.

"I have to go," her brother said.

"The gods keep you safe."

He kissed her cheek, and did not answer.

* * *

IT RAINED THAT night, a hard flat downpour. In the morning the fields were wet and glittering. Rain the midwife came by early for a basket of purple fennel. Then two of Miri Halleck's great-grandchildren arrived, to ask her to take the prickles out of their arms and hands. As payment, they had brought a basket filled with ripe, succulent raspberries. The children sat stoically as she teased the thorns out.

At midday she went down to the river to check her fish traps. One held a large flat eel. She killed it with a stone, filled a crock with water and salt, and put the eel in it to soak. Then, basket of berries on her arm, she walked to the Halland farmhouse. The house was a sea of scraps. Dolls perched everywhere. They lolled on the hearth rug. They sprawled on beds. Maura and Rianna called welcome to her across the chaos.

"What's happened?" Maia asked.

"A merchant from Ujo saw two of the dolls in Nini Daluino's stall in Castria Market and said he would buy the dolls from me and sell them in the south. He asked how many I could make. I told him twenty. He agreed to pay half a ridari for each doll I make. He bought four of the finished dolls to show to people, and he gave me four ridari, so that I could buy the cloth I need. He will return for them in October. What do you think of this one?"

She held up a nearly finished girl-doll. It was exquisite, slender and sleek, clothed in silk and lace. "She's beautiful," Maia said.

Rianna said, "She's a Kameni princess. Papa carved a crown for her. It has rubies in it. See?" She displayed the tiny circlet. It was painted gold, and studded with red beads. "I glued them on. Her name's Angelina. She has a prince. His name is Alessandro." The prince was dark-haired and handsome, wearing a sky-blue cape. He looked rather wistful. "He's handsome, don't you think? Where's Morga? Didn't she come with you?"

"No."

"Why not?"

"She's off hunting. She does that sometimes."

"What did you bring us?"

"Raspberries."

"Yum." Maia handed her the basket. Rianna had grown an astonishing amount over the summer: she was brown, long-limbed, and limber.

"Where's your father?" she asked. She had not seen him in the fields.

"Taking honey from the bees." The Hallands had three beehives at the western edge of their fields. Maia had gone with Angus once to tend them. The smell and sound of the bees had made her nervous, but Angus moved about them easily, touching them with his bare hands, clearly unafraid. He burned puffballs to make the bees sleep.

"Come sit with me," she said to Maura. They walked outside and sat on the step. The ginger cat appeared and weaved around her ankles.

Maura said, "It's good to see you. You look happy."

"I am happy," Maia said. "I saw my brother yesterday."

"Ah. How is it with him?"

"He's alive. His arm is healed."

"And?"

"The lord made a pact with him. He promised to serve and be obedient for one year. If he can do that, the lord will free him."

"Will he do it?"

"I hope so." Savage Treion. Stubborn Treion. Karadur would kill him, else. She trailed a piece of straw for the ginger cat. It rolled on its back, batting the air.

Maura said, "Are you ever sad—sad that you came here, I mean? It is not easy, this life, and little of it was of your making. Do you ever wish to go home again?"

Home . . . Where was home? Reo Unamira's house was gone. Sorvino had ceased to be her home the day she left it, perched on the wagon at her mother's side.

Shall we ever come back here, Mama? she had asked her mother.

Iva Unamira had answered, *No. We never shall.*

She gazed across the fields toward her house. The smell of the rich soil rose from the earth like a blessing.

"No," she said. "I am home."

IT WAS ALL, Marion diSorvino decided, completely and absolutely the Bastard's fault.

It had not been a good month. His favorite hunting horse was lame; left forefoot swollen all the way up to the knee. The grooms were poulticing it, but the horse could not be ridden. He had nearly sent the beast to the knackers. Only the assurances of his chief groom that the horse would eventually recover had kept him from doing so.

A letter—the third—had arrived from his banker, warning him that certain of his expenditures—in particular, the repairs he had ordered on the hunting lodge—were straining his domain's budget. DiSorvino despised budgets. He despised his banker. The man was a fool, with no understanding of how a man of his stature should live.

It was *entirely* the Bastard's fault. The harvest had been good. The olive trees had, according to his factors, yielded exceptionally well. The farmers, after making the usual complaints, had paid their taxes. But diSorvino had had to partially remit the taxes from Alletti, Bruna, Embria, and a half dozen other towns. He had had to replace the mill at

Alletti, and the bridge at Maranessa. That was the Bastard's fault, no question. So were the extra payments he had to make to his troops, who would not have needed to be paid more than usual were it not for the months they had spent hunting the Bastard across every hill and ravine in western Nakase, to no avail. DiSorvino's banker had not been happy about that expense, either. He had not been happy about the very fine set of blown-glass goblets that had been diSorvino's wedding gift to Kalni Leminin's daughter. He had been positively scathing about the two cases of merignac diSorvino had purchased in Ujo. It did not help that in the rush to leave Ujo, the merignac—which he, himself, had bought, paid for, and personally arranged to have delivered to the hotel in a specially padded wagon—had been left on a street corner. Sitting at his desk, staring at the monthly accounts that Colm, his household steward, had left for him to review, Marion diSorvino wondered for the hundredth time what had happened to that wine. It had to have gone somewhere.

He wadded up the meticulously prepared account and tossed it away. The hell with it. Colm would sort it out. That was his job, after all. It *was* entirely the Bastard's fault. Damn his arrogant soul to hell. He was dead now, which was good. DiSorvino's only regret was that he had not been there to watch Treion Unamira die. He hoped it had taken a long time.

Tevio knocked on the door.

"My lord," the boy said. "Captain Nortero is here."

"Excellent! Send him in," said Marion diSorvino. "And bring me a bottle of brandy. This one's empty." He liked Nortero. Unlike his damned banker, Nortero was respectful, liberal-handed, and always ready with a joke. DiSorvino swept the papers off his desk and closed his hand around his glass, preparing to be entertained.

"Gilberto. Sit, sit. It's good to see you. Have some brandy." He pushed a glass Nortero's way.

"Thank you, my lord." Nortero filled the goblet. He was a big man, big in the shoulders and bigger in the belly. "Your health." He raised the glass.

"And yours." He waited until Nortero's ruddy nose had disappeared into the throat of the goblet before remarking, "Gilberto, if I didn't know better, I'd swear you're pregnant."

The soldier sputtered. "My lord, I weigh no more than when you last saw me. It's the jacket. It's cut wrong. I was just complaining to my tailor." He peered with mock anxiety down the slope of his massive chest.

"Ah. And how's Madelina?" Madelina Nortero was a pretty, pious ninny. Gilberto had married her for her money, with the promise that if she would not interfere with him, he would let her do anything she wanted. Since she wanted nothing better than to fill the house with astrologers and canting priestesses, it was a bargain that pleased them both. "Has she converted you to the path of virtue yet?"

Nortero's bluff face grew solemn. "My wife is very well. My wife, my lord," he intoned, "is a good woman." He raised his glass. "Praise be to the gods, that they did not make too many of 'em!"

"I'll drink to that," diSorvino said. He had given up on wives. Both of his had been difficult, deceitful women, and both—might they be damned through all the seven hells—had left him. Susanna had run off to Firense with that spindly-legged mummer of an apothecary. Iva had gone back to her bandit father. Whores were simpler to deal with. As long as you paid them, the bitches could not complain at what you did.

Nortero said, "My lord, Franco Genovese asked me to send you his greetings."

"Huh. I doubt that. Why were you in Secca?"

"Genovese's grandfather died. You remember. Lorca, the one who went mad. I went to the funeral. You asked me to go, my lord."

He remembered then. There had been some trouble on the eastern border, some small dispute about a boundary line. He had asked the Lemininkai to adjudicate it. The Lemininkai had ruled against him there, too. It wasn't fair. He should have won. "How was the funeral?"

"It wasn't," Nortero said.

"What?"

"We were ready to bury him, priestess there, grave dug, family standing about, looking solemn. But they couldn't find the body. Someone had taken it from the house, winding sheet and all. The servants whose task it was to prepare the body for burial all swore they didn't know what happened to it; the guards swore no one had come into the house. . . . Franco was spitting nails."

"He'd already paid the priestess?"

"Of course. But that didn't matter, or not so much. It was the theft of the bones that troubled him."

"Why?"

"Some people believe that you can do mischief to someone if you use the bones of their blood kin to make the spell."

"Hedge-witchery." DiSorvino made a face. "Gilberto, I thought better of you. How can you believe that slop?"

"I don't," said Nortero. "But Franco Genovese does. The day after the funeral, the funeral that didn't happen, he hung the guards. Then he put out word that he would pay a reward for the return of the bones. Fifty nobles. Every mountebank in Nakase has been showing up on the doorstep of Genovese Castle, dragging sheep bones and pig bones and Imarru alone knows what other sorts of bones, dressed up in winding sheets some of them, with rings and bits of lace and finery and such. . . . Franco's front hall is ankle deep in bones."

DiSorvino pictured Franco Genovese's paneled hallway strewn with pig bones, and Franco, brandishing a sack with fifty gold pieces in it, wading through them. . . . He laughed. "Was it Franco who locked the old man in the cellars for twenty years?"

"It wasn't twenty years," Nortero said. "More like ten. No, it wasn't Franco; it was Franco's father, Luigi, who did that. Claimed he'd tried to poison him. Probably he had. He'd already killed his brother, Marcello, and the other boys, his sons, Luigi's brothers. Lorca was always killing somebody."

"How did Luigi die?"

"I believe it was a fever. A natural death, the physician said."

DiSorvino grunted. He disliked physicians as much as he disliked apothecaries.

"Were Franco's brothers at the funeral? Carlino, and—and—"

"Alano. No. Wise of them. Franco's not a loving brother. It's a wonder they're alive at all. They left home quite early."

"Clever of them." His own brother had done the same. He lived in the south, near Firense, and had never shown the slightest interest in returning to Sorvino. "Franco had a sister, didn't he? What happened to her?"

"She's Abbess of the Temple of the Moon in Mako. She probably spends a good deal of time praying for the rest of her family." Nortero grinned merrily. "That reminds me of a story I heard about Fabio Trasio." Fabio Trasio was one of the town's leading citizens. He was also a drunk, a spendthrift, and a notable rake. DiSorvino waved a hand. The story turned out to be quite unbelievable, involving as it did a novice in the temple, a horse, and Fabio Trasio clad only in his socks. But it was a funny story.

"Tevio!" diSorvino called. "Bring more brandy." It was good brandy, from some vineyard in the Lake District. It was not, of course, as good as the merignac would have been. How could anyone steal nearly fifty bottles of merignac? He had had the wagon driver and the guard flogged and dismissed. "What other news do you hear?"

"Let's see. Erin diMako's daughter, the one who married into the Leminin clan, is pregnant. Bork Hal, Gerris Hal's eldest, has settled his trouble in Serrenhold. Though you know that family. Never out of trouble. Already he's in dispute with the Red Hawk sisters over the ownership of some land. There's unrest on the southern border. The Chuyokai are restless. And oh, yes, there's a story being told about your young troublemaker, the one you, ah, mislaid in Ujo."

"Unamira," diSorvino grated. "Treion Unamira. The one who was stolen from me, you mean. I presume it's an old story. He's dead."

"Not according to Egidio diPrima. I met him at the horse fair in Averra. You know him; his caravans go everywhere. He heard from one of his suppliers that *he* had heard from a friend of his, an innkeeper in Castria, that Unamira's still alive. Karadur Atani didn't kill him. After all the misery he put you through, it hardly seems fair."

A scarlet rage crawled up Marion diSorvino's backbone. The Bastard was alive. He could not believe it. Tevio came in, a fresh bottle of brandy cradled in his arms.

"Bring it here, damn you!" He did not want to believe it. He glared at Nortero. "When did you hear this?"

"I told you, at the horse fair. Last month."

"Why did you not mention this before?"

Nortero shrugged. "It slipped my mind."

"What mind?" Nortero looked away. "What more did diPrima tell you?"

"That was all, my lord." Nortero reached blithely for the bottle.

"Take your hands off that! That can't be all. Is Unamira a prisoner? What was done to him? Damn it, find out! I want to know everything."

"You want me to talk to diPrima, my lord?"

DiSorvino looked at his commander in loathing. The man was brainless. "Gods, no. Idiot. I want you to send someone to Ippa."

Nortero's ruddy face went blank. "My lord," he said, "it's November. It's winter in the north. No one goes to Ippa in winter."

"I give you money for intelligence, don't I?"

"Yes, my lord."

"Then show some! Hire a spy, tell him what you need to know, and pay him double." DiSorvino closed his fingers around the brandy bottle. "Tell him not to come back until he knows everything that happened to Unamira, and most particularly, where he is." With all his strength, he flung the bottle at the door.

Naturally, it shattered.

"Go!"

12

"HOY, ONE-ARM," said Anssa, "give me a hand!"

The pot of grease he held was tipping dangerously, threatening to spill on the kitchen floor. Taran went quickly to his aid.

"Careful," Anssa warned, "it's hot." Taran grabbed a cloth. Between them they steadied the pot. "Got it. Thanks." Staggering outside, Anssa poured the hot grease into the snow. Eilon handed Taran a grease-encrusted skillet. He passed it to Pico for washing.

Ruth grabbed his sleeve. "Help me with the rolls." He went with her to the bake oven, and helped her pull the wide flat trays from their shelves. The crusts of the rolls were flavored with honey and cinnamon. They slid the trays into the trestle to cool.

"Smells good," Taran said. Ruth nodded and returned to her table, on which sat rows and rows of savory dumplings, waiting to be dropped into the soup. Taran had never realized what labor it took to feed a household. Every day, Boris and his undercooks thrice fed Dragon, his officers, his guests, if there were any, the forty or so men of the war band, and the more than fifty men and women who served them. The work started before dawn and did not stop. There was always something to be done: fires to be fed, beasts to be butchered, vegetables to be cleaned and chopped, dough to be prepared, sauces and soups to be stirred, pots and pans to be filled, emptied, or scoured, spits to be turned. The work was drudgery. He hated it, especially the pot washing. He hated the grease and spatter and smoke.

A pot holding yellow mustard sauce started to bubble. Taran hissed at Eilon. Together they moved the pot farther from the fire. Eilon was chief of the scullions, soon to be made undercook. He was a big-boned lad, with a placid temperament, quite different from Boris, who made an art of losing his temper, or from Simon, the sneering stew cook. Sour Simon, the scullions called him.

When first Taran came to the kitchen, Eilon had refused to speak to him. The other scullions had been actively malicious: jostling him, tripping him, leaving spoiled food in his blanket. "Ignore it," Boris had said. "It'll stop." But ignoring it had not been easy. The harassment set his teeth on edge. He wanted badly to retaliate, with words, or blows, or with the knife that he had stolen from the knife rack and hidden in his boot.

But retaliation, he knew, would incite more animosity, and if he used the knife, no matter what the provocation, Karadur would kill him. He kept his mouth shut and did what he was told. Eventually, as Boris had said it would, the hostility ceased. Only Simon's had not. That morning he had surreptitiously spilled water at Taran's feet as he was balancing a heavy pot. "Look out!" Ruth had shouted. "Simon, you lackwit oaf. Watch what you're doing!"

"Sorry," Simon said sullenly, "it was an accident."

But they all knew it was not.

Someday, Taran determined, Simon would pay for that, and for other insults. But not now. The door to the yard swung open. Half a dozen children, red-cheeked from the cold, weaved amid the flashing cleavers and the dangling cauldrons. Boris brandished his slotted spoon and roared at them. Laughing, they ducked beneath his windmilling arms, snatching bits of meat from the tables.

Great haunches of elk lay cooling on the slicing table. There was plenty of food, of course, more than enough. Even in the dead of winter, no one went hungry or cold or untended in Dragon Keep or anywhere in Karadur Atani's domain. The lord and his hunters made sure of that.

I saw your sister yesterday, Rogys had said, two days ago. Or was it three? *We brought her meat and firewood. She said to tell you she's well.*

Karadur Atani was a good lord. Taran had come to the opinion grudgingly. He had wanted to hate the man, to name him tyrannical and brutal, but he was not. He asked of his soldiers only what they could give. He rode with them, trained with them, hunted with them. On winter nights, when the air grew so cold that smoke froze leaving the chimney, he stood watch on the walls beside them, lending them his warmth. *Dragon*, they called him.

Karadur rarely spoke to him. But he felt the dragonlord's gaze on him, now and again. It sent a chill through him that the kitchen warmth could not assuage.

Jess said briskly, "Hoy! One-arm, you're dreaming. Wake up." She held out a dirty pot. Taran added it to the scullions' pile. Metal screeched; Boris was sharpening his big carving knives.

Anssa said, "He's dreaming of the treasure." Up to their elbows in grease, the scullions grinned. Dragon Keep was rich, everyone knew that. There were vaults beneath the castle, hollowed by the dragon-kindred out of solid rock. The scullions had plied him mercilessly with tales of those vaults: immense, shadowy rooms piled with heaps of glittering bright coin and blazing jewels. . . . He had dreamed about it at night.

But those were Treion the bandit's dreams. He was Taran, or, more commonly, One-arm. The soldiers, when they spoke to him, called him One-arm. He watched them training every chance he had. The officers—even Herugin—did not stop him. He knew them all now: tough, black-bearded Marek, volatile Lurri, Rogys, the red-haired cavalryman who was clearly one of Dragon's favorites, Raudri the herald, Ruth's brother. . . . The day after he followed Boris to the kitchen, Raudri had dragged him to a shadowy corner of the courtyard and told him that if Taran caused Ruth any trouble, he, Raudri, would break Taran's neck.

"Anything," the herald warned him.

But Taran had no intention of causing Ruth, whom he liked, or Anssa, or Boris, or even Sour Simon, a moment's concern. He would keep his bargain with the dragon-lord. He would win his freedom, and a sword.

And then, somehow, he would kill Marion diSorvino. The passion that coursed through him whenever he thought of the man had in no way abated. He did not know how he would manage it, only that he would find a way, somehow.

What he would do once *that* was done, he had no idea.

Anssa stuck his head out into the hall. "They're coming in," he said over his shoulder. The serving-girls stopped their gossiping and straightened their aprons.

Boris laid the whetstone down and began to slice.

AT THE END of the meal, Karadur called for music. As was customary, the cooks and servers and scullions laid their work aside and went into the hall to listen to the singer. Taran went with them. The reverence the folk of Dragon Keep gave to music had surprised him. There had been no music in Sorvino.

"Riders at the gate! Seven riders at the gate!" Azil's voice filled the hall, compelling as a trumpet. When he ended, there were tears in some men's eyes. Lord and singer left the hall together, and the rest of the household followed; most to their beds, a few to the bitter cold of guard duty in midwinter. The servers cleared the remains of the meal from the tables. The dogs, whining, crowded at the kitchen entrance for the scraps of meat. The scullions scoured the cauldrons. Boris wiped his spoon on a cloth and hung it on its hook in the pantry, above the jar of precious yellow saffron that was his alone to touch.

When all was done, he set the keph pieces out on the baker's table. Finding someone to play keph with at the Keep had been a bounty Taran had not expected. Boris was a good keph player, better than Taran. The cook preferred the Summer pieces. His play reminded Taran of Niello's, a little. Niello was dead. He did not want to think of him. Taran wiped the grease from his fingers and took his place on the stool opposite the cook.

Boris moved his Eagle. Taran moved a pikeman to protect his Princess. Boris leaned back a little, then took the pikeman. Taran moved his Raven up to threaten Boris's King. Boris moved his Eagle to intercept the threat.

Their pieces ambled about the board for a while. Then Boris took Taran's Wizard. Taran scanned the board. He was going to lose this match.

"I'm done," he said. He tipped the Winter King on its side.

Smiling, Boris put board and pieces away and padded off to his apartment. The ovens emanated warmth. The scullions, rolled in their quilts, snored beside the shining cauldrons. Boris had left the lamp alight on the baker's table. Taran felt under his quilt for the wood stave he had hidden there. He tucked it under his arm. Then, carrying the lamp, he went back into the vacant hall.

It was cold and dark as a tomb. A faint warmth rose from the hearth ashes. He set the candle beside the hearth. The stave was nearly four feet long. Holding it as a man would hold a practice sword, he cut, and cut, and cut again ten strokes, twenty, fifty, a hundred. . . . He did figure eights. He advanced, boots stamping, and retreated, slicing into the shadows with strokes he had first learned when he was ten from Emmit d'Andorra, commander of the diSorvino household's guards. DiSorvino had been furious when he learned about the lessons.

Waste of time, teaching a bastard! No more. I forbid it!

Never mind, boy, d'Andorra had said quietly. *We'll find you a teacher*. And he had arranged for Treion to take lessons from Lorin Befaccio, who made his living teaching the children of Sorvino how to hold a sword. Befaccio had fought for the Lemininkai—not Kalni Leminin, but his father. He had yellow eyes and a crooked nose. He was a good swordsman, and a good teacher.

The first rule of swordsmanship is, Watch everything, he had said. *The second rule is, Move your feet!* Taran moved his feet in the way Befaccio had taught him. One hundred fifty, two hundred . . . He pictured an enemy cutting at his legs. He parried the deadly blows. Sweat coated the shirt beneath his heavy vest. When first he started to train like this, in secret, his arm had been clumsy, his wrist weak. It was stronger now.

Two hundred fifty, three hundred . . . His breath steamed in the night air. His lungs burned. The wooden stave felt heavy as iron.

His sword, when he got it, would be heavier.

Three hundred ten, three hundred twenty . . .

The door from the courtyard opened. A cold wind blew into the hall. The lamp's meager flame wavered in the draft. Then it sprang erect. A torch on the wall blazed into life.

Panting, Taran spun.

Karadur Atani stood in the doorway of the hall. Despite the ferocious cold, his arms were bare.

Taran let the tip of the stave drop to the stone. His heart thumped painfully.

The dragon-lord's face was unreadable.

Then he said, "It's late. Go to bed." He glanced at the torch. It went out. He let the heavy door close.

Taran stood still, catching his breath. The sweat dried on his skin. The chill made him shiver.

He went into the kitchen. The ovens still emanated warmth. He picked his way through the chamber to his pallet. Sliding the stave beneath the thin straw, he worked his boots off—it took a long time—and wound himself into his quilts. The wind, moaning softly, crept under the door.

The doleful sound made him think of Niello.

THE ILLUSIONIST CAME to Castria in a snowstorm.

He was a bright-eyed, genial fellow, portly, but nimble as a youth, and not so young, the folk of Castria agreed, as he appeared. He arrived on the back of a sturdy brown mule. He was, he explained to Gerda and Blaise Sorenson, a traveling entertainer, a maker of small whimsies, a sometime animal trainer. He had once, he claimed, traveled through Nakase from Averra to Merigny with a troupe of performing monkeys.

He paid for a room, and Gerda was delighted to rent it to him at quite a low rate, since he was, given that it was February, the inn's only tenant. He had a bag filled with coins beneath his cloak. Blaise Sorenson, who liked his creature comforts as well as the next man, insisted he had heard the ring of nobles amid the clink of less valuable coinage.

He was not, the stranger claimed, an outlaw, nor any sort of malefactor. Though he had, he confided privately to Blaise, fallen afoul of the watch a time or two. *(I have a deplorable weakness for wine. But it must be good wine, mind you!)* He had come north because—a foolish reason—he had never been north. His name was Nino Pecci. He was from Kameni, where his mother *(a wonderful woman)* and his half a dozen brothers and sisters still lived. That he had arrived in the midst of a snowstorm was his own fault. He had simply not heeded the advice he had received in Ujo. That advice had been that he should wait before crossing the border—preferably until April.

"This is nothing," Ferd Parisi told him. "In December the snow was four feet thick, and so hard that the cattle walked on top of it." Ferd then guffawed loudly, which spoiled the joke. Southerners would believe anything of a northern winter.

Dinas Altimura said, "Two years ago it snowed in May." This was not a joke. The listeners nodded soberly. Gerda signaled the girls to refill the mugs. There was a surprisingly large number of people in the Lizard's common room. Word had gotten out that there was a stranger at the inn, and that he was moderately entertaining.

"Three years ago the roads were closed by Harvest Moon, and it snowed every day from October clear through to June," said Blaise. "That was a terrible winter."

Nino Pecci nodded. "Aye. Even in Ujo we heard of it. There were stories of rivers of ice, and wargs, and dragons battling, and chests of gold. . . . I don't suppose you happen to have one of those chests lying about for the taking . . . a small one? No? I thought not." Grinning, he took a silver coin from beneath his cloak and walked it along his knuckles.

"What's that?" someone asked.

"A *dinado*. It's a Chuyo silver piece. Worth about six ridari." He walked it along his knuckles again. Then, grinning, he made it vanish. Expectantly they waited for it to reappear, which it did, in Blaise's hat.

"To tell the truth, it's kind of a good-luck piece. One time I was traveling with the monkeys in Taviz, down by the Chuyo border, and I met a girl from Dorry in the market. . . ." The villagers drew their chairs closer.

Nino was full of stories. Sometimes they were about him, sometimes about his brothers and sisters and cousins, sometimes about other folk. Always he prefaced his most fantastic stories with: *"To tell the truth . . ."* He was a bit of a mountebank, but his stories kept the common room a good deal busier than it would ordinarily be in February, and for this Gerda was grateful. The tricks *were* entertaining. His manners were excellent; he left the women alone. Besides, Blaise liked the fellow. He was easy to like, for he listened as much as he talked, and seemed as interested in the exploits of Gerda's granddaughter Nell as in the deeds of the great and near great. The dogs liked him, too, and they were discerning beasts, known to snarl at folk they did not trust. Whenever he entered the common room they would trot to his side to have their muzzles rubbed. She would be sorry to see him go.

After the second week, Nino confided to Blaise that he was running out of money.

"I have enough to pay my room and board, never fear. But I had best find another source of income, or I shall be reduced to eating with the dogs, and sleeping with Bianca." Bianca was his mule. "Have you any recommendations?"

Blaise frowned. It was hard to see what work could be found for an itinerant illusionist.

"What can you do?" he asked bluntly. "Besides tell stories, and pull coins out of people's ears."

"I can teach a dog to dance on its hind legs. I know, it's not a skill you northerners have much use for. I can cook." He looked at Blaise hopefully. "I don't suppose . . ."

"We have a cook." Blaise thought. "Can you sing?"

"Why?"

"Dragon likes music, especially singers. If you could sing, you could ride to the Keep and earn a purse."

Nino shook his head. "Alas, I croak like a crow."

"They might have use for another undercook at the Keep. Though they say that Boris the head cook has a terrible temper. I can ask."

"I'm not overfond of castles," Nino said. "Too drafty."

"Well, we will see if we can find you something."

Quietly, he let it be known among his friends—Blaise had many friends—that the southerner was looking for some kind of employment.

It was Ferd Parisi who suggested that Nino might be able to find employment at the Amdur farm.

"We breed horses: the best warhorses in Ippa, we think, though there are folk in Mako who'd dispute that. There's a lot to do right now. There's the usual mucking and cleaning and feeding. But two of the lads are sick, and the rest of us are damn near run off our feet. Do you know anything about horses?"

"I have some experience with horses," Nino allowed.

"I'll take you there tomorrow."

"If the weather's clear."

"Even if it's not." Ferd clapped the smaller man on the shoulder. "Don't worry, man, you won't freeze."

"It's Bianca I worry about," Nino said gloomily.

* * *

BUT THE NEXT day indeed proved fair, and Bianca did not object to following Ferd's horse to the Amdur farm. Nino admired the barns, the house, the foaling stalls, the neatly fenced pastures, now lightly burnished with snow. The house was large, fronted in stone, with windows on the side as well as the front. It sported two chimneys.

"It looks new built."

"It is," Ferd said. "There was a fire. Outlaws."

"Aye. We have them in the south, too. What did they want? Gold?"

"They came to steal the horses. It was Unamira and his band: him that used to live on Coll's Ridge. They burned the barn and killed Thorin Amdur and Garth, his second son. But Mellia, his widow, and Hern, his third son, manage the farm between them. They are openhanded folk; you could not find a better place." He shouted to a man with a pitchfork over his shoulder, "Hoy! You know where the lady Mellia is?"

The man called back, "Try Swallow's stall."

"Trouble?"

"She's ailing."

"Now what?" Ferd led the way to a horse stall. Its occupant was clearly suffering: she stood shuddering, eyes wide. Her dun-colored coat was patchy with sweat. A grey-haired woman wearing a man's shirt and pants tried to coax a nosebag over her long face. Tossing her head, the mare backed away from the bag. The stall was hot and odorous.

"What happened?" Ferd asked.

"She ate some bad corn." The woman reached up. The mare bared her teeth. "She won't take the draught. Hern is in the north pasture. Six of the sheep got out last night." She grinned without humor. "The gods only know what they thought they would find in the north pasture in February. Spring, perhaps." She moved toward the mare again.

The animal tossed her head and bared her teeth. "Oh, my poor girl."

Nino said, "Let me try." He opened the door to the stall and sidled inside. A cat colored like a patchwork quilt sidled toward him. He bent to scratch its nose. Without hesitation, he extended a palm toward the mare.

"Hush, my sweetheart, my lovely lady, my buttercup darling, listen to me now, only listen. . . ."

Mellia Amdur said ominously, "Whoever you are, if you disturb her further, I'll set the hounds on you." Nino murmured soothing nonsense to the mare. She rolled her eyes at him and snorted. He did not retreat, only continued to talk. She dropped her head toward him and snuffled at his hand.

"Good girl, that's a good girl. What a fine, pretty lady you are. I knew we should get along, you and I. What's her name?"

"Swallow."

"Swallow. What a pretty fine thing you are, Swallow darling. What's in the bag, ma'am?"

"Salicorn and sage in an oat mash."

"Give it to me." He reached a hand for it. The other stroked the horse's neck. "Listen, my lovely, this will make you feel better, it will. That's my girl, that's my dainty-footed darling. This will make the stomach trouble pass. Next time put some rosemary in it; it will further soothe her system. Aye, pretty girl, you shall have a fine foal come summertime, wait and see."

He slipped the nosebag over the mare's head. Her jaws moved.

"Good," Mellia Amdur said. "Very good. Ferd, who is this?"

"His name's Nino," Ferd said proudly. "He's looking for work, he's a southerner, he trains animals. . . ."

Days later, when he had met Hern Amdur, and been told

what his wages would be, and shown where to sleep, Nino Pecci reflected that luck, as usual, had flowed his way. His friends had often remarked that he had been born under a lucky star, and more than one astrologer had confirmed that yes, it was true. His mother, a devout woman, insisted that his good fortune devolved from her prayers, but Nino doubted that. She prayed equally for all her children, and his sisters and brothers had had no more than the ordinary amount of luck.

Swallow snuffled at his hair. He rubbed her nose.

"Hey, my pretty, are you feeling better now? Good girl, that's a good girl. I can see that you are." He had offered to bed with her for a few nights, in case she had a relapse and needed doctoring. The candle in the lantern flickered through the glass. The place was quite private, as he had known it would be.

He had been in the north less than three weeks, but he had learned a great deal. He had heard from many about the old bandit, Reo Unamira, *Him that used to live on Coll's Ridge. . . .* He heard about the raid on the farm, and about the fire.

The leader of the raiders had been Treion Unamira.

Unamira had escaped Karadur Atani's wrath by taking with him a hostage, Herugin Dol, cavalry master at Dragon Keep. He had promised to send him back, and evidently, he kept the promise: thin and scarred, Herugin Dol had returned to Dragon Keep that winter. And that had been the end of it, until Karadur Atani returned from Ujo this very summer with Treion Unamira tied to the back of a horse. He had run all the way to Kameni, it seemed, to escape Dragon's justice.

"What happened to him?" he asked his informant.

"Dragon cut his arm off." The man refused to say more. Nino had not pressed him, though there was more he wanted to know.

But luck, that inexplicable influence which had accompanied him all his life, had brought him precisely to where he needed to be. Both Mellia and Hern Amdur—so his informant had averred—had been present when Karadur Atani cut off Treion Unamira's arm. They would know what else had happened to him, whether he was dead, or exiled, or locked in a hole somewhere. One of them would tell him about it.

It was one of his gifts, that men and women trusted him, even as the animals did, and confided in him, just as did the animals. They, of course, did not use words.

He pulled his notebook from his pouch, and laid out ink and quill. The patchwork cat that had come to greet him when he arrived looked up from her nest in the straw.

"Merow?" she inquired. She was a friendly little thing.

"Go to sleep, little one. This doesn't concern you," Nino told her.

She blinked, and put her head down again. Laboriously he wrote, in his own personal code, what had happened that day. If he were ever searched, and the little book discovered, no one would be able to read what he had written. But he had never, in twenty years of gathering intelligence for whoever would pay him, been searched, or even questioned. Nino believed that it was because he bore no ill will to those he talked to. He did not try to trap or cozen them. He was an entertainer. He did tricks, and taught dogs to dance on their hind legs, and monkeys to submit to wearing hats.

And if, in the course of his travels, people told him, without realizing it, bits of information that they ordinarily would never reveal, and which might someday do them harm, it was not because he meant to hurt them.

It was simply because he asked, and they trusted him. . . .

13

TERRILL CHERNICO WOKE to the sound of horns blowing.

She lifted herself onto her good elbow. She had not slept well. She had dreamed, restless, painful dreams. One had transported her to a desolate landscape, a labyrinth of rock, where fell voices howled at her. Someone she cared about was lost in that place, and she could not find him. She lifted a hand to her cheek. It was wet with tears.

Pushing the nightmare from her mind, she thrust her head out the window. The sky was clear and cloudless. On the west side of the yard, a clot of half-grown boys were wrestling.

The mismatched trumpets trilled again. From the angle of the sun along the stones of the wall, she knew she had missed breakfast. She dressed, and walked to the kitchen. Ruth, her elbows powdered with flour, nodded companionably to her and passed her half a cinnamon loaf. She took it into the ward to eat.

As she passed the armory steps, she stopped. There was a child lying on the steps. He appeared to be sleeping. It was Shem. He was curled like a newborn, knees to chest.

"Shem," she said, "wake up, sleepyhead." He did not move. "Shem Wolfson!" She laid her hands on him, afraid—was he wounded, unconscious, bleeding?—and realized as soon as she touched him that he was none of these things. He was linked.

She sank on the step beside him. His eyes were open, smoky, and blind. He whimpered. She lifted him, and held him. "Thea's son, Thea's son," she sang, rocking him, "it's well, it's well, be still. . . ." Sweet Mother, he was too young for this. His mind was chaos; his thoughts moved, like ribbons strung with jewels, dancing in the sun. She looked for one that did not move. She found it, and slid her own thought along it, seeking the mind that had entrapped his. . . .

Suddenly, he jerked in her arms. Swiftly she withdrew.

"Hawk?" he said tentatively. He gazed at her, and then wriggled from her arms, frowning.

"He's lost," he said.

"Who's lost, cub?"

"The man. He doesn't know where he is, and he's afraid." His eyes were his again. She stroked his head, wondering how the linkage could have happened. By accident, surely; dear gods, he was but a baby!

"Do you know where he is, cub?"

He waved his arm in a vague easterly direction. "That way."

She reached out with thought. *I am here,* she sent. *Cleave to me, I will help you.* But there were too many people about. Their thoughts chattered and yammered wildly. . . . She pulled back, defeated.

"Hawk?"

"Yes, Shem."

"We have to help him."

"How can we do that, cub?"

"I can find him. I have to find him." His steady, measuring stare, so like his father's, traveled from her booted feet to her cropped hair.

She said, "We shall find him, cub, I promise. I must speak to Dragon. Go put your boots on and bring your cloak. Meet me at the stable. Tell the boys to saddle Lily."

Karadur was in the donjon, meeting with the elders from Castria and Sleeth. They were talking about road repair. Torik went in with her message. In a moment, the dragonlord came out. "Hunter, what is it?"

She told him quickly what had happened, and what she wished to do about it.

"Is Shem hurt?" he asked.

"No, my lord."

"Can he do this thing?"

She said, "I think he must."

He frowned. "Go, then. Take Finle with you. And Olav. He needs something to do." The big northerner had been moping about the Keep for days, ever since his best friend, Irok, had left to visit his family in Hornlund.

She found Finle in the barracks. He was delighted to join the expedition. "I'll get Olav," he offered. "When do we leave?"

"Now," she said.

SHE STOPPED AT the kitchen, and then at her chamber for her bow, the small one, and her arrows, and her heavy riding cloak. Shem was in the stable yard, playing tug-of-war in the dust with Turtle. As she walked into the yard, he came to his feet.

"Enough, Turtle," he told the excited dog. "Behave now.

Be still. You can't come with us." He was wearing his boots. His riding cloak lay folded against the stable wall. His bow and a quiver of arrows stood beside it. She had made the bow for him, out of a length of yew from Liam Dubhain's store. The arrows were fledged with eagle feathers.

"I told them to saddle Lily," he said.

She told Gelf to ready Finle's bay, and Brick, who had a mild temper, and would not jibe at a stranger, and the dun, Guardian, that Olav usually rode.

They took the horses out through the little gate. "Where are we going?" Olav asked.

"I'm not sure," Hawk said. "Shem?"

He pointed in the direction of Castria. "That way. I feel him that way."

The road was largely empty, save for the occasional ox-cart. There were men in the fields, repairing fences. The sound of axes came irregularly—tock, tock—across the rise of the hills. Shem sat before her on the saddle. He hummed, a wordless warble.

He said confidingly, "I had a dream last night."

"So did I."

"I had a good dream! Was yours a bad dream? I know a charm for those. *Light the fire, nightmare run; To my dream no shade will come; sunlight quickens, shadows die; Day will rise, and so will I!*" His voice rose triumphantly.

"Where did you learn that, cub?"

"Kiala taught me."

The bright March day was cold but fair. To the north, the guardian mountains—Dragon's Eye, Brambletor, Whitethorn—towered, tall peaks glinting white. Squirrels, looking for the nuts they had stored that winter, bustled from ground to tree and back again. Two black-winged kites soared overhead. Hawk reached to them. *Cousins, how goes the hunting . . .?* Engrossed in an ecstasy of wind, they did not respond.

At midday they halted to rest and eat. After the meal, Hawk left the others, and walked alone to a clearing. She reached into the distance. She touched the mind of a sleeping grey fox, and a badger in its den, and a woodpecker hunting insects up the bole of a tree. But she encountered nothing human. Past the gates of Castria they left the road for the forest. Shem begged to hold Lily's reins. He steered the horse through the trees. They came into the open again. The hillside was dusted with snow. Jagged stumps of trees lifted through the white.

Lily tossed her head. Shem said, "She's thirsty." He thrust an arm out. "The river's that way."

"How do you know, cub?" Hawk asked.

"I smell it."

So did she. But she was changeling grown. She tried to remember how old she had been when her powers had wakened in her blood. She had been at least nine, surely? Shem was four. Perhaps wolf-changeling developed differently from hawk-changeling. She did not know. Wolf would have known. Lily, snorting, pulled against the bit. She wanted the water. "Go on, you lazy beast," Hawk told her. "Find it. You can find it." The mare ambled purposefully along the ridgetop.

Suddenly the land dropped away into a sloping bowl. Beyond the bowl the river gleamed. Tall sedge grew along the water's edge. Saplings, limber as flames, quivered in the sun. At the foot of the slope stood a small stone cottage.

Shem said, "I know that place." The cottage door opened. A tall, brown-haired woman stepped out on the path. She wore a pale blue shirt, and trousers like a man's. A black dog moved at her side. Shem said excitedly, "Hawk, I know her! She was in my dream."

Hawk said, "What dream was that, cub?"

Shem did not answer. Shading her eyes, the woman gazed up the slope at the riders. Then she turned, and reentered the house.

THEY TOOK THE horses to the water. The river ran low between stony banks. Twenty yards downstream, the bank flattened. The horses drank, lipping cautiously at the icy stream. Suddenly Shem whooped, bouncing in the saddle. "I feel him! He's there!" He pointed east. Hawk sent her thought questing across the snow-covered hills. Abruptly she felt the stranger. His thought was dazed and weak; he was cold, frightened, nearly starving. . . .

"Finle, go left. Olav, right. I'll take the center. Look for a man, or a man's tracks. He won't call to you; he's not fully conscious."

They found him at last, a gangly form crumpled into a snowbank. A pack and the leavings of a fire lay nearby. Finle held his palm to the blackened wood. "It's cold," he said. Hawk ran her hands over the stranger's chest and legs and arms. He was shivering spasmodically, but appeared to have taken no other hurt.

"So is he," she said. "Let's get him out of here."

They brought him down the hill and laid him in the sunlight. As the light fell full upon his face, he muttered, and rolled his head. Olav pushed the youth's straggly hair back from his face. "This is no man," he said. "This is a boy."

At the sound of Olav's voice, the youth opened his eyes. Then, with surprising strength, he tore himself from Olav's grip. Rolling to a crouch, he drew his knife, and faced them.

"I will not go back," he said hoarsely. "I will not."

Finle said, "By the Hunter, it's Juni Talvela!" The boy's gaze turned toward him. "Juni! It's Finle Haraldsen; remember me? We competed against each other in Ujo. Do you remember me?"

"Finle," Juni repeated. The knife tip wavered.

"You are safe. Whatever you are running from, it is not here. This is Dragon's country, and this big, yellow-haired brute on my left is Olav the axman, who wears Dragon Keep's badge, and this is Hawk the archer, who was also in Ujo, and this is Shem Wolfson."

"Finle." He looked at them wonderingly. "Hawk. I remember you." The knife sank. He sagged, and staggered. Olav caught him under the arms and lowered him gently to the earth. Finle pulled a blanket from his pack. He wrapped it around Juni's shoulders.

Hawk, kneeling, held her flask to Juni's lips. "Drink," she said. "Not too much." She had to help him. He coughed as the wine went down. "When did you last eat?"

"Don't know."

"Finle, have you flint on you?" He nodded, and worked his tinderbox from its pouch. "Olav, get some meat from the pack. Shem, see if you can find some dry twigs." Shem trotted off. "Can you feel your toes?" she asked Juni. Shivering, he nodded. "How about your fingers?"

"I can feel them," he said, in a voice like a ghost.

Finle had the fire going. Shem came back with an armload of wood, most of it dry. They sat about the fire, shoving bits of wood into it. Olav passed Juni a strip of dried meat.

"Slowly!" Hawk said. "You'll choke if you eat too fast." His hands trembled. But he did as he was told. His jaws worked on the tough smoked meat.

His eyes stared into the fire. There were stories told in Issho, and in Ippa, too, that the Talvelai were wolf-changelings. They had been known to say it themselves. If Juni Talvela had wolf blood in him, it might explain how it was that Shem had felt his presence across so many miles.

He drank more wine, and then some water, and then wine again. His shivering stopped. After a while, he said, "I think I can move now." He came to his feet.

The sky was grey with cloud. The day had worn close to dusk. She sniffed the air. The wind had shifted. It was blowing from the east.

"It'll be snowing before we reach the Keep," Finle said. He cocked an eye at Hawk. "What do you want to do?"

Olav said, "We can do it."

Hawk frowned. Shem was weary, and Juni's thin face still had little color. "I don't want to risk it. Where can we stay the night?"

"Castria?" suggested Olav. "There'll be room in the guardhouse."

"Too far. The horses are tired."

"The Halleck steading," Finle said. "There's always room in that house, and I'm cousin to the Hallecks, on my mother's side, so they'll not give us an argument, and anyway we're on Dragon's business."

The snow started as they left the ridge. By the time they reached the Halleck steading, it was falling steadily, big thick flakes, and Juni was pale again, and swaying like a reed in his saddle. The house was large and filled with people, most of them Hallecks, but there was always room for more, and visitors from the Keep were always welcome, so Miri Halleck said as she led her guests to a chamber.

"Finle Haraldsen, I'd have known you anywhere. You look just like your uncle Sulien, and he was a handsome man, though with scarcely the wit to milk a goat. I hope your wits are better. You had the sense to come here at least, instead of trying to ride to the Keep in this weather, which is what this big ox out of Serrenhold would have tried to do." Olav grinned. "And you are the lady archer of whom my grandson Rowan speaks." Rowan was a newcomer at the Keep; he had come in the spring levy. "They call you the Hawk, and aye, you have the hawk-sister look to you. And this is Shem, grandson to Serret of Sleeth, whose dog Turtle likes to steal hen's eggs! You see, I know all of you. Save this one." She poked a finger lightly at Juni. "What's your name, lad?"

The heat in the house had revived him. He bowed extravagantly.

"Juni Talvela, my lady."

Her fine pink cheeks reddened. "My lady, is it? Ah, I like that. But it's nonsense, I'm no lady. Call me Mother Halleck if you must. But you are far from home, Talvela's son." She cocked her head. "Na, look not so anxious, I'll not question what's none of my business anyway. Take your boots off and warm yourselves. Supper'll be ready soon."

Supper was ample, though plain; turnip-and-potato stew, cheese, and beer, served by a host of Halleck women, the younger ones giggly at the presence of Dragon Keep soldiers, the older ones brisk of manner, and sharp of tongue.

After the meal, Hawk sent Shem to bed. It took a while; he had found himself a litter of kittens to play with. Yawning, Juni went with him.

"The young mend swiftly," Miri commented, "and despite that he's not so broad as this big yellow one, the lad looks like he's got some strength in him. Have some more ale." Alf passed the decanter across the table. The three from the Keep filled their mugs. It was only courtesy; to drink, and share whatever news from outside they had with folk who might not have heard it. So they spoke of the wedding, and Cirion Imorin, and the competitions, and Lemininkai's red marble palace. The Hallecks spoke of the harvest, and the hunting, and which of their beasts had survived the winter, and their hopes for spring.

* * *

BREAKFAST, TOO, WAS plain, but ample: porridge, with bits of meat in it, but served with bread over which the last of the honey had been spread. Outside, in the new dawn, snow was falling. After the meal, Finle and Olav went to make ready the horses.

"Mother Halleck, the Keep is grateful for your hospitality," Hawk said formally.

"Dragon knows the Halleck land stands ready to serve him," the old woman said. "And tell him to take care of that boy. Something's troubling him. He's got a valiant heart, but someone's been hard on him, too hard for his nature."

As often happened in March, the snow ceased to fall soon after dawn. By midday it was gone from the fields. The sky blazed blue as fire. On their right, the serrated peaks of the mountains gleamed like spearpoints. Juni stared at them.

"They are beautiful," he said.

"Aye, they are," Olav said. "Though not when you are trying to get through them, and you don't know the way, and it's snowing so that you can't see where you are, or even if you are going up or down or in circles . . ."

"Yes," Juni said. "I know."

Hawk said, "Where were you when the snow started?"

"Galva."

Finle frowned.

"It's near Serrenhold," Hawk said. "That shouldn't have been so difficult. From Galva to Derrenhold is a straight line. From Derrenhold you head northeast until you reach Dragon Keep. Only maybe you didn't know that."

Juni said quietly, "I knew it. But I had to leave the road. I was being chased, and if I had stayed on the road they would have caught me. I was on foot, and they were horsed. So I went north. I thought they would not follow me if I could only go high enough. I was right. They dropped back when I went over the pass. But I went farther east than I meant to, and when I finally found the way back, I was tired, and cold, and my food was gone. I tried to hunt, but the game was thin."

"How long had you been wandering?"

"I'm not sure," Juni said. He took a deep breath. "If you had not come, I probably would have died. I owe you my life."

Then they were at the Keep. As they approached the great granite castle, Juni Talvela's eyes widened.

He said, "Gods, it's big. I had not known it was so big."

"Is it bigger than Talvela Manor?" Finle asked.

"Much bigger. Bigger than Serrenhold, too."

"It's Dragon's house. It's where I live," Shem said happily.

THEY WENT IN through the little gate. The boys took their horses. Turtle trotted out of the stable and stood waiting, head cocked. Shem's eyes lit. He slid down Lily's side. Boy and dog tumbled over each other.

Dragon was in the tower. "Wait here," Hawk said to Juni. She went up the outer stair. As she neared the tower chamber, she heard Azil Aumson's voice through the open doorway.

Let love be all and there shall be no weeping;
In every spring, sap rises in the tree;
Sweet summer calls; cold winter lies a-sleeping;
Let all be love when you return to me.

The room was warm, and smelled of wine. Azil sat in his usual place, harp across his knees. Karadur sat hipshot on the scarred table that served as his desk.

"Well, my hunter? What did you find in the wild?"

She said, "My lord, you have a guest. Juni Talvela."

He slid from the desktop. "Juni? The young archer from Ujo? Tell me."

Succinctly she made her report. When she finished, he said, "It's a month's journey from Galva to Dragon Keep, on foot, in winter. He said he was being pursued? By whom?"

"He didn't say."

"Where is he?"

"In the ward."

"Torik!" Torik stuck his head around the door. "There's a young man in the ward somewhere; his name is Juni Talvela. Mind your manners, he's a lord's son. Find him, and bring him here. Hunter, you stay." He seated himself in the chair behind the table. In a little while, Juni appeared. He hesitated on the threshold. He looked very young.

"Juni Talvela," Karadur said curtly, "you have put my soldiers to some trouble. Get in here."

Juni dropped to one knee. "My lord, I ask pardon for my trespass," he said.

Karadur looked him over silently. Then he said, "Get up. Sit over there." He pointed to a stool. Juni obeyed. He was trembling slightly. It was not easy to face the Dragon of Chingura in his own house.

Karadur said, "My soldiers tell me that you came over the mountains to escape pursuit."

"Yes, my lord," Juni said.

"Tell me where you came from, and who was chasing you."

"I came from Serrenhold, my lord. Bork Hal's soldiers were chasing me."

"Why?"

"I left his domain without permission."

"You ran away," Karadur said curtly.

Juni swallowed. "Yes," he said. "I ran away."

"When did your father send you to Serrenhold?"

"In August."

"How long were you meant to stay there?"

"I don't know," Juni said. "My brother Koiiva was there three years."

Karadur said, "I was Erin diMako's cavalry captain for two years. It was excellent training. Erin diMako is a good soldier, and a good man. I still count him as my friend and counselor."

Juni looked at the floor.

"Serrenhold is a harsh climate, and the lords of Serrenhold are not much celebrated for their kindness."

Still Juni did not speak.

Karadur said, "Look at me." Juni looked up. "So you left Serrenhold and went north to escape your pursuers, which was a stupid thing to do, though effective. Then you turned south and could not find a way out of the hills. How old are you?"

"Fourteen, my lord."

"Still a boy. Ydo Talvela is a lord of Issho. Two years ago, when I needed them, he sent me horses. Tell me," Karadur said, "why I should not bind you, set you on a horse, and send you under guard back to your father?"

The color leached from Juni's face. "If you do, he will send me back to Serrenhold."

"And so?"

Juni looked at his hands, and then, directly, at Karadur. "I will not stay there. I will find a way to escape, my lord. If necessary, I will go outlaw." He shut his teeth. There were tears on his cheeks. He took a deep, ragged breath, and another.

Rising, the dragon-lord walked to the low table beside Azil's chair. It held a decanter, and glasses. He poured wine from the decanter into a glass and handed it to Juni.

"Drink," he said. Juni drank. Karadur gave him a moment to regain his composure. Then he said, more gently, "Why did you come to Dragon Keep? You could have gone to Derrenhold, or Mirrinhold, or Ragnar. You could have gone to Voiana; the hawk-sisters owe allegiance to no one. You could have changed your name and found work in some nameless village somewhere in the Blue Hills. Why come to me?"

Juni looked at his hands. Then he said, "The music."

Karadur's eyebrows lifted slightly.

"Is there no music in Issho?"

Juni said, "Not for the son of Ydo Talvela."

Azil plucked a harp string. It chimed like a bell. He said to Juni, "Do you sing?"

Juni said, "No. I harp. Not very well."

The singer played the refrain from "Dorian's Ride." *There are riders at the gate! Seven riders at the gate!*

Karadur said, "You are the younger son. Is your brother incompetent?"

"My brother is everything my father wishes him to be," Juni said.

"I see," Karadur said. "Difficult for you." He leaned against the desk. "I think perhaps you are suffering from a high fever."

"My lord?"

"A high fever that has led you to do some extraordinarily foolish things, such as leave Serrenhold without permission. I believe you are still suffering from it, and that given your condition it would be folly on my part to send you anywhere. You will recover, of course, though it may take some months." Hope burgeoned in Juni's face. "Meanwhile, I will send a courier to your father with a letter, suggesting to him that you join my archers. The caliber of the Atani war band is known through Ryoka. I think Ydo Talvela will be happy for his younger son to receive his military training at Dragon Keep. Get up."

Juni knocked the stool to the floor in his haste.

"Lorimir Ness is captain of Dragon Keep's forces and first of the swordsmen's wing. Orm Jensen is first of the archers. You will obey them and all Dragon Keep's officers as you would obey me. Torik! Escort our newest recruit to the barracks." Juni opened his mouth.

"Out," Karadur said.

The door closed behind the youths. As they thundered down the stairs, the harp spoke again, a trill of laughter.

Karadur, echoing it, reached for the decanter. "Imarru, what a tangle! Azil, you'll have to help me with that letter."

Azil said, "I can do that."

"Hunter, let Orm Jensen know he has a new archer in his wing. And keep your eye on the lad. Was it indeed Shem who led you to him?"

"Indeed it was."

"I should give the cub a gift. What do you think he would most like?"

"A pony."

"He shall have one." Rising, he poured wine into Azil's cup. The singer laid the harp beneath his chair. "How is he—Shem, I mean? Is it well with him?"

"I think so, my lord."

"Keep your eye on him, too. I would not have any hurt befall him. For his father's sake, and for his own, he is precious to me."

"And to me," she said.

She went to the barracks, to let Orm know that Juni Talvela, son of Ydo Talvela of Issho, would be training in Dragon Keep, and that Dragon had assigned him to the archers' wing. Juni was already there, with Finle. He jumped up as she came in.

She braced herself for elaborate thanks. He said, quite simply, "Thank you for coming to find me."

She smiled at him; she couldn't help it. He was so young.

He said, "Finle says that you are also an archer, that you were Kalni Leminin's archery master."

"I was."

"I am honored. Please teach me."

His sincerity touched her heart. She said gently, "Orm Jensen and Finle will teach you. They know everything I know."

"The child who was with you—Finle says that it was he who found me. How may I thank him?"

"You needn't. Dragon is giving him a pony."

Later that evening, she went to the apartment behind the kitchen to see Shem.

"He's sleeping," Beryl Gavrinson told her, with some heat. "He's worn out, poor lamb. Wherever did you take him, anyway?"

"Coll's Ridge," Hawk told her. She bent over the child's pallet. Shem's face was smooth in sleep.

But the placidity was deceptive: she could sense his exhaustion, and deep inside his mind, a vulnerability, an *opening* that should not have been there. She did not know what to do about it. She could not teach him; he was simply too young, and they were too different, hawk and wolf.

That night sleep did not come. She lay awake, staring at the ceiling.

In the morning, though, she knew what she had to do. She had paper and ink and stylus in her chest. She set them out on her table.

Shem would not understand. But this is what would be best. His father would have approved.

She wrote, *To Naika Dahranni, of Nyo; from Terrill Chernico, once of Voiana and Ujo, now of Dragon Keep: Greetings . . .*

14

IN DRAGON KEEP, everyone was talking about the musicians.

They called themselves the Golden Sparrows. The folk of the Keep had standing orders to make all musicians welcome, and so they had been escorted to a guest chamber and fed, and their mules cared for.

There were three of them: a burly, mustachioed man, a slender, fair-haired youth, and an elegant, dark-skinned woman. They arrived just after midday. Dragon came to the courtyard to greet them. Lita, who had escorted them to the guest chamber, brought word to the kitchen that they had come.

"They brought letters," she reported.

"From where?" Anssa asked.

"One was printed with the blue arrow. The other was stamped with the wolf's head."

"That's Ydo Talvela's mark," said Ruth. "It must be about Juni. I hope it's happy news."

"He's better off here," Jess said. No one disagreed. The folk of the kitchen liked the youthful archer; he was always polite. They knew his story. *Bitter as the winds of Serrenhold,* men said, and evidently Juni had found them so, since he had walked nearly the length of Ippa rather than stay there. Why he had come to Dragon Keep was not entirely clear to the cooks and servers and scullions, but it seemed to have something to do with music.

The musicians were not the only guests at the Keep. An hour after the arrival of the musicians, Egidio diPrima's caravan rattled through the gate, its wagons filled with oils and spices, silks and ivory, sponges, parchment, and ink. DiPrima, with his guards, scribes, and drivers, was also staying at the castle.

Having extra mouths to feed made Boris testy: he growled his orders at the cooks, and barked at Ruth when she told him that they did not have sufficient leeks to make leek pies.

"What do you mean, not enough leeks? There are fields of them!" He waved a hand. "Send the girls out to pick some!"

She told him, sweetly, not to be a fool.

"Dragon has asked them to play tonight," Lita said. "The visitors. The woman's named Khorrem. The others are Angelo and Donatello. He's *really* pretty."

"Who?"

"Donatello. He looks like a dandelion."

Boris scowled. "Tell him to stay out of my kitchen, or I'll put him in the soup." Pico, who was stirring the soup, giggled. "And if you let that soup boil, I'll put *you* in it."

Pico giggled again. Boris swatted at him with the spoon. The boy ducked: right into the path of Simon, who was carrying a bowl of cream. Pico, Simon, and bowl tumbled in a heap. Boris roared. Simon thrashed out of his path. Taran plucked the spoon from Pico's hand as he fled dripping out the door. Boris chased Pico down the steps. A black cat slithered in through the open door and began to lick the cream.

"What are you smiling at?" Ruth said to Taran.

"Simon," he said.

"Huh." Her mouth quivered.

The meal that night was sumptuous: onion pies, roast boar, vegetables sauced in cream, and cherries cooked in merignac. The castle dogs fawned outside the kitchen door, licking at the scullions' hands as they passed in and out of the kitchen. Anssa, who had a taste for fat, snatched bits of succulent boarskin off the platter when Boris's back was turned.

Ruth passed Taran a roll. He dunked it in the drippings, and slipped it to Pico, who was hiding under the table.

His year was almost up. Amazingly, he had kept his temper, and his promise. He had served the Keep freely; he had not made trouble, nor skewered Simon, nor tried to escape. Soon, in a week, two, a month, Dragon would give him a sword, and let him go.

If I let you go, what will you do?

Kill Marion diSorvino.

And then what? He still had no answer. His solitary training had given him the strength, at least, to wield a sword left-handed. Skill would come.

Perhaps he could find work as a mercenary, or a guard at a brothel: anything, to stay alive. He imagined what his sister would say to that.

Would she hate him if he killed her father? He did not know that, either.

Midway through the feast, Dragon called the head cook out to take a bow. Boris returned to the kitchen smiling beneath the jut of his beard.

"The singing's about to start," he said. "Go out there."

The musicians stood by Karadur's table. The fair-haired

one was indeed pretty, with smooth golden skin and eyes as tender as a baby's. The burly one carried a harp. The woman wore a night-blue robe patterned with silver leaves.

I gave my love a cherry; it had no stone
I gave my love a chicken; it had no bone
I gave my love a river; it had no bend
I told my love a story; it had no end. . . .

A cherry when it's blooming; it has no stone
A chicken when it's peeping; it has no bone
A river when it's running; it has no bend
The story of our loving; it has no end.

Khorrem's voice was cool and clear as water. The blond boy's voice followed hers, weaving in and out of the melody. It was a simple song, one they all knew. Then Khorrem sang a Chuyokai lullaby. Donatello and Angelo sang a set of ribald verses about a boy who went to romance his sweetheart, and ended up in bed with her sister.

"Sing 'Ewain and Mariela,' " someone yelled.

Angelo scowled theatrically through his mustaches. "Never," he said. Everyone hooted.

"Sing 'The Red Boar of Aidu'!"

"No," Angelo said. "That is a song of Ippa, and there is one here who knows it far, far better than we three southerners ever could. We would not insult him." He turned to the dragon-lord. "My lord, is there aught you would like to hear?"

Karadur said, "Sing a song from Selidor."

The three conferred. Then Angelo said, "My lords, ladies, visitors, and friends, we give you the tale of the 'White Ship of Mantalo'."

It was a song of battle; the story of a pirate ship, and of the ship that bested her. It had a steady beat, and a melodic, mournful chorus that went, *And the rains fall, And the rains fall forever, on the white sands of Mantalo!* When it ended, the warriors beat their knife hilts on the table.

Karadur said to Azil Aumson, "Now, you sing."

Azil drank from his cup, then set it aside. He said, "My lord, my friends, guests: tonight I will sing you an old song. It is the story of Ewain of Ragnar and the treachery of Gundahara." Rising, he beckoned. At his place at the far table, Juni Talvela rose. He was cradling a small harp in his arms. He made his way to the singer's side, and struck a chord.

Clear and tender, the singer's voice filled the high-ceilinged hall.

Proud heroes hearken To the doom of Ragnar
And the death of Boris, Derrenhold's king;
And of Ewain the warrior Ever-faithful;
Broken and betrayed By his own liege.

Some of the listeners had heard it before, but many had not. It was a tale of forbidden love, a king's treachery, and the death of a hero.

Ewain takes counsel With his chosen comrades;
Sworn brothers all Through battles dire;
Though treachery waits Strong hearts remain steadfast;
Dishonor disdaining; Ragnar's pride.

In the morning Women are weeping;
For brave Brunhilda, Who killed a king.
Great warriors died In the dooming of Ragnar;
Where darkness gathers And ravens feed.

When the last note of the harp died away, the hall was silent. Then the cheering started. It went on a long time.

"Bow," Azil said to Juni. "They are thanking you; you have to thank them back." Flushing, Juni bowed, and bowed again.

"Taran," Ruth said softly, "you're weeping." Taran touched his face. It was so. It was ridiculous to weep over a dead hero. Silently, he went to the kitchen and wiped his cheeks with a rag.

Eilon came in. "One-arm, there's a man out here asking for you."

"Who?"

"Some wagon driver. He's waiting for you by the whipping post."

"Thanks." Taran could not imagine who it might be. He walked into the yard. A three-quarter moon silvered the dark space. A man beside the post waved an arm. Taran maneuvered around the sleepers to his side. The man dropped his hood.

It was Edric. He'd grown a beard.

"Surprised?" he said jauntily.

"Stupefied. I thought you were dead," Taran said.

"I thought *you* were." He grinned. "I thought they'd killed you, in Lienor. Then I heard you'd been brought here. I was certain you were dead, then. They tell me you've a new name. I hear they call you Taran."

"Or One-arm," Taran said.

Edric shot a quick look at his right sleeve. "Aye. I heard about that, too."

Directly at their feet, a man lying in a bedroll opened his eyes. "Get out of here, or I'll break your face," he snarled.

"Sorry," Taran said. They moved away from the post. "How did you get out of Lienor?" Taran asked. "How have you fared?"

Edric shrugged. "Well enough. I've been doing honest work—sort of. As to how I got out of Lienor: they let me go. Dumped me outside the wall one morning, told me to leave

Kameni and never come back, if I wanted to keep my skin."

Above them, the scrape of a boot heralded a passing guard. Edric looked up unhappily. He dropped his voice to a whisper.

"Is there somewhere we can be alone? I've got something I'd rather say in private. Too many ears here."

"What sort of thing?"

"It's an offer of employment. All you have to do is listen to it, and say then yes, or no." He clapped Taran awkwardly on the left shoulder. "By Imarru's horns, I can't believe you're standing there alive! Leo and Oliver and the rest of the lads, they'd shit to know of it." He looked again at the guard. "Can we get out?"

"Out where?" Taran asked.

"Outside the walls. It's a fair night, no harm in taking a little walk, is there? Surely they don't chain you up at night like one of the dogs." He laughed a bit, to show it was a joke.

Taran wondered what would happen if he were caught outside the walls. Would they think he was trying to run? There were ways to get out without being seen, he knew.

"Come on," he said recklessly. They walked to the storage barns. The hole in the wall Pico had shown him was still there. They wormed through the narrow lightless tunnel. Then they were out. Cicadas called in the fields. The hillside shimmered in the moonlight.

"What's that?" Edric asked.

"The old buttery."

"Let's go there."

They strolled toward the moonlit ruins, past tall green mounds, and across the remnants of an ancient creek bed. The buttery stones were wreathed in thorn-clad vines. A heavy perfume hung in the night air. The June stars blazed.

"This is better," Edric said. He sat on a stone. An owl

hooted nearby. "More private. Good place to bring a girl."

Taran nodded. It was a favorite place for the men of the war band to come with their girls, or with each other.

"What's this offer you have for me?"

Edric said earnestly, "I'll tell you. But I need your promise first."

"What promise?"

"Swear by the Hunter's name that once you hear what I have to say, if you decide it's not for you, you'll forget about it, forget we talked, forget I was even here. . . . Otherwise I can't say more."

"So it's not an honest offer?" He meant it in jest. But Edric shut his lips together. "I swear by the Hunter's name that I'll forget we talked."

Edric looked relieved. "Good." He rubbed his hands together. "So. Here it is. Some mates of mine and I, we were talking, and they said, 'Why not go into the hills?' These are good men, you understand, but not ones to be overfond of laws and rules, if you take my meaning. Some of them have tried farming, or clerking, and found it wanting. Some of them prefer the dark in which to do their business. You know the sort of men I mean."

Taran said irritably, "I know the sort of men you mean. I used to be one of them. Do I know them—these mates of yours?"

"Na. Those you knew, those that knew you, they're scattered, or dead. Leo's in Issho, so I hear. Gund's dead. These are other men. But they'd heard of you: Treion the Bastard, the man who burned Castella. They'd heard of Niello Savarini, too, but he's dead for certain sure, and you're alive. . . . Anyway, these men I'm speaking of had heard of you, and heard too, that I'd rode with you. They'd talk about your swordskill, and your temper, and about how you planned the raid on Castella and got away with the loot. When we first started talking, they thought you were dead. I thought so, too, like I said before. But then we all heard that no, you were alive, in Dragon Keep, and not in no dungeon, neither, but walking around in daylight, and working in the kitchen . . . !"

Had Edric always been so full of words? He couldn't remember.

"Who did they hear this from?"

Edric shrugged. "Don't know. Anyway, they asked me to bring you an offer."

"Go on."

"They're going—we're going—to Issho. Most of them are from Nakase, but Nakase's got too many soldiers in it, too much law. The Lemininkai's strong, and getting stronger, and Lukas Ridenar's men are everywhere in the south, and it's that"—he drew a hand across his throat—"if they catch you doing something they don't like. But Issho's not crowded, and there are not so many lords with strong war bands there: the Talvelai, yes, and the Niroi, but not many others. Not so many fat merchants coming along the roads, of course, but we're not greedy, and there are not so many of us. . . . We'd like you to join us."

Someone was offering him the Bastard's Company, reborn. Taran did not know whether to laugh or weep.

"Why?"

Edric said, "You were always full of plans. We need a man who can think. But there's another reason. My mates think you're lucky."

"Lucky?" The word seemed insane. Taran touched his stump. "You think *this* is lucky?"

Edric said seriously, "It is, in a way. You're not dead, and the gods know you should be. That's the kind of luck every outlaw in Ryoka wants to have." Lowering his voice, he said in a rush, "Listen; I can get you out of here. There's a horse waiting for you, right now. If you want it."

The owl called again.

He was beyond the wall. All he had to do was walk away. No one would know.

For a moment, Taran let his imagination soar free. He rode at the head of a great company. The grassy plains of Issho spread before them. The western lords in their mansions despised and feared him, but, strong as they were, none of them could stand before him. He rode where he pleased, took what he desired, gold, silver, jewels, and left—what?

A tortured child. Ashes on a hillside. The body of a woman, stabbed through the throat.

Though treachery waits Strong hearts remain steadfast;
Dishonor disdaining; Ragnar's pride.

"No," he said. "Sorry."

"Why not?"

"You wouldn't understand."

"Try me."

He did not know how to say it. "I promised Dragon a year."

Edric gaped at him. "What the hell are you talking about?"

"Ah, well. The lads will be disappointed." A stranger sauntered into the tumbled-down building. He was bearded, big-bellied, broad-shouldered as a bullock, and he wore a black cap on his round head. There was a sword in his hand.

"Who the hell are you?" Taran asked.

"My question exactly," said another voice.

It was Herugin. He strolled out from the shadow of a mound.

He, too, was holding a sword.

"*You* I remember," he said savagely, to Taran's companion. "Edric, isn't it? So this is what your word is good for.

How long have you been planning this?" That, unfairly, was to Taran. He opened his mouth to protest.

Then he saw the others running across the grass. Starlight gleamed on a knife blade. Suddenly he was down, with someone on top of him. A forearm stopped his mouth. He bit it. He thrust an elbow into someone's soft parts, clawed someone's privates. There was a knife in his boot if only he could reach it. A boot thudded twice into his ribs. He doubled over. A hand thrust a cloth between his teeth. There were two, no, three men on top of him. He squirmed uselessly. They wound him with ropes. He could not move, not even a finger.

He was lifted at shoulders and ankles and heaved through the air. He landed belly down on the back of a horse. He yelled through the gag.

"Strap him down," a voice said. He thought it was the man in the cap. He felt hands on him. He arched his back, and kicked out. Someone swore quietly.

"Shut him up, now. Hit him," the voice said.

He yelled again.

"Do it!"

Then there was a bright light, and pain, and darkness.

THEY FOUND THE body in the buttery at dawn.

Periel, who had been in Dragon Keep a month and scarcely knew how to hold a sword, was first to see it. He promptly turned aside and was sick.

Hurin, who had been to war and knew a dead man when he saw one, turned the corpse over on its back, and sighed in pity and relief. "Not one of ours." He slapped Periel's shoulder. "Pull yourself together, lad. Go find Orm." Orm was watch commander. "Tell him what we've stumbled on and bring him here. He'll want to see it for himself. Move!"

Periel went as though Imarru the Hunter were on his heels. Hurin watched him run. There was no shame to being sick, as long as you could still follow orders.

When the trumpet sounded, the men asleep in the barracks tumbled from their beds, grabbing for their boots and swords.

"Out, out! Move, you slugs!"

In the courtyard, the merchants' armsmen sat nervously upright in their bedrolls. A few fingered knives they were not supposed to have.

Orm hammered on Karadur's door. The dragon-lord emerged fully clothed, sword in his hand. Azil Aumson stood behind him.

Orm said, "My lord, sorry to disturb you. There's a corpse in the old buttery."

"Close the gates," Karadur said.

"We have, my lord. The men are searching the grounds."

In the courtyard, the dogs were barking furiously. The dragon-lord went down the stairs. The dead man lay on a plank in front of the armory. His face was contorted in a pained grimace. His clothes were dark with blood. Flies crawled over them, and over the two great holes in his body.

"Who is he?" Karadur asked.

"We don't know. He's got no badge," Orm said. "We think he must have come with one of the merchants. He's not a soldier. Perhaps a groom, or a driver."

Karadur said, "Wake the armsmen and the wagon drivers. See if any of them recognize him. If not, wake the merchants." Crouching, he lifted the man's arm and put it down again. "I want to talk to the gate guards, all of them, anyone on the gate since sunset. See if we are missing any horses, either our own, or the visitors'." Orm saluted and left. The horns had stopped. The men of the archers' wing stood on the walls, bows drawn, facing outward.

The gate guards trooped into the yard. Dragon pointed to the dead man. "Do you know him?" They looked. All of them shook their heads. "Dismissed." They melted away from him.

Marek Gavrinson appeared at Dragon's elbow.

"My lord, we've found the marks of shod horses in the grass near the buttery. They came from the south, and go off in different directions. It's an old outlaw tactic."

"How many horses?"

"Three."

A man standing over the body said, "I know that man. That's Edric Edricson."

Dragon turned. "How do you know him?"

"He drives for Egidio diPrima, and so do I. He wasn't with us when we started; he came on at Secca, I think, or maybe it was Sorvino. DiPrima will know."

"Wake diPrima," Karadur said. "Bring him here."

In a very short time, Egidio diPrima, barefoot, with only a robe covering his pink, hairless chest, arrived in the courtyard. He gazed with distaste at the dead man.

"My lord, his name's Edric. He joined us at Sorvino. One of my drivers was wounded in a brawl—he claimed he was set upon—and this man asked for the place. He told me he had worked in the diSorvino stables, and I saw no reason to doubt that. He was excellent with horses, and a very competent driver. I asked why he was leaving his position, and he said frankly that he mistrusted his lord's temper, which I could well understand. So I took him on. Other than that, I know naught of him, for good or ill."

Karadur said, "I understand. Thank you."

The merchant said tentatively, "My lord, about the body . . ."

"We will bury it," Karadur said. That satisfied diPrima. Twitching his robe around him, he pushed through the watching crowd in the direction of his chamber.

It was starting to be light; in the east the blackness had turned grey, and the torches in the courtyard and on the walls seemed less bright. The kitchen folk had awakened; smoke was rising from the chimneys. Orm came once more into the courtyard.

Grimly he said, "My lord, none of our horses is missing, nor are any of the merchants'. But Taran One-arm is gone, and no one knows where Herugin is. Captain Lorimir has ordered the men to form search parties."

"Yes," Dragon said. He walked through the courtyard to the eating hall. Pale light fell through the narrow windows. The hall was cold. Dragon looked at the hearth logs; they flared into life. The dragon-lord sat at his table. Azil sat opposite him. A girl from the kitchen brought soup and buttered bread.

In a little while, Lorimir Ness came to Karadur's side. He looked very tired.

He said, "My lord, I am sorry, I have bad news. Herugin Dol is dead. We found his body in a ditch beside the Great South Road. He had been stabbed, many times. Men are bringing the body."

The dragon-lord walked to the courtyard. Rogys stood in the middle of it, holding his long spear in both hands. His face was white. They brought Herugin's body into the yard on a plank, and laid him at Karadur's feet. He was grievously torn; huge wounds marked his chest and belly. They had wrapped his cloak around him to keep his insides from falling out. Kneeling, Karadur laid a hand on the dead man's shoulder.

"O my friend," he said. "We should have gone to Selidor together, you and I." Tears of flame glittered on his cheeks. Fire moved beneath his skin. The merchants and their armsmen backed from him, their faces distorted with fear. But

Azil did not move. Neither did Lorimir, or Hawk, or the rest of Karadur's officers.

Finally he rose. "Have you found any trace of Taran One-arm?"

Lorimir shook his head. "My lord, we have not."

"Hawk, my hunter, can you find him?"

The one-eyed archer ran her hands through her short dark hair. She said, "I don't know, my lord. I will try."

Finle said, "My lord, Taran spoke of going to Sorvino. You remember."

"I do," Karadur said. He frowned. "Go to the kitchen. Get Boris."

The cook came from the kitchen. "My lord, you wanted to see me?"

Karadur said, "Has Taran said aught to you about Marion diSorvino?"

The cook shook his head. "No, my lord."

A small voice said, "I can find Taran One-arm."

They all looked down. Shem Wolfson stood beside Herugin's torn body.

Hawk knelt and put her arm around him.

"Wolf's cub," she said gently, "what are you doing here? You should be in bed."

He did not look at her. "The trumpet woke me. I can find Taran One-arm," he repeated. His hair was going every which way.

Marek Gavrinson said, "My lord, he's fey."

Karadur laid a hand on the boy's head. Shem looked up at him. The dragon-lord said, "How can you find him, cub?"

Shem said, "I feel him."

Karadur knelt. "Shem, do you feel him now?"

Shem nodded. "He is there," he said. He pointed south.

The dragon-lord glanced questioningly at Terrill Chernico. "Hunter, how can this be so?"

Hawk closed her single eye. Then she opened it. "I don't know, my lord. But it *is* so. I cannot reach Taran, but I can feel the link between them."

"Surely he is too young for this. It is dangerous for him?"

"I don't know that either. It may be."

Karadur's lips pressed together hard. Then he said, "Shem Wolfson, thou art thy father's son, surely." He swept the boy into his arms.

"Rogys, Finle, get your horses. Torik, bring my sword. Shem, you shall ride with me. Smoke will bear us both, and you and Hawk will guide us to Taran. Lorimir, you will hold the Keep until I return to it."

"I will, my lord."

Rogys and Finle rode into the yard. Raudri came from the armory carrying the dragon banner. He handed it to Rogys. Behind them came the grooms with Lily and Smoke.

Karadur set Shem before him on the saddle. Torik trotted across the courtyard. He was holding Dragon's sword in both hands. Dragon took it and fastened it across his back, cavalry style.

"Raise the gates," said Lorimir Ness. Men sprang to the winches. The big gates rose. Karadur rode through the gate.

The men on the walls shouted, and waved their spears.

15

HIS KNIFE WAS gone. His boots were gone. His feet were tied together at the ankles. His arm was doubled up and trussed to his body. His head throbbed where something had hit it. He was lying on sacks. His left eye was shut with something crusted over the lid—probably blood. A rough cloth covered his body. There was also, most unpleasantly, a cloth in his mouth. He smelled beer, and old boots. Had he been drinking? He could not remember drinking. Someone had, though. Edric had been there, and Herugin. No, that was impossible. He was feverish. He willed himself to wake.

He was in a wagon: he could tell by the jolting, and the steady, rhythmic clip-clop sound that moved in time to the jolts. Each jolt shot a little bolt of pain through his head.

Several centuries later, the jolting stopped. The cloth over his body was yanked away. He gazed at the stars. An unfamiliar voice said, "I'm going to take the rag out of your mouth and let you breathe. If you yell, I'll gouge your eyes out." A hand fumbled at the rope. It went away. The sodden cloth was plucked from his mouth.

The relief was enormous. He breathed, and spat, and breathed again.

He whispered, "I have money. Let me go. I'll pay you."

"Nice try. I've been paid." A hand thrust the rag into his mouth. He tried to bite it. A gritty, spatulate thumb settled on his right eyelid. It hurt. He tried to move his head away from the pressure.

"Fight me, lad, and I'll blind you. My orders are to deliver you alive and in one piece. They didn't say in what condition."

He froze. The thumb lifted. The rope went round his head again. His captor, whistling, unhitched the horse, or mule, from the wagon and took it away, presumably to be groomed, fed, and made comfortable. Taran smelled woodsmoke, and heard the crackle of flames. His doubled arm was numb. His feet were numb. The shoulder hurt, a white agony that would have made him yell, had he been able to yell. The inside of his mouth hurt, too.

He heard footsteps. Hands fumbled at his body. His kidnapper hauled him from the wagon and dropped him. The ground was chill. He started to shiver. His abductor picked Taran up—it took him little effort to lift a full-grown man—and dumped him beside a fire.

Taran stared at him out of his one working eye. His beard was black, and his head was smooth as an apple. He was big, big of shoulder, and big in the belly.

He said amiably, "Gods, you stink. You want that rag out again?"

Taran nodded. He felt hands around his head. Then the gag left his mouth. He coughed, spat, breathed. He smelled urine. Sometime during the ride he'd pissed himself.

He whispered, "Water. Please." His thirst was tremendous.

"Here." The stranger cupped his chin and poured wine into his mouth. It burned. He choked, but drank. The man gave him some more. It warmed him. He stopped shivering.

With painful effort, he turned his head and wiped his crusted eye against his shoulder. Now he could see out of both eyes. "Who are you?" he asked.

"Ralf Molto."

"Where are you taking me?"

Ralf Molto laughed. The sound curled the hairs on Taran's neck. "Home, boy," the heavyset man said. "I'm taking you home."

He turned to build up the fire. An owl hooted. The night was alive with crickets. Taran had no idea where he was. The memory of Edric floated again through his mind. It was not a dream: he had been talking to Edric, at the Keep. How had Edric come to be at the Keep? It made him furious that he could not remember.

He said, "My arms and feet are numb. If they get no blood, they'll rot."

"Too bad," his captor said. He did not sound concerned. Nevertheless he rose. Crossing to Taran's side, he loosened the rope that bound Taran's arm to his ribs. The arm flopped free. There was no feeling in it whatsoever. He re-bound it in a different position, and laid a finger for a moment on the nexus of pain in Taran's shoulder joint.

"Hurts right there, doesn't it," he said cheerfully. "How's your head?"

"It hurts, too."

"It'll improve. Or it won't, and you'll die. Better lie down and sleep now." With a practiced gesture, he popped the rag back into Taran's mouth.

He might have slept. Mostly he shivered. Morning came. Molto put him in the wagon. The sun beat down on the canvas that covered him. They were on a road. They stopped twice that day. The first time, Molto allowed Taran to shit and piss. Then he fed him wine. It stung his mouth, which was torn in the corners from the gag. He tried to pull his head away. He strained against the ropes. It did no good.

"Drink it," Molto said. He cuffed him. "Drink it or I'll stop your nose and drown you in it." The drink made Taran's head spin. The wagon slats felt hard as rock. Molto dumped him into the wagon and pulled the canvas cover over him. It was heavy. Sweat poured off him, mingling with the urine.

The day seemed to last forever. That night, Molto was cheerful. He took the hideous gag from Taran's mouth. "If you yell, it goes back in," he advised. "You need to piss again?" Taran nodded. It hurt to speak. Molto untied his belt and yanked his breeches down. "Vaikkenen's balls, you stink like a goat."

They were somewhere off the road. Molto had a fire going; he was cooking. The meat smells made Taran's stomach churn. Molto brought him to the fire and set him in front of it. He forced himself to speak. "Where—Edric?"

Molto raised a bushy eyebrow. "Dead."

"You kill him?"

"You don't remember? I must have hit you harder than I thought. Of course I killed him. I couldn't let him live. He believed it was true, all that nonsense he told you. He told us about you, One-arm. He said you can always see a lie. Some witchery in you. Is it so?" Taran grunted assent. "Useful. How do you do it?"

"Don't know." He had no memory of what Edric had told him, nor of what he had said in return. "How many—take me?"

"At the Keep, you mean? There were three of us, and Edric. At first I thought I might have brought too many people. Turned out to be just enough. You struggled like the devil. Truthfully, I didn't expect it. It was bad luck your scarred friend showed up. Bad luck for *him*." He laughed.

"Herugin." So it had not been a dream—Herugin had been there. "What—what do to him?"

"We killed him," Molto said. He pulled the skewer from the fire and waved it in the air to cool the meat. "I told Sandro and Lorenzo to drop his body in a ditch. I expect they'll think you killed him."

They would, of course. The wine, and the fact that he had had no food for days, was making him dizzy. He stared into the fire, praying that it would hear him one more time. The quivering flames blurred. *Wake! Move!* He imagined a fiery hand reaching through the air to fasten incandescent fingers around Molto's neck.

He managed one more question. "Where?"

"Where are we going? I told you, boy, you're going home. We're on the Great South Road. It'll take us a week to reach Nakase. Three days after that, more or less, we're in Sorvino, and my work's done. I saw the hanging cage they've built for you in Sorvino. It's small, too small for my taste, but solid. It'll hold you."

An iron cage . . . He had seen such a monstrosity once, in Arriccio. It had had a skeleton in it. The horror he felt must have showed on his face. Molto laughed.

"Ah, they've got other plans for you as well." He brought the flask out. "Enough conversation. Drink, now," he crooned.

Taran clenched his jaws together.

"Stubborn bastard. Drink," Molto said, "or I'll break your teeth and make you swallow them."

Helpless, Taran drank.

A FIRE BURNED in his head.

Outside him was the greater fire. That was Dragon.

Sometimes Dragon's fire swelled, growing so huge that the smaller fire was nearly obliterated by its power. But then it would shrink, and he would feel the little fire again. The little fire was Taran One-arm. He was not really inside Shem's head. He was in a wagon. He did not want to be there, but the man traveling with him would not let him go. He was sick, and afraid, and helpless. His misery made a cold pain inside Shem's heart.

It seemed to him that they had been riding forever. They were riding on the edge of the world. If they fell, they would fall forever. But Dragon would not fall, and so neither would he, because Dragon's arm was around him. It held him firmly on Smoke's back, while the road pounded beneath the horses' feet. Ahead of them the dragon banner, gold on white, snapped and glittered. Travelers on the road saw it and moved aside for them. Rogys had the banner. Finle was behind them. Hawk rode on their left. When he turned his head he could see her, but he did not have to turn his head to know she was there: she was in his head, too.

They stopped at a traveler's shelter. Rogys gave the horses water. Hawk brought food. She fed it to him, bits at a time. It tasted of ashes. He felt suddenly dizzied, sick, as if he were falling. He yelled. Strong arms caught him. A deep voice spoke to him. "It's all right, cub. You're safe."

"Hurts," he said.

"What hurts?"

"Here." He touched his shoulder and his mouth. It was Taran's sickness, Taran's pain, but it made him hurt, too. His head was muzzy, and the emptiness in his stomach—no, it was not his stomach, but it felt as if it was—made it ache. Herugin was dead, Dragon was angry—that made his stomach ache too. The twisting pain was so strong that he was afraid he would not be able to breathe. . . .

Then somehow Hawk was there, between him and the pain.

Hurts, he said to her.

I know, cub. She said aloud, "Poor babe, he has no skin."

Dragon said, "Can he endure it?"

I can, Shem thought.

Hawk did not answer.

Then they were riding again.

JUST BEFORE THEY got to Estancia, the wheel came off the wagon.

Taran, head hazy with wine, half-asleep, felt the wagon lurch. There was nothing he could do, of course. The floor beneath him canted. He rolled as it tipped.

Molto swore, "Gods-cursed flimsy piece of wreckage . . . !" Taran heard a snapping sound. The world slid. He was slammed against the side of the wagon. Pain pierced his left shoulder, vicious and penetrating as a sword cut.

Fingers gripped his leg. Molto said softly, urgently, "Keep still, or I'll kill you right now." Steps approached the wagon.

A man's voice said, "Hoy, you need help?"

Molto said heartily, "Thanks, it's fine. The axle pin's broken, that's all. I'll make another."

"You're lucky the wheel's not split. Did you lose your goods?"

"Naw. Everything's tied. What's the nearest town?"

"Estancia. It's south about four miles." Molto moved away from the wagon, talking. Like a giant's hand, the heat pressed down on the canvas. It squeezed the air from Taran's lungs. He gasped for breath. Sweat poured from him. He tried to move his legs. He could not even wriggle.

Molto called commands to the mule. The wagon lurched

and rolled. It stopped. The heat lessened. A songbird called. The sound was very close. Molto was whistling.

Suddenly he stripped the cover back. Taran gasped at the relief. "Gods, what a stench. Get up." Molto dragged him from the wagon and thrust him against a tree. Pain coursed through his shoulder. It felt like the bones had separated. For a terrifying moment he thought that he might vomit. If he did, gagged as he was, it would suffocate him. He fought the sickness with all his strength. Molto took the gag from his mouth.

"Are you going to be sick?"

Taran shook his head. "Water."

"Here." Molto held a waterskin to Taran's mouth. His lips were hot, gluey, and swollen. He sucked like an infant. The water ran down his chin and onto his soiled, fetid clothing.

Molto watched impassively. Then he said, "I'll leave the gag off if you promise not to yell."

Taran nodded. He did not think he could yell; his mouth was swollen, and the tissue of his throat was so inflamed that it was torment to swallow.

"More," he whispered. Molto gave him more water. Then he went away.

The sky was pulsating, and blue as he had never seen it before. Taran closed his eyes. He was in the shade: a blessing beyond price, after the heat of the wagon. He knew roughly where they were; north of Estancia, still in Ippa, and close, very close, to the Nakase border. Molto unhitched the mule and led the patient beast to a patch of grass. He bent to rummage in the wagon. Taran heard the sound of ax blows.

Then Molto returned to the shade, carrying a split of wood.

He slid his knife from its sheath and bent to his task. "My uncle was a wheelwright. Taught me how to mend a pin, fix an axle, bind a split wheel. Useful."

"Uh."

"A man needs a trade."

"Uh." He shifted. The grass beneath the tree was softer than the wagon planks. Birds twittered overhead. Taran looked up, into the canopy of leaves. The sunlight made his eyes hurt. He wondered how far from the road they were. Far enough so that if he were to yell, no one would hear him. He would yell anyway. He yelled. Molto swore, and jumped up, knife in hand.

He heard horses, coming fast.

Suddenly there were voices all about him, and horses, huge and dangerous. Molto was running. He saw the flash of sunlight on a spear. Molto screamed and went down. He felt the ropes about his chest and back fall away. The relief was enormous. Strong hands helped him to his feet. He recognized Finle, then Hawk the archer. Beside her stood a little boy. It was Shem Wolfson. What in the name of all the gods was Shem Wolfson doing in this place?

Karadur walked across the grass. Flames danced along his arms and through the wind-twisted gold of his hair. His eyes were white-hot. He looked supremely dangerous.

Taran croaked: "Herugin—I didn't kill him."

"Are you hurt?"

"No."

His gaze swept past Taran. "Bring him here." Rogys dragged Ralf Molto in front of him. Molto's face was tallow. Blood streamed down it from a cut on his scalp. His face was bruised. His right arm dangled by his side, clearly broken. Rogys thrust him to his knees. Dragon said, "Who sent you?"

Molto did not answer. Rogys jammed the butt of his spear into Molto's stomach. He folded, arm over his gut. Taran would have smiled, except that his mouth hurt too much.

"Who sent you," said the implacable deep voice.

Molto said, "Gilbert Nortero hired me. Marion diSorvino's man."

"What were your orders?"

"To get this man out of Atani Castle, and to deliver him to Sorvino in one piece. If I couldn't arrange to do that, I was simply to kill him."

"Did you kill my officer?"

Molto said, "No."

It was a lie. Taran opened his mouth to say it, and saw that he did not need to. Karadur hit Molto with his fist. The blow tore Molto out of Finle and Rogys's hands. He spun like a doll, and fell, face down, in the mud.

Finle prodded him with a foot. He did not move.

Karadur said, "Bring him to the Keep. I will deal with him later."

Then a great sheet of blue-white lightning fell out of the sky.

Taran closed his eyes. His hair stood on end. The lightning scorched the grass; he smelled the hot iron scent of it. He opened his eyes. He was nearly nose to nose with the golden dragon. Steam coiled from its nostrils. Its huge eyes, indifferent, pitiless, stared at him.

There was nothing remotely human in that gaze. He could not tell if it knew him or not. The fanged mouth opened in a terrible, bone-chilling roar.

Great wings unfurled. In one smooth bound, the golden dragon climbed into the sky, and shot south.

TOUCHED BY ORDINARY fire, fences burn, meadows strewn with dry grass burn, haystacks burn, wooden walls and buildings burn.

The fire that drips from the wings of a vengeful dragon is not ordinary fire. Beneath its withering caress, rivers boil to steam. Air heats until it cooks the lungs. Tools and cooking cauldrons and cages melt. Stone burns.

Inside the privacy of his big wooden house, where he was hosting a party, Marion diSorvino did not see what the citizens of his city saw as they went about their business on the streets: a great winged golden beast, arrow-shaped, arrow-swift. Fire shimmered on its wings. It traveled across the sky from north to south and fell blazing toward the city.

Seated with his companions at his lavishly appointed table, diSorvino heard a clamor in the hallway. Then the dining hall door crashed back upon its hinges, and a man entered.

Furious at the intrusion, diSorvino rose. He drew breath to shout for the guards.

Then he saw that it was Karadur Atani.

He sat down again, grinning, and reached for his wineglass. The northerner was angry, he could see that. But this was his house. "Care to join our party, my lord?" he said with elaborate courtesy. "Do come in. Teo, pour a glass of wine for our guest."

Teo did not move. Stupid boy.

"Come, my lord," he said again, "share a glass of wine with us." His guests looked from him to Atani apprehensively.

Gilberto Nortero, who was sitting at the other end of the table, near the doors, rose from his chair and started for the door. Atani turned his head and looked at him. He froze in midstep.

Atani said, "Who are you?"

"N-N-Nortero."

Idiot. He was stammering like a child. DiSorvino wanted to laugh. It was ludicrous to make so much out of what was really a private dispute. Atani had stolen something from him. He had retaliated. It was no great matter. He was sorry the plot had been discovered, but at least the bastard was dead. He hoped the death had been painful. His smiths had nearly finished forging the cage. He had been looking forward to locking the bastard into it, minus some significant portions of his anatomy, of course.

He raised his glass.

"A toast!" he said. "To justice!"

His guests slowly reached for their glasses.

Atani said, "The coward's way would have been wiser."

"What?" diSorvino said.

The room filled with light. Blinking from the dazzle, diSorvino at first could not understand what had happened, why the room had grown so hot. Suddenly the roof of his house was gone. Fire played about his feet. He glimpsed bright wings, claws the size of scimitars, and a barbed, coiling tail. He gasped, and fell, breathing flame. Huge lambent eyes stared down at him. There was nothing human in their depths.

He died then. About him the wooden walls of his mansion shriveled like straw. The wealthy, wellborn men who had been dining with the lord of the city crawled, choking, away from the ravaging fire. It followed them, chuckling. In the kitchens and laundry and stables, the maids and cooks and grooms screamed and scrambled to escape. It found them, too. Aster Minnasdatter, her unbound hair streaming fire, climbed from the window to the water barrel to the roof, and stood on the roof-pole, her youngest child in her arms. Outside the walls, between the burning mansion and the city cisterns, stood a line of men with buckets. Like all wooden cities, Sorvino had had its share of fires, and had created over time a cadre of experienced men who knew how to extinguish a fire, what would feed it, what restrain it. They knew their flimsy efforts could not exterminate this fire, but they hoped they might contain it. The man who led them—

whose parents had named him, with uncommon prescience, Illuminato Moro—stood in front of Marion diSorvino's house with a bucket of warm water in his hands. "Fornicating dung-eating bastards . . ." He felt a prick of pain. He swore steadily and indiscriminately at the fire, at the stupid, terrified people who huddled in the road, and at his sandaled feet. Word of the savage blaze had brought him from his house too swiftly; he had neglected to put on his boots.

"Hoy!" called Ignacio, his second-in-command, and not incidentally, his brother. "Lumio! What d'you think? Should we—" He gestured toward the house.

"Absolutely not. No!" Lumio bawled back. Gods, his feet were on fire. "Stay where you are, you demon-begotten donkey!" Nacio always hoped that somewhere in the hottest blaze there might be a survivor. The heat from this fire was enormous. There would be no survivors. So fiery a blaze was unnatural. He could not imagine what had caused it.

Then the man in black walked out of the smoke. He was a very big man, very fair—and he was whole. The son of a bitch was whole. That was impossible. It was impossible that anyone should have walked unscathed out of such a conflagration.

Lumio started to shout at this madman, to tell him to hurry, to run, before the fire found him again. He was holding something. It squalled. A baby. Imarru's balls, he was holding a baby. He slung the screaming brat at Lumio. Lumio dropped the bucket just in time. He drew breath to swear at him.

Then he saw the inferno in the stranger's eyes, and saw the shape of the band coiled like a living thing around his bare forearm.

PART FOUR

16

BEYOND THE WALLS of Sorvino, in Alletti and Maranessa and Bruna, farmers and shepherds and herdsmen saw the grey cloud hanging above the city, and smelled the unmistakable odor of burning flesh. "Sorvino is burning," they said to one another.

High above the smoke and ash, the golden dragon made circles in the azure sky. "The dragon has burned Sorvino."

Those who remembered it—and some who did not, but pretended they did—reminded those who didn't of the madness of the Black Dragon and the burning of Mako, twenty years before.

On the day following the fire, Angel Angelino returned from Sorvino to his home in Bruna. An olive farmer, he had been in Sorvino visiting his daughter, who had married that good-for-nothing horse trader and left with him to live in the city.

"Sorvino stands," he told his family and a cluster of wide-eyed neighbors. "The walls are intact. DiSorvino is dead, though, and his house is gone. Nothing left of it but a pit in the ground."

His wife, Maria, shuddered. "May the Dark Lady be kind to him."

Lauda, her sister, said, "Marion diSorvino was a pig."

"Lauda!"

"He was. You all know it." Lauda put her hands on her hips. "But what will happen to *us* now? Who will guard the roads, and mend the bridges, and keep the merchants from cheating us of our profits?"

The folk of Bruna looked at one another. It was a serious question. A region without a ruler risked anarchy, lawlessness, and even bandits. They all remembered the outlaws who had raided them a year ago. They had paid money to get them to leave.

Maria said, "DiSorvino has a daughter. . . . Doesn't he have a daughter?"

Angelo frowned. "Aye. There's a boy, too."

"The boy wasn't his," Frisio said.

Lauda said, "I thought the girl wasn't either."

"Oh, aye, he said that. But *I* heard she was. And there's a brother in Kameni, a scholar of some sort. . . ."

"I thought he was an astrologer," Angelo said. The folk of Bruna looked anxiously at one another. Astrologers were notoriously otherworldly, and some, it was said, were sorcerers. Not the sort of man one would choose to rule a city. It fell to Frisio, who had served as town constable and had even held officer's rank in the local militia, to reassure them.

"Don't worry. The Lemininkai will see to it. DiSorvino was his vassal."

Maria said, "The Lemininkai knows nothing of us; why should he care what becomes of us?"

Frisio said, "Because it's his business to care. You'll see. He's a good lord. They say his soldiers are honest."

Which, they all agreed, was more than could ever have been said of Marion diSorvino.

IN UJO, KALNI Leminin heard of the burning of Sorvino from Lorenzo Tullio, his intelligencer.

Tullio said, "DiSorvino is dead. So are twoscore of his friends and associates." He named them. The list included four of the town's six magistrates, all its senior military officers, the recorder, and its two bankers. "The house is gone. The city stands, though buildings nearest the Sorvino mansion took great damage."

"You're sure it was Atani who ignited the fire?" the Lemininkai asked.

"Yes. He was seen in dragon form, hovering above the house. And a fair-haired man, wearing black, with a gold band shaped like a dragon on his right forearm, walked out of the house as it was burning, and the flames did not touch him. I spoke to the chief of the bucket men, who saw him."

"I see," said the Lemininkai. "Thanks, Tullio." The intelligencer withdrew. The Lemininkai gazed out into the garden. The flower beds were bright with blossoms: roses of every description, red and pink and yellow, white lilies—his favorite—and purple irises. The trees were green and lush, just as they would have been in Sorvino.

"You were right," he said to Sarita. She sat in a chair beside the fountain. The jewel at her throat was worth the price of a house. "You said he was as dangerous as his father."

"I am often right," his wife said. "Dangerous as Kojiro Atani, yes, perhaps. But at least he was not mad."

"How do you know that?"

"He could have let the city burn. He didn't." She rose in a whisper of silks, and glided across the red-tiled floor to stand beside him. "I wonder what provoked him."

"Some stupidity of Marion's, I'm sure of that." Kalni Leminin turned from the window. "Damn Marion; he gives me trouble even with his death! There's not even an acknowledged heir. I shall have to appoint a governor."

"I thought he had a brother."

"Cosimo; he lives outside Fuld. He's an astrologer. He was the elder; by rights, Sorvino came to him. But he never wanted it. He signed a paper relinquishing his right to rule; I saw it. *He'll* be no help.

"No, I shall have to find someone else."

RALF MOLTO DID not regain consciousness.

Finle and Rogys rolled him under the wagon. He lay there, face slowly purpling, his breathing slow and labored. Molto's mule, and all the horses, including Smoke, had fled in terror at the dragon's roar.

"They'll come back," Hawk said. "Sit down, before you fall."

Taran folded into the grass. Finle brought him dried meat and fruit, and a waterskin. His mouth hurt, and his teeth were loose. He chewed slowly. It hurt to swallow.

"How did you find me?" he asked.

Hawk said, "Shem found you." The little boy sat in the hollow of Finle's arm. He looked exhausted.

Taran said, "Thank you, Shem." Every muscle in his body ached.

Finle said to Hawk, "Where is he?" She looked at him. "Dragon. Where did he go?"

She said, "Sorvino."

Taran remembered the dragon's great horned head stooping near him, and the heat of its breath, and the white rage shimmering in its eyes. Finle opened his mouth, as if to ask another question, then shut it.

Rogys said, "I wonder if that bastard's awake yet." He padded off in the direction of the wagon. He returned, frowning. "He's dead," he reported. "Now what do we do?"

"Bury him," Finle said.

"Here?"

"No," Hawk said. "Wait till the horses come back. See if that cart will roll."

The horses drifted back. Molto's mule was with them. They carted the body to Estancia, and paid the long-faced innkeeper to bury him. It was not the first time he had been asked to do such a service. Traveling, he informed them, was unhealthy. People died on the road, of all sorts of ailments. Better a man should stay where he was.

"What sort of rites would your friend wish?" he inquired.

Rogys said shortly, "He wasn't our friend. He was an outlaw."

Hawk said, "Say whatever ritual seems good to you. Have you a bathhouse? Our companion needs to bathe. He needs clean clothes, too." She passed the man some more coins. "Trousers, a shirt, boots."

The bathhouse behind the inn was small, and it smelled of sewage, but the stones in the fire pit were hot. Taran sat on the narrow seat, drinking water, and sweating, while the filth peeled off his skin. They ate in the inn's common room. The food was passable. They slept at the inn that night. In the morning they rode north. Taran rode Rogys's horse, while Rogys rode Smoke. Hawk took Shem before her. They left the mule and cart with the lugubrious innkeeper, in payment for the night's lodgings. They went slowly; Taran was still weak, and there was no need to tax the horses.

The first night they stayed in a travelers' shelter. It rained.

The second night they camped in a farmer's apple orchard. They made a ring of stones and built a fire, more for the comfort of the light than for warmth. The night air was mellow, ripe with the scent of apple blossoms. The farmer's wife brought them lamb stew, seasoned with apples, and a jug of apple wine. Finle and Rogys passed it back and forth. Hawk shook her head. They offered it to Taran, but he waved it away. Just the smell of wine made him queasy.

Finle, finally, said, "You'd best tell us what happened, One-arm. How did you come to leave the Keep?"

Taran told them about Edric's offer, and about the men who had taken him.

Finle said, "What did diSorvino want with you?"

"He wanted to put me in a cage."

"Truly?"

"Yes."

Finle said, "He must have really hated you. Why did he?"

"I never knew," Taran said.

"I thought you'd killed Herugin," Rogys said.

"I didn't."

"I know that now."

Shem said suddenly, "The house is burning."

They all looked at him. Finle said, "What house, cub?"

"The angry man's house. He's dead." He sighed gustily, and knuckled his eyes. Hawk smoothed his hair.

Rogys said, "What's the boy talking about? What man?"

She said, "I think he means Marion diSorvino. Dragon's killed him and burned his house."

"How can he know that?" Finle asked.

"I don't know," Hawk said. "He shouldn't."

So diSorvino was dead, burned to ash in his big house, just as he had wished for so long. . . . Taran wondered why he did not feel exultant. Maia would have to be told that her father was dead. He did not think she would grieve.

Their fire was nearly out, its fuel consumed. He gazed at the flutter of red thrusting between the stones. *Wake*, he said to it in his mind, *move*. . . . It rose out of the ash like a wave to shore. He felt it in his mind. His muscles locked. He stared at the bright leaping flame, astonished, uncertain. The yellow tongue of flame subsided. *Move*, he said to it again.

But whatever had happened did not come again. He glanced at his companions. Rogys, clasping the jug, was staring at the moon. Finle was removing his boots. Neither he nor the redhead had noticed anything. But Hawk was looking at him out of her single eye.

Careful, she said. Her lips had not moved. She had spoken inside his head. *Be very careful, One-arm.*

MAIA DISORVINO WAS picking raspberries on a hillside when she saw the dragon fall.

He came down fast, on folded wings. She dropped her basket. He was moving so swiftly that she did not see how he could stop in time. Without thinking, she began to run.

At the ridge, she climbed, legs and lungs burning, terrified of what she might see from the crest. At first she could not see anything. Then she saw him: a fair-haired, fair-skinned man, prone in the fireweed, head turned to one side as though he were sleeping. She clambered down the hill. Kneeling, she laid a scratched, berry-stained hand on his back. His skin was warm, his breathing even. She felt his pulse with trembling fingers. It was strong as the river in spate.

Ice coated his hair. His shirt was caked with ash. She shook him, gently at first, then harder. "Karadur," she said. "Karadur Atani, wake . . .!" He rolled over, and sat up.

Morga bounded up the hill. Tail thrashing, she thrust her nose at him. She sniffed his hands, then his sleeves. The fur on her back stood up in a ridge. She growled, deep in her throat, and backed from him, still growling.

"Fool dog," Maia said, "what's wrong with you?"

Karadur said, "She smells death."

Treion, she thought, *something has happened to Treion. . . .* She sat back on her heels, and laid her hands in her lap.

She said, "Whatever it is, tell me quickly."

He said, "Maia diSorvino, I am sorry. Your father is dead."

It was not at all what she had expected. She wondered how it had happened: a fall from a horse, a sudden sickness. . . . No. Karadur Atani would not have come racing across the sky to tell her that.

"Did you kill him?" she said. He nodded. "How?"

"I burned his house."

Surely a daughter should mourn a father. There were words a child was supposed to say, prayers to speed a parent's spirit on its journey. She had said them for her mother.

But she had not loved Marion diSorvino, and he had not loved her. He had killed Master Eccio. He had dishonored her mother. She felt no grief, only a strange and compelling lightness.

"Why did my father send men to Dragon Keep?"

"They came to take your brother."

She caught her breath. "Taran tried to leave the Keep?" Stupid Treion; savage Treion, whose name was Taran now . . .

"No. It was a design of your father's. He paid men to kidnap Taran, to bring him to Sorvino. All's well, we found him. He's sore and weary, but not hurt."

Vaikkenen, god of thieves and beggars, thank you for that mercy.

Dragon waking, Dragon flies, Dragonfire fills the skies, How many candles by my bed, snuff them out you sleepyhead. Ten, nine, eight, seven . . .

"Did you burn the city, too?"

"No," he said. "I could have. He sent men to my domain, to *my* Keep. They killed Herugin, my cavalry master. But I did not do it. I am not my father."

Herugin was the man Treion had scarred. She wondered if he had left a wife, children. . . . Karadur's face was light-filled, shining with the dragon-glamour. Mother of the gods, he was beautiful. His skin glowed like polished metal. If she touched him she would burn. She would not wait any longer. She put her hands on his forearms, then on his face, and drew his head down. He kissed her forehead, her eyelids, her mouth. They disengaged. She was shaking. Her legs did not want to move. Karadur's arm came around her, and the shaking stopped.

He lifted her, and brought her down the hill. At the foot of the hill, he set her on her feet. He lifted her hands lightly, and kissed her palms.

"Maia."

"My lord . . ." His smile silenced her. "I don't know what else to call you."

He said, "My friends call me Kaji."

"Kaji," she repeated. They walked together to the cottage. She pushed the door open. "Come in," she said. Karadur did not move. She held out a hand. "Please."

He said, "Maia, are you sure?"

He was Dragon, dragon and human, together; he would never be other.

"I'm sure."

He took off his clothes, letting her look at him. Over the last two years she had treated the wounds of farmers, hunters, trappers: she knew what men's bodies looked like.

His body was perfect. He took off her clothing, slowly, a piece at a time. He kissed her eyelids, her breasts, her belly. His hands moved on her, gently, then hungrily, but she did not fear his desire, or his strength, or the fire that shimmered in his hair and on his skin.

He said, "They say it hurts, the first time."

"I know."

"Shall I . . ."

"Yes!"

AT MOONRISE THEY went to the river to bathe. Karadur waded to the middle of the deep, swift stream and held out his hands. She plunged toward him, gasping as the water enveloped her. She stood within his arms, and did not feel the cold.

They returned to the cottage, to the bed. She lay naked, head pillowed on his arm. Despite soreness in unaccustomed places, her body felt pliant and languorous as a cat's. Morga lay on the rug, paws neatly crossed, head erect, watching them. She had whined outside the door until Karadur unbarred it.

Hip to hip on the narrow bed, they talked.

"Tell me about your mother," he said. "Was she tall like you? Was she kind? Was she beautiful?"

"She was beautiful," Maia said. "She wasn't tall, she was tiny. She was always kind to me. She was courageous. Even when she lay dying, she would only let me give her enough poppy to dull the pain." She twined her fingers with his. "Tell me about your father. You were very young when he died. Do you remember him?"

"A little. I remember the way he filled the room. He carried me on his shoulders, and taught me the names of the stars. He gave me my first knife." His voice grew meditative. "In the domain, and outside it, they tell stories of his cruelty. Lorimir Ness, the Keep's senior captain, once told me that there was only a little tenderness in him, and that he did not dispense it freely. But with me, with my brother, he was always gentle."

Of his brother he said, "We were womb-brothers. We were friends when we were young. But he envied me, that I had inherited the dragon-nature from our father, and he had not. It made him bitter, and vengeful. He was truly a sorcerer, but he sold his gift to the darkness that he might destroy me. He almost succeeded."

He stayed the night, and left in the morning. All morning she moved within a dream, pursued by heat that seemed to rise from her feet and travel up her frame to the crown of her head in inexorable waves.

At sunset he returned, soaring through the purple sky, immense and golden. Despite their breadth, his pale gold wings seemed delicate as the wings of butterflies, far too light to bear his weight.

"I brought you this." It was a fur cloak. The luscious brown pelt was sleek and sensuous as satin. He wrapped it around her shoulders.

"It's so warm. . . ." She stroked it. "What beast has fur like this?"

"A beast out of the northern ocean. It has fins, like a fish. They hunt them in Skyeggo." He lifted it from her shoulders and spread it across the bed. "And this." He held out a necklace: chunks of roughly polished amber, strung on a gold chain. She stood naked in the middle of the cottage while he fastened it around her throat.

The fire in the amber gleamed. "It's beautiful."

"You are beautiful."

* * *

IN DRAGON KEEP, the cavalry riders washed the body of their dead captain, wrapped it in winding cloths, and laid it in the earth. At meals a place was set for him, and a glass of wine poured, to honor him and comfort his shade.

Marek Gavrinson and Irok the northerner, the Keep's best trackers, each took a party of men and the dogs to follow on the heels of the fleeing outlaws. In the barracks, the men were unusually silent. No one was quite sure what had happened, or what would happen. Lorimir, who had seen such moods before, set the men to sword drill and repairs. The barracks' roof required patching, and Bryony needed new laundry tubs.

In the kitchen, Ruth was red-eyed, Eilon sullen, and no one was speaking to Simon. Even the dogs sulked in the kennel. Turtle hid in the stable, and snapped at Luga when the dogboy tried to coax him out, and would not eat.

The trackers returned, without success. They had followed a trail to the Great South Road, but lost it there.

The Golden Sparrows left the Keep, with a fat purse and fine new curtains on their wagon, a gift from the girls in the laundry.

"Where shall you go now?" Azil asked Angelo.

"South, to Ujo, then to Rowena and Salvati and Allegria. From there, if the border is still open, we'll cross to Chuyo. Then east, to Kameni, where my wife and children live."

"I didn't know you had children."

Angelo said, "Four sons. They live with my wife, in Colonna. Khorrem has a son and a daughter in Al-Assar. Donatello is a virgin, of course."

FOUR DAYS LATER, the Golden Dragon came gliding across the sky at sunset, with the red sun shining on his wings. He circled once about the castle before plunging to the Dragon's Roost. Azil Aumson, sitting in his chair in the tower chamber, heard the rushing thunder of the dragon's wings. In a little while, Karadur came into the chamber.

Azil laid his harp aside. Karadur's hair was windblown, and there was a faint shade of stubble on his cheeks. His face was impossible to read.

"Tell me," Azil said.

Karadur said, "Taran did not kill Herugin. He was taken against his will. Shem Wolfson found him. He is safe."

"And?"

"Marion diSorvino is dead. I killed him and burned his house."

"And?"

Color touched his face. "The girl . . ." He did not say any more. He did not have to. They had both known this moment would come.

"Say something," Karadur said. Azil shook his head. The dragon-lord moved, then. He crossed the chamber in three strides. His big hands came down hard on Azil's shoulders.

"Azil. It changes nothing."

"You are wrong," Azil said. "It changes everything."

SUMMONING HIS OFFICERS to the room in the tower, Karadur told them that Hawk, Rogys, Finle, and Shem would be back soon, with Taran One-arm, and another man, named Ralf Molto.

"Let the war band know, Taran is blameless in Herugin's death. Molto took Taran from the Keep against his will. Molto killed Herugin. He was sent by Marion diSorvino."

The officers looked at one another. Lorimir Ness said, "Will there be a reckoning for that, my lord?"

"There is," Karadur said. "There was. DiSorvino is dead."

Letters went out that day from Dragon Keep, penned by the dragon-lord's own hand. Two went swiftly, by courier: one to Kalni Leminin, and one to Erin diMako, in whose cavalry Herugin had served before he came to Dragon Keep. A third was written and set aside, to be given to the next merchant or musician who came to the castle. It was addressed to Dennis Amdur.

That evening, in the hall, the dragon-lord chose to sit not at the table near the hearth with his officers, as was his custom, but with the riders, with Federico, Arnor, Raudri, and the others. They told stories of Herugin's loyalty, to his lord and to his men, of his courage, and of his skill with horses.

Arnor said, "I mind the time I fell into the river below Castria, and he pulled me out."

Karadur said, "He learned to swim in Selidor. He was a good swimmer."

Federico said, "He was a good swordsman, too. No one can say he wasn't."

Raudri said, "We should sing for him." He looked at Azil Aumson, sitting quietly at Karadur's left.

Azil said, "Juni, get your harp."

The young archer went quickly from the hall. In a little while he returned with a rosewood harp cradled in his arms.

"What would you hear?"

They looked at one another. Raudri said, "Sing 'Dorian's Ride.' It was his favorite song."

Azil sang "Dorian's Ride." Folk came from the kitchen to listen. Ruth, Raudri's sister, stood with her fists knotted into her apron and tears rolling down her face. When the music ended, the dragon-lord rose, and the cavalrymen rose with him.

Karadur said, "He died in battle. No warrior can ask for

more than that." He drained his glass. Then his fingers closed firmly on the singer's wrist.

THAT NIGHT, THE page whose task it was to sleep in the hall outside the dragon-lord's bedroom went elsewhere to sleep. Within the elegant room, neither man rested. Karadur's appetites, at least, had not changed. His hunger was as demanding, and his ardor as relentless, as it had ever been. At last he lay satisfied, eyes closed.

Beside him, Azil lay, breathing hard. There were bruises on his ribs, and on his wrists, where Karadur had held him. Blood stained the quilts. The scars on his hands had split in the passionate struggle. A cool breeze blew through the chink in a shutter. The candle flame flickered in the draft. The chamber smelled of sex and sweat.

He wondered if Maia diSorvino lay awake at this moment. In the most noble portion of his nature, he wished for her what he had: passion without stint, unwavering trust, constancy and friendship. In the basest region of his thought, he hoped that she would be content with whatever wealth or honor Karadur might choose to give her: that, and her children.

He stretched luxuriously.

Traitor. I see you, traitor.

The quilts beneath his body were soft. Next to him stretched his lover, his lord, his dearest friend. Karadur was not asleep. Azil had only to turn to him, to say his name . . . But he could not move. He could not speak. He lay in the darkness, trembling. Deep within his mind, the hateful, never-to-be-forgotten voice whispered: *You are mine, traitor. You will never be free of me. The ice runs in your veins, in your heart.*

I will make you the instrument of his destruction. His downfall will be your doing. Through you his seed will rot; through you his land will wither; through you his hope will be forever silenced. Through you his line will end, and as he dies, in pain, he will know it, and know it was your doing.

You are mine. To death, and after, you are mine.

17

THE MORNING AFTER Karadur's return, Taran, with Finle and Rogys and Hawk, and Shem Wolfson perched before Rogys on the black horse Smoke, arrived at Atani Castle.

Throughout the journey north, Taran had kept from his mind all thought of what might be, or could be. Nevertheless, when the road curved suddenly, revealing the dark stones of the castle stark against the green of the hills, he felt an unanticipated eagerness. He laughed. Finle, riding beside him, shot him a curious look.

A horn blew on the wall. They went in through the little gate. Gelf and Angus and Jules came running from the stables. Barking, Turtle dashed across the courtyard, tail a blur. Shem slid from Smoke's back and fell upon him. The smells of horse and bread and laundry soap mingled in the soft summer air.

How long had he been gone—a week, a year, a day? Suddenly he wasn't sure.

A gaggle of the castle brats, led by Devin Marekson, charged from the stable and encircled Shem, pummeling him happily. Dog and children rolled in the dirt. Then Shem sat up. He wound his fingers in Turtle's collar.

"Dragon coming," he said softly.

Karadur, with Lorimir and Orm at his heels, entered the courtyard. Sunlight danced on his skin and his hair, and on the armband coiled about his forearm, and his face was fixed in the perilous stillness that his soldiers knew well.

"Ralf Molto?"

"Dead, my lord," said Finle evenly. "He never woke."

A memory of fire moved across the dragon-lord's skin. Taran held his breath. Then Karadur left the yard. The riders came from stables and field and hall, and closed around Rogys.

Taran watched them for a little while. Then he walked through the courtyard, past the armory, to the kitchen. The door was open, held so by a stone. Faces turned to him through a blur of steam.

Eilon said, "Hoy, look what's come!" He reached a hand out. "What are you standing there for? Come in!" He pulled Taran inside. As always, the big room smelled of smoke and grease and baking bread.

Jess said joyfully, "See, I told you he'd come back!" She put a hand on his sleeve. "They said some man took you. Is it true? Is that what happened?"

"It's true."

"Where were you?"

"Trussed like a turkey, in a wagon on the Great South Road. I was a prisoner."

Pico crowded close to him. "Dragon rescued you."

"Yes."

Boris said, "Let the man breathe, you hollow-headed

donkeys!" They backed up precipitously. They were all smiling at him.

"I thought I'd lost my keph partner," the head cook said. "You're too tough to kill, I guess."

"Too stubborn, perhaps," Taran said. "A stubborn bastard."

"It's good to see you."

"You, too."

Ruth touched his arm. Her hands were yellow with flour. Her hair was smooth and shining as the gloss on an apple.

"Are you all right?" she asked. "You look thin."

"My captor didn't feed me very well," he said. They looked at him in horror. Ruth handed him a cinnamon bun. Eilon thrust a beef bone under his nose. Jess held out a goose leg, the skin still warm and dripping with juice.

Simon, surly Simon, stood in his corner, pretending that nothing unusual was happening. Taran grinned at him. Simon scowled and looked away.

Eilon poked Anssa with his wooden spoon. "That's ten pennies you owe me. Pay me!"

THE NEXT DAY, Hern Amdur arrived at the Keep, accompanied by two of his sturdiest grooms, and a black-haired, skinny youth bound across the back of a horse. His face and arms were marked with scratches, as if he had been crawling through brambles. Karadur was in the training ring, watching the riders with their horses. They brought the captive to him. The riders stopped their practice to listen.

Hern said, "My lord, we caught him in the stable, trying to steal a horse. We found his own wandering across the pasture, lame. He said his name was Damian, and claimed to be visiting a brother in Castria, but when we asked the brother's name it was a name none of us knew. He had this among his belongings." Hern held out the hilt of a sword. Its blade was broken off two inches above the wrist guard. The guard showed the emblem of a running horse.

The riders murmured. Rogys said, "That was Herugin's."

Karadur took the broken sword and turned it in his hands. Then he bent his blue gaze on the frightened youth.

He said, "You will not lie to me, I think. What's your true name?"

"Lorenzo."

"Where are you from, Lorenzo?"

"Faggio, my lord. It is a village near Ostia."

"Do you know a man named Ralf Molto?"

The young man froze. Rogys stepped forward and struck him across the face. "Answer!" said the rider fiercely.

"Yes! Yes, I know him."

"How do you know him?"

"He's my uncle."

Karadur said, "The man who bore that sword was sworn to me."

Lorenzo, gasping a little in terror, said, "I didn't kill him! My uncle struck the blow. I am guiltless of his death! I swear it."

"But you were there, were you not? You watched him die, and flung his body into the waste for the wolves to find, and took his sword as a memento. And you helped ambush another man, a man with one arm, who is also my servant. Didn't you?"

"Yes," Lorenzo whispered.

"For trespass in my domain, assault, and kidnapping, the punishment is death. How old are you?"

He could barely speak. "Nineteen."

"So. You are young, but a man." The dragon-lord looked

at Rogys. "Rogys. Is there room in your grieving heart for mercy?"

Rogys, in turn, looked at the riders. One by one, they shook their heads.

"So be it," Karadur said. "Hang him on the wall."

Ashen, Lorenzo sank shaking to his knees. Four of the riders stepped forward. They hung him on the wall. As the hard summer sun beat upon the dark stones, they could hear him whimpering. He lived three days, which was long, the kitchen folk agreed, though perhaps not that long, given that he was young, and unwounded, and had not had his arms or legs broken first. Eilon said, "They die quicker in the winter."

ACROSS DRAGON'S DOMAIN, in inns and market squares and other places where people gather to talk, the news that Karadur Atani had killed the lord of Sorvino, and burned his city—or perhaps not—was scarcely mentioned. Merchants in their caravans, traveling tinkers, and mercenaries looking for an inn to guard made occasional reference to it, but the inhabitants of Dragon's domain had little to say. Most had never been to Sorvino; it was far away, in Nakase. Those that had been had no comment. They knew Marion diSorvino's reputation. And Dragon's enemies were Dragon's business, unless they came to the gates of Chingura waving swords and spears, in which case they would get a rude welcome.

Of more interest to the drinkers clustered in the common room of The Simple Lizard was the news that Taran One-arm, once a bandit, more recently a washer of pots, who had vanished from the Keep the night Herugin Dol died, was back, seemingly unscathed. There was argument in the common room: had he tried to escape, or not?

"If he'd tried to escape he'd be dead," Gerda Sorenson declared.

Kernan, who had served in the swordsmen's wing for two seasons, before returning to Castria to take over his father's farm, wondered aloud why Dragon had bothered to rescue a pot washer, and a one-armed one at that. "He's a thief, after all."

In the hills around Coll's Ridge, the shepherds' children watched the flights of the dragon and also wondered; but, young as they were, they knew not to talk of Karadur Atani's comings and goings. Miri Halleck warned her sons and daughters and grandchildren to mind their speech away from home. Maura and Angus Halland could not help but be aware of the dragon-lord's visits to their nearest neighbor. Maura said nothing to anyone, and Angus, of course, did not speak.

But others did. Tel the ironworker, come at dawn to cut a round of salt from the salt mound on the ridge, saw the black horse Smoke tied to the birches near the herbalist's. That night at The Simple Lizard in Castria, he described what he had seen to Corwin the cartwright and Small Rory. Corwin Cartwright was a closed-mouthed man. But Small Rory—so called to distinguish him from his cousin, also named Rory, who was tall—liked to gossip. In the forest the next day, he mentioned to Tall Rory what Tel had seen.

Tall Rory, being older and wiser than his cousin, said, "I would not make too much of that."

Small Rory said, "Dawn's not usual hour for visiting. I wonder what he's up to."

Tall Rory said dryly, "Best not wonder, lad. It's Dragon's business."

In Castria Market, Henk the butcher, come from the Halleck steading, where he had directed the slaughter of four of the Hallecks' pigs, spoke of the passage of the golden dragon over the farm, not once but twice in three days.

* * *

FERD PARISI HAD never visited the herbalist before. But he had a boil festering on his palm, a big one, filled with blood and pus. None of the horse ointments the folk at the Amdur farm traditionally used to doctor their own ailments seemed to affect it.

"Go to the herbalist," his wife said. "She will give you something to heal it."

"It will heal of itself," Ferd said. But it did not.

So Ferd, having first sought leave from Mellia Amdur, rode the yellow mare across the fields to the stone cottage where the herbalist lived. Graciela had told him how to find the cottage.

"You cross the Windle at Tangle Ford. It lies between the river and a round high hill. The door's west-facing. She's made a garden against the south wall, and a goat pen to the east. It's easy to find."

Indeed, it was easy. He left the mare by the riverbank and strode silently through the tall grass. As he came around to the west he heard laughter, and a man's voice. The sun's strong glare beat against the house walls. He put up a hand to shield his eyes.

A man and a woman stood before the door of the house. The woman was quite tall; she wore a long gown of emerald green, and a garland of daisies in her hair. She looked like something out of a story. The man was taller. He wore black. His hair was sun-colored, and his skin gold as summer. They clasped hands. The woman looked up. The man bent his head. A golden armband gleamed on his right arm.

Silently, Ferd retreated.

That night, in bed, he told Graciela what he had seen.

At the market the next day, she told her friend, the draper Nini Daluino.

Taran One-arm heard the news by accident. Crouched in the pantry one day, sweeping spiders and their webs from the lowest shelves, he heard Simon speak first his name, then his sister's.

"Her name's Maia. She lives outside of Castria. She's tall as a man, but pretty enough, they say. It's about time Dragon found a woman."

"You say she's One-arm's sister?" That was Gelf, from the stable. He liked to gossip.

"Half sister. That's what I heard."

"You think Dragon will wed her?"

"Some village bawd? Of course not. Why would he need to?"

Taran emerged from the pantry, then. Simon and Gelf looked up in alarm. Taran brushed Gelf aside. He wound his arm about Simon's neck. Ignoring his struggles and shouts, he marched the flailing cook out the door and ran him headfirst into the kitchen midden. "You keep your comments about my sister to yourself!"

Then he went to the tower chamber. He had never been there before. Dragon was not in the sunny chamber, but Azil Aumson was. As Taran burst in, he looked up, nodding cordially.

Taran said, "Where is he? I want to see him."

"No, you don't," said the singer. He was seated in a high-backed chair. He had a harp on his lap. "Not with that temper on you. What is it you wish to say to him? Something about your sister?"

Taran gaped at him. "You know about it?"

Azil ran his fingers along the harp strings. "Don't be a fool, Taran Unamira," he said curtly. "Of course I know about it."

"And are you at peace with it?"

Azil's face took on some of Dragon's hardness.

"That is not your business, and never will be. But *you* had best make your peace with it, and quickly."

TARAN WENT TO Boris. "I need to leave the Keep. Give me permission."

"Why?" said the cook.

"I need to see my sister."

The head cook said, "Ah. Are you sure that's wise?"

"I don't know if it's wise. But I need to talk to her."

Boris gave him permission. In the stable, a sullen Gelf helped him saddle Lace. He rode out through the little gate and turned east. The sun was strong; the sky a bright clear blue. The hills about the Keep were brown and sere. High overhead, a hopeful eagle scryed slow circles across the burnished sky. He dropped into the valley. Here the hills were greener, the pastures golden, the wheat engorged and tall. Shorn sheep drifted in placid ranks across a hillside. He had helped his grandfather steal sheep out of a pen, once. He had been drinking merignac, and thought himself heroic: Unamira the Bastard, the prince of outlaws. Vaikkenen's balls, what an idiot he'd been.

The holly was thick around the cottage door. Maia was sitting on her step. She rose to greet him.

"I'm glad to see you," she said. "No escort?"

"None." He kissed her. Her face was nut-brown from the sun. Her hair smelled of lavender. She brought him into the cottage. Morga lay stretched on the hearth rug. She opened her eyes. Her tail thumped twice. Slowly she rose, and came to him, and thrust her head against his knee.

"Would you like wine?" Maia asked.

"Gods, no. Just water." She brought him water in a cup. She put bread and strawberries on the table. The cluttered cottage seemed unchanged from the last time he'd been there. Drying herbs dangled from hooks and racks. The shelves were piled with pots and jars. Maia wore trousers and a loosely flowing shirt. Her hair fell about her shoulders and down her back. The lacings of the shirt were open. A bright green jewel dangled from a chain at her throat. It looked like an emerald. Perhaps it was an emerald.

"You look well," he said inadequately.

She said gravely, "I am well. And you? You had a bad time. Are you recovered?"

"I am." A heavy leather-bound book lay on the table. Gold lettering across the leather binding said, *A Pharmacopoeia For Physicians*.

He said carefully, "I heard a rumor at the Keep. About you, and Dragon."

Color flooded her face. "You heard that we are lovers." He nodded. "It's so."

"Are you happy?"

Her mouth curved. "Do I look miserable?"

She did not look miserable. She looked resplendent.

He said, "You know he has another lover."

"The singer. I know. It doesn't matter."

He thought perhaps it might. But it was not his business to dispute with her, or advise her. "Will you come to the Keep?"

"He has not asked me to come to the Keep."

He took a breath. "I have to ask you something," he said. "Don't be angry." She nodded. "Are you pregnant?"

"Not yet."

There were potions women took to keep from having children. He knew nothing about such things; they had never concerned him before. Pregnancy was women's business. But everyone in Ippa, everyone in Ryoka, knew that Karadur Atani's birth had killed his human mother.

He said, "I love you. I don't want you to die."

She said, "I won't die. I am strong, stronger than you think."

THEY DID NOT speak of Marion diSorvino's death, or of the fate that had been planned for him. It was not something he could speak of, yet. Karadur, he was sure, had told her about the rescue. He asked about her work, about her neighbors, Angus and Maura.

"And the child, the little girl?" he asked. He had forgotten her name. "How is she?"

"Rianna," she said. "She's very well."

When it was time for him to leave, Maia brought a carrot for the horse. Lace nibbled it from her palm. She stroked the gelding's nose and told him he was a handsome beast. A bird trilled in the birch tree, exultant.

Taran gathered the reins in his hand, and mounted. Maia said, "Come back when you can."

"I will."

"Don't fear for me. All that has happened, happened by my choice."

Her certitude silenced him.

He urged Lace up and over the ridgeline. In the east the darkening sky was clear, but in the west a feathery mass of clouds spread across the horizon, and the sun as it descended lit them, so that light streamed along them and through them. They blazed like shining wings. Wind hissed through the bowing wheat, bringing with it a hint, a whisper, of winter's chill. Summer was ending. The year he had promised the dragon-lord was gone.

At supper that night there was a guest: Murgain Ohair, once archery master at Dragon Keep, who had come to tell Dragon of the birth of his son. They toasted the child's coming with ale and wine.

After the meal, spurred by some wildness in the dragonlord's mood, the revelry in the hall grew boisterous. The men raced through the ward, and along the shadowy, treacherous ramparts. They hung ropes from the ceiling beams to see who could scale a rope most swiftly. Jon, who fancied himself with a spear, challenged Rogys to a competition with the throwing spears; the loser to clean the winner's boots for a month. He lost. The swordsmen rolled a tub from the laundry into the yard, filled it with ale, and challenged the riders and archers to see who amongst them could keep his head under longest. Evan, an archer from Estancia, who stood six feet tall and had a chest the size of a barrel, won that contest. Edruyn nearly drowned, and had to be held upside down to let the ale drain out of him. When the contest was over, they drank the ale.

When it was gone, Olav the axman, hair and beard sudsy, bellowed, "I cry challenge! I am strongest! I can pin any man here!" Whooping, they returned to the hall. One after the other, the strong men of the war band set themselves opposite the axman and clasped his hand, while the spectators counted down from ten: *"Nine, eight, seven, six, five, four, three, two, one . . . Go!"* One after the other each was solidly beaten. The final match, with Lurri, took a long time: Lurri was powerful, and Olav was tired, and both were drunk. But at last, amid the yells and exhortations of the gamblers, Olav slammed Lurri's arm to the wood. He rose, arms upflung, crowing.

"I win!"

"Not yet," said Karadur. He slid onto the bench opposite Olav, "I challenge you." He raised his right arm and wiggled his fingers.

The shouts and laughter died. Men glanced sideways at one another. Olav was a big man; nearly as tall as the dragon-lord, and with shoulders as broad. But they all knew Dragon's strength. Gamely, Olav sat, and lifted his tired right arm.

"As my lord wishes."

Azil leaned to whisper in the dragon-lord's ear. Dragon nodded.

"The singer suggests I accept a handicap," he said. "Your two arms, against my one, and the left one at that. Does that seem more equitable to you?" He cocked his head at Olav.

"Done!"

The men yelled and ranged themselves around the table. The folk from the kitchen crowded forward to see. "Ale!" Karadur commanded. Half a dozen men held out mugs. He drained two of them.

"Count for us," he said to Azil.

Olav clasped his right hand around his own left wrist. Dragon's huge hand closed around Olav's fingers. Azil chanted, and half the hall with him. *"Nine, eight, seven, six, five, four, three, two, one . . . Go!"*

The contest went on longer than anyone thought was possible. Olav's broad face purpled, and the veins stood out so on his forehead that more than one man wondered if they might burst. Karadur did not redden, though the sweat leaped on his brow, as on Olav's. But his arm, despite Olav's pressure, did not waver from the vertical. Finally, shoulder swelling beneath his shirt, he forced both of the axman's arms to the table. Olav slumped. The soldiers, shouting, flung the contents of their mugs, drenching both men.

Laughing, Karadur rose. He wrapped a long arm around Azil Aumson's shoulders.

"Give us some music!"

The soldiers shouted their approval. Azil beckoned. Juni Talvela came forward with the rosewood harp in his hands. Azil sang "The Red Boar of Aidu," and the soldiers stamped and yelled the chorus, until the hounds rose barking from beneath the tables.

When it ended, the soldiers shouted for more. Karadur, rising, gestured them to be still. The tumult diminished. The torches flared in their iron holders.

Karadur said, "Rogys."

The redhead rose from his seat. "My lord."

"Dragon Keep's cavalry needs a captain. Will you take the post?"

"My lord, you do me honor."

"You may choose your own lieutenant." The dragon-lord looked across the hall. "Taran Unamira. Come here."

The dragon-lord's shirt was wet with ale, and his skin shimmered faintly gold. The glow came from him, not from the torchlight. As always, when one drew close to him, the size of him shocked the senses.

"We made a bargain, a year ago. You promised to serve me faithfully for a year. I promised that if you did so, that when it ended I would give you a sword, and let you go." He beckoned. Edruyn, holding a sword, stepped softly from the shadows. He gave it to the dragon-lord. Karadur drew the blade from the scabbard and spun it singing with a twist of his wrist. "It's a Chuyo blade," he said. "Very sharp." Light shimmered on the steel. "It came from Dragon Keep's hoard. Some forgotten warrior carried it into battle." He thrust the sword back into the scabbard and held it out. "Take it."

Taran hesitated.

"Take it!"

He took it. He held it a moment, feeling its weight and balance. It was a lovely sword. The elegant hilt shone as if it had been newly worked. The scabbard was carved with vine leaves. The beauty of it made his throat ache.

He said, "My lord, I can't take this blade."

The soldiers murmured.

Karadur said, "Why not?"

He tried to smile. "It's too good for me. I'm a thief, an outlaw. Everyone who sees me with it will think I stole it."

Karadur said, "You were a thief and an outlaw. What you are now we will see. Take the sword, Taran. It's yours; I give it to you. You are free. You can take it, and walk out my gate."

His blue gaze sharpened. "Or—if you choose—you can stay at Dragon Keep and fight for me."

The stones of the Keep seemed to shift beneath his feet.

He could refuse. He could walk through the courtyard, and out the castle gate. He could change his name, and sell himself to someone, some merchant or petty lord, who might hire a one-armed mercenary to guard a warehouse, or a brothel, or to collect taxes. He could learn to drink wine again; as, surely, he would. He could remain solitary, without comrades or kin or history, never trusted, never trusting, lest someone, employer, lover, friend, learn that he had once been Treion the Bastard, the man who burned Castella. . . . Or he could stay at Dragon Keep.

"Make your choice," Karadur said.

Dragon sleeping, Dragon wakes, Dragon holds what Dragon takes. . . . The dragon-wraith emerged suddenly from the wall. Its silver eyes gleamed at him.

He said, "What must I do?"

Karadur said, "You must swear to me."

"Here? Now?"

"Now and forever."

Shaking, he knelt on the hard stone. Karadur's palms settled on his shoulders. The heat of them burned through the cloth.

"Do you know the words?" the dragon-lord said. He shook his head. "Azil. Help him."

The singer's beautiful voice said, "Speak after me. *I, Treion Unamira, called Taran One-arm, swear fealty to Karadur Atani, lord of Dragon Keep.*"

"I, Treion Unamira, called Taran One-arm, swear fealty to Karadur Atani, lord of Dragon Keep."

"At your bidding I will come and go."

"At your bidding I will come and go: my knife to your hand, in war and peace, in speech and silence, until you release me, or my life fails, or the world ends."

Karadur's powerful fingers tightened. "I, Karadur Atani, receive this service. As it is offered, so it shall be returned: fidelity with love, courage with honor, oath-breaking with death."

Lifting his hands, he stepped back.

18

ON COLL'S RIDGE, a badger had taken up residence in the hollow log.

It was a big badger, squat and powerful, with shovel-like claws, and a wide white stripe running from the top of its head to its nose. Shem could feel it, and he could smell it. It smelled like a skunk. It was there now, curled in a ball, and dreaming inchoately of food. It often dreamed of food. It ate ground squirrels, and snakes, and frogs, and mice. He was not sure, but he thought it was a male, because it had no babies. The bees had swarmed in August. The badger had come soon after. He had been worried, when first it came, that Morga would harry it; badgers, Cuillan told him, were fearless, and even dogs used to bigger prey could be badly torn by a badger's claws. But Morga evidently knew that; she was not the least interested in the badger, certainly not today. She lay beside him in the tall grass on her back, paws limp, belly exposed.

It was Morga who had first given away his hiding place.

He had feared when first Maia had found him, hidden beside the boulder on the slope, that she would not allow him to stay. But she had. More than that; she told him he could come to visit her whenever he liked.

"You shouldn't say that. You don't know who I am," he said. "I could be an outlaw."

"Morga would not have made friends with you if you were an outlaw."

And that of course, was true.

She had heard his name before, Maia told him. Even at that first meeting she had seemed to know a lot about him. She knew that he lived at the Keep, that he was a wolf-changeling, and that his mother and father were both dead.

"Do you miss them?" she asked him.

The question had given him a strange feeling in the pit of his stomach.

"Sometimes," he said.

She said, "My mother died four years ago. I miss her very much."

"Is your father dead, too?"

"Yes," she said. "Never mind that. Come and meet my milch goat."

The milch goat's name was Joella. She lived in a pen behind the house. She had no horns. She was brown and white, and her long fine hair was very soft, almost as soft as a cat's. She was very friendly. She liked to be rubbed on top of her nose.

"Where's her kid?" he asked.

"At my neighbor's farm. He is almost grown."

A small brown hare peered from behind a clump of rushes. Shem whispered, "Morga. Rabbit." She did not wake, but her paws twitched. He gazed down the hillside. It was covered with spiky purple fireweed; it was a perfect place for a small boy to hide, undetected. Finches skittered through the grass.

The woman with the red hair was leaving the cottage, basket on her arm. Maia stood at the gate to watch her leave. Then she looked up the slope of the hill, and waved. She was wearing her blue gown, and her hair fell loose past her shoulders. Shem thought she was beautiful.

"Dog," Shem whispered. "Wake up, dog."

Morga opened her eyes, sneezed, and rolled to her feet. Side by side they loped down the hill.

"Hello," Maia said. She smiled and trailed her fingers through his hair. He liked it. "There's bread and honey and milk in the cottage. Do you want some?"

He did, of course. Maia's cottage was not like any other place he knew. It smelled wonderful. Dried herbs dangled from the ceiling. It was rather like what he imagined a witch's house would be, but Maia was not a hedge-witch, but an herbalist. She made teas and potions and ointments. He was not the only person from the Keep to visit her. Taran One-arm came. So did Bryony Maw.

So did Dragon. Shem had not told anyone in the castle that he had seen Dragon visiting the herbalist who lived on the ridge, but people knew.

"Who was that lady?" he asked around a mouthful of bread. "The red-haired one."

"Her name is Graciela Parisi."

"What did she want?"

"A tea for headache, and to talk."

"What does she talk about?"

"She tells me what is happening in Castria."

"What did she tell you?"

"Many things. Let's see if I can remember some of them. Sinnea Ohair has had her baby at last: a boy. They named him Conal." He listened, not to the words, though he heard them, but to the cadence of her voice, which reminded him of something he had loved. "The red mare at Amdur farm foaled last week. That's uncommon, so late in the year. They were up all night delivering her. Now, you tell me the news from the Keep."

So he told her that Beryl Gavrinson, wife to Marek Gavrinson, mother of his best friend Devin, was pregnant, and that Juni Talvela had learned to play "The Red Boar of Aidu," and that Taran One-arm had sworn fealty to Dragon. He was training with the war band, wearing a dagger, not a sword; training with a throwing spear, and sleeping in the barracks with the soldiers.

"Yes," she said, "I heard that. When is Beryl's baby to be born?"

"Sometime around New Year's Moon. He's big enough to kick now. I felt him."

"How many children does she have?"

"Brian, Devin, Mira, Elise . . . Four. There was another, she told me, but it died. But this one is strong."

"How do you know?"

"Beryl says so. And I can feel it."

He had felt it from the beginning, like a little piece of warmth inside her. He had not, at first, known what it was. At first it had seemed fragile and tiny, smaller than a seed. But now it was bigger, more solid. There was a seed inside Maia, too. It was different from the being inside Beryl: it was smaller, and fiercer. It glowed, like an ember in the darkness. He thought perhaps Maia did not know it was there.

He stayed a little longer with her. Then Arafel, from the Halleck steading, came to get a potion to stop her mother's cough. So he left. Maia gave him a carrot to give to Bella. He fed it to her. She blew bits of it back at him affectionately. He unlaced her reins from the birch tree. He had to use a stump to mount, but he was used to that.

He stopped at the well in Castria for water. The hills,

which had been green all summer, were yellow and crimson and brown. The tock, tock sound of the woodcutters' axes echoed through the forest. The first time he had come this way, with Hawk, on Lily, he had thought it a long, wearisome ride. But now it did not seem long to him at all.

He rode through the trees and out again to an open meadow. Mice scurried through the stubby brown grass. A fearful grouse fluttered up from its nest. Its mate followed, squawking, *Hunter, hunter!* He looked up, expecting to see the shape of a falcon or hawk, but the white wide sky was empty.

Suddenly, a human figure rose up out of the burnt grass. Bella shied violently. Shem clamped his legs hard on her ribs. "Easy!" She danced, and finally quieted. He patted her neck. "It's all right," he told her.

The stranger's eyes were yellow as sunflower; she wore leather breeches and a pale shirt, and a jerkin, and tall boots. Her tawny hair gleamed at the tips, as though it had been dipped in molten silver. She smelled of cinnamon and new green grass, and something else, something subtle and unfamiliar. . . . She wore a small knife at her right hip, no sword, no bow. He wondered where her horse was. Perhaps it had thrown her, and run into the hills. Or perhaps she had none.

She held up both hands, palms out, to prove they were empty. As he had seen the men do, Shem put his hand on the hilt of his knife.

"Peace to you," he said.

"Sorry to have startled you," she said. "Is this the way to Dragon Keep?"

He knew then she was a foreigner. Everyone in Ippa knew the way to Dragon Keep. He pointed north. "Dragon Keep is that way. If you follow the road, you'll find it. I'll help you catch your horse if you like."

She said, "I'm on foot. Thank you for your offer, though."

She stepped back. Clearly she meant him to ride on past her, and so he did. Halfway across the meadow he looked back, but could not see her.

AT THE KEEP, a caravan clogged the way to the main gate. The caravan guards sat in the sun beneath their flapping flags. In their brightly colored caps they looked hot, and bored. Shem weaved Bella carefully through the press of big horses.

The merchant stood before the gate, talking earnestly with Derry. Shem liked Derry, who had once been Dragon's page, and was now grown, and in the war band.

"Hey," he said, "it's me."

"Shem. What are you doing on this side of the gate? Go ahead, go in."

He brought Bella to the stable. Turtle frisked from a stall, tongue lolling, and jumped to lick his face. "Down. Sit." Kneeling, he pressed his face into the dog's fur. He gave Bella water and rubbed her down, taking care to check her hooves for cracks. Then he went to the forge. The forge was hot; it was always hot, even in winter. Devin stood beside Rannet, Telchor Felse's tall son, helping him pump the big bellows. Sparks flew around his ears. His face was smeared with soot. They grinned at one another.

Devin said, "Hey. Kiala was looking for you earlier."

"Whyfor?"

"Something about a shirt."

Kiala was always fussing at him about his clothes. He grew quickly; it was, Hawk said, the changeling blood in him.

"What did you tell her?"

"I told her I didn't know where you had got to."

They grinned at one another. When first he had started

stealing away to Maia's house, he had created a maze of half-truths, telling Devin one thing, Rogys another, Kiala a third, so that no one would know that he had left the Keep. He did not mind lying to Kiala. But Devin was his friend, his best friend, and he hated lying to Devin. So he told Devin about Maia. So far, Devin had kept his secret.

Rannet made an irritated noise. Devin bent to his task. A spark lit on his shoulder. Shem brushed it away quickly before it made a hole in his shirt.

Devin said, "You know, I'm thirsty."

"I could do that," he offered. He put his hands round the bellows poles.

"Steady," Rannet warned.

"I know," Shem said. He pumped in a steady rhythm, keeping the fire hot, while Rannet held the tongs with one hand and worked his hammer with the other. Devin slipped out to get a drink of water and wipe the soot from his eyes. Then he came back. Shem relinquished the poles. They took turns pumping, until Kiala came in.

"How come you're never where I want you to be when I look for you?" she said. She glared at Devin. "Where have you been all day? Gods, you're filthy! Come on. You can't stay like that."

"Why not?"

"Because it's disgusting." She dragged him to the laundry and made him stand in a tub and be scrubbed, and pulled a clean shirt to wear from out of his chest, and a partially clean pair of breeches, and made him put them on, despite his protests. "And stay out of the dirt!" she ordered.

It was an impossible prohibition; every part of the Keep had its own kind of dirt. Shem climbed the stairs to the roof, to the place near the kitchen chimney, where no one would find him and make him do anything he did not want to do. Scents from kitchen and stable, forge and field washed over him. A drift of cloud like lambswool scudded across the sky. He drew a deep breath in through his nostrils. The weather was changing. Frost was coming; he could smell it. Dragon was in the tower; Shem could feel the hidden heat of him across the castle. It warmed him.

He heard the scrabble of claws on stone. A cold nose poked his chin. A warm tongue lapped across his cheek. "Dog," he said softly. "You dog."

BY THE TIME the horn blew to call the Keep to supper, he was hungry again. As he went into the hall that night to eat, Devin caught his sleeve.

"There's a stranger at Dragon's table, a woman," he whispered. "She's odd: not a merchant, and not a messenger, either. Go look."

Strangers were interesting. Curious, Shem strolled between the tables, Turtle at his heels. Dragon had not come to the table yet. But Lorimir was there, and Orm, and Marek, and Hawk, and beside Hawk sat the sunflower-eyed woman who had loomed like a revenant out of the field. He smelled her scent, the cinnamon-grass scent he had smelled in the field, but deeper, more intense. Something in his mind cried *Danger, danger*. He started to retreat. But she had seen him. Her yellow eyes met his. He felt a prickle of sensation in his head.

Turtle growled his singing growl. "Hush," he said to the dog. He slid his fingers under Turtle's collar. The hair on the brown dog's back was raised and bristling.

Hawk said, "Shem, this is Callista Dahranni, your father's sister. She has come from Nyo, in Nakase, a long, long way."

"Why?"

"To greet you."

Callista said, "Greetings, Shem Wolfson, brother's son. My mother, your grandmother Naika, sent me."

Your father's people live in Nakase, by the Crystal Lake, where the river ends. It is a long, long ride from Dragon's country, farther even than Ujo. Someday they will come for you, and you will go to them.

Shem stared at the stranger, the first of his own kind he had ever met, and hated her. He backed from the table, dragging Turtle with him. His heart was pounding. Then Dragon came into the hall. Everyone stood. The servers came from the kitchen with the big platters filled with meat, and baskets of soft white rolls.

Devin bobbed up beside him.

"What's happened?" A moth fluttered past them, on its way to oblivion in a candle flame. "Something's the matter, I can tell. What is it?"

"Nothing. Go away, leave me alone." He sidled into the corner where the servers kept the brooms. It was a shadowy place, away from the torches, a place from where he could watch, and listen, and not be seen. *Danger, danger.* He listened to the men talking. They were talking of hunting. A trapper had stopped at the Keep that morning to say that he had seen elk in the northern woodlands.

"It's early for elk," Marek said. "It hasn't even snowed yet. Last year it was November before they came."

Lorimir said, "It will be an early winter."

Azil the singer sang, and Juni Talvela played, his fingers dancing on the harp strings. Azil sang "The Red Boar of Aidu," and "Tirion's Hunting," and "The Riddle Song."

Then Dragon asked Callista Dahranni if there was a song she wished to hear.

She said to Azil, "Do you know 'Benta's Lament?' It is a song from Issho."

"I know it," the singer said. He took the harp from Juni.

Shem had never heard the song, and so he listened intently. It told the story of a warrior who returns to his home after a terrible battle, and finds all changed; his wife and children gone, and strangers in their places. He walks around his manor, and speaks to people, but no one can hear him. At last he realizes that these are his descendants, and that he is a ghost.

Grieved, but content—for the land is rich and fruitful, its people fed—he lays his broken sword upon the hearthstone of his hall, and walks into the mist.

Let the mountain be my gravestone, and let no man speak
my name,
That I may sleep, that I may sleep.

The music was sad, but it stirred the blood like one of Raudri's horn calls. When it ended, the men shifted on the benches, their faces hard and thoughtful. The servers brought the wine round a final time. Slowly the hall cleared, as men left for their posts, or for their beds, until only the folk at Dragon's table were left.

A deep voice spoke inside Shem's head.

Shem Wolfson. Come here.

Shem walked across the hall to the table where his lord sat, with Azil the singer, and Finle, and Rogys, and Hawk, and Callista Dahranni. Lorimir had gone. So had Marek and Orm and Lurri. Juni Talvela sat at the end of the bench, running a soft cloth over the rosewood harp.

"My lord, you sent for me," he said.

Dragon said, "You didn't eat."

"I wasn't hungry," Shem said stiffly.

"My wolf cub not hungry? Impossible," Dragon said. A smile flickered at the corner of his mouth. Then the smile went away.

He said, "Your father's sister Callista came from Nakase, a long journey, to meet you, and you would not speak to her. Tell me why."

"I don't know her."

"She is your kin, your father's sister. She is wolf, like you."

"I don't care," Shem said.

"You have kindred in the west, cub. It is fitting that you meet them, and know them."

A black wind of despair blew through his heart. "I don't want to know them. I don't want to leave Dragon Keep. You said, 'Dragon Keep is your home.' You said so. You must remember."

Dragon said, "I did say so. I say it now again. Dragon Keep is your home, forever and ever. You are mine. Your father pledged you to my service when you were not a year old. You shall serve me, and when I am gone, you shall serve my son or daughter, whichever it shall be.

"But it is right that you should know your father's people. Therefore, it is my command that you shall go with your aunt, cub, and when you have learned what your people can teach you, you will return. A warrior goes where his lord commands. Do you understand?"

"Yes," Shem said.

Dragon reached a hand out and ruffled his hair with his long fingers. "It will not be so bad, cub. You will see."

Then Dragon rose, and the officers, too. Dragon left, with Azil Aumson at his heels. The servers came from the kitchen with their brooms and cloths. The dogs snuffled beneath the tables. Shem looked at the sunflower-eyed woman, and she looked gravely back at him.

He said, "When must we leave?"

"In a few days," she said.

"Is Nyo far?"

"Reasonably far. A few weeks' journey at best. Longer if the weather turns bad."

Turtle pressed against his leg. He said, "I would not like to go without my dog. I raised him from a pup. It would break his heart to be left behind."

She said, "Of course he shall come with you."

"Bella, too?"

"Who is Bella?"

"My pony."

She said, "Yes, of course. Both can come." And somehow that made it not so terrible. She beckoned. "Let us go from here. I want to show you something."

They walked into the courtyard. Night was approaching fast, and with it rode the frost that he had smelled in the air that afternoon. High above, on the wall, halos ringed the torches. He sniffed the moist, chill wind, tasting it in his throat.

He said, "It smells like snow."

She said, "I smell it, too."

But Cuillan could smell snow, too, and so could old Jon Duurni, and Lorimir, too, sometimes. Was what he smelled different from what they smelled? He did not know.

He said, "What do you want to show me?"

She knelt, and pulled the shirt back from her throat, exposing a bright jewel on a golden chain. "This. Do you know what it is?" He shook his head. "Look closely." He looked, and saw that it was a lump of yellow amber, rough carved in the shape of a wolf's head. "I made it, when I was fourteen. It's a talisman. It is changeling-magic. Every changeling makes a talisman: it is the device through which we receive and direct our powers. Dragon has one: the ring he wears on his arm. Your father had one, a silver pendant. You will have one, too."

"Every changeling has a talisman?" he repeated. "Hawk doesn't."

"Terrill Chernico's talisman was lost. That is why she cannot fly."

He had known that. Surely he had known that.

"May I touch it?" he asked. She nodded. He brushed his fingertips against the amber. It was warm from her skin.

"It's pretty," he said guardedly. "How does it work?"

She said inside his head, *Like this.* Light shimmered across his vision like a curtain blowing in the wind. He blinked. His heart jumped. Sleek as shadow, a wolf with a tawny, silver-tipped coat stood before him. It gazed at him out of sunflower eyes.

The light came again. The wolf vanished. Callista stood looking at him. They stared at one another. *When you are older, you will learn to do that. I will teach you.*

He shivered a little, at that touch inside his mind. The hairs on his arm lifted, then settled.

What might it feel like, to be wolf, to have a wolf's grace and agility and power, to know the world as a wolf would know it, with its secret scents and whispers?

He said, "I can find things that are lost. Buttons. Buckles."

"Can you find people?"

"Yes. I found Juni Talvela when he was lost. And Taran One-arm."

"Your father found me, when I was lost." She smiled. "I was scarcely two, a cub, and I wandered away from my mother's door, and could not find my way home. It was late in autumn, nearly winter, and I was frightened and cold. I hid in a blackberry thicket. He found me and brought me home."

He said, "Did you know my mother?"

"No. It's a grief to me that I never met your mother. But your father loved her, and so I know she was clever and tender and good. I know that she made him happy."

The gentle words made Shem's throat close up. He swallowed. He could still recall the shape of his mother's face, and her smell. But he could no longer hear her voice.

His stomach fizzed. He was, abruptly, ravenously hungry. How silly he had been not to eat. Perhaps Devin had saved him something, a roll or a bit of goose tart. . . . His stomach grumbled, more loudly.

Callista said, "I'll wager there are leftovers in the kitchen."

They went to the kitchen. The scullions were scouring the last of the pots. Simon was there, Simon, the stew cook, whom Shem did not like, but so was Ruth, who was always kind, and Boris the head cook, and Taran One-arm, seated at a little table over a checkered board, with a knife in his belt, and no apron, playing keph by lamplight. And there was food: bread, and bits of goose in a rich wine sauce, and something sweet. Sitting on a stool, with a platter on his lap, Shem ate it all so swiftly that he barely had time to taste it.

Then they were alone, in the chamber behind the kitchen. He could see the red glow from the fire, where Devin slept. His stomach was full. He was warm again, and sleepy.

Something niggled in his mind. He said, "Can I ask you a question?"

Callista said, "You can ask me anything, cub."

"When I become wolf, will I still be me?"

She looked down at him. "You will always be you. Who else would you be?"

"When Dragon Changes, he forgets that he is human."

She said, quite sharply, "Who told you that?"

"Captain Lorimir said it to Marek. I heard him. He said, *Never forget, he was Dragon in the womb. When the dragon-rage takes him, all you can do is run, and pray that he remembers who he is before everything around you has turned to ash.*"

"Ah," Callista said. "It is true that when they are angry,

the dragon-changelings have been known to forget that they are human."

"When I am wolf, will I forget, too?"

"No," the wolf-changeling said firmly. "You will not. It is not a thing that happens to wolves."

HE SAID GOOD-BYE to Beryl, which was hard, and to Kiala. She cried. He went to all his favorite places in the Keep and said farewell to them, to the warm place by the kitchen chimney, the old buttery, the green mounds where the ghosts walked. . . . The dogs in the kennel whined and licked his face when he told them he was leaving.

"I'll be back," he said to them. "I promise I'll come back."

He said good-bye to Mira. *She* cried.

"I'll be back," he said to Devin. "Dragon Keep is my home. Dragon said so."

"I know," Devin said. "I heard him."

He gave Devin the glittery sharp piece of dragon's claw he had found in the buttery. He gave Mira the scrap of velvet that he had picked up from the floor of the sewing room, and kept because it reminded him of the color of his mother's eyes, a color he could no longer remember. . . . He said good-bye to Rogys. It was hard to do. He liked Rogys very much.

"Safe journey, cub," the rider said, and gave him a brief hard hug about the shoulders.

It saddened him that he could not say good-bye to Maia and Morga, but Maia he knew would understand, and Morga, he thought, would not miss him very long.

The night before he was to leave, he sat at Dragon's table, with Rogys on one side and Hawk on the other. "Here, cub," Dragon said, and poured wine into a cup. Shem sipped—he knew if he drank it all at once it would make him dizzy, or sleepy—and ate, and listened to the officers' talk. At the end of the meal, when the servers had taken the plates from the tables, and left the wine, Dragon said to Hawk, "Hunter. Tell us a story."

Hawk said, "What would you hear, my lord?"

"Let Shem choose." They all looked at him. Dragon was smiling.

He said, as he always did, "Tell a story about a dragon."

"As you wish," Hawk said. She leaned her elbows on the table.

"I shall tell you a story of the First Dragon.

"They say that when the First Dragon fell to earth, thousands of years ago, at the very beginning, when the world was new, he was wholly dragon, not human, and his nature was of starstuff. For Tukalina the Mother had plucked him from the Void, and shaped him with Her hands into dragon form. Wings She gave him, and shimmering scales, and a great proud head, and talons mightier than any eagle's. And when she had finished, She flung him toward the earth. *Go, child of fire*, She said, *and make thy home*.

"Burning, the First Dragon fell through the sky. And the denizens of the world looked up and saw that bright burning being falling toward them, and did not know what it was, save that it was beautiful. And the beasts said, 'Surely this is a new kind of thing.'

"But as the dragon fell closer, they saw that he had wings. And the birds said, 'Surely this is a bird, the most beautiful of all birds. We shall call to it and welcome it.' They spoke to the dragon and said, 'Come, bright one. Come make a home among us.'

"So First Dragon looked at all the places where the birds

made their home. He saw grouse resting in fields, and sparrows in bushes, and jays and magpies and mockingbirds in trees, and owls in barns. But none of those places seemed good to him. The fields were too low, and the trees too small, and the barns were cramped and dark, and they smelled strange.

" 'I cannot live here,' he told the birds.

"They said, 'Go to the sea, and look there.'

"First Dragon flew to the sea and found birds nesting in the cradle of the waves. But the sea was wet and windswept. 'I cannot live here,' he told the birds.

"They said, 'Go to the ice, and look there.'

"First Dragon flew to the ice, and there he found fat, stubby-winged birds that swim, and do not fly.

" 'I cannot live here,' he told the birds. 'It's cold.'

" 'Go to the desert,' they said.

"He flew to the desert, and found wingless scaly beasts nesting in the sand, who gazed at him with knowing eyes. But the desert had too much sand, and no place to roost. 'I cannot live here,' Dragon told the birds. And First Dragon was very tired, for he had been to fields and sea and ice and desert, and in none of them had he found a resting place.

" 'Go to the mountains,' the birds told him.

"So First Dragon flew to the mountains. They were high and inaccessible and wild, with powerful winds upon which he could soar.

"I could live here, he thought.

"Then he heard a noise unlike any that he had heard before. He followed it, and found a nest, and four little beings in it, with their mouths open. Then a white bird with huge wings holding something in its talons spiraled out of the sky. It dropped into a hollow of rock.

"First Dragon said: 'White bird, what is thy name?'

"The white bird said, 'I am Condor.'

" 'Where dost thou live?'

" 'I live here. This has been my home from the beginning of the world.' And as Condor spoke, she opened her talons, and dropped what she held into her nest. For at the beginning, Condor's nature was not as it is now, an eater of the dead. At the beginning, Condor was a hunter.

"First Dragon looked at Condor's nest. And he said to Condor, 'Go away. I want this place. I want to live here.'

"First Condor said, 'I shall not. I was here first. You go away.'

"But First Dragon did not want to go. So he breathed against the rocks, with his fiery breath. Condor spread her wings, and fled before the fire. But the condor chicks could not fly, for they had just been hatched into the new-made world. And so they died.

"And First Dragon folded his wings, and landed in the place where the Condor's nest had been.

" 'Go,' he said. 'This is my place now.'

"First Condor screamed in grief and rage. So great was Condor's grief that Tukalina, Mother of all, heard it. Spreading Her dark wings, She flew through the sky like a storm cloud until She came to the mountains.

"She said, *Why dost thou lament, my child?*

"Condor answered, 'O Goddess, Mother of us all, my babies are dead. This bright burning thing has killed them.'

"And Tukalina, looking down, saw First Dragon, and knew him. And Dragon looked up, and saw his maker, vast and terrible, with stars in Her hair, and all of night riding on Her wings. And he bowed, for even Dragons bow before the gods.

"Tukalina said to him, *What hast thou done, child of fire? Thou hast killed Condor's children*.

"Dragon answered, 'I sought a home, Mother.'

"And Tukalina looked at First Dragon, and saw that he did not know what he had done, for though his form was flesh, his nature was still wholly that of starstuff. She passed the shadow of her left wing over First Dragon as he stood amid the rocks. And as the shadow of the goddess's left wing passed over him, First Dragon changed. His wings and tail and claws and fangs dissolved. His integument grew soft and without covering. His eyes shrank. His spine straightened. He grew legs, arms, hands, feet. In short, he became human.

"And First Dragon looked at his new shape, and said to Tukalina, 'What is this? Where are my wings and fangs and claws?'

"Tukalina answered, *This is thy new form.*

" 'What wrong have I done, that you so punish me?'

"That thou will learn. Go thou, and make thyself a home among men.

" 'I hear and obey,' First Dragon said. And First Dragon walked down the mountain toward the houses of men. But even though he wore a human shape, those houses still seemed small and dark to him, and they smelled strange. So he halted midway between the human places and Condor's nest, and there he built a shelter. It was a rude place, built of stone. Men called it—still call it, though it is much changed—Dragon's Keep.

"But First Condor stood over the blackened corpses of her children, and shrieked her grief, and would not be comforted.

" 'Give me back my babies!' she cried to Tukalina. 'You are goddess. Make them live!'

"But Tukalina said to her, *I cannot. Cendrai the Gatekeeper has admitted them to the Void, and even I cannot bring them back. To do that would displease Grandmother.* For even Tukalina the Mother Goddess, Maker of the world, fears to displease

Grandmother, Whose bones are the universe itself. She sleeps now, and in the fabric of Her dreams all beings, gods and stars and beasts and changelings and humans, have their being. But if Grandmother were to wake, all, all would change.

" 'Then give me vengeance!' First Condor cried.

"What vengeance dost thou desire?

"And Condor looked down upon the Dragon's Keep, and said, 'Let me eat him.'

"It shall be so, Tukalina said. And she passed the shadow of Her right wing over Condor's head. Condor's nature changed: she became, not a hunter, but a scavenger. The peak where Dragon first acquired human form became known as the Dragon's Aerie. We call it Dragon's Eye. Condor still lives in the crags above Dragon Keep. And Condor hates the dragon-kindred. Her greatest lust is for the flesh of dragons.

"But the dragon-kindred know this, and for this reason, it is said, that when dragons come to die, they do not die as others do, in the arms of friends and kindred. When their time comes to die, they leap into the sun.

"No one ever finds the bones of dragons."

When it finished, Callista said, "Ah, that was a fine story."

Hawk bowed her head. She said, "Thank you, Callista of Nyo. Your brother, too, enjoyed my stories."

Then Dragon drew a knife from his belt. It was beautiful. The sheath was crimson leather. Shining blue gems studded the hilt.

"Shem Wolfson."

Shem's heartbeat made a little skip. "My lord?"

"I gave this knife as a gift to your father. When he died, it came back to me." Drawing it from the sheath, he turned it to the candlelight, showing the delicate cloudlike pattern on the narrow blade. "It's yours, now. Take it, and wear it. It will remind you of my pledge, that Dragon Keep is your home forever." He slid the knife back into the sheath.

Callista's voice spoke inside Shem's head. *Go. Take it from him, cub.*

Squirming from the bench, he walked around the other side of the table to where Dragon sat, and reached both hands for the knife.

Karadur laid it in his palms.

19

MIDMORNING, AFTER THE hunters had left the castle, Azil Aumson packed for his journey.

He had spent plenty of time in the castle's map room; he knew where he had to go and how to get there. Spare breeches, a warm shirt, his warmest, it would soon be fully winter, leggings, gloves. He looked for, and found, the scarlet wool scarf which Thea Serretsdatter, Shem's dead mother, had made for him. He stuffed it into the pack.

His harp lay beside the pack. All the strings but one were tucked into his inside pocket, next to the elk-horn pick Liam Dubhain had fashioned for him.

The hunters had left at dawn. They would be halfway up the flank of Dragon's Eye by now, Karadur in front, his whole face shining with his delight in the chase, his spirit untroubled and happy. Azil had counted on that. The Keep was not empty, of course: Hawk was about, and Lorimir, and Taran. None of them had much taste for the hunt.

His mother, too, was somewhere in the castle, doing the

honorable, meticulous work she had been doing for twenty-five years. He did not intend to say good-bye to her: it would break her heart, and he had done that already. He would take no weapons, save his little knife. He did not expect to need them, and there were none his hands could grip. A voice in his head yammered at him steadily, telling him not to be a fool, there had to be another way, he did not have to do this. . . . He knew that voice well; it was only fear. He ignored it.

The other voice, which sounded like Tenjiro Atani's, and was not, was also silent. It rarely spoke during the day. It would return, in the night, to torment him, and the next night, and the next, as it had for months. It knew his plan, and it did not like what he was doing, at all.

Traitor, it hissed into the darkness. *I see you, little traitor.* Somehow, he had learned to ignore it, too.

Opening the door, he stuck his head into the hall. Brian was practicing sword parries down the length of the corridor. He said, "Tell Juni Talvela I want to speak with him."

The boy went off. In a little while, Juni came up the stairs. Despite his skill with the bow, he hated hunting, and Karadur had given him permission to remain in the castle.

"Come in," Azil said. Juni stepped across the threshold. His gaze moved swiftly over the bed. "Sit, please. I need you to write something for me."

Juni said, "Of course, sir." He seated himself at the desk. He pulled the paper to him, checked the tip of the stylus, and eased the wax stopper from the mouth of the ink bottle. "To—"

"You can omit the salutation." Azil closed his eyes a moment. He knew exactly what he wanted to say. His heart was thudding hard. "Write this.

"I must go. By all that has been between us, I beg you not to look for me.

I do not go for the reason men will think, nor for any reason that you can imagine, but it is for a reason.

I love you more than life.

I will love you always, whatever form you wear."

He walked to the desk, and read the words over Juni's shoulder. "Give me the pen." He closed it in his fist, and drew his initial below the carefully written words. Lifting the page from the desk, he blew on it to dry the ink.

Then he carried it down the hall, into Karadur's bedchamber. He drew the bed hangings back and laid the note on the pillow. He dug the loose harp string from his sleeve. As he laid it across the note, the pain of what he was doing tore through him, bowing him double. He wondered if there was any way he might take his heart out of his chest and leave it, still beating, for Karadur to find.

A small brassbound chest sat unlocked against the wall near the bed. It was stuffed with gold: coins mostly, nobles from the Lemininkai's mint, coronas from Lienor, bracelets, rings. . . . Without hesitation, he filled a pouch with coins and thrust it into his shirt. He left the lid of the chest up and returned to his room.

Juni was sitting at the desk, white-faced.

Azil said, "I am trusting you to keep it secret, that I am gone. In three days, more or less, he'll return from the hunt. When he finds the note, he will ask who wrote it. Tell him. He will ask you what I said and did. Tell him everything, hold nothing back. He will ask you if you know where I am going. You don't." He could not smile, but he patted the boy's shoulder. "Answer whatever he asks you, and don't be afraid."

He reached to close the straps of the pack. The leather was stiff. Juni did it for him. Then he said, "Will you tell me something?"

"Maybe," Azil said. "What is it?"

"What am I to say when he asks me how it happened that I let you go alone?"

He did not know what to say.

Juni said, "You are my teacher. It is my obligation to travel with you, wherever you go, to serve you. That is what a student does for a teacher." His young voice broke, then dropped half an octave, as it was beginning to do. His gaze was steady. "I will get my pack, and my weapons, and tell them in the stable to saddle two horses. If anyone asks, we're going to Chingura. You need something at the market." He left, walking swiftly, but not running.

In a short while he was back, wearing his cloak, with loaded pack, bow and quiver over his shoulder, and his sword stuck in his belt. He picked up Azil's pack.

Azil slung the harp over his shoulder.

They walked into the yard. The boys brought the big roan, Guardian, and the grey filly, Aster, from the stable. The horses' breath steamed. The sky was ice-blue. Behind the castle, the great wall of mountains lifted into emptiness, three taller than the rest.

A mile or so down the road they passed a troop of men going toward the Keep.

"Hoy, singer!" It was Wegen. "Where are you off to?"

"Chingura Market," Azil said. "You?"

"The barracks, and bed, thank the gods. Morgan just relieved us."

They went around the gates of Chingura, past farmhouses and shepherds' cottages, until they reached the Great South Road. The horses were eager and fit; it would not take long for them to get to the Mako border. There were no fences, no guard posts between Dragon's domain and Erin diMako's lands, but men bearing Dragon Keep's badges patrolled the road near Estancia, questioning travelers as to where they had come from, and where they were going. The men on patrol would recognize Dragon's singer. If they asked his destination, he would say he was on Dragon's business.

The irony of that made him smile. He glanced at Juni. The boy had said nothing to the soldiers. His youthful face was resolute and remote. It would do no good to tell him to go back. Clouds scudded across the bright pale sky. Beyond them in the east lay darkness. A storm was brewing in the Grey Peaks. By the time it struck they should be well south. With luck, they would reach the border before dark.

Past noon, they halted in a travelers' shelter to rest and feed the horses. Finally Juni asked, "Where are we going?"

He would have to know eventually, and there was no good reason to keep him ignorant. "South."

"I know we're riding south," the boy said patiently. "But where?"

"First to Ujo," Azil said. "Then down the Great South Road as far as we can go, to Rowena, and Salvati, and Allegria."

Juni said, "You're following the Sparrows!"

"I hope to join them, if they'll have me."

"Of course they'll have you! How could they not?"

Azil said, "They might be too afraid."

Juni's face closed tight. "Afraid of Dragon?"

"Yes."

"Are *you* afraid of him?"

He had known Karadur Atani all his life, had loved him all his life. He had never feared him. "No."

"Won't he look for you?"

"I hope not. I asked him not to."

"What if he does?"

"If he wants to find me, he will. I'm not hiding from him, Juni." He could see the boy's confusion. "You will have to trust me."

They could rest at the Golden Cup in Sogda, north of

Mako. It wouldn't matter how crowded the inn was: a good inn always had room for jugglers and singers, and he was a singer. He would sing in the common room the songs they knew and loved: "The Old Man's Beard," "Ewain and Mariela," "The Red Boar of Aidu," "Dorian's Ride."

His mind was empty, now, quite hollow. The yammering in his head had stopped. Grief remained, though.

He pulled his hood up, so Juni would not see his face, and let the tears fall.

BENDING OVER HER work in the carpenter's shop, hands busy, mind fixed on the grain of a stave of wood, Terrill Chernico did not immediately hear the captain's step.

"Hawk," he said. Reluctantly she drew her attention from the length of red yew. Lorimir Ness's face was set and grim. He looked like a man about to go into battle.

She stood. "What is it? What has happened?"

He said, "Do you know where he is? Can you find him?"

There was only one *he* in Dragon Keep.

"Why?"

"Azil Aumson's gone. He and Juni took Guardian and Aster from the stable yesterday, to go to Chingura, they said. But they are absent still, and so are Juni's weapons—bow, arrows, sword—and Azil's harp. I sent men to Chingura. They are not there. They never were there. Nor are they in Castria or Sleeth. And there's a letter in Dragon's bedchamber, on the bed, with a harp string coiled about it. Lita found it when she went to fill the oil lamps."

"What does it say?"

"I don't know. I didn't open it."

"What are you thinking?" she asked him.

He said, "I don't think anything. I don't know anything. But I believe you should call him."

"All right," she said. She laid the stave aside and walked into the courtyard. Lorimir followed. The sky was vast and grey. Dragon had taken ten men with him, mostly men of the cavalry and the archers' wing. The Keep felt empty. It was not, of course: there were people in the stables and the kitchen. She could see the savanna in her mind; an endless rolling country blanketed with soft green grass, orange poppies, blue lobelia, and the grey geese wheeling above it. . . . But no, she thought, it's winter now.

She closed her eyes, blocking out Lorimir and the Keep, and directed her thought northward.

Suddenly she felt him, blazing across the distance.

Hunter!

Come, she called, *you must come. . . .*

Lorimir said, "Did you find him?"

"Yes," she said. "He comes."

They climbed to the Dragon's Roost to meet him. Thunder rolled through the vast grey twilight. A white-gold shape plunged from the sky. Bright wings unfurled, the Golden Dragon circled once around the castle. Then, talons spread to grip, he plunged downward. He settled on the granite. A crystalline light crackled across the sky. Then the dragon-form vanished, and became the man. A golden dust, like pollen, touched his skin. His hair was windblown. His eyes shimmered with a white light.

"What's happened?" he said. "Why did you call me back?"

Lorimir said, "My lord, if I have erred, I beg your pardon. But Azil Aumson has left the castle, with Juni Talvela. Neither has returned, and no one knows where they have gone. There is a message for you; a note. I don't know what it says."

"Where is it?"

"In your bedchamber."

* * *

AZIL HAD NOT written this.

Azil could not have written it; he could not hold a pen. But the words were his, and the nearly unrecognizable letter *A* scrawled beneath the round, carefully scripted letters.

I will love you always, whatever form you wear. He had said something like that once, to Azil, in the ice.

I do not go for the reason men will think, nor for any reason that you can imagine, but it is for a reason. The reason men will think: he was talking about Maia, of course. Men thought all sorts of stupid things. He could not imagine any reason that would drive his friend to leave him. Juni had penned the note. Juni had gone with him. That was good. He picked up the bronze harp string, then laid it gently back across the pillow.

The lid of the little chest was up. Azil had taken some gold, then. That, too, was good.

He said aloud, "You should have told me you wanted to leave. I would have sent an army with you, to protect you."

I beg you not to look for me.

Azil never begged. Three years a prisoner in the ice, tormented, starved, beaten, he had refused to speak a word, rather than beg. He had never asked Karadur for anything, except a horse to ride.

I beg you.

Where would he go? Not west, surely, toward Derrenhold, Serrenhold, Voiana: those places were too cold. South, perhaps, to Ujo. East, perhaps, into Nakase. Issho was windy and inhospitable, except near Lake Urai. Chuyo was warm. But Chuyo was far.

Thank the gods Juni had gone with him. He was so vulnerable, unable to hold a pen or a sword, or even saddle a horse.

But Juni, though quick and willing, was only a boy. There was so much danger in the world. He might die, and Karadur would not know it.

I thought him dead before.

I beg you not to look for me.

"I *must* look for you," he said. "I can't do without you, you know that."

Only silence answered. Anguish, and a savage rage rose inside him. A hot wind moved through the chamber. The curtains flapped like banners. The paper flared to ash in his hand. It did not matter. The words were seared into his heart.

He walked out of the bedchamber. Lorimir and Hawk had followed him. Their faces changed when they saw him.

He said, "Who was on the gate when they left?"

Lorimir said, "Derry."

"Bring him. I want to speak to him."

Lorimir Ness was pale, but the old man had been a soldier all his life. He said, "You can't. I sent him away."

The rage blew out of him then. Almost without volition, his fist moved. Lorimir's head snapped back. Boneless, he slumped to the floor, and lay there, not moving.

No. . . .

Hawk, kneeling, laid the fingers of her right hand against the hollow of Lorimir's throat. Then she shook her head.

Karadur closed his eyes. *Gods, what had he done? . . .* Sparks streamed from his fingers. If he stayed where he was the Keep's walls would explode. Let it burn, he thought insanely. Let it all burn, as Sorvino had burned, and Coll's Ridge, and Mako, if only the inferno in his heart would stop.

He moved then, along the corridor, out the door, to the Dragon's Roost. Changing form in midleap, he flung himself from the rock, wings spread to catch the mountain wind, driving upward through the moist, snow-laden clouds. Ahead of him loomed Dragon's Eye's summit. He soared over the peak, skimming the snowcapped rock. Something shrieked: the black condor, flung from its eyrie by the wind of his passage, spread its wings and croaked its outrage.

He had killed Lorimir. He had not meant to do it, but he had done it nevertheless. The sun, a blood-red ball, was falling into the west. He wondered what would happen if he flew into it. Perhaps it, too, would explode.

Like a bright arrow he rose, up and up. Then he heard the voice speaking in his head.

Greetings, bright one.

All the instruments of sound humans had ever made, or ever could make, lived in that voice. He looked up. Above him hung a white, winged, naked man. Streamers of frost wreathed its head.

This is my kingdom. Hast come to play again? That was a fine chase we had, last time.

He said, *No, god of winds, I do not come to play.*

Dost seek again thy kindred? sang that exquisite voice. *I have told thee, they are gone.*

No, god of winds. The air was thin. He could scarcely breathe. Darkness pressed about him. His wings moved slowly. *There is nothing I desire, save my friend, who has left me.*

Ah, Inatowy sang, *I understand. Thy friend is dead, and thou wouldst join him. That is easy. Go thou a little higher, bright one. There is death in this place.* He gazed into the pitiless emptiness. *Come,* Inatowy sang.

Sanity returned. He had come too high. Lungs heaving, he retreated. He let himself drop downward, away from the domain of the wind god, to his own country.

* * *

HE LANDED ON the Dragon's Roost, and Changed. He went downstairs, half-expecting to see Lorimir's body in the hall outside his bedchamber, but it was not; they had moved it. He went into the chamber and sat on the bed. The rage that had fueled his flight had receded, leaving him exhausted; he did not want to move.

In a while, Marek Gavrinson spoke through the door. The words had Lorimir's name among them. Karadur did not listen.

Later, Hawk spoke to him. *Don't do this,* she said.

Go away, he told her. *Leave me alone.*

Your people need you.

Her persistence infuriated him. Wielding fire like a knife, he cut the link between them. The chamber grew dark. The night wind plucked at the shutters. He would have to leave the chamber eventually. The needs of his human body would drive him from it. He did not want to be human; it hurt too much.

The harp string lay across the pillow. Picking it up, he wound it about his wrist.

LORIMIR NESS WAS laid in the earth, and the swordsmen stood watch over the grave. Across the domain, the folk of the villages mourned him, for though he had come from outside the domain, he had served Dragon Keep for thirty years.

"He was a good man," the women said.

"He was an honorable captain," said the men who had served in his command.

A letter went to Averra, to his people, telling them that he had served his lord well, and died in honor. It was written by Aum Nialsdatter, and bore Karadur's seal.

Winter came early to Ippa that year. The first frost arrived in October, and by November the roads were closed, with snowdrifts high as a man's head. The fur trappers were happy, for the heavy snow had driven lynx and beaver and white foxes south early. The harvest had been good; there was plenty of hay for the horses and cattle, and vegetables for the pots, so no one starved, but the sheep grew thin.

On Coll's Ridge, the cottage by the Windle sat empty. The herbalist had gone to stay at the Halleck steading.

"You cannot stay alone this winter," Maura had said, when first Maia's condition became evident. "Stay with us."

Rianna jumped in delight. "Yes! Stay with us." Angus signed his agreement.

Maia demurred. "Your house is small, and it will be smaller with Morga and myself within."

"You cannot stay alone. Maura gestured toward the high swollen mound of Maia's belly. "If you will not come to us, go to Miri Halleck."

And Miri said firmly, "Certainly you will come to me."

So Maia went to live in the Halleck homestead. She shared a sleeping chamber with Linnet, Ursule's youngest daughter. At first, she found the presence of so many people difficult. She was accustomed to solitude, and the big sprawling house was never empty, never still. Even in the middle of the night the walls creaked, sleepers snored, children cried, and mothers rose to comfort them. . . . Within weeks, though, she found she had grown accustomed to the clamor.

Morga, wary at first among so many strangers and strange dogs, found her place in the household. Indeed, she seemed to like being part of a pack.

Miri's daughter Arafel and her daughter-in-law Ursule, wife to Alf, treated Maia like a sister. Ursule made her cup after cup of nettle tea, and brought her treats when her appetite failed. Arafel, who had borne three children, rubbed her legs when they cramped. The house seemed filled with children. The youngsters were enchanted by the stranger in their midst. They showed her their toys, and made her part of their games. It was pleasant, at first. But idleness made her cranky.

"Let me work," she said to Ursule. "I feel well, I'm not sick. I can clean, and sew, and bake."

"Why should you work? You are our guest."

But Miri said, "Of course she should not be idle! She can tend the herbs in the sunroom, and watch the little ones in play."

So Maia spent her days in a tiny warm chamber filled with pots of dill, basil, sage, and mint. The herbs in their pots made it fragrant; the smell reminded her of home. She had brought little with her to Miri's house; only her books, and her clothes, and the cloak Karadur had given her. News from the Keep was infrequent and troubling. She knew—everyone knew—about Azil Aumson's disappearance, Lorimir Ness's death, and Karadur's grief.

Alf said, "They say the lord speaks to no one. They say he stays in his chamber and will not come out." She wanted to go to him. But of course, she could not.

Her body changed.

How do you feel? the women of the household asked her. *Are you sweated? Are you chilled? Is there aught you need*? They brought her fresh meat, which she could not eat—the odor made her sick—and soups, which she could. Their solicitude was sweet, but she knew well that it was not for her, but for the child she carried, the babe that might be a dragon-child, and was in any case Karadur Atani's heir.

IN DRAGON KEEP, the mood was grim. Marek Gavrinson, unbidden, assumed Lorimir's duties. The dragon-lord spent his days in the tower, or in the castle map room, and his nights in his chamber. He spoke to no one.

"This is stupid," Rogys said one evening in the kitchen. Brian had just brought a platter back from Karadur's room. The food on it had not been touched.

"It is stupid," agreed the head cook. "You tell him."

"I will," Rogys said. And the rider captain, who loved the man he served—would have killed for him, died for him, gone to his bed without a second thought—strode to the tower chamber. "My lord!" He hammered on the door.

It opened suddenly. Karadur loomed in the doorway. The dragon-lord's face was haggard, and his cheeks, habitually smooth, were rough with stubble. His eyes burned with a deep blue flame.

He said, "You have news for me?"

Rogys said, "My lord, I do not." The words running through his mind—about hope, and fidelity, and the fears of his men—seemed worse than foolish now. Nevertheless, he drew breath to speak.

Karadur said, "Then go away." Quite gently, he shut the door.

More troubled than he had ever been, even in the time of the wargs, Rogys spoke to Finle. That evening, together, they spoke with Hawk.

Rogys said, "He'll kill himself if he does not eat. Go to him. He calls you friend. He'll listen to you."

But the one-eyed changeling said, "Do you think I have not tried? He will not."

"Why does he hold himself apart from us?"

"He's afraid," the hawk-changeling said bluntly.

"Of what?" Finle asked.

"Of himself. Of what he has done. Of what he might do."

* * *

IN THE DAWN after New Year's Moon, they lit torches in the villages, and banged the drums, to call Imarru the Hunter back from the Country of the Dead. In Dragon Keep, Raudri blew the horn to welcome in the year. The mournful sound echoed along the icy flanks of the mountains.

A week after New Year's Moon, Rain the midwife came to the Halleck homestead. She felt Maia's breasts and listened to her belly.

"Aye, the babe is well," she said, "and you also. How do you feel?"

Maia said, "My feet are too fat, and my sides hurt."

"That is as it should be," Rain said severely. "Your body stretches to hold the child."

The squirming baby's heel thumped firmly against a rib. Wincing, Maia laid her hand on her belly. "Little one, be still a moment." The wriggling quieted. "Is it boy or girl? Can you say?"

"Sometimes I can tell," Rain said, "but not with this one. You will know soon."

"How soon?"

"April, I think."

Maia blinked. "Surely not. I bled in August."

Rain shrugged. "Babies come when they will. And this one looks to be in a hurry."

Thoughtfully, Maia pulled her gown back down about her legs. Hana Diamori Atani's babies had come early, too. But she was not Hana Diamori Atani, who had died giving life to her children. She was Iva Unamira's daughter. She thanked the elderly midwife, who had struggled through snow to reach her. Despite her complaints, she felt quite well. Her appetite was changeable, and her belly itched constantly, but Ursule and Arafel assured her that they, too, had experienced this: all women did.

Also, there were other changes. Her senses had sharpened. Her night sight had grown keen. The taste of food was more acute.

February came, and March. Winter's grip on the land lifted. Frozen rivers cracked and trickled. It rained; ice melted; roads turned to mud. The light deepened, and lingered longer. Red buds appeared on the trees.

At the Halleck homestead, the women scoured the baking ovens. Maia tried to help. "Get away," Miri scolded. Alf and the boys dragged the plow from the barn.

AS THE DAYS lengthened, Karadur emerged from his refuge. He confirmed Marek Gavrinson as captain. He named Lurri first of the swordsmen's wing. He ate in the hall: not every meal, nor even every day, but often enough. And he wrote letters, and sent them, to the Lemininkai, Lucas Ridenar, Allumar Marichal, and to Cirion Imorin, in distant Kameni. Each said the same.

My friend, the singer Azil Aumson, and the archer Juni Talvela may be traveling through your country. Of your courtesy, I ask you to receive them should they come to you, and give them whatever they need.

MAIA DISORVINO GAVE birth to her baby on a soft April morning, while the white mist hung about the hills. The pains began about midnight; they were mild at first, but soon grew fiercer. Her back ached. She walked about the house. As the speed of the cramps increased, Arafel and Ursule soaked her belly with hot cloths. Heat coursed through her arms and legs. She crouched. The room was hot, and filled with women: Rain, Sirany the priestess, Miri and her daughters, and Maura, who had come across the fields in the middle of the night to be with her. They tried to feed her sweet stuff.

"It will keep you strong," Ursule said.

"I don't want it." She did not want to eat. The contractions coursed through her. Rain had told her that her womb was full of water in which the baby lived. She imagined it swimming toward the opening between her legs. "Come, little fish," she whispered to it, "hurry." Sweat stung her eyes. Maura, kneeling beside her, wiped her face. "Hurry."

"It comes," said Rain. "Push! Again." She gasped for breath. "Now, hold still!"

There was one very urgent sensation, and then, amazingly, a baby cried.

"A girl-child!" Rain said triumphantly. Sirany spoke the blessing.

"Am I torn?" Maia whispered.

"No," Maura said.

"Good." She rolled onto her side. Her legs ached. "Is she—?"

"She's fine," Rain said. "She's perfect. She's beautiful."

"Give her to me." They laid the howling baby in her arms. She stroked the huge head with one finger. It was covered with red-gold stubble, like the skin of a peach. The hair went all the way down her back to her tiny tailbone. She was not beautiful; she was wrinkled and damp as a new-hatched butterfly. Her eyes were shut. Her minute fingers were furled tightly into fists. "Hush, now, little one," Maia crooned. The crying stopped.

Maura said, "You must give her a name."

"Her father will name her." She was very sleepy, and also very thirsty. Her throat hurt. Fluid gushed between her legs.

"A use name," Maura said.

"Little one," Maia whispered. "Lovely one. Thy name is Jewel."

As if she approved, the baby made an amused, bubbling sound, and opened her eyes. They were immense, blue as sapphires. She bubbled again, and waved her arms. Her fists unfurled.

Claws, small as a kitten's, tipped the end of her perfect fingers.

IN JUNE, MAIA diSorvino rode to the Keep.

Alf, Angus, and Lew, Alf's middle son, rode with her: Alf, who had served in the war band during the years Karadur Atani lived in Mako, wore his sword; Angus and Lew carried bows. Mounted on plow horses, they made an incongruous escort.

The day was warm. Cloud shadows dappled the hills. Iridescent butterflies fluttered over the grass, which was bright with yellow mustard and blue thyme and every color of wild lilies. From the crook of Maia's arm, Jewel gurgled with delight. She waved her arms at the sunlight.

An orange-and-black butterfly lit on Bessie's neck. Crowing, Jewel snatched for it. The startled butterfly sailed upward, away from the clenching hands. Jewel frowned. "Thou canst not have it," Maia told her. "It must fly free, as wilt thou someday." She put her little finger into the yearning baby's palm.

Jewel grunted and tried to tug the finger to her mouth. Already her grip was strong. Her claws had sloughed off about a week after she was born. They would return, Rain said, when she was older.

They halted thrice for Jewel to nurse. By midafternoon they reached the Keep. The dark granite castle towering over them looked as if it had been made by giants. As they rode up the narrow path to its gate, Maia repressed a shiver.

Taran met them at the gate. His face was brown; above

it, his hair seemed almost white. She dismounted. He put an arm about her shoulders. "Gods, I'm glad to see you." He gazed at Jewel. She looked at him serenely. "She's so small."

"Not really. She grows swiftly," Maia said. "Little one. Lovely one. This is thine uncle."

Taking Bessie's rein, Taran led the plow horse beneath the great archway. Behind its impregnable wall, the Keep revealed itself to be not one but many buildings, some low and squat, some narrow and tall. She smelled the odor of hot iron. A heavy, rhythmic hammering came from one of the buildings. Someone, somewhere, was baking bread.

A large-headed dog came to sniff her boots. His hackles lifted as he caught Morga's scent on her clothes. A ragged boy thrust his head out the entrance of the dog kennel. He clicked his tongue.

"Savage," he called. "Savage, come here." The dog trotted to him.

Jewel arched her back and said, "Aha, aha." It was one of her favorite noises.

"Where is he?"

Taran jerked his head toward the great stone spire of the watchtower. "Up there."

"Wait here for me," she said to her friends.

Taran took her into the castle. Light from narrow windows shed a soft irregular glimmer through the corridors. The halls smelled faintly sour. The wall tapestries were so begrimed that she could barely see the colors. They climbed a stair. A girl, arms full of linens, pressed against the wall to let them pass. Her eyes went wide when she saw the baby in the crook of Maia's arm.

They climbed a second, even steeper, stair. At the top, a boy sat on the floor opposite a doorway. The door was shut. The boy rose as they approached.

Taran said, "Tell him Maia diSorvino is here to see him."

The boy said, "He won't answer. The mayor of Castria came this morning to see him. He wouldn't open the door."

"Tell him."

The boy knocked, and said clearly, "My lord, Maia di-Sorvino is here to see you."

There was no answer.

"Is the door locked?" Taran asked.

"No," the boy said.

Taran opened the door. The room was dark; shutters covered the windows. A single candle flickered on the desktop. The air smelled stale.

Karadur was seated at the desk. He was dressed, as always, in black. He was bearded, which Maia had not expected. Beneath the golden bristles, his face was drawn.

He looked at her without expression. Then he said, "What are you doing here? I didn't send for you."

She said, "It's dark in here."

Taran found a second candle, touched its wick to the first, and stuck it in a holder. Maia unfastened her cloak and laid it on the desktop. She set Jewel on top of it. The baby waved her arms and legs. Her blue eyes gazed widely, knowledgeably at the dragon-lord. She gurgled, and reached toward his beard.

"My lord," Maia said, "I came to introduce you to your daughter."